MW00879147

MOTHER
PIG

HOUNDSTOOTH BOOK 2

TRAVIS M. RIDDLE

www.travismriddle.com

Book Layout © 2017 BookDesignTemplates.com

Cover design by Deranged Doctor Design

Mother Pig/Travis M. Riddle. —1st ed.

ISBN 9798705158034

Also by
TRAVIS M. RIDDLE

Houndstooth
Flesh Eater

Ustlian Tales
Balam, Spring
Spit and Song

Standalones
Wondrous
The Narrows

For Carly Rae Jepsen & Dua Lipa

Coal Ereness is not having a good time.

A little over a year ago, there was an earthquake in his home city of Muta Par, resulting in the utter destruction of the library in which he and his father Von worked. The two of them were trapped in a back room for weeks, surviving on mere droplets of water, before Von ultimately passed away. In an effort to survive, Coal had to make the impossible decision to eat parts of his father. He did this with the knowledge that doing so was strictly outlawed by the Dirt King, and that the punishment was severe.

Eating the flesh led to the appearance of his father's ghost in the room with him. Von told Coal that he was speaking to him from the other side, that he could feel the presence of the afterlife around him. This bizarre happening repeated every time Coal consumed any of his father's flesh.

When Coal was finally found, things only got worse. Upon seeing his father's corpse, Muta Par's officers marked him as a Flesh Eater. He was to be apprehended and sent to a prison labor camp designed specifically for those who have eaten flesh. But with the help of an old family friend, Coal was able to escape and has since lived his life on the run, heading south through the kingdom of Ruska.

While laying low in the southern city of Vinnag with his childhood friend Zank, Coal was looped into doing a job for a man named Garna Nomak. Nomak was one of Vinnag's many crimelords, a wealthy anteater who stops at nothing to obtain whatever he desires. Together with Zank, a rabbit named

Venny, and a wolverine named Marl, they set out in the dead of night to fulfill Garna Nomak's request.

During the job, however, Coal is nearly caught by Palace Stingers: special soldiers employed by the Dirt King to seek out the most dangerous criminals in Ruska. After narrowly avoiding capture yet again, Coal decides he needs to take steps to secure a peaceful future for himself.

Zank hooks him up with a woman in Vinnag who can offer him services to wipe his slate clean, but the price is high. Far out of reach with his current funds. He would have to complete countless jobs for Garna Nomak in order to afford it, and time is not on his side now that the Stingers know his location.

But then he learns that Nomak will soon be heading to the rivertop city of Soponunga for a spiderback race. The grand prize is hefty: a diamond anteater claw that is worth thousands of tups. If he can enter the race and win the claw, Coal knows he could sell it to Nomak and be able to afford the woman's services and clear his name.

But to compete in a spiderback race, one needs a spider, which Coal is lacking. So after arriving in Soponunga, he makes a quick detour to the nearby Flesh Eater prison known as Faranap. Under the cover of night, he infiltrates the camp and witnesses the despicable conditions in which the prisoners must live, kept under guard by abominations the likes of which Coal has never seen. Smooth-skinned, eyeless creatures with limbs that can stretch and morph into any weapon. It's a struggle, but Coal manages to steal an orb weaver which he dubs White Rose before making his daring escape from the camp.

In Soponunga, Coal meets Garna Nomak's assistant, a mild-mannered woodpecker named Ilio. The two spend their days together exploring the city, growing their bond. After a few days, Coal is caught off guard by a kiss from the man. But it is a good surprise, one that Coal reciprocates, and their relationship deepens despite Coal's animosity toward Ilio's employer.

Finally, the day of the race is upon them. Competition is fierce, and it is not helped by a monster attack in the middle of the track. The racers are set upon by creatures that look like a typical animal called a retno, but with disgusting malformations and intense aggression. Coal and the other racers must swiftly deal with the assault, during which Coal is savagely wounded by one of the beasts.

But another racer, a raccoon named Noswen—along with her bat companion Yurzu—harbor an odd investment in seeing Coal win. Noswen is able to magically heal Coal's wounds, an ability that he never would have dreamed possible.

Feeling better than ever, he is able to continue on with the race, narrowly beating out the others for first place.

The diamond claw is his, and his future seems secure.

That is, until he meets with Noswen and Yurzu after the race. They tell him they know about his innate magic, and then reveal that they possess abilities too. Coal is hesitant to believe that magic is real, but he is convinced by the fact that Noswen was able to heal him out on the race track. Yurzu divulges that his magical ability is being able to detect illnesses within people. Coal reluctantly tells them that he is a Flesh Eater, and that he can speak to people after they've died by consuming their flesh.

Noswen goes on to explain that there are three others like them in Ruska, individuals infected with magic who call themselves the Blighted. They have been sent on a secret mission by the Dirt King to retrieve six ancient artifacts throughout the kingdom, one of which is the diamond anteater claw. With the claw in hand, they would only need three more objects to complete their mission.

According to the Dirt King, the massive, immutable tree called the Houndstooth at the northern tip of the kingdom is leaking dark magic, leading to the creation of monsters such as those they encountered during the race, as well as infecting the six Blighted with magical abilities. If they obtain the six artifacts and channel their own magic through them, they can seal away the infection and save Ruska.

Once Coal is promised that his Flesh Eater record will be cleared if he helps, he agrees to join Noswen and Yurzu on their quest. He bids a fond farewell to Ilio, swearing he will see him again soon, and then sets off with his two new companions toward the town of Sadatso to meet the other three Blighted.

1

ILIO AND COAL'S FACES brushed against each other. Warm. Soft. Feather and fur.

They were on the floor of the supply room of the Uncut Gem, pressed into the back corner. Music drifted up from the jukebox downstairs. A jazzy number that Coal didn't recognize. Fanaleese's love for the genre dipped into the obscure.

Their breathing was fast and heavy, punctuated by snappy drum beats and blasts of brassy horns.

Coal looked into the woodpecker's bright orange eyes as the man pulled away. His glasses had been knocked aside a moment prior. Ilio's eyes flicked downward to Coal's lips. His beak parted, just slightly, then he pressed forward—

—and Coal was startled awake by the unimaginably loud clang of Yurzu dropping his bag on the ground a couple feet away.

Coal's eyes flitted back and forth, absorbing where he actually was. To call it a rude awakening would be an understatement. Sleeping in the old marten's supply room had not exactly been the most comfortable place in the world, but it beat the rough, uneven forest floor. Being practically smothered by Ilio wasn't too bad, either.

"What the hell are you carrying in that thing?" Coal croaked groggily, sitting up in his sleeping bag. Specks of dirt and a long twig plagued the orange and black fur atop his head. His pointed ears flicked irritably at the noise. "It sounds like you have enough pots and pans to run a high-end restaurant in there."

"Not one of your snappier quips," Noswen commented, no more than a disembodied voice. Coal looked around and spotted the raccoon behind him, rolling up her own sleeping bag. Her pack was already loaded up. Coal was the last to stir, it seemed.

Yurzu gave him an apologetic frown. The bat's already scrunched-up face scrunched up even more. "Sorry," he said meekly, sniffling his flat nose. He hastily gathered up his bag, stuffing the few items that had fallen out back into it.

"I'm only giving you a hard time, it's not a problem," Coal assured him, now feeling guilty. He offered the guy a friendly smile. "Just woke me up from a good dream, is all."

Yurzu smiled back, though Coal could tell he still felt slightly embarrassed.

The three of them had been on the road for a few days now, just under a week, and it was taking a while for Yurzu to warm to him. They were friendly with each other, but the bat was exceptionally shy and generally kept to himself. He was also prone to embarrassment and shame.

Noswen, on the other hand, had taken to Coal almost immediately. She was just as snippy and prickly as when he'd met her, but he quickly ascertained that that meant she liked him. They enjoyed trading barbs, which sometimes left Yurzu feeling uncomfortable if he did not pick up on the fact they were messing with each other.

"Time for you to get up anyway," said Noswen. There was then a plop to Coal's left, where he looked and saw three thin, deflated waterskins and a small cloud of dust rising. "Go fill those up, would you?"

Coal scooted out of his ruffled sleeping bag and snatched the waterskins. He traipsed past Noswen, stepping between the thicket of trees and approaching the Lunsk River a short way beyond.

As he knelt at the river's edge, dipping the spouts of the waterskins into the gently flowing river, his mind wandered back to his dream. His spine tingled.

He watched the waterskins enlarge as they filled with water. They were crafted from the skin of a ventem and had to either be very old or very expensive, as these types of waterskins were no longer regularly produced. The invention of canteens and the ban on killing animals had made them obsolete.

The soothing trickle of the river eased him into wakefulness. He took a minute to sit by the riverside after he finished his task.

He was still wracked with disappointment about being woken from his dream. His hands yearned for Ilio's. It was sappy, but true. His stomach still fluttered at the thought of their young romance, rudely torn away by this ridiculous quest from the Dirt King.

It was a stunningly beautiful day in Ruska, though. It was as if the kingdom was reminding him what exactly they were fighting for. Sunlight peeked through the canopy above and glinted off the water's surface. Coal skimmed a fingertip along the river's surface, his long, curved nail slicing through it. He needed to trim his nails. A small piece of personal hygiene that had fallen by the wayside during his recent tumultuous travels.

According to Noswen, they would reach Sadatso in only a few hours. Which was a great relief to Coal, given how sore his feet were with all the walking he'd been doing. Not only from Soponunga to Sadatso, but also Vinnag to Soponunga before that. He had hardly any time to rest since embarking on this whole endeavor.

The only time he'd gotten good, deep sleep was after being beaten half to death by Garna Dend's bodyguards and Meretta Noyles. Coal shuddered at the memory.

Their travels since departing from Soponunga had been stress-free, though. Coal had confidence in Noswen's sense of direction and trusted she was taking them along the most efficient path to their destination, which would definitely not be the case if he was left in charge of planning their route.

They had not encountered any wild animals in the woods, nor had any unfortunate run-ins with the Houndstooth's malformed abominations. After the scrape with the not-retnos during the spiderback race, Coal could safely say he was done with those things. He did not need to meet any more, thank you.

There were occasional moments when, during a lull in conversation, Coal thought he heard a rustle in the treetops above. A piece of him wondered if it was White Rose keeping a watchful eye on him, but he never saw the massive spider up there. It was highly unlikely, anyway.

He returned to the others, distributing to each of them their respective waterskin. To Yurzu, he asked, "What's on the menu this morning?"

The bat's face lit up at the question. Yurzu was their designated chef for the duration of the short trip. The little guy had a great fondness for food, and Coal had a fondness for his cooking. Despite the dearth of ingredients on the road, the bat still managed to knock out tasty meals for breakfast, lunch, and dinner.

Yurzu started, "Well, we're running low on supplies, so…"

"Some would call that masterful planning, since we're going to arrive in Sadatso today," Noswen chimed in before taking a quick pull from her waterskin.

"…so it's gonna be light," Yurzu continued. "Just bread with spiced mealworm butter and an apple."

"We've all gotta split an apple? We really are running low. Not so masterful, in my book," Coal joked. Yurzu giggled and clarified that they all would be enjoying their own apple, thankfully.

Coal packed away his few belongings while Yurzu began doling out everyone's breakfast. One of the only things Coal had to his name was the diamond anteater claw he'd miraculously won in the Soponunga Spiderback Showdown, but even that was tucked away among Noswen's possessions.

He leaned back against his rolled-up sleeping bag with the apple in his lap and buttered bread in hand. It was a fluffy piece of bread with a thick, crunchy crust, just the way he liked it. A generous heaping of Yurzu's spiced mealworm butter was spread across the top.

While putting away his things, Coal had observed Yurzu preparing their food. The butter was made by sprinkling some zippy special seasoning blend into some ground-up mealworms, which was then all mixed into softened butter. Absolutely delicious. Coal scarfed down his whole piece of bread in only three bites before deigning to give his fruit even the slightest consideration. But the apple was equally scrumptious, nice and sweet with crisp red skin.

Sitting across from Coal among his own bags, Yurzu was taking his time with his bread, daintily nibbling on it. Noswen sat far away from them, obscured by bushes and tree trunks. She typically kept to herself in the mornings, wanting some time alone before they set off. When Coal had asked Yurzu about the ritual a few days prior, the bat shrugged and said that she probably just wanted some silence and time to herself. With the amount of time he had spent nestled away in library corners reading books, Coal could relate to the impulse.

Coal told Yurzu, "I always wished I knew how to cook."

Yurzu blinked rapidly a few times before responding. For some reason, he always seemed surprised that anyone felt the desire to speak to him. "I wouldn't exactly call this *cooking*," he then said, grinning. It was rare to hear the bat make a joke. Coal smiled.

"I'm useless when it comes to preparing any sort of food," Coal went on. "Even something as simple as this. It's beyond me how people can throw stuff together like your spice blend and just *know* what will taste good. Seasonings and sauces are fascinating to me."

"A lot of it is trial and error," Yurzu said before taking another meager bite of his bread. Spitting crumbs, he said, "You end up eating a lot of bad food before you get to the good stuff."

"How many iterations of this mealworm concoction did you have to go through before you landed on this one?"

Yurzu smirked, then answered. "Well, actually, this was my first time making it…"

"Wow!" Coal exclaimed. "First of all, proving me right that putting flavors together is some magical ability I don't possess. Maybe *that's* your thing, not detecting diseases or whatever." Yurzu laughed heartily at that theory. "But if you're not a magical chef, then why in the world did you give us your test batch? What if it tasted awful!"

Yurzu laughed even more and said, "*Someone* has to try it, right? Do you think it needed anything else?"

Coal pondered for a second, trying to recall the exact taste of the creamy butter, then shook his head. "It was pretty delicious to me."

"It's good," Yurzu nodded, "but could use a bit more black pepper, I think. It has less bite than I wanted."

"'Butter with bite.' There's your slogan. Jar it up and slap that on the label."

"I might have to, actually."

"Once it's perfect."

"Of course."

Coal then asked, "Where'd you learn how to do all this, anyway? Your parents?"

Yurzu nodded. "They were both gifted chefs. Not professionals—they didn't cook in restaurants or anything—but they coulda been famous in the kingdom if they had, I bet. My mom's mushroom stew is one of the best things I've ever eaten. I still can't make it as good as she did, but maybe I'll get there."

"She never taught you how to make that one?"

"She didn't get the chance. She and my father both passed away eleven years ago." There wasn't any sadness in his voice, it was simply a matter of fact. A wound long since scabbed over. Or at least one he was skilled at concealing.

"Sorry to hear that," said Coal.

"It's okay," Yurzu said, though given his own experience, Coal knew it was not. Just one of those phrases people say because it's easier and cleaner than the truth. "But anyway, what I learned from them were a lot of the fundamentals, and they left behind a small but detailed recipe book."

Coal smiled. "That's nice, at least. A piece of them to carry with you."

"Mhmm. I think I've mastered her blueberry muffins by now, but the mushroom stew is still out of reach."

"You'll get there, I'm sure."

Yurzu grinned. "I hope so," he said. "I find myself craving it often. It was my favorite dish of hers."

"My father wasn't much of a cook. Everything he made was certainly passable, but it never blew me away. He definitely didn't leave me with any cravings." Coal shivered at his own unfortunate turn of phrase. Yurzu stared on, blissfully ignorant of the fact that desperate starvation had driven Coal to eating part of his own father's corpse. Coal swallowed and continued. "I can't really think of anything he left me with, to be totally honest. He's who got me into spiderback racing, but it's not like he himself taught me how to ride. He wasn't worth a shit on the back of a spider, but you better believe it didn't stop him from yelling out advice and criticisms at every lesson I went to."

Coal took another moment to think back over his childhood, grasping for any activity he and his father might have bonded over, but there was nothing. They always remained at arm's length from each other, even until the bitter end.

"You never did *anything* together?"

It was Noswen who spoke. She trundled into their conversation, wiping crumbs from her gray chin and sliding a notebook into her bag. She walked past them, still standing and staring off into the distance while waiting for a reply. Looking toward direction in which they would be walking soon.

"No," said Coal. "Not really." The answer saddened him, somewhat. Yurzu frowned too.

Noswen turned to face them. "I can't seem to get any of my kits to leave me alone for even a second when I'm at home," she said. "I wish I could impart anything at all as useful as cooking, though. I don't think 'hanging from Mommy's arms' is going to particularly help them out much in the future."

"You not much of a cook either?" Coal asked her.

She shook her head. "Not for lack of my mother trying to instill it in me. I'm like you, though. The act of balancing flavors is mystical to me. If I'm not following a recipe, I'm completely worthless. And even then, I usually manage to under-season it and it all turns out bland and I get pissed off and want to swear."

"The kids probably don't notice or care," Coal offered.

"They don't! Or at least they don't voice it. And neither does my husband, but it makes me mad anyway. With every bite, I ask myself if I even put any damn salt in the food, even though I know I did."

"Just dump a bowl of salt into the pan next time you make them something," said Coal with a shrug. "I'm sure you'll be able to taste it then."

"A bowl of pepper, too," Yurzu added.

"Thank you for your culinary expertise," Noswen said, her words dripping with sarcasm.

"Well, with how hopeless it sounds like we are, I'm glad we've got you on the team. You're our greatest asset," Coal then said to Yurzu. "Otherwise, instead of butter spread over bread, I think our breakfast would've been mud spread over tree bark."

"I know you're joking, but I actually know a few good preparations for tree bark..." said Yurzu.

Coal smirked. "I'll say this much: if you know of a way to make tree bark taste good to me, then you genuinely are imbued with some sort of magical cooking power, because it has yet to happen even once in my life."

"I'll take you up on that challenge," Yurzu beamed.

Coal was about to ask where Yurzu was from when Noswen said that they should finish packing up and get going. Coal was beyond ready to throw himself onto a bed in a real inn, so he did not argue. He was sorely missing the luxury suite in the Longowosk Hotel. Waking up every morning with dirt in his fur had grown tiresome fast.

Although, he did not know how much time there would actually be to relax once they reached Sadatso. He assumed they would at least stay the night there, but he also knew that the rest of the team was waiting and probably eager to get back on the road. Noswen had already made it abundantly clear that she was ready to get back to her home in Holluwak as soon as possible. Even if the kids exhausted her, she was anxious to see her family again. There were surely others in the group who were similarly ready to get this adventure over with sooner rather than later.

She had told Coal a little bit about the rest of the group, but not much. He knew Jatiri was a soft-spoken saola, and that the boar, Biror, was essentially the complete opposite. Quick to anger and short with everyone. A real joy to be around.

Yet the person Coal was most nervous about meeting was Lop, the orangutan. Noswen described him as a stoic guy who was best pals with Zsoz, the slime who was traveling with them. But Lop apparently worked as a Palace guard before being thrust into this mission, and Coal was unsure how the ape might react to the knowledge that he was a Flesh Eater. Even if they were now playing on the same team, there was sure to be some tension between them if Lop truly bought into all of the Dirt King's philosophies. The man might demand they clamp a muzzle on him as soon as they met.

But he'd cross that bridge when he got to it. Perhaps he could avoid the sticky subject altogether.

As they were hoisting their packs onto their backs, there came a rustle from behind them in the direction of the river. For a split second, Coal once more found himself hoping that it was White Rose. But when he turned to investigate the source, confusion rippled through him.

It was Marl.

The dark-furred wolverine was flanked by two other men who Coal presumed to be under Garna Nomak's employ as well, both rabbits. Thankfully neither of them were Coal's friend Zank, or Zank's on-again off-again girlfriend Venny.

Coal had not seen the man since they parted ways outside Garna Nomak's office way back in Vinnag City after completing their one job together, obtaining Nomak's leaked private photos. After the turn his life had taken, Coal did not figure he'd ever see the wolverine again.

Marl appeared much less confused by Coal's presence than Coal was by his. The man's face sported its usual impassiveness and mild grumpiness.

For once, Noswen did not take the lead. She seemed alarmed by this sudden development.

Coal felt he should handle things, given his brief history with Marl. He stumbled over his words, but eventually asked, "What in the world are you doing here?"

The wolverine glanced from Coal to Yurzu to Noswen and back to Coal. Sizing them up. Coal didn't like the ferocious glint in the man's eyes. He'd seen what Marl was capable of in a fight, and it was not pretty.

Marl said, "We've come for the claw."

Coal reflexively rolled his eyes. His body sagged at the horrible battle that was surely about to commence.

"Of course you did."

2

YURZU LOOKED FROM COAL to the hulking wolverine. The man was easily double the size of Yurzu, both in height and girth, and subsequently he felt very fragile all of a sudden.

He then glanced in Noswen's direction, but her focus was solely on the intruders. Her body was tensed, but he knew that her only weapon—a pistol that Lop had provided her before they left for Soponunga—was stuffed in the bag currently looped around her shoulder.

Not the brightest idea to keep their only real weapon packed away, but there was nothing to do about it now. Coal evidently recognized the wolverine, so at least he seemed to have the situation handled. Maybe.

"The Garna tried to do this the right way, but you didn't want to sell," said the wolverine. His voice was a low growl. Deep, hardened.

"I gotta say, Marl, this is the most I've ever heard you speak," said Coal. "And I didn't want to sell the claw because I didn't want Nomak to have the claw. Simple as that."

"That's why he's resorting to these measures," the wolverine, Marl, grumbled.

One of the rabbits at Marl's side was making Yurzu's senses tingle. There was some kind of sickness in the man, though Yurzu couldn't tell what it was. Nothing serious, as of yet, but he got the feeling it would grow over the next few days.

The other rabbit cracked their knuckles, like a thug in an old pulp novel getting ready to beat someone in a side alley.

Regardless of how cliché the action was, it still made Yurzu want to shrink into himself until he disappeared completely.

He still hadn't fully recovered from their fight with the monsters during the race. Noswen had healed his wounds, of course, so physically he was fine. But the brawl had left him rattled, and he was not ready for another. He knew he wouldn't be a match for any of the three men who were eager to wail on them, and Noswen would only really be useful with the gun that she didn't have access to. Perhaps Coal could take down one of the men, but certainly not all three. Yurzu silently wished for the fox to talk them out of this one.

Marl took a step forward. Yurzu instinctively took a step back, but to their credit, neither Coal nor Noswen moved an inch. "Look, I like you. But I don't care if I need to make this bloody. That's fine with me. It's your choice, though," the man said, looking Coal in the eye.

"You like me?" Coal laughed. "If I had to put money on it, I would've bet you didn't even register my existence when we worked together. Did you even speak to me during that job? I genuinely don't remember."

Marl ignored him and took another step. The rabbits trailed close behind. All three of them locked their eyes on Coal. None were paying any attention to Noswen or Yurzu.

Yurzu's mind raced, trying to dream up ways they could slip out of this awful scenario without any bloodshed.

Aside from willingly giving up the claw. That was not an option.

It was clear that in a hand-to-hand fight, they would lose. Marl outweighed them all and was comprised of pure muscle, while the rabbits were lean and agile and would duck and dive around them before anyone could get one measly punch in.

He pondered their situation. What could he do?

Yurzu's skills in blending complementary seasonings together, passed down to him from his mother Muneer, extended beyond the culinary world into one quite the opposite: poisons.

That aspect had been taught to him by his father Zanhu. Back in Toothshadow, the family had a sizeable garden outside their home, in which they grew a multitude of vegetables. Both for their own consumption as well as pickling and selling for their family business. But sometimes bugs and animals would try to eat the vegetables, and that was when his father employed various powdered solutions.

The most common was a sleeping powder. Zanhu did not want anything ruining his garden, but he also wanted to inflict little to no pain on the creatures. They were simply following their instincts, trying to survive; he did not fault them for that. So, whenever possible, he would dust the vegetables with a sleeping powder of his own making. Every morning and afternoon, Yurzu was in charge of going out to scoop up the sleeping insects and carry them back into the woods, safely depositing them.

One breed of insect, however, proved to be immune to any type of sleeping powder Zanhu concocted: vodflies. Vodflies were fingernail-sized pests with tiny horns on their foreheads that they used to burrow into the center of vegetables, where they would then lay eggs before tunneling the rest of the way through and emerging out the other side. Muneer also failed to put together anything that was effective against them, so unfortunately, Zanhu had to resort to a powder that instead killed the pesky things. His killing powder was only used during vodfly season, and it did regrettably affect some other insects during that time. He gravely cautioned Yurzu on the safeties of handling the killing powder. If even the smallest bit was ingested, that would be the end.

At some point, Zanhu tried one of the sleeping powders on himself when he was going through a patch where he had trouble sleeping. It worked like a charm, as the man had expected. Deep, restful sleep all through the night. It even kept him asleep during a thunderstorm once.

Yurzu continued the practice after his parents passed, when the house and the garden were his to care for. He knew all the recipes for each type of powder by heart, and he would dutifully dust the crops with the appropriate powder according to the season. Thankfully, vodflies only came around for a few short weeks before winter.

Before setting off on this wild journey with Lop so many months ago, he had thought to grab his supply of powders. He had healthy doses of both the sleeping and killing powders tucked away in his bag, just in case. There was no telling what the journey would entail.

And it was now proving to be a smart decision as these men stood before them with threats of violence.

If he could blow some of the sleeping powder onto the men, it would knock them out for at least an hour or two. Possibly even up to eight hours, if they inhaled enough of it.

But like Noswen's pistol, he couldn't reach into his bag without drawing Marl or the rabbits' attention. Somehow they needed to be distracted long enough for him to retrieve the powder.

Coal was still prattling away at his former coworker, asking something about how Marl had reached them so quickly, when Yurzu decided to collapse to the ground.

His head slammed into the dirt, sending a dull ache throbbing through his skull. He let out a wild, pained yelp. It was partially playacting, but it did actually hurt a lot more than he was expecting. He clamped his eyes shut and sprawled one arm out, the other resting atop his bag which was slung behind his back, mostly out of view of the men.

"Shit," he heard Coal mutter several feet away. "Yurzu? You okay?"

Yurzu breathed steadily but remained silent, not giving up the ruse.

"What the hell happened?" one of the rabbits grunted suspiciously.

"He scares easily," Noswen answered. Yurzu was slightly embarrassed by how swiftly she had the response ready. "He fainted. It happens a lot."

Not exactly true, but not exactly a lie, either. He had fainted the first time he ever encountered both Noswen and Coal, after all. His embarrassment deepened.

Yurzu waited a few moments, unsure when all eyes would be off him and unable to check.

Marl grunted and said to Coal, "Claw. Now." Yurzu could hear the man take a single step forward. His heart pulsed faster. He needed all three men to stay close together if his plan was going to be effective.

Coal sighed heavily. "I can't give it to you. I can't explain why, but it's important. Trust me. If I could, I would've given it up to Nomak in an instant. I need money a lot more than I need an anteater claw, no matter how shiny it is."

Yurzu hoped enough time had passed and that everyone was looking to Coal again. He slowly slipped his hand into the top of his bag, gently rummaging around with as subtle movement as possible.

The sleeping powder was in a velvet pouch, while the killing powder was in a leather one. His father had explained why the latter needed to be housed in leather, but the reason had long since drifted from Yurzu's mind. It didn't really matter why, as long as he remembered to do it.

Marl was saying something to Coal, but the words were dulled in Yurzu's head. He couldn't tell if it was due to the pain of hitting his head or his intense concentration on the task at hand.

His fingertips grazed the leather, and for a second he considered going with that instead. If he could cease searching now, that would give the men less opportunity to realize he was not actually passed out. The result would be the same: the men would be incapacitated and they could escape unharmed.

But Yurzu did not want to kill them.

That was not who he was.

He continued sifting through the bag until finally he felt the soft pouch. He grasped it in his palm and—painstakingly slowly—extracted it from the bag.

The next part would be tricky. There was maybe twenty or thirty feet between him and the attackers. But he was small and fast, so he could probably cover the distance before they were fully cognizant of what was going on. As long as he could hop to his feet quickly.

Coal being so close to them would be an issue, though. If he inhaled the powder and passed out, Yurzu and Noswen were in no position to lug his unconscious body all the way to Sadatso.

Please move, he thought to Coal, wishing in that moment that his blight allowed him to speak through someone's mind.

Noswen was starting to say something with vitriol when she was abruptly cut off by Yurzu leaping to his feet. He dashed forward, screaming *"Move!"*

Everyone, his friends included, was wildly confused by what was now transpiring.

Coal realized it was him being spoken to. He jumped backward, his boots slipping in the dirt and sending him plummeting onto his ass. He let out a pained yowl.

Yurzu skipped across the ground, grabbing a pinch of green powder with his free hand. A pinch was all it would take. Marl and his two rabbit companions stood at the ready, poised to knock him flat once he reached them. He skidded to a halt a few feet away, holding out the palm of his hand and blowing on the powder.

Noswen took the opportunity while the men were distracted to dig through her bag in search of the gun, but it proved unnecessary.

The powder shot forward with the force of his breath, clouding the three men. They coughed and wheezed as it shot up their nostrils and down their throats.

"What's th—" the wolverine sputtered, attempting to wave away the green out of the air, but that was all he managed to say before careening face-first onto the ground. There was a nasty crack as his snout collided with the forest floor. The rabbits soon followed suit, landing hard on their backs.

Seeing their bodies limp on the ground and eyes shut tight, Yurzu felt his own body suddenly relax. He did not realize how tense his muscles had been. He breathed out a sigh of relief, drooping his shoulders.

And he was more than a little proud of himself.

Coal was still sitting on the ground, staring straight ahead at Marl and the others. He then turned his head toward Yurzu and asked, "What just happened?"

Noswen held her gun pointed at Marl's heaving body, unconvinced that the threat had been dealt with.

"It's a sleeping powder," Yurzu explained. "An old family recipe."

"You and your family recipes," Coal groaned with a smile, pushing himself up off the ground. He patted dirt off his pants. All his clothes were always so dirty, though, Yurzu did not know why he bothered.

Noswen cocked an eyebrow and asked, "They're out cold?"

"For at least an hour or two, if not more," Yurzu nodded.

The raccoon trusted him and lowered the pistol.

She then rushed over to him, grabbing him by the shoulder with her free hand, and looked his body over. "Are you okay?" she asked him with genuine concern in her eyes. She grabbed him by the head and examined it for any bumps or gashes. "I'm fine," he told her. She tended to be overly concerned about his wellbeing. Yurzu appreciated her concern, but it did make him feel childish. Like she was his mother preening over him. But he did not want to say that and offend or upset her, so he remained tight-lipped. It wasn't the worst thing in the world having someone wanting to make sure you were safe.

"That was a pretty rough fall," she said. "You certainly had me convinced."

"Me too," Coal chimed in. "I even thought for a second that maybe you sensed Marl had some magic powers that he was about to blast me with."

Noswen continued inspecting him for any injuries, but he knew she wouldn't find any. Even his headache was fading away by now.

"You're sure you're okay?" she asked him again.

He nodded.

Then she smirked and said, "Nicely done, by the way."

Yurzu smiled.

Coal approached the wolverine and knelt down by the man's face. He let out a light laugh.

"They must've been traveling day and night to reach us," he said. "Last time I saw Marl here was in Vinnag. Nomak got word back to him pretty damn fast. Unless Marl was with him in Soponunga and I just didn't know it." He rose and looked to Yurzu. "You may not be much in a fight, but neither am I, and at least you can think fast. You've got me beat there, that's for sure."

Yurzu thanked him and asked, "Who is that guy?" His curiosity was piqued.

"Just some guy I did a job with back in Vinnag," Coal replied, gracing Marl with one last look. "I don't know him very well. We barely spoke. Just a friend of a friend."

"Who's Nomak?" Noswen asked, turning to face Coal. "You've mentioned that name a few times."

Coal nodded. "Nomak is some bigwig in Vinnag. Nasty, rich asshole. I'm sure you know the type." Noswen affirmed. He went on, "Marl does jobs for him and I was roped into one, so I got to know Nomak a little. He sponsored a racer, too, hoping to win the claw. He was…quite a bit miffed when I won instead and wouldn't sell it to him."

"And he's clearly not above using thugs to steal it instead," said Noswen with no hidden disdain.

"Nope. I'm not surprised by that, but I would've thought we were in the clear at this point. Like I said, I don't know if Marl was already with him and I just didn't know, or if Marl made it all the way here from Vinnag in that short amount of time."

"Seems unlikely," said Noswen, "but money and obsession can buy you a lot of shit I'm sure none of us could ever dream of. Maybe your pal Nomak found a way."

Coal simply shrugged. Yurzu didn't have any theories to contribute either; he had never been as far south as Vinnag. The farthest he'd been was Soponunga, and before all this started, he had only even left Toothshadow a handful of times.

"Is Nomak the type to keep trying?" Noswen then asked. "Or was this his one attempt to wrestle it away from us?"

"I don't think he'll be satisfied until he gets the claw. He's deluded enough to think he's entitled to it, somehow. I can't say I know what lengths he'll go through to get it, though. I haven't spent a whole lot of time with the guy, and most of that was just spent drinking and eating, to be honest."

"It sounds like we should stay on our toes," said Noswen. "We let ourselves get too comfortable. Pretty much no one in Ruska knows what we're doing and what we're after, Nomak included, so we didn't really think anyone was watching us. But Nomak *does* know that we have an item he wants. It's a good thing we're at least aware of his plans now."

Yurzu returned the sleeping powder to his bag. Meanwhile, Noswen wisely equipped her holster and slid the pistol into it for easier access in case Nomak had sent more goons after them. Yurzu was uncomfortable with the prospect of killing anyone, but he had to admit that he felt somewhat safer now.

With the three men indisposed, Noswen asked, "Are we all ready to go now?"

Yurzu had no doubts about the potency of his powder, but still, he wanted to put as much distance as they could between them and Nomak's men. He nodded eagerly.

"I'm good to go," Coal said. "Aside from my ass hurting. And my legs hurting. And my feet hurting. Can you heal any of that?"

"I'm not touching your ass," said Noswen, strolling down the pathway without another word.

Coal asked, "Yurzu, do you have some sort of powder you can blow onto my ass, then?"

Yurzu chuckled and said, "No, sorry. No family recipes for that."

The fox laughed heartily, and the two of them set off after Noswen.

3

COAL WAS PROUD OF himself for keeping his complaints to a minimum on the rest of the walk to Sadatso. When the village finally came into view, he almost shrieked with excitement.

Sadatso was nestled deep within the woods, like most other townships in the territory of the deer. They tended to enjoy the shade that the canopy provided, as well as being surrounded by the greenery. Coal could see the appeal. There was something cozy and rustic about it.

Trees were only cleared as much as necessary to construct a building. Otherwise, the natural world was left untouched. It made navigation slightly tricky, as there were no real designated pathways through the town since they would have been weaving through so many trees and bushes. A person really had to know where they were going to navigate a place such as Sadatso.

It was several hours past lunchtime. The group opted not to stop for lunch, instead snacking on dried insects and fruit while they walked to reach their destination sooner. As Coal looked around a bit at the village, he realized his dreams of buying some shitty vending machine vegetable chips were dashed. The Sadatso villagers were seemingly uninterested in such mediocre luxuries. His stomach was rumbling as fiercely as it had when he was making his way through the dung tunnels the previous week.

He was not cut out for traveling by foot. It was unfortunate that so much of the past year of his life consisted of it.

Noswen did not want to waste any time sightseeing. Not that there was much to gander at; it was a fairly modest village, consisting of tall, stone buildings. In an effort to cut down as few trees as possible, the deer typically built upward rather than outward. Many of the buildings in their towns and cities towered nearly as tall as some of the trees. It was impressive at first sight, but the buildings themselves were plainly decorated and there was nothing in the town square like Soponunga's many water features. Coal wasn't sure there even *was* a town square.

Every building looked the same to Coal. Just gray, looming, unmarked cylinders nestled amongst the trees. It was lucky that Noswen seemed to know where she was going.

As they followed her through town, Coal asked Yurzu, "Is there anything else I should know about the team before I meet them?"

The bat mulled the question over for a few seconds. "I think we've covered it all, really," he replied. "Just don't be too offended by Biror, I guess. He's very blunt and kind of rude. That's just how he is."

"And you all just take it? No one tries to put him in his place?" Not that Coal was likely to feel comfortable doing so himself.

Yurzu shrugged. "We all have to work together no matter what, since we're the ones infected by the blight. So it's easier just to smooth things over or ignore them. No one wants to get in too big of an argument and make things awkward."

That was fair. Coal was not usually big on confrontations either. But it didn't make him any more excited to meet the boar.

Noswen brought them to a nondescript tower that she assured them was the inn. The interior was as simple as the exterior, with no decorations of any sort. No potted plants, no framed paintings on the walls, nothing at all. Just a man sitting behind a (plain) stone desk. They marched straight past the reception desk and began climbing the narrow staircase.

They had to ascend six flights before they reached the correct floor. Coal's legs were jelly. If there wasn't a bed already waiting for him in the room, he was going to throw himself onto the floor. He might not even bother meeting the others yet.

"Here we are," said Noswen, stopping in front of a door with a metal plaque declaring it Room 621. She rapped her furry black knuckles on the door and waited.

A few moments later there came the *click* of the lock and the door swung open, revealing who Coal had to assume was Lop.

The orangutan was huge, easily filling the width of the doorframe. He would have to turn to the side and duck his meaty head to enter and exit. His jowls hung loosely on the sides of his round face, curving down toward a long, bright orange beard in contrast with the darker orange of his fur. His eyes were dark, almost sinking back into his skull. He wore light brown, loose-fitting pants with suspenders looping over his thick shoulders and no shirt to speak of, exposing the wrinkled red skin of his chest. Really letting it all hang out there.

Lop gave a curt nod to both Noswen and Yurzu before turning his attention to Coal. To him, he said, "A visitor, or an ally?" His voice was low, guttural. It boomed through the hall.

"He's the sixth," Noswen answered.

Lop's eyebrows raised and his mouth curled into a wry smile. "Our company is complete!" he boomed. He moved out from the doorway, allowing them entry.

Coal edged past the large man, accidentally brushing against his stomach. Lop closed the door behind them and Noswen led the way into the seating area of the room.

The first thing Coal noticed was the brightly-colored orange slime, Zsoz, stuck motionless to the wall. He had never spent any extended period of time with a slime, so he did not know if this was normal behavior for the creatures. Lop moved past them and took a seat on the floor beneath the slime, leaning his back against the wall and letting out a deep, contented sigh.

Seated in a chair with his arms crossed, suddenly awoken by their arrival, was Biror. His rough fur was mostly white, tinged with brown. The man was large like Lop (though not quite at the orangutan's level), but in contrast, his bulk was primarily muscle. His floppy ears were a deep black, a coloring which also covered his eyes and trailed down to his damp snout, which was slightly crooked. As if once broken and never properly set. Yet there was an undeniable attractiveness to the man; his bent nose was charming, rather than off-putting. He remained silent, staring at Coal with indifference.

Standing over by the window was Jatiri. Coal was momentarily transfixed, having never met a saola before. She was a slender, brown-furred woman with white streaks on her cheeks and above her eyes. Long, thin, pointed horns extended out from her forehead, a little more than half the length of her arms. She was dressed in a billowing white long-sleeved shirt, buttoned up to her neck, with a black corset and black leather pants.

She gave Coal the friendliest greeting of any of them: a wide smile and a wave.

"Welcome back," she said to Noswen and Yurzu. The former took a seat opposite Biror, while the latter remained stationary at Coal's side. "Who is this?" Jatiri then asked.

Noswen looked over to their newest recruit and said, "Our sixth member. Believe it or not, he was participating in the race, too."

"Lucky break for us, then," Biror huffed. He spoke in a heavy Mudlands accent, each word thick and throaty, with strange intonation. "Did any of you manage to get that claw?"

"I did," Coal said, his first words to this strange group he had unwillingly joined. He found himself wanting to impress them, wanting to prove his value. "I won it in the race."

But it did not seem to faze Biror. All he said was, "Good." Quite the understated response to learning they had succeeded in obtaining another ancient, world-saving artifact, in Coal's opinion.

"Shit got messy, but we got it," Noswen said, pulling the claw out from her bag, still encased in its glass cube. She placed it on the low table before her. "You want this thing, Zsoz?"

The slime said nothing, but began to crawl down the side of the wall, leaving a wet trail behind it. It slithered past Lop and moved over to the table, then said in its strange vibrational speech, **Yes, please.**

Noswen popped open the casing and grabbed the shimmering diamond claw. She held it up for everyone to see and asked if anyone wanted to take a look at it before Zsoz got ahold of it. No one was interested, so she plunged its sharp end into the slime, who then sucked the rest of it inside itself.

Upon closer examination, Coal could make out other objects in the slime's translucent orange jelly. There was a small, four-pronged antler in addition to a three-inch oval that Coal suspected might be a scale of some sort. The anteater claw nestled itself snugly between the other two items.

I will keep this safe, Zsoz promised them.

"We are aware," said Biror. "You do not need to be saying this every time."

The slime then returned to its previous position on the wall above Lop, who looked pleased.

"Another successful quest," said Lop.

"But three more to go, which means three more chances to fuck up," Noswen sighed. "This one was almost a blunder, too. They wouldn't let us buy the claw. Like he said, we had to actually race. Yurzu and I are pitiful racers, so it's a good thing we had him on our side."

"And who is *him*, exactly?" asked Jatiri, taking a step away from the window and toward the rest of the group. "I definitely want to hear what sounds like a fascinating story, but that can wait for dinner. Perhaps we should introduce ourselves?"

Coal decided to take the initiative, wanting to endear himself to these people. "My name's Coal Ereness," he said, granting each of them a friendly smile.

Each of the others introduced themselves in turn. He already knew their names, but refrained from saying so. Biror's eyes were already shut again, and he scratched at his chin.

"I know Noswen can heal and Yurzu can sense stuff in people," said Coal, "but they didn't tell me what the rest of you can do."

"Should we put on a little demonstration?" said Jatiri with a grin. Her voice was smooth, soothing.

Without waiting for a response, she held up her hands and closed her eyes. Her face bunched up in concentration. With her hands held up to him, Coal noticed a blue-inked tattoo on the woman's palm. It depicted a bowl of some sort, wide-rimmed and standing on three prongs. Jagged lines like lightning bolts encircled it.

She stood there for a second, doing and saying nothing, and then Coal nearly yelped in surprise when the woman's fingertips suddenly vanished.

The invisibility trailed slowly down her hand, first appearing as if she had no fingers at all, then half her palms were gone, until finally both her arms ended in nubs.

Her hands then abruptly popped back into existence and she opened her eyes, frowning apologetically.

"That's as much as I can do right now," she said. "I keep practicing, but I still can't do more than my hands."

"Wow," Coal muttered, truly amazed by the display even if it was only her hands. "That was incredible. Definitely flashier than what Yurzu does," he teased. He gave the bat a grin to let him know he was only messing with him. "Invisibility's *pretty* useful in a fight, but why don't any of us shoot icicles from our eyes or something more fatal like that?"

Jatiri laughed and said, "Maybe Lop's blight is more your speed."

Coal turned to face the orangutan, who was dragging himself up off the floor. The straps of his suspenders grazed his nipples as he raised his arms like Jatiri had.

Suddenly the man's skin began to ripple, and his chunky fingers engorged until they pressed into each other, solidifying into one big mound of flesh that curved and sharpened into an axe on the end of each arm.

Coal was too horrified to say anything, his mouth hanging open dumbly.

It was exactly what the abominations in Faranap could do.

Noswen chuckled and said, "He's flabbergasted. Look at him. Never seen anything like it."

I wish, he thought.

When he found his words, he asked, "Can they...change into other stuff?"

Lop responded by morphing one limb into the shape of a broadsword and the other into a gun barrel. That intrigued Coal; he had not seen either of Faranap's ghastly guards transform their arms into guns. Did he have to load bullets into himself somehow?

"And can they stretch?" He already knew the answer, but he wanted to confirm it anyway.

The orangutan nodded and his gun arm floated in the air, stretching out his hairy orange arm, snaking it around Noswen's head before coming to rest with the barrel pointed at Coal's face. It then morphed back into a hand, with which he waved at him.

Coal let out a sputtering laugh, and Lop asked him, "How did you know?"

"I've, uh…encountered something before that could do that," Coal said.

"Where the hell would you have done that?" asked Noswen.

But Lop already knew the answer. "A Flesh Eater prison," the ape said, retracting his arm. He formerly worked at the Palace, so it was reasonable for him to be in the know about the prison abominations. His voice was tinged with distrust already and Coal hadn't even freely admitted yet that he was technically a Flesh Eater.

Coal nodded.

"Why were you there?" Lop wanted to know. He remained standing, his body towering over everyone else in the room.

"He's a Flesh Eater," said Noswen.

As expected, Lop was not happy to learn this information.

Jatiri looked shocked as well, and the news even got Biror to open his eyes again.

Coal was mortified by how nonchalantly Noswen had tossed the fact out into the room to let it explode like one of the Palace's Fireballs. It felt like his fur was aflame.

"I'm…yes, I'm a Flesh Eater, but the situation is complicated," he said, stumbling over his words. There was no way he was going to dive into the full explanation right now, but he wanted to defend himself. "I wasn't imprisoned."

"So you're a fugitive?" said Lop.

"Calm down," Noswen groaned, standing to face the orangutan. Behind her, Biror was grinning at the drama unfolding. Noswen continued, "He's trustworthy."

"He is a Flesh Eater," Lop said with a scowl, glaring at Coal.

"And Biror's a dickhead. Who cares? We're all on the same team here, and I said he's trustworthy. Without him, we wouldn't even have the claw. Isn't that worth something?"

Lop said nothing further, but it was obvious he wasn't letting this go yet. He slid back down onto the floor below Zsoz, who had not moved an inch during the momentary tension.

Noswen said to Coal, "Might as well tell them what you do, now that it's out in the open."

Yeah, thanks for that, Coal said in his head.

Aloud, he told them after a brief pause, "I can speak to a person's spirit if I eat their flesh." He glanced at Lop to gauge the man's reaction, but he still wore the same perturbed expression as before. "But really, I'm not...I'm not rabid, or a criminal, or anything like that. There were some extenuating circumstances."

"Circumstances that led you to *eat someone?*" Lop growled.

Even Coal would admit it sounded flimsy. He was in no mood to tell the sordid tale, though.

"Shut up," Noswen shot at the man, and Lop grimaced but kept his mouth shut. She had clearly taken charge of this group at some point and everyone respected her. With the exception of Biror, maybe.

Jatiri looked disturbed by Coal's power, but she tried to steer the conversation back toward a more jovial tone. "Another piece of magic that isn't helpful in a fight," she said, forcing a smile.

"Not at all," said Coal.

Lastly, Biror sat up straight in his chair and said, "I do not know my power yet."

Coal stood for a second, perplexed by the admission. "How do you not know?"

"Nothing strange has happened. I have done no such thing like this woman's disappearing hands."

"Then…how do you know you're magical in the first place?"

The boar shrugged. "I do not know this."

"Yurzu sensed it in him," Noswen stepped in. "There's something there, but we're not sure what it is yet."

Coal remembered how defensive the little bat got when his abilities were questioned back in the Longowosk, so he didn't prod this time. If Yurzu sensed magic—or a *blight*, rather—within Biror, he was inclined to take the guy's word for it.

Lop at least had a useful ability if they found themselves face-to-face with more disgusting monsters. But if Biror wasn't shooting out icicles either, it seemed the group would have to rely primarily on his and the orangutan's brute strength.

I carry the artifacts, said Zsoz from the wall.

"The most important of us all," Jatiri smiled.

So that was the crew. The Blighted.

With the friction between himself and Lop, a part of Coal feared the man might sabotage him and leak their whereabouts to Palace Stingers to get him arrested.

That would be foolish, though, Coal knew. All six of them were required to seal the infection back in the Houndstooth. Surely he had nothing to worry about on that front.

But still, that paranoia lingered.

As if on cue, Noswen said, "Guess we need to get word back to the Dirt King and let him know we found the sixth."

She stood from her chair and walked over to a nearby desk just behind Jatiri, who took the raccoon's place. There was a pen and pad of paper resting on the desk, on which Noswen began scribbling.

Lop rose as well, but did not move from his position by the wall. The short orange hairs on the top of his head could almost brush against Zsoz. He said, "The Dirt King will be pleased to hear we've found everyone, though I know he had the utmost faith that we would. It was only a matter of time."

Coal scooted past Jatiri and Biror and shuffled over to the desk, peering over Noswen's shoulder. On the page he saw the word *spirit*. He whispered, "What exactly are you telling him?"

"Don't worry," said Noswen, her voice low. "I'm not gonna mention your status. No reason to. He specifically requested being told what each person's ability was, though. I'm just saying that you can speak to spirits. Not mentioning the specifics of *how*." She finished the brief letter, signed the bottom (with some impressive swoops on the tails of her N and S), and folded it in half once, then again.

Knowing what was expected of him, Zsoz came back down from the wall and approached the raccoon.

She pushed the paper into the slime's goo, along with a few tups. "Pay for the fastest courier possible," she told it. "After you're done, we'll be dining at Mojila's. You can meet us there, if you want."

I will hand off the letter to the fastest courier available so that it can be delivered to the Dirt King as soon as possible, said Zsoz. **Afterwards, I will return to Room 622's door and await the completion of dinner.**

"Okay then," Noswen nodded. "Thanks."

From the sound of it, the group had booked at least two rooms at the inn. If Coal could bunk in the room without Lop in it, that would be fantastic.

Zsoz then crawled leisurely toward the door, where Lop opened it up for him before resuming his position by the wall. Coal would swear the man was keeping his eyes fixed on him. He needed to do something to earn the man's trust, but he was failing to think of a way he might do so. Maybe Yurzu would have an idea.

"So we are going to Mojila's, then?" said Biror. With his accent, every sentence sounded perturbed.

"Yep. That a problem?" Noswen asked sternly.

"I am getting pretty sick of this."

"You'd rather eat at The Bumpy Log?"

"I am sick of this place too."

"Well, there are only two restaurants in town, so I don't know what to tell you."

"I would like Mojila's," said Yurzu softly from the other end of the room.

"The kid wants Mojila's, so that's where we're going," Noswen declared. That was that.

Biror groaned but did not press the matter, shoving himself up out of his chair. He was even bulkier than Coal had realized, now that he was standing tall. Not accounting for magic, Coal was unsure who would win in a straight brawl between Lop and the boar.

Noswen, as always, led the way out the door. She was followed closely by Yurzu, then Lop, then Biror. Coal and Jatiri brought up the rear.

"That got kind of uncomfortable," the woman said to him with a chuckle.

"Yeah," Coal said, joining in her strained laughter. "I was given some warning about Biror, but Lop was…more intense than I expected."

"He's a good guy, but yeah, he can be a little intense," Jatiri nodded. "He'll warm to you, though. You seem like a good guy too. I've got a sense about things like that. I'm maybe not as accurate as Yurzu with his blight, but still." She grinned.

"Thanks," Coal said.

The saola gave him another warm smile and squeezed his shoulder amiably. Then she turned and headed toward the doorway.

Beyond her, Noswen called to Coal. "Hurry up, newbie! I thought you were starving. You wouldn't shut up about it!"

Maybe he had not kept his complaints as minimized as he thought.

He rushed toward her out into the hallway, joining his new-found friends.

4

THE INITIAL MEETING DIDN'T go as poorly
as it could have, Yurzu thought. It wasn't totally
smooth, though. Biror behaved himself and was less
abrasive than usual, but maybe he was simply tired and hungry
and the forthcoming meal would fire him up. Lop had reacted
to Coal's secret with much more vitriol than Yurzu had ever
seen him exhibit, however, and he had known the orangutan
the longest out of all them.

They all trailed behind Noswen through the wooded town
toward Mojila's. Sadatso's other restaurant, The Bumpy Log,
had not set right with Yurzu's stomach the last time he ate
there, so he was eager to avoid it.

Truth be told, he thought both restaurants were mediocre at
best, but at least Mojila's was not *bad*.

Sadatso was a small village, with only one inn, two restaurants, and one general store. The rest of the buildings were
homes stacked atop one another.

In a way, it reminded him of his hometown, Toothshadow. It was a similarly small village, just south of the Palace and the Houndstooth. Said by its founders to be in the colossal tree's shadow, hence the name. It was not literal, of course; the Houndstooth lay just beyond the Palace and was inaccessible to anyone but those who lived inside.

But like Sadatso, Toothshadow received very few visitors and had a single inn. Where they had them beat, though, was that they had *three* restaurants and *two* general stores.

Yurzu's family had originally been planning on selling their pickles to both stores, but one offered a better price for exclusivity, so his parents opted for that one. After they passed and the business was left to him, he decided to not renew the contract when it expired and sold his wares to both stores. He felt it was more fair. It created a lot more work for him, but it was work that he enjoyed doing.

Almost ten months had passed now since he was last home. He had departed Toothshadow with Lop during Drymonth. Some of his peppers had been harvested, but not all had ripened yet. Unfortunately, he had not gotten to dig up his potatoes or pull up his carrots either, and pickled carrots were some of his best sellers.

He sold raw vegetables to the stores, but he also attempted to pickle anything he could get his tiny hands on. Pickling was the most fun he ever had. Ginger-dill pickled carrots were what he sold the most of, closely followed by the same brine (with only slight modifications) for cucumbers. He also tried pickling spinach as well as potatoes, but those did not sell nearly as well. It seemed he might be the only person who was actually a fan of those. But still, it was fun to experiment with atypical vegetables and flavors.

Yurzu was thinking about his wasted crop when the group arrived at Mojila's. The only thing that distinguished the restaurant from the rest of the buildings in town was that it was considerably shorter than all the other towers. Mojila's stood alone, without any other establishments above or below it, though the restaurant was still two stories tall to account for both the dining room and the kitchen.

Despite their large number, their party was immediately ushered to a hefty table at the back of the restaurant, near the staircase that led to the kitchens. There were not many patrons tonight. Aside from their own, there were only three other groups seated: two couples and one family of four.

The restaurant was sparsely decorated, filled with stone tables and chairs, but it was a little flashier than their inn. Most things in Sadatso and other deer villages were constructed from stone, not wanting to kill more trees. A few wreaths hung from the walls, as well as some handwritten signage with "inspirational" phrases attributed to Mojila.

One such sign hanging near their table said: *"The older you are, the wiser you become. Never let your dreams slip away."*

Yurzu wasn't exactly sure he understood the correlation, but he supposed it was not untrue, if a bit trite.

The table had one chair on each end and two on either side. Lop sat himself down at one end of the table, and Coal sat at the opposite, as far away from the orangutan as he could manage. Yurzu sat on one side of the table, near Coal, with Noswen beside him. Jatiri took the other seat near Coal, while Biror sat next to Lop and across from Noswen.

"So, what's good here?" Coal asked the table, grabbing a menu and flipping through it.

Yurzu almost said "Nothing," but held his tongue.

Jatiri was the first to respond. She had seemingly taken a liking to the fox. Or, at the very least, she was making the greatest attempt to ease him into the group and make him feel comfortable. She said, "I think their cauliflower steak is pretty nice."

"I had a really good one in Soponunga," Coal said before licking his lips. "I might be in the mood for another..."

At the other end of the table, Biror grumbled something about being sick of eating nothing but vegetables. "I need an insect. I need a *crunch*," the man moaned irritably.

The menu at Mojila's was completely vegetarian. It was difficult to obtain insect-based products at such a remote location without going out and hunting or breeding the bugs oneself. Yurzu figured the head chef (was that Mojila?) was uninterested in the extra work.

"The Bumpy Log has waspballs," said Jatiri, trying to be helpful.

"We are not at the Log. And anyway, their waspballs taste of dirt and old rags." The boar mimed spitting on the ground, thankfully refraining from actually doing so. Yurzu would not have put it past him.

But what Biror said was true. Yurzu had eaten the waspballs there too, and they were far from the best he'd ever eaten. Waspballs were made by combining wasps, breadcrumbs, and herbs, plus a binder, then forming them into small spheres that were either baked or lightly fried in oil. Given the taste of those at the Bumpy Log, though, Yurzu would not be shocked to learn that some dirt was indeed carelessly scooped into the mixing bowl along with the dried wasps.

They each ordered their drinks. Waters across the board, and glasses of longwine for both Noswen and Lop. Yurzu was nervous about the orangutan getting some drink in him and yelling at Coal more, but he could usually hold his alcohol well.

Noswen kicked back half her drink in a single gulp, the rest of the murky purple liquid sloshing around as she placed the thin-stemmed glass on the table. She smacked her lips in satisfaction.

Yurzu never had the taste for longwine, or for any alcohol, really. Sweet, fruity cocktails were about all he could stomach, but even those he felt were generally cut by too much bitterness. He was content with his water.

Again, Jatiri was the facilitator of conversation while they perused their menus. She said to Coal, "So, tell us about the race."

"It was actually a fucking mess," Noswen said before the newcomer could get a word in. "A shitload of blightbeasts showed up in the middle of it."

"Is 'blightbeast' the official term?" Coal asked. "I was calling them not-retnos or not-ventems."

"Seems a bit wordy."

"At least it's more specific. Do you just call them *all* blightbeasts?"

"They *are* all blightbeasts. They aren't retnos or ventems or whatever else. But yes, I guess those ones did look similar to retnos. One guy ended up dead," she said.

The group let out a quiet collective gasp.

"Who?" Lop asked. Yurzu knew he was pretty into the spiderback racing scene, and had actually wanted to go to Soponunga to retrieve the claw (and watch the race). But they all decided Zsoz should stay behind, and so Lop remained in Sadatso with his buddy.

"Uh…" Noswen struggled to find the name.

"Manova Mandolat," Coal answered for her.

Lop's expression was inscrutable. Yurzu couldn't tell if he was familiar with the racer or not.

"That's horrible," Jatiri frowned.

"It was rough," Coal nodded. "There were a ton of them surrounding us. I wouldn't have gotten out of there alive without their help," he said, gesturing toward Noswen and Yurzu.

The raccoon giggled before taking another sip of her drink. "His ass was laid out pretty badly before we got there," she then said. "You probably would've been the second casualty."

"Don't remind me," Coal muttered.

Jatiri stared slack-jawed, horrified by what they were saying and their casual attitude about Coal being fatally wounded. Noswen briefly explained how she had to plug up multiple holes in the fox's back, which elicited more shock and disgust from Jatiri.

Biror had a more pragmatic rather than empathetic reaction. "So we almost lost the claw *and* the sixth is what I'm hearing. I knew you two were not cut out for this job."

"Clearly we *were* cut out for it, because we're back here with the claw and the sixth, jackass," Noswen said, rolling her eyes and slurping down more longwine. The glass was nearly depleted.

Yurzu was impressed by her restraint. He expected a much more ferocious snap back.

"Yes, only by the swish of your fucking tail," said Biror, adopting an old boar idiom.

"Yeah. And who fucking cares? We got what we went there for. *More* than what we went there for, since we found Coal *and* the artifact." The fox's ears perked up, not wanting to find himself in the middle of this argument. "The beavers weren't budging. We offered them triple the value of the claw and they still wouldn't sell it, so we did what we had to do. I'd like to see your ass climb up onto a spider and try to race for it. Is there even a spider out there that you wouldn't crush?"

Biror huffed, more amused than offended by the barb.

Beside him, Lop spoke up. "What breed did you ride?"

Surprisingly, the question was directed at Coal. Perhaps they would find some common ground and smooth things over after all.

Coal was clearly caught off guard by the question too. After processing it, he said, "An orb weaver."

Lop's eyebrows shot up. "You can handle one of those?"

"They're my specialty," Coal nodded with a grin. "I grew up learning on an orb weaver. That's what I feel most comfortable on. This was the fastest I've ever seen, too. You wouldn't believe the speeds it could hit."

"He didn't even use a saddle," Yurzu chimed in, assuming this would be an impressive factoid. He wanted to hype up Coal in Lop's eyes.

His ploy worked. Lop let out a low whistle and tugged at his beard. "A saddleless orb weaver is a rare sight. I can't recall if I've ever seen a professional rider do that, come to think of it."

"It was more out of necessity than anything else," Coal confessed, "but I made it work." He added with a grin, "These two were riding hacklemeshes." As he spoke, he jabbed a thumb toward Noswen and Yurzu.

Lop guffawed. "No!" he exclaimed.

Coal laughed too and nodded.

To them, Lop said, "That is despicable. No wonder you needed him to win the claw for us. *Hacklemesh weavers?* Pah!" More booming laughter.

"Yeah, okay, well—I think we did pretty well for ourselves under the circumstances," said Noswen. "Maybe you missed the part where he said he wouldn't have won without us."

Coal and Lop continued to laugh together at their choice of spider. Yurzu was at least glad that his incompetence could bridge the divide between the men, even if only momentarily.

Their waiter then returned and took their meal orders. Yurzu went with something different this time around, hoping it was an improvement on the last dish he ate there. It was something simple—roasted sweet potatoes with ginger and scallions—but it would hit the spot. Assuming it did not taste vile. He was hard-pressed to think how a chef could screw up something as easy as roasting potatoes, though.

He always loved listening to other people order food. He felt it revealed a lot about them. And besides that, he simply loved food in general and enjoyed seeing what types of dishes people he knew liked. It was always fun seeing how chefs prepared the meals, too.

Coal and Jatiri both went with the cauliflower steak, while Noswen ordered a light pasta tossed with oil and fresh herbs (and another glass of longwine). Biror got something called a "vegetable loaf," which Yurzu figured was probably just the closest approximation he could get to insect meat. Lop was too far away for Yurzu to eavesdrop on his order, much to his disappointment. He'd have to take a peek at the man's plate once it was brought to the table.

Coal went on to describe the spiderback race in detail, including aspects that Yurzu was unaware of, such as his tangles with Cassallia Juj and a nasty scrape with geigexes. Lop, Jatiri, and Yurzu sat with rapt attention while he told his tale, but Noswen and Biror were fairly uninterested.

Conversation then segued from the diamond claw to their next target: the crystal tiger fang.

In addition to the anteater claw, they already had the silver deer antler and the copper lizard scale. After the fang, they would then need to acquire the jade hoof from the boars and the obsidian beak from the macaws.

But those were problems for later.

"Thankfully, the Dirt King knew exactly what city this one is located in," Lop began, keeping his voice low so that the other diners would not overhear them. The people were all pretty far from their table, so there was little worry. "We don't have to scour for clues throughout the whole tiger territory. We will be going to Nitulo."

Everyone else nodded knowingly except for Yurzu.

It was not a city he had ever heard of. He lived a relatively sheltered life back in Toothshadow, so most places were unknown to him. This ten-month journey had been eye-opening in many ways.

"According to the Dirt King," Lop continued, "the person in charge over there is a woman named Ghoresn Daanarb. She has the fang in her possession."

"Did your king have any suggestions on how we make her to give it up?" Biror asked.

Jatiri piped up before Lop could respond. "There might be a different issue," she said. "The town I'm from isn't terribly far from Nitulo, and there have been rumors circulating for months now about Ghoresn going missing."

"Perfect," Biror grimaced, slouching back in his chair.

"Is there a different, more helpful rumor, about where she possibly disappeared to?" Noswen asked.

The saola shook her head. "None. All I've heard is that she's gone, disappeared from public view a while back. And also that in her stead, the Calitarash are running things now. I think the last time anyone saw her was Newmonth."

"Who are the Calitarash?" Coal asked. Yurzu was wondering the same thing.

"They're a religious sect," Jatiri replied. "I'm afraid I don't know much more about them, though. I've never actually been to Nitulo."

"Do you know anything about them?" Noswen asked Lop. The orangutan shook his head. No one else had any information to offer on the subject either.

Lop sighed, and Noswen looked defeated as well.

"It doesn't change anything though, right?" Yurzu said. His voice cracked as he spoke. He cleared his throat, then said, "We still go to Nitulo. It's more of a lead than we had on the antler or the scale. Either the fang was left behind somewhere, like Ghoresn's house, or we can search for clues to her whereabouts. Someone there might know something."

"If these people could not be able to find her for months, do you think our dumb asses are going to do it?" said Biror.

"I don't know," Yurzu said, shrinking away from the boar's harsh words. "But if it comes to that, we have to try. We don't have any other choice."

"The kid's right," Noswen nodded. "The beavers wouldn't take our money, so we had to compete in the race to win the claw. The same thing applies here. We'll do what needs to be done to track down the fang."

They quietened their talk of the artifacts as their waiter returned with food.

The plate of roasted sweet potatoes didn't look terrible. There was slightly more char on the tops of each slice than Yurzu would have preferred, but when he pierced the blackened layer with his fork, he discovered soft, creamy potato underneath.

Before taking a bite of his own food, he glanced over at Biror's vegetable loaf. It looked as unappetizing as its name suggested, and the boar seemed disgusted by his own choice.

Sitting in front of Lop was a bowl filled with various grains (of which Yurzu could not identify), whole roasted carrots, and a creamy dressing drizzled on top. Pumpkin seeds were sprinkled over it, dotting the cream.

Coal ribbed Jatiri by telling her the cauliflower steak here was not as good as the one he ate back in Soponunga. She laughed and told him he couldn't be so picky out on the road. Even Lop, Noswen, and Biror seemed to be getting along better than usual, all of them making quips about the awful loaf Biror had to eat. Surely the longwine was improving Noswen's mood.

Yurzu smiled. Even if he wasn't joining in on any conversation, it warmed him listening to everyone else's. Jovial chatter bubbled all around him. He always liked keeping to himself anyway.

Listening to everyone enjoying each other's company, he was feeling much more confident about their ability to work together now than he did only about an hour before. He loved how a meal really could bring people together.

Finally, he took a bite of his potato. It was incredibly oversalted.

But he ate it anyway and merrily listened to the others.

5

AFTER DINNER, THE GROUP sauntered back to the inn with full bellies (and a bit of swagger in their gait, in Noswen's case). Zsoz was stuck to the door of Room 622 as it said it'd be, and everyone filed into their respective room.

Jatiri, Lop, and Biror took 622, while Coal was corralled into 621 with Noswen and Yurzu. He was happy with that division. Things had grown more cordial with Lop over the course of the meal, but he still wasn't particularly comfortable around him.

Now Coal lay in his cramped bed, in a similarly cramped room that was an offshoot from the sitting area where he had earlier met everyone. There were two bedrooms: a tiny one with a tiny bed (which he was currently trying to get comfortable in), and a slightly larger one with two beds, where Noswen and Yurzu were already dozing.

He stared up at the ceiling, grateful for the bed, yet still longing for the one he'd had back in Soponunga. Where he could stretch out and truly relax.

Thoughts of the Longowosk inevitably drifted to those of Ilio. For a few brief moments, he returned to the fantasy of the Uncut Gem supply room, running their hands up and down each other's bodies—but then he began reminiscing about their day together at the festival. Playing that stupid, rigged water jug game.

Even before he distracted himself with thoughts of Ilio, he was feeling restless. The bed was small, the room bitterly cold. Not exactly prime conditions the night before setting off on yet another week-long journey.

Coal sat up, blinking in the dark. There wasn't a window in this room, so he did not even have dim moonlight to guide him. It was not much of an issue, though, with his impeccable night vision. He leaned over the side of the bed and grabbed his bag off the floor, slamming it onto his lap.

He rifled through the bag until he found what he was looking for. The book was a relatively slim volume, typical of its genre. He ran his fingertips over the cover, then traced each letter of its title, relishing in the swoops of the Ps and B.

There had not been a great opportunity for him to start *A Popular Bargain* yet, but on a few occasions he had taken the gift from Ilio out of his bag to admire it. The illustration was rendered beautifully; enough fine details to give it a sense of realism, of texture, but still lacking enough to give the whole piece a tinge of mysteriousness. Of danger.

Now is as good a time as any, he thought, resigning himself to his sleep schedule being ruined regardless.

He opened the cover, flipping past all the boring front matter—what did he care who the story was dedicated to?—until he hit the meat of the book.

Danai Loroto certainly had a unique writing style. The prose was a lot more flowery than Coal typically expected from the mystery genre. Usually the writing was much more direct and to-the-point, keeping the reader grounded and in the moment. In *A Popular Bargain*, though, things were much more dreamlike and surreal. It was an interesting shift, and Coal was intrigued by it, but he had always found it difficult to be hooked by that style. He could only read so much of it at a time before everything got muddled and confusing or he grew distracted.

After wrapping up the prologue, he closed the book and placed it back in his bag. He tossed himself backward into his flat pillow and clamped his eyes shut, willing himself to sleep.

Thirty minutes later, it still hadn't worked. He crawled out of bed, yanked on his boots, and quietly slipped out of Room 621.

His footsteps beat against the stone as he traversed the narrow inn stairs, echoing up and down through the numerous flights of steps. Coal wrapped his arms around himself, trembling in the cold.

Out in the open, Sadatso was still. A huge change from the past few weeks spent in Soponunga and Vinnag. Nobody was outside at this hour, and even earlier in the evening, he had seen hardly anyone milling about. Come to think of it, he might not have seen anyone at all. If there hadn't been other people dining at Mojila's, he may have feared they were in a ghost town. But it was a small village with a low population, and surely everyone had better things to do at home rather than wander around. It wasn't like there was anywhere to go, anyway. Nothing to see.

Coal walked through the empty town, weaving between trees and kicking up leaves and dirt as he navigated the streets. If they could even be called streets. Aside from the stone buildings, every other part of Sadatso was natural. No unnecessary structures or roads. Letting the forest gift its own vibrancy to the village. Ruska was its decorator.

Which meant there were no streetlights to speak of. The moon struggled to cast its light on the town through thick-leaved treetops. A possible reason for its residents to remain indoors at night. Coal could see just fine, though.

It was too late when he realized that he would be unable to tell which building was the inn whenever he was ready to go back. They all looked the same, and he had not picked out any landmark such as an unusual bush or a tree stump or anything to help guide him back to that unfortunate bed.

He was starting to find the quiet more unnerving than relaxing. His mind started to race, imagining that Sadatso was a town frozen in time, and he was the only person who could still move through it. The sway of leaves in the gentle breeze was a dead giveaway that this was not the case, but still, he latched onto the idea.

In the distance, behind a stout building that he guessed might be the town's other restaurant, he spotted a faint purple glow that caught his attention.

His pace quickened, titillated by the discovery. He soon rounded the building and let out a soft gasp.

It was a small clearing of purple flowers, all glowing with brilliant luminescence. Their petals were a deep, rich purple while the stamens slithering out from their centers were a cool blue that glowed as well, but were overpowered by the petals. Coal was transfixed by the sight when there came a familiar voice to his right. "Hey."

He looked and Jatiri was sitting on the ground, her back against the stone structure, knees pulled up to her chest. She smiled at him, and he took another look out at the clearing before taking a seat beside her. He was actually happy to find the saola here.

"They're beautiful, huh?" she asked him, nodding toward the field of flowers.

"They are," he affirmed. "I've never seen them before."

"That's because this is the only place they grow. I'd never seen them before either, before I came here. I'd heard about them, though, and I knew they bloomed at night, so I come out here every night. They're called sadas."

"Ahh. Sada flowers. Sadatso."

Jatiri grinned. "You're cleverer than you look."

"Thank you. I read mystery novels, so it was easy for me to piece that one together."

"Brilliantly done."

They shared companionable silence while looking out at the sadas.

"Can't sleep?" Jatiri then asked after a minute.

"Unfortunately, no," he replied with a sigh. "I've been completely exhausted all day, wanting nothing more than to lay in bed, but I just can't."

"Nervous about the next leg of the mission?"

"I don't know if it's that or if the bed is just trash. It's so small! I barely fit!"

"Ahh. You're in the solo room, I'm guessing? That's where Biror is in ours. My bed has plenty of space for me."

"Rub it in, why don't you?"

"Sorry," she chuckled. She turned from him and gazed out at the glowing flowers. "I'm worried about not being able to find Ghoresn. After being missing for so long, what are the chances she's even still alive out there somewhere?"

It was a concern of Coal's as well. "What happens if we can't find her and the fang?" he asked.

"Ruska succumbs to darkness and is wiped off the face of the planet, I'm guessing," Jatiri shrugged.

"Not a great outcome."

"No."

"Do we have some sort of time limit imposed on us? Noswen didn't mention to me if there's some specific timeframe we're working with."

"We just have to find everything as soon as possible. The Houndstooth could burst open tomorrow, for all we know. You'll have to use your keen detective skills and find the fang quick."

"I'll do my best."

"Probably the only person with any real idea of how much time is left is the Dirt King. He's the one who's been around for hundreds of years and has seen this happen before."

"You'd think he'd be more proactive about preventing it," Coal grunted. "Not letting it get to this point in the first place." His tone presented it as a joke, but Coal found himself believing the words. If this kept happening, and the Dirt King knew it, why was he not doing more?

"I guess preventing worldwide disasters is harder than we'd think," said Jatiri with a smirk.

"Maybe you're right. Was it hard tracking down the other artifacts? As hard as it seems like finding the fang will be?"

Jatiri inhaled deeply, then exhaled slowly. She said, "I'm not sure about the copper scale. They found that before me. I was actually the last to join the group, before you."

"Oh, yeah?"

"Mhmm. The town I'm from isn't terribly far from here or from Nitulo. Relatively speaking, anyway. It's a bit farther north than Nitulo. Have you heard of Kilutsk?"

"No," Coal confessed.

"Ahh. Well, it's nestled away in the forest underneath the Houndspine. It's small and unassuming, just like this place. It's not named after anything amazing like these flowers, though. Our flora is much more normal. Kind of boring in comparison, honestly."

Coal was familiar with the Houndspine; he had traveled it on his way south from Muta Par to Vinnag. It was a massive bridge in central Ruska, spanning countless miles, raised up high into the sky above the kingdom's forest. It was a structure meant to ease and speed up travel, allowing people to move between north and south Ruska without needing to traverse the dense forests. It was vital for merchants, and many others made use of it as well.

He also knew that the saolas kept to themselves in that central forest beneath it. Their population had declined heavily over the years, but Coal had never learned the reason why. He liked Jatiri, and felt they had a nice rapport going, but he did not think they were at a place yet where he could ask such a sensitive question.

The woman went on. "The antler was no problem, though. It was in an art museum in Vuela. All we had to do was buy it from the curator. Vuela was also where we caught wind of the race in Soponunga and realized the grand prize was the claw we were looking for, so that was convenient. We decided to hole up in Sadatso rather than Vuela, though, since it's so much more low-key. As I'm sure you've noticed."

"Oh, is it?" he joked.

"We figured there'd be less prying eyes on us here than in a major city."

"I can't imagine there have been any eyes on you at all, let alone prying ones."

"Exactly. Things have been quiet here. I like the quiet." After a pause, she said, "Vuela was pretty overwhelming. I'd never been in a city that big before."

"Really? I've only ever lived in a big city. I'm from Muta Par."

"I haven't heard of it."

"I guess we're even, then. It's just some place up north. Nothing special. Nitulo is a city too, isn't it? Are you ready for that?"

"From what I hear, it's not on the same scale as Vuela, but yes, it's a step up from Sadatso."

"Honestly, I think a typical birthday party would be a step up from Sadatso, in terms of liveliness."

Jatiri laughed at that. "Do you miss Muta Par?"

It was a complicated question. Coal wrestled with the answer for a moment before responding.

"I think I miss…I don't know. I miss the idea of what my life was, rather than the city itself. Does that make sense? I like Muta Par, but I'm not specifically yearning to walk down its streets or to look at its sights or anything like that. It's more that I miss how simple and easy things were back when I lived there. The one thing I do miss that I can't get anywhere else, though, is this food stall there called Ants To Eat You. Truly horrific pun. Doesn't even make sense in any regard; not with the 'eat you' part and also 'ants' doesn't really work to replace 'nice,' but that's beside the point. All of the guy's food was delicious."

She couldn't contain her laughter at the name. Coal joined her. It really was a ridiculous name for a food stall. He craned his head back, laughing, and smacked his head into the building behind him. He yelped in pain and rubbed the back of his head. Jatiri then laughed even harder, clacking the sharp tips of her horns on the stone.

"Oh, sure, laugh it up," he said, feigning offense. "We'll see if you're still laughing when your beloved 'sixth' is brain-dead and can't complete the ritual of destiny or whatever the hell and save the world."

"Nah, I think we'd be fine," said Jatiri. "Noswen has magical healing and I have normal healing. One of us can patch you up."

"You're a doctor?"

"Yep. One of two in Kilutsk."

"So now just one person is left keeping everyone in town healthy?"

"Luckily we're never really overrun with patients, so I'm not worried about my partner being burdened while I'm gone. It did give me pause, though, when the others were recruiting me. I didn't want to leave."

"That makes sense. If they had found me in Muta Par, there wouldn't have been much keeping me there. I was just a librarian. Nothing fancy or useful like you."

"Libraries are useful!" she objected. "They provide knowledge and entertainment."

"You provide *health*. Which is vital for life, last I checked."

"Knowledge and entertainment are both vital for rich lives, though, no?"

"Knowledge, sure. But with some of the books I've seen, you might have a hard time defending entertainment." He shuddered, thinking of *Valiant Memories*, one of the drabbest, most generic books he'd ever encountered in the library.

Jatiri scoffed. "Nah," she said with a shake of the head. "Entertainment gets us through all our roughest times. Our saddest, our loneliest, our most *bored*. It's a light that gets us to the end of the tunnel. To the other side."

"Maybe you're right," Coal conceded. He smiled at the woman's positive outlook.

She smiled back at him, raising the white streaks of fur on her cheeks. "You were just as vital as I was."

"I appreciate that," he said, tearing his eyes from her and looking back out at the calming sadas. "I noticed your tattoo earlier." He pointed stupidly at her hand, as if she did not know where her own tattoo was. "It's pretty. I've never seen blue ink before."

She turned her hand over with a smile. "Thanks," she said, looking down at the three-legged bowl surrounded by crooked lines. "It's a fenté bowl."

"I'm not familiar," Coal admitted.

"I'm not surprised," she laughed. "Fenté is a drink specific to saola culture. It's poured into a bowl like this and the whole group drinks from it. The tattoo symbolizes community and hospitality. Fenté's consumed at a lot of important events."

"So is that a tattoo that lots of people get? Or was it something you wanted?"

"Both, I suppose," Jatiri replied. "Being tattooed is common in our culture, and there are many traditional designs that people get. This was important to me, so that's the design I chose when it came time for me to get tattooed. There are other more literal designs like this, but some are abstract designs which carry meaning to saolas."

"The ink is beautiful," said Coal. It seemed to almost shimmer in the moonlight. Glittery.

"Thank you," she smiled. Then, after a minute of silence, "I'm sorry about Lop." They were not words he had been expecting to hear. He forced himself to continue staring ahead at the flowers. He did not want to meet her gaze.

"It's okay," he said, after an embarrassingly audible gulp.

"For the record, I don't think any less of you."

Coal's breathing quickened. He was suddenly very conscious of how loud his exhales were from his nostrils. The delightful rapport between them was slipping into awkwardness. Mostly on his end, but he couldn't help it.

"Thanks," he whispered, not knowing what else to say.

Apparently she didn't either, because the conversation faded after that. Maybe she had assumed he would dive into his own complicated history, explain what the "extenuating circumstances" were that led to becoming a Flesh Eater, but he did not want to talk about it. Did not want to relive those moments. Not right now. Maybe never.

A minute passed, and she broke the tension by saying, "I'm glad you're here."

"Yeah?" For him, the verdict was still out on that.

"Yeah. I'm not the newbie anymore."

"Ahh," said Coal, nodding and smiling. "So it's for purely selfish reasons."

"Yes, of course," she grinned.

"I'm the one now who doesn't know what the hell is going on and asks all the questions and gets made fun of by everybody behind my back."

"Oh, yeah, we're a rude bunch. Always talking behind each other's backs. When we got back to our room, Biror told me he thought you were a *doofus*."

"Wow. Harsh words. And definitely sounds like the type of insult he'd use."

"He can be savage, it's true."

"I'm not convinced you know much more than I do about this whole situation, though," said Coal, rubbing his chin thoughtfully. Playing the detective role, analyzing his suspect. "You've only got one artifact under your belt, after all. You're even greener than sweet little Yurzu. I think you and I are on equal footing here."

"I'm up to *two* artifacts now, actually. The claw counts."

"That's bullshit!" Coal laughed. "You were all the way over here looking at flowers! You had nothing to do with the claw. I did pretty much all the work on that one, actually. Noswen didn't even tell me what was going on until after I'd already won it."

Jatiri shrugged, donning an expression that said *I don't know what to tell you.* "The fact of the matter is that I've been part of the group when it obtained both the antler and the claw, so that's two on my record. You've only got the claw. Sorry."

"I—"

"I don't make the rules, Ereness!"

"Fine," he grumbled. "I will accept the role of the newbie."

"You kinda *have* to," Jatiri said. "You're the newest member of the group. It kinda lands on you by default." Then her face lit up and she said, "Come to think of it, you'll *always* be the newbie. No one else is gonna be joining the group." She cackled with glee at this realization.

"Wow," he sighed. "So I don't even get the chance to hang it over someone else's head like you are right now."

"Nope. Sorry."

"Well, I'm glad you are taking it upon yourself and acting with dignity," he teased her.

"Thank you."

He squinted out at the clearing filled with sadas, more closely examining the blue stamens. They each looped two or three times before coming to a bulbous tip, some even tangling up with each other. He was reminded of the tendrils on the heads of the abominations in Faranap. A chill coursed through his body.

But then Jatiri let out a sigh, and he was put at ease again, being shaken from his memory and reminded of her presence. It felt good to have already made a friend. He and Yurzu were pals, but the bat was still very guarded, and he could already sense a deeper connection with Jatiri.

After a while, she said, "Should we head back?"

"Yeah, probably. I hope you know the way, though, because I definitely don't."

Jatiri giggled and said, "I've been coming out here every night for the past two weeks, so I've got the path locked down by now." She stood, taking in the flowers one last time, then slowly made her way through the village, Coal by her side.

Neither of them said anything, taking in the stillness of the moment. This time, Coal did not find the quiet unnerving. He felt relaxed.

Back in his bed, it did not take him long to drift into sleep.

6

YURZU KNOCKED GENTLY ON Coal's door. He needed to wake the fox up, but he did not want to come across as too aggressive or intrusive.

"Yeah?" came a muffled call from inside the room after a few seconds.

"Noswen says it's time to get up."

"Mmkay."

Yurzu waited in the sitting area for both Noswen and Coal to be ready. His belongings were already packed and he had eaten a light breakfast. He tended to be an early riser; he had already been awake for around an hour. His parents had gotten him on Noctgone early in his youth and he'd basically flipped from his nocturnal ways: now he awoke early in the morning and was tired by early evening. It was a better fit for his gardening and farming lifestyle.

Soon Coal emerged from his room holding his bag, which he flung forward. It rolled a few feet along the ground before colliding with a chair.

The man looked worn out. His usually perky ears flopped down and his eyelids drooped. He let out a beleaguered sigh as he sat near Yurzu.

"The bed was awful," Coal explained. Yurzu realized he'd been staring at him and was suddenly embarrassed. "Couldn't get to sleep until late, and even that was toss-and-turn."

"Sorry." His own bed was not the most luxurious, but he had slept fine.

Noswen popped out of their room, looking much more put-together than Coal despite her drunken swagger the night before. Her gray fur was neatly brushed and her black-rimmed eyes were bright and full of life.

"Ready for a long, hard day of walking?" she asked Coal with a cheeky sneer upon seeing the man's exhausted slouch.

"Why are we walking? Why not rent a carriage or ride the Houndsvein or something? Doesn't the Dirt King have deep pockets? You had all those damn tups to spend on the claw…why not use them on something that will make us less miserable?"

"Walking's good exercise. You'll thank me for it someday. And we need to save the money for when it's truly necessary, such as if we need to drop thousands of tups on buying the world-saving artifacts. Or what if we spend all our money on a beetle ride now, but then in a few weeks poor Yurzu here breaks his leg and can't walk, yet we can't afford another ride?"

"You can magically heal him. That won't be an issue."

"True. So I guess we won't ever need to spend our money on rides, then."

Yurzu chuckled. Coal moaned and slumped further in his chair like a scoop of ice cream melting in the Highmonth heat.

"You'll be alright," Noswen told him. "Keep whining, it'll help. Let's go get the others, shall we?"

Together they trundled out of Room 621 and Noswen proceeded to pound on the door of 622. A disgruntled yelp came from the other side, and the slab of wood swung open to reveal an annoyed Biror.

"What?"

"What do you mean, 'what?'" Noswen asked before shoving past the man and barging into the room. "Everyone ready to go?"

It was Lop who had commenced this whole expedition, launching from the northernmost tip of Ruska at the Palace, making his way south and collecting Yurzu from Toothshadow, then Biror after. Noswen was the fourth recruit, and yet she had somehow positioned herself as its leader. Yurzu wasn't sure if it came to her naturally, having to corral six children back home, or if she just had little patience for anyone in the group. Maybe the two were related.

Yurzu knew she desperately wanted to get back to her home in Holluwak, though. That was undoubtedly a big motivator in her wanting to move things along at a faster pace.

It was a sentiment Yurzu related to. Noswen wanted to return to her children, and he wanted to return to his vegetables.

He and Coal entered the room behind Biror, who quickly disappeared into one of the side rooms to finish packing. Everyone in Room 622 had time to get a lot more comfortable, having spent a couple weeks in Sadatso while Yurzu and

Noswen gallivanted around Soponunga. They had much more to load back into their bags.

Zsoz was up on a wall again, which seemed to be the slime's preferred nesting place. The three artifacts they had acquired could be seen suspended within its translucent orange jelly. Zsoz was a fairly light shade of orange, but it had noticeably darkened over the course of the past several months Yurzu had been on the road with it. He estimated the slime was probably close to a year old, halfway through its lifespan.

Hello, Noswen, said the slime.

"Hi, Zsoz," she nodded to it.

Hello, Yurzu.

"Hi."

Hello, Coal.

"Hey."

It is nice to see the three of you this morning. I am looking forward to the continuation of our journey. I am well-rested. Noswen and Yurzu look well-rested. You do not look well-rested, Coal.

"Thanks, Zsoz," said Coal, amused by the slime's assessment.

With Zsoz lacking a face, Yurzu had no idea how to determine the slime's mood or whether it was well-rested. He was kind of surprised to hear that it required sleep, though why wouldn't it?

Lop was once again sitting hunched over by the wall underneath Zsoz. Looking at the room's tiny chairs, it was obvious the furniture was not designed with the ape's bulk in mind. He nodded a greeting toward all three of them, Coal included. That last nod seemed reluctant, though, Yurzu would say.

Then Jatiri entered the room, looking bright-eyed and ready to embrace the day. She smiled at the sight of Coal, and he smiled back. She said hello to all of them.

While they waited on Biror, Coal said, "Is anyone else gonna try convincing Noswen we should hop on a beetle in the Houndsvein? Or hire a carriage or something? Am I the only one tired of walking?"

Yurzu was a little tired of it too, but he was not one to complain. He would rather go with what the majority wanted than incite any conflict.

"I'm actually looking forward to stretching my legs a bit," said Jatiri. "We've been sitting around here for so long, I'm in need of some real movement."

Coal's mouth hung agape, struck by her betrayal.

"Have you looked around?" Lop then asked the fox.

There was irritation in the man's voice that knotted Yurzu's stomach. His instinct to avoid conflict was urging him to flee from the room.

"We're in the middle of nowhere in what's practically a ten-person town. There are no wagons to hire here. No one's coming and going. The people here don't leave. Even if we *wanted* to waste the money on such a thing, we couldn't. In addition to that, we've got to travel through the Innards to reach Nitulo. No other way. Have you ever traveled the Innards?" Without waiting for a response, he went on. "The trees are too dense for much more than a footpath, let alone roads for a wagon. And the nearest Houndsvein gate is in Vuela, but that is northeast from here, and we're headed northwest. Think before you speak."

Coal opened his mouth to offer a rebuttal, but then thought better of it. Noswen and Jatiri kept quiet as well. Lop's harsh words hung awkwardly in the air between them. Yurzu was now especially thankful he had not voiced his agreement with Coal.

Biror entered the room with a chipper expression on his face, which Yurzu had never seen him wear before. "I heard a fight out here," the boar said, grinning. "I heard Lop sounding pissed off. You are pissed at the fox, yes?"

"Are you ready to go?" Noswen asked, ignoring his attempt to egg things on.

"Kotcha se," he nodded with a sardonic smile. Yurzu was pretty unfamiliar with Ronog—the language of the boars—but over the months, he had picked up that the phrase essentially meant *yes.*

"Good," said Noswen, understanding the meaning as well. "Let's get out of here. Come on down, Zsoz."

Yes, Noswen. I am looking forward to our journey, even if it is on foot and not through the methods of transportation that our new friend Coal would prefer.

Jatiri laughed at that, which broke the tension that permeated the room. Even Coal chuckled. Lop was unamused, but pleased that the slime was on his side.

The ape rose and stood with his back pressed against the wall as Zsoz made its way downward, leaving streaks of wetness that should dry relatively soon. It crawled onto Lop's shoulder, where it would cling to his hair for the duration of the trip.

"Oh, so that's why you're fine with it, Zsoz," Coal muttered. "You pretty much have a wagon to ride on!"

Everyone else laughed at the joke, including Yurzu, but Lop did not seem to appreciate being compared to a wagon.

He rolled his eyes as he edged past Yurzu and headed for the door.

LOP HAD ALWAYS BEEN a pretty serious guy. Well, "always" in Yurzu's book was merely the past ten months since he had met the man.

Every Drymonth, the city of Banak Tor held a celebration called the Rechando Festival. The city surrounded the Palace and was only a few hours from Yurzu's home in Toothshadow. Having the opportunity to sell his pickles there would hopefully net him a great deal of tups, and most importantly it would be a lot of fun, too.

Yurzu applied for a vendor stall at the festival every year for the past five years, ever since he'd turned twenty, and was routinely denied. Last year, though, his application was finally accepted. He was positively giddy throughout the months leading up to the festival. He worked tirelessly stocking up on extra jars of pickles—cucumbers, carrots, beets, peppers, even his maligned spinach and potatoes—in several varieties of flavors. He wanted to make a good impression and sell a lot of product.

He knew his food was delicious, and he wanted to share it with the world.

The Rechando Festival was filled with street vendors selling various crafts, clothing, and other products. Stalls lined the streets of the city, and at its epicenter, in the park, a stage was constructed for concerts to be performed all day every day for a week. Yurzu's stall was going to be set up in the farmer's market, also located within the park.

It was northern Ruska's biggest celebration of the year, and people traveled from all over to partake in the festivities. The festival was said to originally be in honor of some long-forgotten accomplishment of the Dirt King, but the man had not attended the festival himself in countless years and no one remembered or cared about what they were honoring. All that mattered was that they were having fun, eating food, and drinking booze.

When he finally arrived in Banak Tor, hauling his crates of jarred pickles behind him, Yurzu was buzzing with anticipation. He made his way through the impressive city, with buildings taller than he ever could have dreamed of, and found the farmer's market set up in the central park.

A woman was singing on stage, accompanied by no more than a drummer. Her crooning wasn't to Yurzu's tastes, but the modest crowd gathered before her seemed to be enjoying themselves. The bigger draws would be performing later in the evening.

Yurzu got his stall situated in the market, nestled amongst other proud, eager farmers showcasing their food. Some were selling raw fruits and vegetables, while others specialized in jams and jellies. There were several others peddling pickles, though Yurzu was confident in his flavors. Unlike those other people, he had thought to supply samples. Bite-sized pieces of his best-selling products were portioned onto a tray at the edge of his table for passersby to taste and be enticed by.

And his ploy worked. For the next several days, many festival attendees stopped to munch on a bite of cucumber or carrot and were dazzled by the flavor. A lot of them would then buy a jar or two before gleefully moving on down the line of booths.

It was a good feeling, seeing so many strangers enjoying his creations. Toothshadow was a small town, and he knew almost all of his customers by name. He did not interact with them face-to-face very often, though, since his pickles were sold in the local stores. There was something magical about seeing a person (who before that moment was a complete stranger) biting into something he made and being so delighted by it. It filled his stout body with unbridled satisfaction and pride.

He swore to himself he would continue applying for a stall every year. Even if he was only accepted every one out of five times, it would be worth the time and effort. He had never been this happy since his parents had passed.

On the fourth day of the festival, just past lunchtime, an intense headache started to set in. At first, Yurzu thought he was simply dehydrated and chugged a glass of water to assuage the pain, but the feeling quickly deepened.

He did not know it at the time, but it was because Lop was approaching, and he was sensing the man's blight. For years Yurzu had known about his ability to sense sickness in others, but he had never encountered something like this before.

The orangutan was stopping at every booth in the farmer's market, chatting every single vendor. As he later told Yurzu, he had been provided special instructions from the Dirt King to seek out individuals with symptoms of magical abilities. He had an unfathomably long list of potential signs, which he had spent the past two weeks memorizing up and down in preparation for the festival.

When Lop reached Yurzu's booth, pain pounded against his skull like a hammer. It was almost too much to bear, but he tried to to push through it for the sake of this new customer.

"Hi," Yurzu muttered, forcing a smile. In retrospect, he probably looked like he was losing his mind. It did not feel far off from the truth. Any second now, his brain was sure to start leaking from his ears.

The towering figure cocked an eyebrow and asked him if he was alright. He affirmed, and so Lop pointed to a piece of pickled carrot and asked, "May I?"

Yurzu affirmed again, so Lop delicately grasped the orange sliver between his leathery fingers and tossed it into his mouth. He bit down with a loud crunch and nodded approvingly.

"Delicious," he said.

"Thank you," Yurzu said, hardly above a whisper. He had to clutch a hand to his head, as if he could push the ache out.

"You really do not seem alright," Lop informed him.

Indeed, he felt like he was going to be sick. It would not be a good look, vomiting all over his wares. No one would want any samples then. But he shook his head, insisting to this stranger that he was fine.

At that point, he passed out. Which was also not a good look.

He awoke an hour later, dazed and in unfamiliar surroundings. The sounds of the festival still blared in his ears, people laughing and cheering and music emanating from the stage. He was in an alley somewhere near the park, but he was too new to Banak Tor to know where exactly he was.

The orangutan sat before him, and Yurzu was disappointed to find his headache had not subsided. More horrifying was the fact that this unknown man had abducted him and carried him off into a dark alley. Even more horrifying than that was that his pickle booth was currently unmanned.

"My name is Lop," said the man.

Yurzu did not introduce himself. He was too frightened, and his headache was too severe to form words.

"It seems like your head is killing you."

Yurzu nodded.

"This was on the Dirt King's list. The Dirt King is wise beyond all others. Let me ask you this: you know when people are sick, don't you?"

His breathing stopped for a second, and for that second he forgot the pain in his head. How did this man know that? He had never told anyone before, not even his parents.

Yurzu thought it best to keep his mouth shut and neither confirm nor deny Lop's suspicions. The orangutan went on to explain what he was doing at the festival, what the Dirt King had tasked him with. Yurzu stared wide-eyed as Lop demonstrated his own ability, at which point Yurzu confirmed that he was right. He could sense illness in people.

He clutched a hand to his head, willing the headache to dissipate. It didn't work.

"The Dirt King said someone like you would react harshly to my presence. He said you would be able to feel the magic in me, and that it would overwhelm you. It was obvious from the first words we spoke to each other what was going on."

Being around the orangutan was unbearable. It had never been this bad, even when his parents were at their sickest.

"His notes even said you might faint," the man chortled. "The Dirt King is wise beyond all others, it's true."

Even during that first conversation, it was beyond obvious that Lop was deeply loyal to the Dirt King. He was a Palace guard; his whole life was dedicated to maintaining the wellbeing of Ruska's ruler. Protecting his life, fulfilling his whims, and upholding his laws. Unquestioningly.

At that point, Lop divulged the truth of what was transpiring in Ruska. Yurzu did his best to concentrate, but it was nearly impossible with his headache.

He agreed to accompany Lop on his quest to find the four other Blighted, but that was out of fear that he would be reprimanded by Lop or even the Dirt King himself if he refused. It did not seem as if he truly had a choice.

But deep in his heart, he did not want to leave his garden. He did not want to leave his home. He simply did it because he knew it was expected of him, and he did not want to put up any resistance.

There was also a fear that he would be living the next however many months in constant, unendurable pain. While that was true at first, as the days wore on he grew more accustomed to the feeling of Lop's blight and he could finally maintain a conversation. The pain would become easier to wrangle with each subsequent Blighted they recruited, although it did always hit him pretty hard during the initial encounter.

So, with Lop's assistance, the next day he loaded up his supplies and departed for Toothshadow to return home and pack whatever he needed for the journey. There were still a few days left in the festival, though, and he was admittedly disappointed to miss out on them.

Lop, feeling guilty, purchased a jar of pickled carrots from him as they rode the wagon for the roughly one-hour ride back to Toothshadow with Zsoz in tow. He crunched on them delightedly, complimenting Yurzu's talents.

When asked what he wanted the Dirt King to provide for him in return for his service to the kingdom, Yurzu's request was simple: all he wanted was a booth at the Rechando Festival every year so that he could share his pickles with the festivalgoers.

"That's all?" Lop asked him.

Yurzu nodded.

"Easy enough," said the man. "Consider it done."

Yurzu smiled, anxious for next year's festival to arrive.

7

I T TOOK A LONG, grueling week to reach Nitulo in the heart of Ruska's Innards.

The Innards were the expanse of dense forest that comprised central Ruska, the piece of land that the Hound-spine was built to avoid. It was the most untamed part of the kingdom, with no major cities or structures of any kind. A lot of it was either unoccupied or, when they did encounter a settlement, it was much like Sadatso. No designated walkways, buildings nestled amongst trees, a distinct lack of flair.

The seclusion that the Innards offered was appealing to the deer and the tigers, which was why many of them made their homes there. Established villages were small and scarce, and a lot of the territory's residents simply built their homes wherever they felt like it. On several occasions, the group passed by freestanding homes, far from anything else of note.

Coal had always heard the Innards were teeming with wild-life, but that did not appear to be the case as they navigated it over the past week. In all their hours of walking (and walking, and walking), he had spotted only a handful of retnos. He thought he might have heard a geigex or two above them in the trees, but he wasn't sure.

There were also no encounters with any not-monsters—or *blightbeasts*, as Noswen more eloquently called them—so the trip was mercifully uneventful.

Just endless walking. Day in and day out.

Coal was sick of looking at trees. He desperately needed to get out of this unending forest.

He did his best to steer clear of Lop. On the occasions when interacting was unavoidable, he made every attempt to endear himself to the man, but nothing seemed to be working. No longer was he outright hostile, which was an improvement, but the glares he shot at Coal told him he still wasn't trusted.

The people he was getting along with the most were Jatiri and Yurzu. The latter still did not speak much, always receding into himself for hours at a time, but when they did talk it was pleasant. Jatiri, on the other hand, was always game to chat. Her kindness outweighed Lop's bitterness in Coal's mind.

The only breaks they took were to eat, so Coal had no time to dig into *A Popular Bargain* more during the day, and in the evenings when they finally stopped he was too exhausted to bring himself to read a bunch of words on a page. He knew he wouldn't be able to focus. He was left thinking about the pro-logue and where the story might go from there.

Finally, they came to Nitulo, and Coal got his wish to see something other than trees.

Previously, he did not know anything about the place, but Jatiri told him a bit as they walked. Nitulo was the largest city in the Innards, but it was still only roughly half the size of behemoths like Vinnag and Soponunga. At some point, some old tiger years and years ago determined that it was important for the territory to have a capital of some sort, and he set to constructing it and declared himself the mayor. The city, once it was finally finished, held elections every few years but the man always ran unopposed and continued reigning as Nitulo's mayor until the day he died. Jatiri had heard rumors he ran unopposed because he always covertly killed anyone who was even considering running against him, but those rumors were never confirmed.

The city was much more structured and organized than Sadatso seemed to be, but it still held onto the design tenets that everywhere else in the Innards adhered to. Trying as much as possible to not disturb the trees or wildlife was of the utmost importance. Where it differed was that it was built on the western edge of the forest, with a majority of its structures built directly into the Yuluj Mountains.

That old, possibly-corrupt tiger mayor had instructed his workers to build upward, just like in Sadatso, but here in Nitulo that meant climbing up and up into the mountainside. Endless flights of stairs were carved into the mountains, stopping off at various platforms chiseled out where rows of buildings stood embracing the cold mountain air.

Now I have to climb stairs, too? Coal thought with a defeated sigh.

Near the city's entrance, there were various stone towers built amongst the trees, most of which were the same height as the inn they'd stayed in back in Sadatso. These towers were actually painted different colors and had signs hanging from them, with some flowers and other light decorations around them. The tigers were evidently not as into the flat, barren aesthetic as the deer. These were apartment buildings, where most of the city's population lived. The wealthy among them could afford standalone homes up in the mountaintops with glorious views of Ruska below.

Another thing Jatiri had told him about were the hot springs up in the mountains. If he could obtain some tups from the Dirt King's coffers, he wouldn't mind taking a hot dip in his free time…

Although he'd be lucky if he managed to squeeze any free time into this visit. Lop was marching full speed ahead toward the mountains, not intending to waste any time that could be spent tracking down the crystal fang. The man was annoyingly dedicated to the Dirt King.

"Could you slow down a damn minute?" Noswen called to him. If even she was vouching for a rest, it was a clear sign that Lop was being impatient.

The orangutan swiftly swung around to face the rest of the group, but Zsoz clung tightly to his shoulder.

"What do you propose we do instead?" he asked her. "It would be foolish and inefficient not to immediately seek out the Calitarash. As was said before, now that Ghoresn Daanarb has been missing for over half a year, we cannot be sure where the fang is. We may have to launch a whole new investigation after speaking to the Calitarash. We do not possess the luxury of being able to squander our time. Ruska is at stake. The Dirt King is relying on us."

"No one is disagreeing with you," said Noswen, "but we're also tired, so chill the fuck out and let's recuperate for a minute before we try to negotiate with some weird cult that decided to take over a city. How's that sound?" She then turned to Jatiri and asked, "*Are* they a cult?"

The saola shrugged.

Over the past week, she had told them what little she knew about the Calitarash. They were overseen by a tiger named Yhorio Calit, son of the late founder Banrea Calit. The religion centered around the belief that all life in Ruska was created by a race of beings that Banrea Calit called the Valohir. The glowing eyes sometimes seen watching over the valley up above the mountaintops allegedly belonged to these Valohir.

The Calitarash preached that the Valohir created life in Ruska and now watched over it from afar, observing how their creations flourished and floundered. Most believed that Ruska contained the only non-Valohir life in the entire world, while some others speculated Ruska was one of many experiments the Valohir were running, and that there were other isolated valleys being watched.

That was as far as Jatiri's knowledge extended. There were no practicing Calitarash outside of Nitulo, so she did not know in what traditions or rituals their followers partook.

It sounded cult-like to Coal, but a part of him could buy into their beliefs. He had never heard any other explanation for the massive creatures that lived outside Ruska. Why not declare them their gods?

Biror had already sided with Noswen and was sitting on the ground, leaning his back against a gnarled tree trunk with his eyes closed and arms crossed over his broad chest. Coal was not going to invite Lop's wrath on himself by joining the boar.

"Sit around here if you'd like," said Lop with a huff. "I will go seek out the location and meeting parameters of Yhorio Calit and return here with whatever information I find."

"Sounds great," said Noswen.

Jatiri took a step forward and said, "I'll go with you."

"Very well," Lop nodded, turning to continue toward the mountains.

Coal was torn between wanting to rest his weary legs and wanting to smooth things over with the orangutan. It could be a good show of faith going into Nitulo with him rather than being "lazy" and sitting around with the others, no matter how immensely appealing it sounded. Having Jatiri there as a buffer might make it easier as well.

He hurried along and caught up to Jatiri, whose expression showed she was just as surprised by his decision as he was himself.

Coal is accompanying us as well, said Zsoz up on Lop's shoulder.

Lop glanced over his shoulder with a small scowl. He caught himself and wiped it away, making an attempt to not appear annoyed by Coal's mere presence.

That's something, I guess, Coal thought. *Not a total dismissal or a "Get fucked, Flesh Eater."*

The three of them began ascending the stone stairs into upper Nitulo. A stiff breeze blew, ruffling their fur. Up ahead, Coal could smell spices on the air. Only halfway up the first flight, his sore legs were already screaming at him to fling his body over the side and return to the peacefully resting group below.

Unlike other towns they'd passed through, Nitulo was much livelier, with its denizens actually walking around, shopping, eating at restaurants. Simple, normal things, but a welcome sight after feeling so isolated in the forest for so many days.

"Do you have any inclinations as to where we may find Yhorio?" Lop suddenly asked.

Jatiri mulled the question over, then said, "No. Sorry. I have never actually been here before, so I don't know a ton about the city. No idea where he might be."

"*Up* would be my guess," said Coal. Lop said nothing, as if he hadn't even heard him, so he elaborated. "People with money and power like being above everyone else, right? I say we just keep going up. Even if my legs are protesting against that idea."

"Our only choice is to go up," Lop said. "So obviously we will be going up."

"Fair."

Jatiri shot him a smile, as if to tell him it was a valiant effort.

They reached the first platform, which had three buildings: one was a cozy-looking restaurant, which was the source of the delicious smells on the wind; one was a clothing store with some incredibly flashy outfits in the display windows; and the last was a spiritual shop that sold candles and texts and other Calitarash-related items.

In the center of the platform was a mass of people, all wearing different clothing but with yellow represented somewhere in their outfits. Mostly tigers, but some deer and martens and rabbits as well. They were all on their knees, in two winding lines, with each person placing their hands on the head of the person sitting before them. The two lines ran all the way back to a single woman, a tiger adorned in a billowing yellow robe, who stood with her hands on the heads of the people at the start of each line. Everyone's eyes were closed and they were softly humming in tune with each other, so quietly that it was only audible as Coal and the others approached the strange display.

"Okay, so this is clearly a cult thing, right?" Coal whispered to his companions.

Lop nodded sternly. "We shall wait until they conclude this ritual and then speak to the robed woman."

They must have stumbled upon the spectacle near its end, because the tiger at the head of the group removed her hands from the two peoples' heads only a couple minutes later. Then each subsequent person removed their hand from each other's heads one by one, down their respective lines. Everyone stood and dispersed without another word, though they looked remarkably relaxed and joyful.

Coal took a deep breath and followed Lop forward through the crowd, toward the yellow-robed woman. She smiled at their approach, her aged face wrinkling. The orange in her fur had faded over the years.

"Good day to you," she said, bowing to each of them. "Blessings from the mountain."

"And to you as well," said Lop, taking a short bow. Zsoz remained unmoved on the man's shoulder, drawing the attention of the woman for a moment before she returned her gaze to Lop.

"I do not recognize you," the woman said, taking a good look at each of their faces. "Are you newly arrived in Nitulo? The Calitarash are honored to count you among us."

"We have just arrived," Lop confirmed. "My name is Lop Mornotico. This is Jatiri Notts and Coal Ereness."

"Very nice to meet you all," the woman said with a smile cut across her face. "I am Medjia Renevi."

"Forgive our ignorance, but is Medjia a Calitarash honorific, or your name?" asked Jatiri.

"It is indeed my status in the church," Renevi replied.

"I'm afraid we are here on some urgent business," Lop continued. "Is Yhorio Calit still in charge around here? Or has Ghoresn Daanarb been located?"

The woman's eyebrows shot up at the mention of Ghoresn's name. She said, "Magister Calit is still helping to run the city in Mayor Daanarb's absence."

"May we speak with Magister Calit? As I mentioned, time is not on our side."

Renevi nodded, but gave them an apologetic frown. "Unfortunately, the Magister is unavailable today. His schedule is quite full. Keeping an entire city up and running is no easy task." She chuckled as if it were some kind of joke. "If there is an important matter you need to bring to him, you may opt to schedule an appointment with him, or I can take you to see the other Medjiam."

Lop pondered their options for a few seconds, then said, "The Medjiam may be able to help us."

"Excellent," said Renevi, her expression lightening again. "I can take you to them immediately, if you'd like."

"That would be great."

Renevi was turning to leave when Jatiri asked Lop, "Do you really think that's best? Shouldn't we go grab the rest of the group?"

"Oh, there are others?" asked Renevi curiously.

"Yes, but they're fine where they are," said Lop, dismissing Jatiri's concern. "We do not need them as of this moment."

Coal was personally in agreement with Jatiri, but the whole point of him tagging along was to demonstrate to Lop that he was on his side, so he chose not to contradict the decision.

As they walked, Jatiri asked Renevi, "What were you all doing back there? It looked very rejuvenating."

The pitch of Renevi's voice lifted when she answered, pleased by the question. "That was one of our daily meditations," she began. "We were transmitting our love and our spirits and our bodies to the Valohir. I and the other Medjiam share a deep connection with our Creators. We are able to share ourselves with them any time we wish. By touching other followers of the church, we are able to help them share themselves with the Valohir as well. It is quite a beautiful thing."

No one had any further questions for Renevi as they followed her up another two flights of stairs before coming to a narrow path branching off around the side of the mountain. The stairs continued upward toward another platform, but they carefully walked across the offshoot and soon came to a relatively small church carved into the mountainside. It was bigger than many of the other buildings they'd passed, but it was fairly unassuming considering this church was now in control of the whole city.

As if reading his mind, Renevi said, "We have a new facility under construction higher up, but for now we are still operating out of our original church."

"It looks lovely," said Lop, ever the diplomat.

The building's entrance was inset in the mountain, with pillars carved on either side of the entryway and depictions of what Coal assumed to be Valohir adorning the walls. Each of the colossi stared gravely down at those entering and exiting the church. Always watching over their beloved creations. It was the most elaborate craftwork Coal had seen yet in the Innards.

Renevi led them inside, which consisted of a single, torch-lit spiraling hallway. They followed it around to the inner chamber. The circular chamber at the building's center contained a statue of another Valohir, one with a thick head and floppy ears, with a meaty snout drooping down its face past its chin. There were no pupils in its eyes, and eight horns protruded from all sides of its bare head. The body was wide-set, with four clawed arms and a spiked tail wrapping around it.

The Medjia caught Coal admiring the statue and said, "That is Fuillaime. He is thought to be the king of the Valohir."

"They have a king?"

"Some sort of leader, yes. He is the oldest of the Valohir. The Creators' creator, if you will."

Ugly guy, Coal thought, wondering absently if he was insulting the thing that had borne him.

He asked, "How did the sculptor know how to depict him?"

"Magister Calit convened with Fuillaime in the dreamscape and relayed his appearance to others," said the woman nonchalantly.

"Oh, of course."

Not counting the hall from which they'd come, the chamber had three exits, one of which was through a set of double doors. Coal assumed through there might be where the church held its sermons, if the Calitarash even held sermons at all.

Renevi ushered them through an unmarked yellow door to their right, through another short hall lit by torches, then into an empty room containing nothing but three tigers and a deer all sitting on the floor meditating. They sat huddled up close to each other, all of them with their hands on the heads of the two closest to them.

At the sound of the door opening and closing, the four ceased their humming and removed their hands from each other. The lone man in the room, a withered tiger, looked up at their guests. Everyone's attention was immediately drawn to the ape with a slime resting on his shoulder.

"Hello, Medjia Renevi," the man said to his colleague. "Who have you brought to our chamber?"

"Hello, Medjia Bhuri. I am sorry to interrupt, but they insisted it was urgent business. This is Lop, Jatiri, and Coal. They are newly arrived in Nitulo."

The man, Bhuri, stood while the others remained on the stone floor. His yellow robe hung loose from his thin frame. It looked as if the man hadn't eaten in months.

He said, "Good day to you all. Blessings from the mountain."

"Blessings from the mountain," the seated Medjiam echoed.

"Thank you," said Lop. Coal almost chuckled at the man's mundane response to the creepy greeting. "We will not keep you long. We were in search of Ghoresn Daanarb, but from what I understand, she has not been seen in many months."

"This is accurate," Bhuri nodded. "Unfortunately, our mayor has been indisposed. Thankfully, Nitulo has been under the guidance of Magister Calit in her absence."

Lop was opening his mouth to say something, but Jatiri beat him to the punch. "Indisposed?" she said. "Not missing?"

Bhuri shook his head. "No, of course not. Mayor Daanarb is right here in the city," he said casually. "She simply fell ill last Newmonth and has been unable to lead Nitulo nor make any public appearances. Early on in her illness, she specifically requested that Magister Calit lead in her stead."

"Well, I am sorry to hear she has been ill for so many months," said Lop, "but I admit it is a relief to learn that her whereabouts are known. You see, we are seeking an object that we believe to be in her possession. A crystal fang. We would appreciate being taken to her so that we may negotiate a trade."

"I know the fang of which you speak," Bhuri said. Renevi nodded in agreement. "Mayor Daanarb treasures it and wears it as a necklace. I can actually confirm that I know for a fact she is wearing it right this very moment. Unfortunately, going to see her would be...unwise."

"Is whatever ails her contagious?" Lop asked.

"We are unsure, though it does not seem so. It is not an illness we are at all familiar with."

"What are her symptoms, exactly?" Jatiri wanted to know.

Bhuri frowned, trying to formulate the best response to the question. "It is complicated to explain," he finally said. "The mayor is...not herself. Quite literally."

"What does *that* mean?" Coal blurted out, unable to stop himself.

Bhuri explained. "The disease that has overtaken her has somehow changed her demeanor and even her body. She has become quick to lash out. Attempting to interact with her would be quite dangerous, I believe."

"And she's still wearing the necklace?" Lop wanted to clarify. All of the Medjiam nodded confirmation.

"Our number actually used to be one greater," said Bhuri. "Three months ago, when she started taking a turn for the worse, we sent a Medjia in to touch her, to convene with the Valohir and bring forth wellness and light into her, but it was unsuccessful. She struck out at him, and he unfortunately passed later that day from loss of blood." The Medjiam all bowed their heads in silence for a moment in remembrance of their fallen ally.

The relief Coal and the others surely all felt at the news of Ghoresn Daanarb still being in Nitulo had been just as quickly dashed. He couldn't discuss it with Lop or Jatiri yet, but to Coal, it sounded like Ghoresn was suffering from the same sort of infection that was spreading through Ruska. Getting the fang from her would be harder than they thought. Suddenly a scavenger hunt through the Innards sounded vastly more appealing to him.

Jatiri said, "I'm a doctor. If you take us to see Ghoresn, perhaps I could ascertain a treatment."

"With all due respect, ma'am, we have had the city's best doctors make examinations at every stage of her illness, and none came to any positive conclusions. All treatments have been ineffective."

"I'd still like to try, if that's alright. It doesn't hurt to have another set of eyes on a problem, does it?"

Bhuri considered her proposal, then said, "I suppose you are right. I have been granted permission to speak on behalf of the Magister, and I believe bringing you to her should pose no problems. She is currently confined in a secure location. You will not be permitted to approach her, but you may observe from afar. This is for your own safety. Is this understood and acceptable?"

"We accept," Lop answered for the group.

To him, Jatiri said, "We really should get the others for this, though."

Lop agreed. He said to the Medjiam, "Before we go, we must fetch our companions from the bottom of the mountain. They are invested in this as well, and they come from many different backgrounds. It is possible they could shed some light on the mayor's affliction with their perspectives, and perhaps we could come to some sort of solution."

"I admit, I am doubtful," said Bhuri, "but also hopeful. It is clear to us that she is in pain, and if that could be alleviated in any way, we are in favor of it." The rest of the Medjiam stood, and Bhuri said, "Come, let us find your friends and pray that the mountain may bless us on this beautiful day."

8

THEY GATHERED THE REMAINING members of their crew (with protestations from Noswen about having talked to the Calitarash without everyone present) and returned to the base of the mountain. Medjia Bhuri ushered them away from the stairs that led back up into the city proper and instead headed further along the edge of the mountain, away from civilization.

The six Blighted kept their distance from the five Medjiam so that they could talk privately amongst themselves.

"So she hasn't been missing at all?" Noswen asked.

"Apparently not," said Coal. He took it upon himself to explain the situation when they reached the others. Lop had simply wanted them to follow without question so that the situation would be resolved in a timely manner.

Noswen asked Jatiri, "Did they describe her symptoms to you? Does it sound like something you're familiar with? Something curable?"

Coal was the one to respond. "Actually, it sounds like she's a blightbeast."

Noswen blinked. "The fuck do you mean it sounds like she's a blightbeast? She's a person, not a blightbeast. Therefore she can't be a blightbeast."

"I know," said Coal, "but the way they were describing her...I dunno, that's just the sense I got. They described her like the not-retnos in the race." He knew it sounded far-fetched, but a decrepit, blighted mess was what he expected to find in whatever cell these cultists had locked Ghoresn Daanarb away in.

"So we will have to kill her," said Biror from the back of the group.

"No," said Noswen resolutely.

"If she wears this fang and is dangerous as the freaks say, then I am thinking we must be needing to kill this tiger if we want to get close."

"I'm going to inspect her and see if there's anything I can do," Jatiri said.

The boar huffed. "Okay. I am sure this goes swell."

Coal hated to admit it, but he had to agree with Biror's sarcastic and cynical remarks. He had his doubts that Jatiri would be able to do anything for the poor woman, despite her best intentions.

They were now a great distance from Nitulo, easily fifteen or twenty minutes of walking, when they came upon a hole dug out in the side of the mountain. Coal peered into the darkened tunnel, but it was unlit and he could not see more than a few feet inside. Once he actually went in, his vision would adjust and he'd be able to see perfectly.

The opening was big enough for most of them, but even Bhuri had to hunch his wiry body over to step inside, which meant Lop was going to be very uncomfortable navigating the space. Bhuri entered first, followed by Renevi, then the six of them followed while the last three Medjiam brought up the rear.

Coal did not like being corralled by the Medjiam. He was creeped out by the cultists. Somehow it felt like they were being led to an execution or a torture chamber or something. As his vision adjusted and he saw just how barren the tunnel was, how secluded and out of the way they'd brought them, his skin tingled with nervous anticipation.

"This is where you keep your prisoners? Doesn't seem very wise. Not hidden or guarded at all," Noswen mumbled, always unafraid to voice her opinions.

"Mmm," Bhuri purred from the head of the convoy. The old man cleared his throat and said, "This is not where we keep prisoners. The Calitarash do not *keep* prisoners." Coal idly wondered if that was meant to imply they never had prisoners or rather that they simply killed anyone who got in their way. Bhuri continued, "Ghoresn Daanarb is not a *prisoner*. She is sick. She is a danger to herself and the citizenship of Nitulo. She is confined here out of concern for everybody's safety."

"Confined against her will, right?" said Noswen. "Sounds like a prisoner. Maybe I'm wrong, though."

Bhuri did not have a rebuttal for that. Biror let out an amused grunt. He liked the friction between the groups.

The winding tunnel came to a large opening. It funneled into a wide, round chamber that was lit by rows of torches on all sides except for the far back wall. The Calitarash were evidently not fans of the Dirt King's electricity. The front half of the room, where they all filed out of the tunnel to stand, was nothing but dirt and a single chair where a yellow-robed deer sat reading a book. Unlike the solid yellow robes the Medjiam wore, this one was striped with white at the end of the sleeves around the deer's wrists. Someone important, but not at the same level as the Medjiam.

The back half of the room, just behind where the now-confused deer sat, was entirely cordoned off by thick iron bars. Most of that side of the room was shrouded in darkness, unlit by torches. Coal could see the outline of a large figure near the back wall if he squinted, but he would need to get closer to see Ghoresn more clearly.

"Looks like a prison to me," Noswen muttered, mostly to herself. If Bhuri heard her, he made no comment.

The deer bolted out of her chair, slamming her book shut, standing up straight in the presence of Bhuri and the other Medjiam. She let her book plummet to the ground as if it did not matter to her at all. It kicked up a small cloud of dust that floated around her feet. "Greetings, Medjiam," she said before scanning the faces of the six strangers who accompanied her superiors. "Blessings from the mountain. I was not expecting you."

"Relax, my child," said Bhuri with an assuring smile. The tiger approached the woman and placed a hand on her shoulder. "How is she doing today?" he asked.

The deer guard looked over her shoulder, past the iron bars into the darkness beyond. She said, "No change. So I suppose that's good, right?"

"A change for the better would be preferred, but *no* change for the worse is good, yes," Bhuri agreed. He absently waved a hand toward the Blighted and said, "These visitors came to

Nitulo seeking out our esteemed mayor. I informed them of her ailments, and they want to try helping her, if they can."

The woman nodded her understanding, though the expression on her face betrayed the utter confusion she was feeling. It was obvious to Coal that this woman believed Ghoresn to be too far gone. Beyond help.

Bhuri turned to them and said, "Please, come forward. Take a look. Make your examinations." He sported a fake smile, convinced that it would be fruitless.

Coal and Jatiri were the first to step toward the iron bars. Jatiri grasped a bar in each hand, leaning forward to push her face in between them, peering ahead. The sides of her horns clacked against the iron.

"I can see her, but I can't *see* her," she whispered to him. "Can you?"

He could.

Huddled by the wall, Ghoresn Daanarb no longer looked like a normal, healthy tiger. For starters, her body was at least three times the size of Lop, who was one of the biggest people Coal had ever met. She was no longer bipedal, instead stalking back and forth on four obscenely muscular legs. There were stray shreds of fabric stuck to her skin, as if her clothing had ripped and frayed as she grew. Rubbery growths sprouted all over her body, some flopping around as she walked, others dragging on the dirty ground behind her or hanging from her distended belly. Her head was misshapen, the lower half jutting out in an intense underbite, with saliva dripping from her maw. Her eyes, now nothing but white, were sunken into her skull. Oozing out from her pores was green and yellow pus. It rhythmically pumped out from her skin, as if in time with the beating of her heart.

And, just as Bhuri had said, dangling from her mottled neck and hanging between her two front legs was a thin, silver necklace with the crystal fang.

The nastiness she discharged was exactly like the colored pus Coal had seen on the not-ventem in the Houndsvein, as well as the not-retnos in the forest.

And like the scab on Bontrug's torso, he suddenly realized, thinking about Soponunga's mayor.

Mayor Bontrug had no legs and instead rode in an insect-like mechanical lower body. While collecting the diamond claw and his winnings from the Spiderback Showdown, Coal had witnessed the beaver lugging himself out of the mechanical chair he rode around in. The man's body ended at his torso, which was covered in a green scab that seemed to still be wet, still fresh. Was Bontrug currently in the midst of a horrific transformation like Ghoresn? Or was he trying to be proactive and lobbed it off before it infected the rest of him?

"Well?" Jatiri prodded Coal.

"Yes," he said, brought back to the present moment. His mouth was dry as he answered. "I can see her."

Then the others approached them. Noswen and Lop each stood on one side of Coal and Jatiri, while Yurzu and Biror lingered behind the four.

"Fuck me," Noswen swore immediately, uncaring if foul language was frowned upon by the Calitarash. As a raccoon, her night vision was just as good as Coal's, if not better.

"Can you have her come closer, somehow?" Jatiri asked the Medjiam.

"I don't think you want her to come closer," Coal said, taking a step back. "It's not good." He was definitely under-selling it. Noswen chimed in with her agreement.

"We cannot control her," Bhuri replied. "And we do not *want* to control her. She is not our prisoner," he said pointedly. "But she also no longer responds well to normal speech. She either cannot understand it or chooses to ignore it; we are not sure which is the case. In our humble opinions, it seems as if she has mentally regressed and now possesses no more than pure instinct."

"You don't believe she can think for herself anymore?" said Jatiri.

Bhuri shook his head. "At first she was simply feeling unwell, which progressed into her being bedridden. Her body then began to change, and her cognitive function has been steadily declining over the months. She can no longer speak our language, and she will attack if anyone draws too close. All that concerns her now is her next meal, I'm afraid."

Jatiri looked back through the bars with a frown. "If I could just get a better look…" she whispered. Lop appeared similarly at a loss, unable to peer through the darkness.

Biror stepped toward the bars and immediately began pounding on the metal. A dull clang echoed loudly through the chamber, and on top of it the man started shouting gibberish.

The effects were immediate. Ghoresn bounded toward them, skidding to a halt a few feet from the bars, but still her face slammed into them and she let out an angry yowl.

Everyone jumped back from the bars in alarm, and Biror laughed heartily to himself. "There you go," he said to Jatiri. "You spoke no lies. That is one ugly fucker."

All five of the Medjiam scowled at Biror's coarse insult toward Ghoresn, but they remained silent.

Some of Ghoresn's growths that dragged on the ground had torn from her belly with the fast, sudden movement and she was now leaking green and yellow pus, though that fact did not seem to perturb her. She snarled at her new visitors. Thick, broken whiskers extended from her flabby jowls.

The Medjiam maintained their calm demeanor in the presence of the city's deformed mayor, but the deer guard appeared to be disturbed by the sight of her.

Being so close to the monster now did not make Coal feel particularly good or secure, so he couldn't blame the deer. Yurzu had backed away even further too.

Lop glared at the massive, malformed tiger, trying to assess what should be done. "If I reached for the necklace, she would attack?" he asked the Medjiam.

Bhuri nodded. "She tends to never lose her appetite, it seems. And I would not advise going into the cell to get close enough to grab the necklace. In fact, I would not even allow it in the first place. For your own safety."

The orangutan sighed. Bhuri did not know about the man's ability to stretch his arms out, which would render going into the cell unnecessary, but that didn't change the fact his hand would probably be snapped off before he could snatch the crystal fang.

Jatiri's curiosity lured her back closer to the bars, though this time she did not risk slipping her snout in between them. Her eyes roved across Ghoresn's ruined flesh. At some point all of her fur had sloughed off and what remained was the pink skin underneath, with discoloration from being stained by the pus.

"I have something in mind," Jatiri then said.

"Are you serious?" asked Noswen, disbelieving. Biror laughed again. The man was endlessly amused by their current disastrous predicament.

Lop wanted to know what she was thinking. Bhuri seemed interested as well, taking a step toward the saola as she spoke.

"There's a detoxification potion I could brew that might help her. Obviously it was never intended for something like *this*," she said, gesturing wildly toward Ghoresn, who was eyeing them all hungrily, "but I think it's generally the same principle. The potion contains a few different nutrients and liquids that should aid her in rehydration and start to force her body to expel the toxins through vomiting and sweat."

"She looks like she's quite literally sweating toxins already," Coal pointed out. Seeing the pus pump out of the creature made his skin crawl.

Jatiri ignored his remark and said, "We'd need a big dose for someone her size and who's so clearly enveloped by…whatever the hell this is. And it's generally administered in two doses, fifteen minutes apart, so it'd be wise to sedate her first. I can brew a sedative that should knock her out for half an hour. Again, a big dose."

Bhuri raised a dubious eyebrow. "You think it will work?"

The saola shrugged. "It's a long shot, but it's the only option I can think of."

Coal was sure that the woman was an amazing doctor, but it seemed like a foolish endeavor trying to cure Ghoresn Daanarb. Especially with something as simple as a potion. Some meager potion was not going to cure the Houndstooth's infection.

"And how do you intend to administer any of this?" asked Bhuri. He apparently did not have a great deal of faith in her plan either.

"We can handle it," Lop said, casting another sideways glance at Ghoresn. "When we're ready, just clear your people from the room. We can do what needs to be done." Based on that, Coal knew the orangutan's plan involved a lot of magic that he did not want the Medjiam to witness.

Bhuri seemed unsure, but after pondering it for a few seconds, relented. "Very well. Brew your potions and try, if you'd like." He had to force a smile when he said, "It would be truly wonderful if Nitulo could have its leader back. I am sure Magister Calit would be thrilled by the news." He then stepped away to let them finish their discussion.

Of course he would, Coal thought. *People in power are always excited to give it up.* Not that the Medjiam could reasonably deny wanting a cure for their sick mayor.

"You really think we should try this?" Noswen asked Jatiri. Coal knew she trusted her, but he was sure that Noswen concurred with his personal belief that Ghoresn was too far gone for any common medicine.

"Yes," Jatiri nodded. "I confess, I am not convinced it will work. But I also don't see what else we can do. Do you?"

"We could go with my plan and kill her," Biror interjected. "It will be easier, I tell you true."

"No," said Noswen.

Biror shrugged. "Whatever you say. We will call mine Plan B."

Noswen did not respond to the man. She asked Jatiri, "What do we need to scrounge up for the potion and sedative?"

Jatiri took a deep breath, exhaled, and said, "I'll make a list."

Behind the iron bars, Ghoresn loosed a low, raspy growl.

9

THEY LEFT GHORESN'S CELL and separated from the Medjiam, much to Yurzu's relief. The sight of the infected tiger had left him feeling nauseous. What he had sensed in her wasn't immediate and overwhelming like when he first met each of his companions, but it left a lingering feeling of dizziness and unease inside him. A bitter aftertaste. His magic did not allow him to diagnose what exactly was wrong with a person, so he could not say what specifically was ailing Ghoresn, but the group had all come to the same conclusion.

"So whatever's leaking out of the Houndstooth is in her, right?" Coal said, voicing the thought on everyone's mind.

They were back in the forest, far from both Nitulo and the entrance to the chamber that held the city's sickly mayor. Before hunting down Jatiri's medicinal supplies they decided to have a quick discussion out of earshot of anyone else.

"That seems accurate to me," Lop nodded.

"No shit," said Biror.

"Have any of you seen something like that before?" Coal asked the group. "I'm new to all this shit, so pretty much all of it is a shock to me, but—"

"No," Noswen answered. "Lop and Yurzu can correct me if I'm wrong, but I don't think any of us have seen this happen before."

Yurzu had definitely never seen a person infected by the Houndstooth. It was possible Lop had some inside information from the Palace, but the orangutan shook his head.

"Well, that's troubling," said Coal. "Didn't you tell me that if we didn't stop whatever's happening from happening, it would start to infect people? That's what the Dirt King said?"

Noswen nodded. Yurzu shivered, having not realized the implication before that moment.

"Okay, so that's *incredibly* troubling," Coal muttered.

"Were you able to glean any insights?" Lop then asked Yurzu.

Yurzu shook his head and tried to control his trembling. "No," he said. "It doesn't work that way."

"Very helpful," the boar chortled.

"Shut up," Noswen chided him. "Are you feeling okay?" she then asked Yurzu.

Was it obvious how bad the meeting left him feeling? He suddenly realized he was holding a hand to his stomach. He said, "I'm okay. Just a little nauseous. It'll pass soon." But then he added, "Actually, I don't know that. This has never happened before. Usually the feelings I get go away as soon as I'm not near the person anymore."

Now Noswen looked concerned. "Do you think what she had was contagious? Are you picking it up from us now? Is that why it's still hitting you?"

It was a good question, one that he hadn't considered. Yurzu concentrated, focusing on each of them in turn.

"I don't think so," he said. "You all seem fine to me."

The raccoon thought for a second, scratching at her furry gray chin. "You don't think it infected just *you*, do you?"

Yurzu shook his head. "I don't think so," he said, but her questions were filling him with doubt. It wasn't as if he was particularly well-versed in how his own magic worked. Even though he'd been experiencing it for over a decade, he had never been truly cognizant of what was going on. It was still largely a mystery to him.

He felt like Jatiri, only able to disappear her hands but not the rest of her. There was possibly some sort of potential within him that he still couldn't unlock.

"Speaking of magical nonsense," said Coal, "don't you think we could skip all this potion brewing and just have you touch her and cure her right up?"

"Absolutely not," Noswen replied, her tone implying he was a buffoon for even suggesting it. "First off, would *you* wanna touch that fuckin' thing? Second, I don't have the faintest clue what is going on in her. If I see a bleeding wound, I know it needs to be patched up, so I can channel my energy into that. Same with a broken arm, or whatever else. Whatever's affecting her is too unknown, too abstract for me to know what sort of energy to put into her to fix it."

Hearing Noswen voice her own inexperience made Yurzu feel slightly better about his own. None of them really knew what they were doing with these blights. They were as much hindrances as they were tools.

"Can you just channel a bunch of different stuff into her? Keep trying shit until something works?" Coal then asked.

"In all honesty, I've never tried, but I doubt it," said Noswen. "Think about during the spider race when you had a bunch of holes in your back. How do you think things would shake out if I channeled, say, magic for re-growing bone into those wounds?"

"I would probably have antlers jutting out of my back right now."

"You would probably be *dead*," she said. "There's too much risk throwing a bunch of random magic at her and hoping that something sticks. I think that's an easy way to kill her."

Biror butted in. "Why do we not want this?" he asked. "Easiest solution, I say. Easy to take this necklace off a corpse. Corpses do not bite or thrash."

"Because we're not fucking psychos," said Noswen.

"We have not made our affiliation with the Dirt King known, but regardless, it would probably be best to avoid killing a government official," Lop added.

His point was hard to dispute.

"If we can help her, we should," Yurzu said. "Maybe we won't be able to, but we should try. It's the right thing to do."

The boar scoffed. "I did not sign up to *do right thing*," he said. "I sign up to get artifacts and throw them at an ugly tree. Easy to take this necklace off a corpse."

"The kid's right," Noswen said. "We should try to help. Not only is it the right thing to do, but also these Calitarash fucks give me the creeps, and it rubs me the wrong way that they just swooped in to take control of the city and threw her in a cage. If we can cure Ghoresn and get her back in charge, that sounds like a good idea to me. If worst comes to worst and we can't save her, then...we'll do whatever we need to so that we get the fang." She paused, and Biror grunted his approval. "This is just another minor setback, like how we were forced to compete in the race back in Soponunga to get the artifact there. This is part of the job, like it or not." The last sentence was pointed toward Biror, though he did not seem to notice or care.

Yurzu looked to Jatiri, who had been oddly quiet throughout the conversation. The saola appeared deep in thought, sitting on the ground with her back against a tree and her knees pulled up to her chest. She was busy writing on a notepad, taking a few moments to stop and think in between each piece of information she wrote down.

He took a few steps toward her and asked, "What do we need?"

She looked up, shaken out of her trance. Surprised to find someone speaking to her. "Right," she said. "There's a bunch of stuff." She held up the list, which was quite lengthy. There were easily fifteen or twenty ingredients they'd need to find in the city, though it didn't seem like an outrageous amount to Yurzu, considering they were brewing two different concoctions.

"Should we split up?" Noswen asked. "Cover more ground, get things done quicker?"

"I don't think so," Jatiri replied. "A lot of these will probably be in the same store, if they're sold here at all. And besides, I'd like to confirm it's the correct thing before anyone spends money on it. Probably best that I just go on my own and meet you guys back here with everything."

She stood to leave, slipping her notepad back into her jacket pocket. Coal said he would accompany her on the shopping trip. He could help search for ingredients in the medicinal shops and provide her with some company.

The two then set off for the steep staircase leading into Nitulo. A part of Yurzu was disappointed he still hadn't gotten a chance to see the city, but he didn't make a fuss.

"If we will just be waiting, I will take a nap," Biror declared, plopping himself down in the grass. He meshed his fingers together behind his head and laid it down in his palms. "I will be rested well to fight the beast."

"We're not gonna be fighting the beast," Noswen reiterated.

"Whatever you say."

The energy among the group was dour.

Biror lay resting, daydreaming about killing the mutated Ghoresn. Lop was a few feet away, hands on his hips, standing and staring in silence in the direction of the mountainside tunnel that housed Ghoresn. Zsoz was still latched on to his shoulder. Noswen paced back and forth near Yurzu, mulling something over.

Yurzu certainly was not confident in their plan to cure Ghoresn, and he did not suspect anyone else was, either. It was noble of them to try, and he trusted that Jatiri was a skilled doctor, but they were fighting against something otherworldly. This was not a simple matter of clearing up a cold. No one knew how to combat whatever darkness had infected Nitulo's mayor.

There were a few minutes of silence shared between them before Lop turned from the mountain and began to speak.

"Here's what I'm thinking," he started, tugging at his beard. "First of all, no Medjiam in the room."

"Of course not," said Noswen. "I'm not convinced they have the mayor's best interests at heart, anyway. Obviously they can't come out and say they hope she dies or just stays in that cage; they have to put on a show, say they wanna help, so that they look like they did their best. But if we screw up and Ghoresn ends up being a slab of meat, I'd bet Yhorio Calit would throw a private party in that church of his."

"Agreed," Lop nodded. "We want little to no interference from them. And with them out of the room, we can act uninhibited. The best plan would be that Jatiri turns herself invisible and simply walks into the cell with the medicines to administer them. She is the doctor, she knows what must be done. And with her magic, Ghoresn will have no idea she is in there and will not attack."

"It's a lovely thought, but you know Jatiri can't do that. She's been practicing every night for weeks and still can't get up to her shoulders. Plus, who's to say Ghoresn's senses aren't enhanced now? We have no idea what that infection does to a body. Maybe she could detect Jatiri's body heat or something. I think the girl's great, but she's no fighter. If Ghoresn pounced, she'd be dead in a second, and Ruska would be fucked."

"Fine," Lop conceded. "Plan B, then."

"We kill?" said Biror, still laying on the ground with his eyes closed, largely uninterested.

"No," Noswen and Lop said in unison.

"This is Plan B. We agreed."

Lop said, "Plan B is that Jatiri tells me where and how to administer the sedative, ideally somewhere on Ghoresn's backside, and I stretch my arm through the bars to do so. If my hand is far enough away from her mouth in the first place, I'm sure I can react quickly enough to dodge any attacks if she spots me."

"It's not great," Noswen said, "but it's maybe the best option we have."

"Or shoot her in the head," said Biror.

This time, no one even bothered chastising him. Lop continued laying out his plan. "After that, we wait for the medicine to kick in and put her to sleep. Then Jatiri can go in and do what she needs to do, while one of us removes the necklace."

"So we get the necklace whether she's cured or not. I like the sound of that," said Noswen.

"What can I do?" Yurzu asked nervously. Getting near Ghoresn scared him, but he wanted to contribute in some way. He didn't want to be dead weight.

"Just hang back," said Lop. "If all goes according to plan, we'll only need two people in there."

"And what if it doesn't go according to plan?"

Biror was the first to answer. "Then we do my plan. Plan C. Shoot her in the head. Or any other part of the body. I am not picky-choosy."

Yurzu didn't like how casually the boar was describing such a grim outcome, but neither Noswen nor Lop were objecting to what he was saying.

"Ahh, this is what I can do while we wait," Biror said, sitting up with a groan. "I will clean my gun."

COAL AND JATIRI RETURNED close to an hour later with a sack full of bottles and baggies containing various liquids and powders.

"Sorry it took so long," the saola apologized. "We had trouble finding some things and the medicine shop was pretty high up, so there was a lot of walking."

"I regret running errands," said Coal, taking a seat on the ground and stretching out his legs. "I tried to convince her we should make a stop at the hot springs to soothe our aching bones, but she insisted that we should go help the mayor or whatever."

Jatiri chuckled and said, "I'll get to work brewing the potions. It shouldn't take long to mix everything up, but the detoxifier will need at least an hour to sit and let everything meld together. Longer would be better, but I don't know if we really have the time."

"Sounds good," said Noswen. "While you do that, why don't you explain what the plan is, Lop?"

As Jatiri sat and began unloading her ingredients, the orangutan dived into his idea for how they should approach the task at hand. Coal and Jatiri nodded along as he spoke, neither raising any objections. Lop did take a second to ask if she thought she'd be able to turn herself fully invisible, but she apologized and said no.

Lop then asked, "Where exactly would the sedative be injected?"

Jatiri responded immediately. Clearly she had been thinking this over while shopping. "The quickest and most effective place to inject would be in a vein, but obviously that is not going to happen, since we can't get close enough to her for any sort of precision. So really, we can just jam it anywhere. Injecting it into the muscles will make it take longer to knock her out, but it'll still work. It'll just take fifteen or twenty minutes rather than thirty seconds. And it'll maybe leave her with some mild bruising."

"If that's safer, I think we're totally fine with a little wait," said Noswen. "And I think bruising is probably the least of her concerns."

"So I can reach in and inject her hind legs or her back? Something like that, away from her head?"

Jatiri confirmed that would be fine.

Once the plan was laid out and the different liquids and powders were organized into two piles (one for the sedative and one for the detoxifier), Jatiri got to work.

Coal laid out flat on the ground to rest like Biror had earlier. The boar had finished cleaning and inspecting his gun and was now taking a walk through the forest, promising an irritable Noswen that he would not stray too far.

Yurzu wandered over to where Jatiri was and sat down beside her, observing how she combined the ingredients.

"What are these?" he asked her, curious. He spotted one small packet of green powder that he thought might be minith, a substance he used in his father's recipe for sleeping powder. There were probably hundreds of green powders in the world, though.

Jatiri smiled and pointed to each substance as she said its name. "This is fint. This one's lavender. Bok. Minith. Passionflower."

"I know minith," Yurzu said excitedly. "So these are for the sedative?"

She nodded. "A lot of these cause calming effects, or make the person sleepy."

"I've used minith for that exact thing. I tend to a garden back home, and sometimes I need to knock out pests. I don't think my powder would work on something as big as her, though," he said. "I combine the minith with some other things, but none of this stuff." He had told her a bit about his pickling business before, though had not gone into much detail.

"Where are you from, again?"

"Toothshadow."

"Ahh. Yes, I don't think you would commonly find passionflower or bok that far north. If it was imported, it'd probably be too expensive to be worthwhile, since there's nothing that makes them more unique than any other sleep aid. They're plentiful in the Innards, though."

"Is bok a flower too?"

"Not a flower, but a plant, yes. Dried and ground up, like the passionflower." She pointed to a bottle of clear liquid that looked like water to Yurzu's untrained eye. "This is rennus. It'll absorb the powders, be infused with their properties, and then we'll inject it into Ghoresn. Honestly, this mixture is a bit overkill. Normally I would just use bok, passionflower, and fint. I thought I should be extra cautious, though, given her size and the general unpredictability of her condition."

Yurzu nodded. He hoped it would be enough to sedate Ghoresn long enough to obtain the fang and administer the medicine. He felt bad watching her behind those bars, all life drained from her eyes. Reduced to nothing more than a wild beast.

"Do you mind if I watch?" he then asked her.

Jatiri chuckled. She said, "It's not going to be very interesting, but sure."

"I think it is."

He sat and watched her mix together everything for the sedative in a small bowl, using a tiny, finger-sized whisk she had bought at the store. Once the powders had sufficiently dissolved into the rennus, she set the bowl aside and rinsed off the whisk with water from her canteen. She then, without Yurzu asking first, explained what each of the ingredients were for the detoxifier and got to work combining them.

Stuff like this had always fascinated Yurzu. He thought of it in the same way as the pest control powders he made, or the pickling solutions for his vegetables. The way different substances could combine and interact with each other to make something wholly new was interesting to him. Even something as simple as rubbing a few spices onto some vegetables before roasting them was like magic to him. Sometimes he thought that made him simpleminded, but he didn't care.

It was only a few minutes before the detoxifier was finished, and Jatiri pushed that bowl aside as well to let it sit for an hour.

"I always get worried before seeing a patient," she suddenly told him. "The anticipation is always horrible. Never knowing if what you're planning to do will be successful or not. Even when you know the correct procedure or medicine to use, there's always the possibility it goes wrong or that there are unintended side effects." She sighed deeply and closed her eyes, rubbing her forehead.

Yurzu did not have a ton of experience with people. Since his parents died, he had spent most of his life alone. He had a few friends in Toothshadow, but no one he was especially close with. The time he'd spent with these five people was the most time he'd spent with anyone. So he was not accustomed to consoling others, but he gave it a shot. It was the right thing to do.

"You're smart," he told her with a smile. "You know what you're doing. I don't think you have anything to be worried about. We're all doing the best we can do here."

Jatiri laughed. It was a hollow sound. Frail. "Thank you," she said, offering a brittle smile. "I appreciate that."

He wasn't sure what else to say, and he wasn't sure his words had even reassured her at all. But he had done his best.

And with that, they waited.

10

COAL HAD HOPED DOING a mundane activity such as shopping would ease his anxiety about their upcoming task, but it barely worked. Maybe if he hadn't had to climb so many damn stairs.

He slept for most of the time Jatiri's potions were brewing or marinating or whatever word she wanted to use for it. It was perfect timing when he awoke to see that she was filling her two syringes with the liquids.

She handed one of the syringes to Lop, the one filled with light purple liquid. The other, which was more of a muddled brown, she kept for herself.

"And I can just jab this anywhere?" he wanted to confirm again.

"Yes," she said. "Her skin is very pale and thin. I noticed you could see some veins underneath, so if you're able to aim for one, do that. I know it'd be difficult, though, so it's not totally necessary."

Lop nodded. "I'll try."

By then Biror had returned from his jaunt, and they all went over the plan one more time. It was simple enough, assuming nothing went terribly wrong.

They returned to the mayor's cell. It was a solemn walk. Everyone was tense and uncertain about what they were about to attempt. Everybody except Biror, apparently, who was keen to roll with the punches and had little sympathy for Ghoresn Daanarb's plight. Zsoz was left behind back in the forest, instructed to plant himself high up on a tree trunk, out of sight. The slime would be much safer there.

Bhuri, Renevi, and the other Medjiam were all awaiting them in the chamber. The nervous deer guard had been dismissed in the intervening hour. Ghoresn was back in the shadows, but with Coal's heightened hearing, he could make out the sound of her padding back and forth near the wall.

"You found what you need?" Bhuri asked them.

"Yep," said Noswen. "Your Magister didn't wanna come down and wish us luck?"

The aged tiger smiled crookedly and said, "As your friends were earlier informed, the Magister is booked solid today. Unfortunately, he cannot be torn from his duties, even for a minute."

"Ahh. What a shame. Just thought he'd want to give his predecessor well wishes. Pray for a speedy recovery, and all that."

"We speak for Magister Calit when we say that we pray the mountain blesses us all on this fine day," said Renevi, placing a hand on Bhuri's shoulder. "Should your efforts be successful, I am sure the Magister would be able to come and welcome back our beloved mayor."

"Wonderful," Noswen said, plastering a toothy smile across her face. It was more like a snarl. Coal was glad to see she felt the same way about the Calitarash as he did. Something was off about them.

"As I said before," Lop then started, "once you all clear the room, we'll do what we need to do."

Bhuri did not appear eager to acquiesce. "Are you sure you would not like our assistance?"

The orangutan nodded. "We shall be alright, I think. But thank you for the offer."

Lop had only worked as a guard at the Palace, but the man had seemingly been trained well in diplomacy. Coal wondered how Noswen or Biror would have responded to the Medjia.

Bhuri slowly looked to each of their faces, giving them a fake smile, before finally relenting. "Very well. I must state plainly that you have been well-informed of the dangers and so the Calitarash cannot be held accountable for any injuries or fatalities you may sustain. We shall wait outside the tunnel entrance with bated breath. Best of luck to you." He instantly lost the smile, his wrinkly orange face sagging as he exited the chamber. The other Medjiam followed him in reverent silence.

Some of the tension evaporated from the room as Bhuri and his cohorts departed. When the Calitarash were out of earshot, Biror said, "I would like to punch that tiger in the head."

"Maybe later," said Noswen.

Coal was impressed that the boar had shown restraint and waited for Bhuri to leave before stating his desire.

The whole group took a collective deep breath and marched toward the iron bars. Yurzu remained a few feet behind everyone else, keeping his distance from the cage. Sitting on the chair where the deer guard had been reading earlier was now a thick, dark iron key. Coal snatched it and held it in his hand, ready for use. For now, he decided to keep the cage firmly locked.

Lop breathed steadily in and out, in and out. He asked again, "Just jab it anywhere?"

"Yes," said Jatiri patiently. It was the first time Coal had seen the orangutan express any sort of worry or fear. It was subtle, but Lop was understandably nervous.

Lop held the syringe in his large, leathery hand. He moved it around a bit, watching the purple liquid slosh about inside. Like always, he was wearing his suspenders with no shirt and his nipples were hard, either out of excitement or fear. Coal wasn't sure which, but he tore his gaze away from the unseemly sight.

"Okay," Lop said, trying to psyche himself up. He took another step toward the bars and squinted, peering into the darkness. "I can't really see her," he then said.

"I will bring her forward," Biror said, gearing up to slam on the bars and scream again.

Jatiri was the one to stop him. "No, no," she said, jumping between him and the cage. "If you rile her up, it'll be basically impossible to inject the sedative." Her voice was trembling with every word she spoke. She was even more nervous than Lop.

"I'll guide you," said Noswen. "Just do exactly as I say as soon as I say it. Do you trust me?"

Lop nodded but said nothing.

The raccoon grew closer to the bars, sticking her nose through them. "She's in the back left corner," she told him. "Sniffing around the wall, for some reason. Her back's turned to us. Try to go fast."

He knew what Lop was capable of, but Coal still nearly gasped when the man's hairy arm started to expand and stretch forward, snaking through the metal bars. The skin showed no signs of distress; it was as if his arm was always ten feet, fifteen feet, twenty feet long. It was a dizzying sight, one that defied reality. Coal felt uneasy watching it. Not to mention the fact that the last creatures he encountered that had been capable of the feat were trying to viciously tear him apart.

Noswen directed him, and Coal watched in the darkness as Lop's hand veered through the air, pointing the tip of the syringe outward. Ghoresn was still interested in whatever she was smelling in the corner and had no idea what was coming for her.

But then her massive form began to turn. Noswen whispered hurriedly, "Go up. Go up. Higher, higher!"

Lop's arm curved upward, almost knocking against the ceiling until Noswen told him to stop. Ghoresn finished her rotation and was gingerly stepping forward, still remaining close to the left-side wall. Lop's hand was safely out of her line of sight, but a portion of his arm was still essentially floating in the center of the cage where it began to curve toward the ceiling.

If she decided to walk in that direction, Coal was sure she'd want to take a curious bite out of the mystery flesh. Lop needed to act fast.

"Go forward, but stay at the same height," Noswen said, keeping her eyes locked on their target.

"How far can your arm stretch?" Coal asked.

"Shut the fuck up," Noswen snapped at him. "Keep going, keep going. You're gonna need to move a little faster, pal."

"It doesn't feel great when I can't see where I'm going," Lop shot back.

Noswen disregarded his concerns and continued urging him on. "Okay, now down, down—hold on, she stopped moving. She doesn't see you. Move forward and to the left..." She paused for a moment, then said, "If you jam forward right now, you'll hit her thigh. Go for it. *Now!*"

Lop's hand shot out, jamming the needle into Ghoresn's massive hind leg. His thumb pressed down on the plunger, and the deformed tiger let out an irritated screech.

"Is it empty? Is it empty?" Lop asked, panic creeping in.

"I can't fucking tell," said Noswen.

But Coal could. "Yes, it is," he said.

"Pull back!" Noswen shouted, no longer keeping her voice low now that Ghoresn knew they were here.

The tiger flung her body around, pulling away from Lop's hand, the syringe still embedded in her leg. She leapt toward the floating hand, but Lop's arm retracted speedily, zipping across the length of the chamber. Ghoresn bounded across the dirt floor, gnashing her teeth and trying to catch her attacker. The syringe flopped around in her leg a couple times before flying out and skidding across the ground.

Coal watched with horror as Ghoresn grew closer and closer to Lop's hand. She was incredibly fast. Her underbite almost grazed the orangutan's long, thick fingers.

But luckily his arm shot through the iron bars at the very last second, returning to its normal length. Ghoresn's face slammed into the cage and she let out a wet, angry roar. Her breath wafted over them, smelling of bile.

"She goes very fast for one who is sedated," said Biror with a chuckle. "She almost eat your arm, friend."

Ghoresn growled, pacing the length of the cage. Her pupil-less eyes glared at the intruders. The crystal fang glittered in the torchlight, dangling beneath her head.

"The sedative isn't instantaneous," Jatiri reminded him. "If it's injected into the muscles, it'll take a few minutes to start working."

"I will prepare for Plan C," Biror said in response, un-holstering his revolver. The gun had a long, rounded barrel sprinkled with gold accents and a golden trigger. It was shock-ingly pretty.

Yurzu looked absolutely petrified by the tiger's fury. He had taken a few more steps back from the group. Noswen went over to make sure he was okay, while the rest of them watched Ghoresn.

She did not take her eyes off them, even when her eyelids started to flutter and her pace began to slow. Around twenty minutes had passed, and Coal was starting to wonder if the sedative wasn't working. But Ghoresn came to a halt a few feet from the bars, laid herself down, and drifted to sleep.

Everyone stared, bodies still, waiting to see if it was a fluke. If she was about to pop back up and pounce at them again after taking a power nap.

There wasn't a ton of time to waste, though. Jatiri reminded them the sedative wouldn't last forever. She had never admin-istered one to a creature so large, and had only been able to make her best guess at the appropriate dosage.

Lop gulped and stretched his arm back out into the cage apprehensively. Coal could see the appendage trembling in the air. Lop reached his fingers out, and the tips of them tickled the fang before fully wrapping it in his palm. He started pulling it up to remove it from Ghoresn's neck, but very quickly encountered a problem.

"I can't get it over her head," he whispered.

They had failed to consider Ghoresn's misshapen head, her massive underbite. The necklace's chain could not be stretched far enough to loop over her jutting chin.

"Yank it from her," said Biror.

"No," Lop argued. "It's too risky."

"You're gonna have to," Noswen said. "Maybe it'll wake her up and we won't be able to give her the medicine, but at least we'll have the fang. Curing her was only secondary to that."

Jatiri nodded her assent, holding her own syringe in hand.

Lop sighed, but swiftly tugged at the necklace. The chain snapped on Ghoresn's neck, and he immediately retracted his arm. He smiled, relieved, holding the fang in hand on their side of the iron bars.

Coal was of the opinion that they should just leave now that their true mission was accomplished, but Ghoresn was still sleeping soundly, so he knew deep down that they needed to try helping her.

Again, they waited a minute to determine that Ghoresn really was still knocked out. Lop tossed the fang to Yurzu, who caught it deftly and tucked it away safely into a pocket.

Coal walked toward the door and timidly inserted the key into its keyhole. He turned it with a satisfying click and stepped away, allowing someone braver than himself to pull it open.

That person was Jatiri. She cautiously entered the cage, leaving the door hanging open.

The heaving mass that was Ghoresn was curled up twenty or thirty feet from the doorway. Her breathing was lethargic as she slept, and her body was pumping out the multicolored ooze less frequently. It rolled over her skin, down the side of her belly, pooling on the floor around her.

Coal wanted to bathe himself after simply looking at the creature.

His heart pounded in his chest as Jatiri inched nearer to the slumbering Ghoresn. She was going to inject the medicine into a vein on one of the hind legs, only half the syringe, then inject the second dose a few minutes later. Coal did not understand why it was necessary to dole it out in two separate doses, but he was not a doctor and trusted the woman's judgment.

Jatiri finally reached Ghoresn. Everyone observed her in silence. Even Biror's expression showed respect for the situation despite how clearly he wanted things to go sideways so he could enact his own plan.

Coal's breathing stopped as his friend leaned forward, placing her free hand on the tiger's enormous leg to steady herself. Her palm pressed into the bare pink flesh. She inspected the leg for a clear, healthy vein. Upon finding one, she swiftly injected the needle.

And Ghoresn's eyes shot open.

The tiger roared in pain, immediately standing and kicking her leg out. Her foot collided with Jatiri's stomach, sending the woman careening through the air, landing with a rough tumble near the back wall.

Coal did not think twice. He didn't even think once, though he should have. He raced forward into the cage, darting past Ghoresn and making his way toward Jatiri's limp body.

Noswen and Lop both screamed at him from behind the bars, while Biror let out what sounded like a war cry.

He ignored all of them as he leapt out of the way of Ghoresn's first assault. She swiped at him with a blotchy claw, narrowly missing him and tearing through the dirt instead. Coal lost his footing, though, and rolled forward, crashing his head into the ground and performing a painful, impromptu somersault. One in which he did not land gracefully on his feet, but rather sprawled out on his back with a huge monster charging toward him. It was more of a fall than a somersault, if he was being honest with himself.

A shot fired in the chamber. Coal had no idea if it connected with Ghoresn, but regardless, the sound was enough to distract her. She turned to track the source of the noise, providing Coal with a window of opportunity to get up off the ground and not be devoured.

He made a mental note to thank Biror later. The boar had to be giddy about his beloved Plan C going into effect.

The shot must have missed or not hurt Ghoresn much, because only a few seconds later, she was running toward Coal again. He had no way of fighting back against a creature so large and ferocious, so he silently prayed that his companions would act fast on his behalf.

Up ahead, Jatiri still hadn't moved. He feared the worst, but had to hope that she was only unconscious or just too pained to move. Neither of those was particularly desirable, but they were preferable to death.

More shots rang out, and he heard Noswen scream, *"Yurzu, stay back!"*

There came more frantic shouting, and whatever the others were doing, they effectively captured Ghoresn's attention. She once again halted her pursuit and turned to face them.

Coal fell to his knees at Jatiri's side. They hurt, impacting with the tough ground, but he banished the pain from his thoughts as he rolled her over onto her back. Her horns dug into the dirt.

Her eyes were open, and she whispered to him, "Help."

"I will," he promised. "Just hold on."

The wind had been knocked out of her. With the force of Ghoresn's kick, it was entirely possible a rib—or multiple— had been broken. He tried to sit her up, but she yelped in agony. He set her back down.

"Can you breathe okay?" he asked her.

She nodded. "Hurts. But okay."

Coal guessed that meant no ribs had punctured her lungs, but there was no way for him to actually know. All of this was based on assumptions and no real knowledge.

He glanced up at Ghoresn and was relieved to see she was far away, contending with Lop and Biror.

Both men had entered the cage. Lop's arms had morphed into long, curved blades which he sliced through the air, lopping off the pustules growing from Ghoresn's body. The tiger screamed at him with every cut of the blade, spraying viscous gunk from her gaping wounds.

Biror was firing off his revolver as quickly as he could, dodging attacks from Ghoresn every few rounds and ducking away to reload. All of his shots were connecting (and it would be absurd if they didn't, given how colossal Ghoresn was), but they were not slowing her down. Bullets did not bother her any more than mosquito bites.

"Shoot at the growths!" Lop yelled at his comrade. Up until that point, Biror had been firing anywhere on Ghoresn's body, tearing holes in her shoulder, her stomach, even a few in her chin.

Biror shifted his strategy and started aiming for the floppy, pus-filled growths extruding from Ghoresn. With smaller targets and the erratic movement of the monstrous tiger, he was missing a lot more often now, but when one connected and the growth exploded in a spray of pus, Ghoresn roared in fury and redoubled her efforts to eliminate the two pests in her cage.

Coal once again tried lifting Jatiri to her feet. She groaned and scrunched her face, but he was able to hoist her up. She stood shakily, an arm wrapped around his waist, putting a lot of her weight on him.

They took a few hesitant steps forward, testing themselves. Something was wrong with her legs, too; she was able to walk, but she nearly collapsed with each small step. It became instantly clear that they would not be traversing the cage with any amount of haste. With the huge scuffle taking place right near the exit, that fact would undoubtedly prove fatal for them.

His mind raced with solutions. None were feasible, except for one. And it would not be great for Jatiri.

He leaned his head toward the saola's and said, "This next part is not going to feel good, but it's the only way. I'm sorry. Get Noswen to heal you as soon as you're out."

There was no time for her to ask what the scheme was, but he doubted she would be able to form the words anyway.

Coal looked to the two men fighting and yelled, *"Lop!"*

It took a few tries before he finally got the man's attention. Lop rotated his wide head to find him in the dark, his jowls flopping with the motion. He leapt backward away from

Ghoresn, who slammed a fist down in the spot where he'd previously stood.

"Grab Jatiri!" Coal shouted. *"She can't walk! Throw her out!"*

He'd seen how fast the orangutan's arms could retract. Lop would be able to pull her across the length of the chamber in only a few seconds. It was her best shot at getting out of there alive. Maybe her only shot.

Despite their differences, Lop did not question his orders. He put some more distance between himself and Ghoresn, ordering Biror to keep her occupied. Then he stretched his arms outward, his hands zooming across the cage. They roughly wrapped themselves around the woman's waist, and she let out a soft whimper.

"You'll be okay," Coal told her. "Just get through these next few seconds."

She nodded.

And then she was gone.

Her scream bounced off the walls as Lop's arms pulled back to him, yanking the battered saola through the air. Ghoresn stopped to stare at the sight for a couple seconds, granting Biror a chance to more easily destroy some of her pustules.

Jatiri's body reached Lop, and then the man swiftly turned and stretched his arms out toward the exit. Ghoresn made a move on him, ignoring Biror and pouncing forward. Jatiri was only halfway across when Lop had to make the choice to toss her the rest of the way. She rolled across the ground, banging a leg on the iron bars as she passed through the exit, in too much agony to even yell out. Noswen rushed to her side, dragged her farther from the cage, and set to work magically healing her injuries.

Ghoresn came down hard on Lop's arms, smashing the limbs to the ground. An audible crack echoed through the chamber like lightning. Both of his arms were broken.

Coal surged forward, not yet knowing what he was going to do, only knowing that he needed to help in some way.

With his injury, Lop could seemingly not retract his arms again. They lay limp on the ground like dead worms. Ghoresn swatted at them, mashing them into the dirt. He put up an admirable fight, but Lop soon passed out from the unendurable pain.

I wish I had White Rose here, Coal thought, yearning for the spider's agility.

He finally reached the scene of the battle and paused, attempting to formulate a plan.

Satisfied with what she'd done, Ghoresn tore her attention away from Lop and focused again on Biror before noticing Coal had entered the fray. The fox intrigued her. She took a couple steps forward, dragging the gigantic growths on her belly across the dirt floor.

The ones on her stomach were vastly larger than the others that sprouted on the rest of her body. It gave Coal an idea.

"Get under her!" he shouted to Biror. "I'll distract her! Pop the ones on her stomach!"

Biror nodded, happy to shoot anything and everything.

He wasn't confident it would work, but it was the only idea coming to mind. At this point, if they did not kill or at the very least incapacitate Ghoresn, Lop was as good as dead. Lugging

Jatiri's small frame out of the cage would have been an impossible task, so pulling the orangutan's huge body out without being mauled first was unthinkable.

For better or for worse, Ghoresn was immensely interested in Coal. He turned her away from Biror, who was charging forward determinedly. The tiger licked her lips, drool cascading over her crooked chin.

Coal stepped back, his boots sinking into puddles of yellow and green goo. Ghoresn readied herself to leap, and Coal preemptively jumped backward himself. But his boots stuck to the goo, faltering his jump, and he fell onto his ass in the revolting puddle. Why did his clothes keep getting ruined?

As Ghoresn aimed herself, Biror saw that it was now or never. He dove forward, sliding on his belly across the rough ground. He ducked his head below the tiger's hulking frame and rolled onto his back. Some of the larger growths slapped against his face, which was now also covered in gunk that he'd slid in, but he seemed unbothered. He was from the Mudlands.

He pointed his revolver at the largest of the growths and pulled the trigger. It burst in a shower of ooze and blood that caked the boar, but it did not deter him. He kept firing, aiming for all the largest pustules on Ghoresn's underside.

It effectively stopped her from pouncing on Coal. She screamed, spraying spittle onto his face and chest, but he would take that over being mutilated any day of the week.

Ghoresn stumbled away, her cries growing weaker until she bumped into the wall. Her stomach gushed yellow and green goo mixed with dark red blood, practically flooding the chamber. Coal could swear she was shrinking, though it was probably just a trick of the light. It almost looked as if she was deflating.

Her roars quieted, then ceased, and Coal watched as she breathed steadily, slumped against the wall. Eventually her eyelids began to droop, obscuring those lifeless white eyes, and her chest stopped heaving. The foul, gooey substance still poured from her gaping stomach, but she was dead.

Biror stood, covered head to toe in the goo and blood mixture. He wiped some from his face with the back of his hand, but seeing as that was covered in it too, it was a useless gesture.

"I waste many bullets on her," he said. "You are clever, little fox." He walked forward and extended a (disgusting) helping hand, hoisting Coal to his feet.

Together, they pulled Lop's unconscious body from the cage. Once they were out, they took extra precautions and locked it up behind them. It seemed Ghoresn was dead, but in reality, none of them knew the first thing about the infection inside her. Maybe she would spring back to life after a few minutes. It was not a risk worth taking.

Jatiri was already looking better, but still fatigued. Coal could also tell that, beyond her own pain, the woman was disappointed that she had been unable to help Ghoresn.

Noswen was now working on Lop's broken arms. No one spoke as she administered her magical healing. The concerned, frantic expression had not left her whiskered face in spite of Ghoresn being out of commission.

Coal shivered, remembering how much it hurt when she had plugged his wounds during the spiderback race. Mending shattered bones had to be brutal. It was a good thing the man was out cold.

Back near the tunnel entrance was Yurzu, who looked traumatized by what had happened to his friends. He had witnessed death during the spiderback race, with the untimely passing of Manova Mandolat, but carnage had never before been so personal.

After making sure she was okay, Coal left Jatiri and approached Yurzu. "Hey," he said to the bat. "You alright?"

Yurzu nodded slowly. "Are you?" he asked.

Coal nodded. "I need to clean all this shit off me as soon as possible, but yeah, I'm fine. Not a scratch on me." He wasn't sure if that was true, but with all the gunk and saliva dampening his fur, he couldn't tell. "I'd give you a hug, but I don't wanna get you all gross like me."

Evidently Yurzu cared less about that. He reached his arms out and wrapped them tight around Coal.

"I'm glad you're okay," Yurzu said. "Is everyone else okay?"

Coal hugged him back and nodded, his chin hitting the bat's shoulder. "They're pretty banged up, but Noswen's helping them out. They'll be fine."

That seemed to soothe him. Yurzu pulled back and let out a deep sigh. He then reached into his pocket and extracted the crystal tiger fang. The whole reason they were here.

"It's pretty," Coal said.

Yurzu nodded.

There wasn't much more to say than that. The bat pocketed the artifact again and finally mustered up the courage to go check on his friends. Coal followed him and sat himself back down next to Jatiri.

"Thank you," the saola said, seeming to get her voice back now. Her words sounded less pained than before.

She was opening her mouth to say more, but Coal stopped her. "You're welcome," he said. "But it was all Lop, really." He looked at the orangutan with newfound respect. The man still hadn't woken up, and Noswen was hunched over him, massaging her magic into his arms.

"Still," said Jatiri. "I—"

"Don't worry about it," Coal said. "Really." He smiled and told her to get some rest.

She leaned her head on his shoulder and quickly drifted to sleep. Coal sat there beside her, watching Noswen work, and tried to steady his breathing.

He'd had several close calls over the past year, between Palace Stingers hunting him down, the monsters in Faranap, and the attack during the spiderback race. But never before had he been so near death. Staring it in the face. Ghoresn's maw hanging open hungrily, priming herself to attack.

His chest was tight, and he wanted to cry, but he didn't have it in him. He leaned his head against Jatiri's and watched the others, wishing Lop a quick and easy recovery.

11

NOSWEN'S MAGIC WAS UNBELIEVA-
BLE. Lop regained consciousness a few minutes
after she began working on his arms. It took less
than half an hour for him to be back in top form, although there
was still some soreness and stiffness in his joints. But his arms
were healed, and there appeared to be no permanent damage.
He could still stretch and morph them with ease as well.

While they were waiting for the orangutan to rest up,
Noswen went outside the chamber to inform the Calitarash
Medjiam what had transpired. No one else felt particularly in-
spired to join her. Yurzu was still standing by the tunnel opening, too stunned to move a muscle.

He stood there in silence, watching his friends. Friends who
he could do nothing to help in their time of need. Some of
whom nearly died. Never before on this journey had such harm
befallen any of them.

And he had been frightened into immobility.

Sure, Noswen had ordered him to stay back, but that was just her being protective over him like always. He should have done something. In retrospect, he had no idea what he could have realistically done, but he was ashamed having stood back while the chaos erupted before him.

Some friend he was.

Jatiri had leaned against Coal for a while, resting, but the fox was now pacing anxiously around the chamber. He noticed Yurzu's nervous expression had not yet softened and decided to approach him.

Placing a hand on his shoulder, Coal said to him, "It's alright if you're still feeling shaken. That was really intense, and it basically *just* ended. We're all feeling the same way."

His words were reassuring, but only slightly. Yurzu was glad to not be alone, both physically and emotionally. But in his heart, he knew he had let them all down.

When Noswen returned, she filled in the rest of the group on how the Medjiam had reacted.

"Well, they seem pretty happy," she started. "They were trying not to act that way, but it's obvious. They were acting angry at our recklessness and mournful about losing the mayor, but I could tell they're giddy about their precious Magister being permanently in charge now."

"Did they put up any fight for the fang?" asked Lop from the ground.

She shook her head. "They could give a shit about it. What they just think of as a piece of jewelry is more than a fair exchange for being handed all of Nitulo."

"Excellent," he said. Now that he was recovered, he was in brighter spirits. As if he hadn't been an inch from death, from being torn limb from limb by a gargantuan, monstrous tiger. Just another day on the job.

Somehow, the normalcy of his attitude made Yurzu feel even guiltier.

"Are we okay with leaving a cult running this city?" Jatiri piped up.

Everyone took a moment to ponder the question. It had not crossed any of their minds.

Biror was the first to respond. "This is not my problem."

"I don't feel fantastic about it," Coal said, "but what could we do about it, really?"

It was a fair point. Yurzu had nothing to offer.

"I have to agree with Coal," said Lop. "The circumstances in Nitulo are unfortunate, but it is beyond our power to do anything about it. Even if we could, we are in too big a hurry. The artifacts take precedent." He took a breath, then said, "I can relay what has transpired here to the Palace once we reach it."

No one put up a fight. It was a miracle that they had beaten Ghoresn; they were in no position to take down Magister Calit and his band of cultists.

"Do the Calitarash need anything else from us?" Lop asked Noswen. "Do we need to fill out some reports about what happened here, or anything of that nature?"

"They didn't say anything about that, so I'm guessing not. Like I said, they were just trying to contain their excitement about this poor woman being dead and gone. That's good enough for them."

Lop nodded. The others had nothing to contribute. Biror was standing apart from the group, his arms folded across his chest like usual, either deep in thought or devoid of thought entirely. Jatiri was seated on the ground, staring blankly.

Yurzu suddenly remembered he was the one in possession of the crystal fang. He took it from his pocket and gazed down at the artifact, glittering in his palm. His nails clinked against its smooth, hard surface.

He looked up at Noswen, who was watching him. She offered a weak smile, then extended her hand. He soundlessly handed the fang over to her.

"We should get this to Zsoz," the raccoon said.

Lop then noisily pushed himself up off the ground, a movement orchestrated with grunts and groans. "You are right. Let us retrieve Zsoz and plan our next steps." He lumbered toward the tunnel.

Coal's ears perked up at this. "Wait," he said, stopping Lop in his tracks. No one else had begun to move. "Next steps? Are you joking?"

"No," Lop replied, turning to face him. His eyebrows sharpened into a glare. "We now have the fourth artifact. There are six in total. Therefore, we need to continue onward in order to complete our mission. Next steps." This time, his last words were tinged with impatience.

"I get that," said Coal. "I know that four is not six. But *come on*. We're all rattled. Even *you* must be rattled, whether or not you wanna put on this tough front. For fuck's sake, we just got here *today*! We got here *today* after walking through the woods for a week and we immediately jumped into a fight with a huge monster. Two of us nearly died, and *you* are among that number. I understand that there's a bit of urgency to what we're doing here, but still—if we burn ourselves out, we're gonna be useless to the Dirt King and we're never gonna get those last two artifacts. We should've gone straight to the damn hot springs when we got here and taken some time to unwind and rest."

Lop now looked like he had blown past *impatience* and landed squarely on *pissed off.* He was opening his mouth in rebuttal, but Coal started speaking first. It looked like an idea had suddenly come to him.

"In fact, that's what I'm gonna do," he declared. "I'm going to the fuckin' hot springs. I'm gonna toss myself in that water and I'm gonna try to forget this truly awful day. After I am sufficiently wet and relaxed, we can meet at an inn or a stewery or whatever you want and talk about your next steps." He then pointed a finger at Yurzu and said, "You're coming with me. You need it too. Let's go."

He marched past Noswen and Lop, who was too fuming to conjure a reasonable argument against him. Yurzu blindly followed Coal through the tunnel and back out into the open air. They could hear Lop now bellowing irately, his indistinct words bouncing off the tunnel walls.

Unsurprisingly, the Calitarash were no longer loitering at the tunnel entrance. All that awaited them outside was a gentle breeze and the rustling of nearby tree leaves.

They both stood there blinking for a moment, their eyes re-adjusting to the sunlight after being in the dim chamber for so long. Then Coal set off for the city, with Yurzu trailing shortly behind.

The farther they walked, the more Coal seemed to calm down. Putting distance between himself and Lop seemed to help. Yurzu wished he could smooth things out between the men.

If he couldn't fight monsters, perhaps he could at least do that much. But today would not be the day.

"What's a stewery?" Yurzu asked. "Is that even a real term?"

Coal laughed. "I don't know," he said. "It just sounds like the type of place Lop would like to eat. A bunch of thick, nasty stews with mushy vegetables and wet bugs."

Yurzu could easily imagine the hulking orangutan shoveling spoonfuls of brown, chunky stew into his mouth, letting it dribble down his chin into his bright orange beard. He chuckled.

As they began their ascent into Nitulo, Yurzu asked, "Why did you want me to come with you?"

Coal shrugged. "It seems like you need some time away from everything as much as I do. If I'm wrong, feel free to head back. I don't wanna force you. I just got kind of wrapped up in the moment."

It was somewhat embarrassing to admit, since he had done nothing to earn it during the battle, but Yurzu said, "You're not wrong."

"Plus, I like hanging out with you. It'll be a good time."

Yurzu smiled. He was still growing accustomed to having a group of friends. His life back in Toothshadow was pleasant and fulfilling in its own way, but it did get lonely from time to time.

They stopped on the first tier of Nitulo so that Coal could ask someone where exactly the hot springs were. Yurzu was happy about Coal taking the initiative, and soon they were on their way to the fifth tier, higher than either of them had been.

"I could never live in this city," Coal said, panting as they climbed the seemingly endless stairs. "This is our first day here and I'm already so sick of this."

Eventually, they came to the city's fifth tier. Unlike all the others, which granted breathtaking views of the kingdom below, it was completely surrounded by walls of jagged stone. The whole area was closed off within the mountain, hidden from the outside world. Stone buildings lined the mountainous perimeter. One was a tall, impressive inn, which Yurzu assumed would be where they'd find the others after their dip in the springs.

They spotted a hand-painted sign that read NITULO HOT SPRINGS hanging from an archway curved above a path leading deeper into the mountain. Yurzu squinted and could see more stairs just beyond.

Evidently, Coal saw the stairs too. "What is wrong with the people here?" he wondered aloud before starting toward the path. "Between the Calitarash and all the damn stairs, I must say again: this place is not for me."

Yurzu laughed and followed him.

The path leading to the hot springs was mercifully short. It brought them higher up the mountain to a fenced-off area with three separate steaming pools. Two were roughly the same size, easily able to accommodate ten people (unless they were all Lop- or Biror-sized), while the other was much smaller, with room for only two. Between the thin fence slats, they had a fantastic view of the forest at the base of the mountains, which stretched as far as the eye could see. The sun was starting to set, painting the sky with vivid pink and purple hues.

"Wow," said Coal. "No entry fee."

Yurzu was surprised by that as well, but it was a welcome surprise.

No one else was currently occupying any of the pools, which was another surprising fact. They were totally alone.

Yurzu had never been somewhere like this, so he was not exactly sure what the protocol was. He let out a tiny gasp when Coal began to undress, tossing his shirt, pants, and boots aside. In an instant, he was down to nothing but his underwear. His short orange and black fur rustled in the mountain breeze, and he shivered harshly.

Okay, then, thought Yurzu, stifling his awkwardness.

He pulled off his own shirt and threw it next to Coal's. It was then followed by his shoes and his pants, which he noted desperately needed a wash, and he was then standing there in the biting cold. He followed Coal into one of the two bigger pools, and let out a deep sigh as he submerged himself in the steaming hot water.

Despite the name, Yurzu was not expecting the springs to be quite so hot. It was a pleasant heat, though, in contrast with the cold mountain air. His fur greedily soaked up the warmth, and for some reason he instinctively pulled his knees to his chest, his body bobbing in the water like a boiling potato.

Coal whistled, leaning his head to dip the back of it into the water. "This is what I've been craving," he said, lifting it back out. Water dripped from his ears. "It's been so long."

"Are there many places like this where you're from?" Yurzu asked. He unfolded his legs, but he had to stand on the tips of his toes to touch the bottom of the pool. It looked like Coal was sitting, though, so his side had to be shallower. He leisurely swam over and plopped himself beside Coal.

"No," the fox answered. "Not at all. I didn't live near any mountains. I'm from Muta Par."

Yurzu was unsure how they had not talked about this before. "I'm from Toothshadow," he said. They weren't exactly neighbors, but the two places were not terribly far from each other. A simple day's journey, probably.

"Oh, really?" said Coal, staring out at the Innards. He sunk lower into the water. All that could be seen above the surface was his head.

"Yes," said Yurzu. "I lived there my whole life."

"Same with me in Muta Par," said Coal. He turned away from the view and looked at Yurzu. "There was an earthquake there last year, sometime in Brightmonth. Were you still in Toothshadow at the time? Did you feel it?"

Yurzu nodded, splashing water with his chin. He remembered that earthquake well. Luckily his own home was left unscathed, but a few buildings in Toothshadow had collapsed. The rumbling was the most intense he'd ever felt, and it lasted for several minutes. He heard nearby cities were affected too, such as Banak Tor, but this was the first he'd heard specifically about Muta Par. It made sense, though, given that city's proximity to the others.

After relaying all that, Yurzu said, "I didn't know what to do. I'd never experienced an earthquake before. My parents never prepared me for it. I'm not sure they had ever been in one either."

Coal was silent for a minute. Then he said, "That earthquake was when my father died."

The words hung suspended in the air between them. Yurzu did not know how to respond. He knew from experience that sometimes you did not want condolences or pity. Sometimes you just needed to express something and have someone absorb it. Share the burden. Sometimes you just needed the words to be heard and the sorrow to be felt.

The sky was darkening to a lush purple, losing its ferocious pink. Scant stars twinkled into existence.

"What are you gonna do when this is all over?" Coal asked after a few minutes.

It was a good question, but not one that Yurzu had put a huge amount of thought into. All he really knew was that he wanted things to get back to normal. A simple enough request.

"Just go home, I guess," he replied. "My garden is probably dead by now. Most of it, anyway. I'll have to start growing things again. I have enough money saved up in the meantime while I get back on my feet."

Coal grinned. "No big vacation or anything like that? No celebration for saving the kingdom? Just right back to work? You sound like Lop."

Yurzu shrugged, his shoulders peeking out of the water with the motion. "I don't have anywhere to go," he said. "This whole adventure is kind of like a big vacation anyway."

"Calling it an adventure makes it sound more fun than it really is. I guess you can think of it as a vacation, except with a lot more weariness and danger and bad company," said Coal.

Yurzu chuckled, then added, "It's probably the most high-stakes vacation anyone has ever been on."

Coal laughed too, then dunked his head fully in the water for a few seconds before popping back out. He wiped water from his eyes and sighed deeply.

"How about you?" Yurzu asked. "Do you have any big plans?"

"Nothing concrete," said Coal, "but there's someone I want to travel with. I wanted to go to a hot spring with them, actually. Up in Jaq Yul. But I'd settle for hanging out in his apartment, or something. Anywhere he wants to go, I'd go."

"I would think you'd be ready to plant yourself somewhere, with all your complaining about walking," Yurzu joked.

"Yeah, well," said Coal, "I'll walk a little more for him."

"What's his name?"

"Ilio."

"Is he your boyfriend?"

Coal thought about it for a second before answering. "I think so, but I guess we never really talked about it or made anything official. But I think of him that way, yeah."

Yurzu smiled. "That sounds nice," he said.

He had never dated anyone before. There had been a few awkward flirtations in the past, but nothing that ever went anywhere. It always fizzled out on his end. If things seemed like they were even mildly progressing, he would succumb to his nervousness, which inevitably would gradually shut the girl out until she eventually gave up on him.

"Hello, boys," came an unfamiliar wheezing voice.

They both turned to the entrance. There stood a large tiger, hand resting on his protruding belly, already stripped down to his underwear. No other clothes were on the ground nearby, implying that he had walked all the way to the springs in such a state. His fur was faded with age. He took a few heavy steps toward them, and Yurzu had no idea how they hadn't heard his approach.

The man carefully stepped down into the same pool as them, sending small waves rippling toward their side. He grinned cheerfully as he sank in deeper.

"Hope I'm not interrupting," said the man. "Name's Fennigha." His voice was warm and pleasant.

"Not at all," said Coal before introducing himself. Then, "This is Yurzu."

Fennigha smiled kindly. "Blessings of the mountain to you, or whatever it is those people say."

Coal and Yurzu both chuckled. Coal said, "You aren't a follower?"

The tiger waved away the suggestion like it was a bad stink.

"Of course I see the eyes above the mountains, those are undeniable, but I am not sure about all that other stuff those people do with the hands on the heads and whatever else. Sending your energy into the sky? Whatever it is they talk about, I am not one for nonsense such as that," he said. "All the Calitarash do is peddle stories, and they are not even good ones. I am too old for new stories. I like my old ones just fine."

"You seem like a man who knows plenty of stories," said Coal.

Yurzu never felt comfortable talking to strangers, even if they came off as friendly as Fennigha did. He was thankful for Coal being there to steer the conversation.

Fennigha nodded proudly. "I do," he said. "The tigers are full of stories. We were the original storytellers, you know. We brought them all with us. All the stories you've heard, all the books you've read—none would be possible without the tigers."

It was an incredibly bold claim, but Yurzu was not going to contradict the jolly old man.

And neither was Coal, who instead asked, "Brought them with you from where?"

"From Zawraht, of course!" said Fennigha, as if this were common knowledge.

Yurzu and Coal exchanged a look, but neither recognized the name. Which was not a huge surprise, given how many new places in Ruska that Yurzu had learned about over the course of the past ten months.

"I'm afraid I haven't heard of it," said Coal. "Where's Zawraht? In the east?"

Fennigha shook his head, his saggy jowls flapping wildly. "Of course not, boy! Zawraht is in the far north, past the Houndstooth."

They looked at each other again, trying to ascertain whether this man had lost his mind. No one knew what lay beyond the Houndstooth. Scholars theorized, of course, but no one knew anything for sure. The tree had been rooted at the tip of the kingdom's mountain pass for centuries, maybe longer. Immovable and impassible.

"What do you mean?" asked Coal with some amount of apprehension.

Fennigha laughed. It was a loud, booming sound. The sound of pure joy. He was not offended by the question, and was rather happy to expound. "Zawraht is the kingdom where we come from! Not you two, of course, but the tigers. You look at the brilliant colors of the orangutans, and the macaws, and the tigers, and you think that we're from Ruska? You think we're from this forest?"

"Your fur is orange and black. You and I have literally the same colored fur," Coal pointed out.

"Ahh! Maybe now, yes. But when I was young, my coat was bright like a flame!" Fennigha boasted.

"How come we've never heard about Zawraht?" Yurzu cut in. "I've never heard of any other kingdoms."

"That's an excellent question, isn't it?" said Fennigha. "There are some in this kingdom who want history to be forgotten, I think. But I could not say why. Such things are beyond even my wisdom, haha! But the tigers still remember. We still tell the stories of our homeland. Like the plight of Chrestith Nowazu. Or the tale of the egg and the willow. The tigers tell their tales, rest assured."

Yurzu didn't know how to process this. It was entirely possible these were just the ramblings of a crazy old man, but Fennigha did not seem out of sorts. He appeared to be perfectly lucid. And he had no reason to lie to them, either. They were just strangers in a pool together.

"We're traveling with an orangutan," Yurzu said. "If his people are from Zawraht, too, why has he not ever mentioned it?" He was positive that if Lop had ever brought up something as outlandish as another kingdom, he would've remembered it.

Fennigha laughed again. "Orangutans are not tigers," the man said, not losing an ounce of his cheeriness. "The orangutans are willfully ignorant. They choose to forget their past. They live up north, catering to the Dirt King's whims. They are slaves to him, obeying without question. They are closest to the Houndstooth, closest to Zawraht, and yet they cast it from their memory! They burn their stories. I do not know why this is. Again, it is beyond my wisdom. Old Fennigha cannot know it all, try as he might."

"How could they have come from somewhere else?" Coal asked. "Ruska is completely closed off. We're surrounded by mountains and the Houndstooth."

The tiger laughed. "The Houndstooth wasn't always there, of course!" he said. It was like he was talking to children. "The Houndstooth—old ugly thing—has not always been up there, reaching into the sky like a charred hand. Neither has the Palace. The valley used to be open to the outside world, with people coming and going. That is what the old stories say, anyhow. As sure as you can find tigers and macaws and orangutans in Ruska, you can bet you'd find foxes and bats and everyone else in Zawraht and beyond."

Yurzu had never thought about the prospect of the Houndstooth not existing. It had always been a part of his and everyone else's lives. Ruska was not Ruska without the Houndstooth. That was what he'd thought, at least.

They were both deeply intrigued by this man who had clambered into the hot springs. Yurzu was glad Coal had dragged him along, both for the relaxation and for this conversation.

Yurzu wasn't sure if Coal was genuinely curious or if he was simply humoring the old tiger, but he asked, "Who was Chrestith Nowazi?"

"Nowazu," Fennigha corrected him. "His is a classic tale in the tiger storybook. He came from humble beginnings and went on to slay the Sadist. Ooooh…" Fennigha shuddered at the mere mention of the title. "The Sadist was a nasty sort."

"Fitting name, then," said Coal.

"Indeed," said Fennigha. "Ruska has never known a monster such as the Sadist, and I am doubtful it has ever known a hero such as Chrestith Nowazu. He was also sometimes called Daggerfang."

Yurzu grinned. He liked the cheesy yet sort of cool nickname. "Could you tell us the story?" he asked.

Fennigha grinned. He was missing two teeth near the back of his smile, but it was a smile full of life.

"Nothing would please me more, boys," he said.

The sun had now fully set, and the only light illuminating them was the moon and a handful of torches set up around each of the steaming pools. Yurzu and Coal shared a smile as the tiger dove headfirst into his ancient tale.

"Chrestith Nowazu came from a small, unassuming village by the sea, one that many thought had long since been lost to the sands…"

After only a single sentence, Yurzu interrupted the man. "What is the sea?" he asked. He had never heard of such a thing in Ruska. By the looks of it, neither had Coal.

Fennigha let out his bellowing laughter again. "Silly Ruskan boys," he grinned. "Listen to what Old Fennigha's got to say." He tapped the side of his head and said, "There's a lot rattling around up here. More than you could even dream of."

They listened to the old tiger speak with breathless attention.

12

THEIR TIME IN THE hot spring had rejuvenated Coal after the tragic bout with Ghoresn. His muscles now felt relaxed, his fur had retained a pleasant warmth, and his mind was clear. It was great leaving behind his worries, if only for an hour or two.

Now he was much more willing to tolerate Lop.

The stories told by their tiger acquaintance in the pool had entertained yet perplexed him. It was the first time he had ever heard someone mentioning the world outside Ruska in any concrete way. Of course everyone knew there was land beyond Ruska—they all saw those eyes gleaming over the mountaintops—but no one had ever put a name to it. And he had definitely never heard that the orangutans, tigers, and macaws came from those distant lands. Everyone assumed that everyone had always been here, that the Houndstooth had forever stood tall and unyielding in the north.

No one had ever questioned it. History really was being forgotten.

But not by the tigers in Nitulo, apparently.

Coal wanted to learn more about Zawraht, but he didn't know where to start, aside from foolishly attempting to interview every tiger he met from now on. In all his years working in the Muta Par library, not once had he ever seen a text about lands other than Ruska.

On the other hand, Fennigha was a goofy old man who lived up in the mountains. Maybe he was simply messing with them. Entertaining himself.

Coal and Yurzu dried off and departed from the hot springs, bidding the tiger a fond farewell. They marched across the mountainous platform toward the inn they'd spotted.

"I need some food," he told the bat as they walked. "I dunno about you, but I worked up an appetite during that fight and for some reason, soaking in the warm water just made me even hungrier." The moon had long since graced the sky, and it was far past Coal's preferred dinnertime. Yurzu mumbled his agreement.

They entered the inn and greeted the receptionist, who seemed to recognize them. He told them that the rest of their party was already upstairs and gave Coal the room number. Evidently someone (probably Noswen) had told the man to keep an eye out for a fox and bat pair.

Coal and Yurzu trundled up the stairs, both of their stomachs grumbling with discontent. The group's room was located at the very end of the hall. Coal knocked lightly on the door and was soon greeted by Noswen.

"Finally," she said in lieu of a real greeting. "We've been waiting for you two to go to dinner. I know he's always pretty testy, but Biror might actually kill you for real this time." She stepped aside to let them in.

As they entered, Coal was surprised to find how huge the room was. They had booked a suite big enough to house their entire party. Everyone was looking at them as they settled in.

"Did you enjoy your hot water bath?" Biror asked them mockingly.

"Yes," Yurzu answered. Coal laughed.

"Big fun bathtime, huh?" said the boar in his sharp Mudlands accent. "Meanwhile, here we are all sitting, dying of hunger and of thirst."

"Don't worry, I know you won't want us to attend your funeral," Coal said. Biror did not look amused.

Lop sat near Biror and was rubbing his sore arms. While Noswen had considerably sped up the healing process, she told him he would probably still have some pain and stiffness for around a week. It might be best to refrain from using his power for a little while.

His buddy Zsoz was rooted to the ground near the chair. The crystal tiger fang had joined its companion artifacts within the slime's gelatinous form.

Jatiri was laid across a couch. Her eyes fluttered open as Coal and Yurzu approached the group. "Hey," she said to them.

"Hey," said Coal. "How are you feeling?"

"Fine," she answered, sitting up and making room for the two of them. "Just some soreness, is all. And a pretty killer headache."

"Enough of this chatter," said Biror. "We all got hurt. It is over. Let us dine."

But the saola ignored him. "How were the springs?" she asked.

"Amazing," said Yurzu before Coal could respond.

Usually the bat was reluctant to speak up when they were with the full group. He had been much chattier (relatively speaking) when it had just been him and Noswen on the road to Sadatso. Coal was pleased to see him coming out of his shell.

Yurzu went on to describe the beautiful views up there, and how they had met an exceptionally friendly tiger who regaled them with interesting stories about the world beyond Ruska. It was clear by their reactions that the others took that to mean he was telling them fables and fairytales rather than anything based in history. Coal couldn't really refute that notion himself, so he let it be.

"Okay," said Noswen, "I need to lug my ass up there. Is it open late? Can I go after dinner?"

"Probably," Coal said with a shrug. "There were no employees or anything like that. It's just a natural hot spring, open to the public."

Learning that there was no fee got her on board even more. Jatiri also expressed interest in checking it out after they ate.

No one pressed for any further details about Fennigha and his stories, which was maybe for the best.

The two women had then landed on the topic of the best natural sights they had seen. Noswen was much more well-traveled than Jatiri, who had primarily spent her life hidden away in the Innards with the other saolas. It had been a long time since Noswen had taken a trip anywhere, though, now that she had her six children to care for. She was talking about how that was the one bright side of this journey when the cheery conversation was suddenly interrupted.

"Let us dine!" Biror roared.

Finally someone acknowledged him. "We will dine soon," said Lop. "First, we should plan our next steps while we have some privacy."

That effectively got the conversation on track. Everyone concurred with both of the men.

"Thanks to the Dirt King's exhaustive research, we know what the final two artifacts are and where to find them," Lop began. "One is the obsidian beak, which is being held by the macaws. More specifically, it is in the possession of a woman named Ranatt Waraspoke. She is a city council member in Moonoshk, in the eastern part of the kingdom.

"The other is the jade hoof, which lies deep within the Mudlands with the boars. It is located in the northwestern city of Vuntagonyeo. Are you familiar with it?"

The question was directed toward Biror, who nodded. The boars who resided in the Mudlands were fairly secluded from the rest of society. Not many people ventured into the territory. "Of course I know it," said Biror.

Lop nodded, pleased.

Coal had never heard of either city. If he searched the annals of his mind, he might scrounge up something about Moonoshk, which he thought he recalled was a city built in the eastern treetops. But definitely nothing about Vuntagonyeo. Practically everything about the Mudlands was a mystery to him.

"They're pretty far apart from each other," Noswen stated. "Like, as far apart as they could possibly be, really. It'll take a lot of time to reach even the Mudlands from here, and then even longer to reach Moonoshk after. I don't feel great about that. Not only because I want to get the fuck home, but also after what we saw with Ghoresn—"

"You and I are on the same page, it seems," Lop interjected.

"We need to split up," the raccoon nodded.

"Wait, what?" said Coal. By the looks on their faces, Jatiri and Yurzu were just as concerned by this revelation as he was. Biror's expression was totally unchanged and uncaring. The man wanted to eat. Nothing else was of any concern to him.

Lop was the one to elaborate, though everything he said was punctuated by nods from Noswen. "What happened to Ghoresn is something we have never seen before. The Dirt King did say that eventually, if the Houndstooth's condition grew too unstable, it would start infecting people. Clearly that is starting to happen. We cannot let the same fate befall others throughout Ruska."

Coal thought about Mayor Bontrug back in Soponunga and hoped that the man was doing okay.

"This means things are worse than we previously thought," Lop continued. "We believed we might have more time to track down the artifacts, but the clock is ticking. We need to get to the Houndstooth sooner rather than later. Our best option is to split into two groups. One can go get the hoof while the other obtains the beak, then we can come together again at the Palace."

"Isn't that way more dangerous?" said Coal. "We pretty much got our asses handed to us in that fight with Ghoresn. Half of the group nearly died, as I mentioned before. What if we encounter something like that again now that the infection's spreading?"

"We won the fight," said Biror. "It is not a problem."

"Our lack of coordination was an issue," said Lop. "Perhaps dividing into smaller groups can help with that, as well."

"I don't think so," Coal argued. "I think it'd just be an easier way for us to get stomped by whatever monsters are out there."

Lop's brow furrowed. He was not expecting this to be an argument, and the last person he wanted defying him was Coal. "If we remain together and increase the time it takes to put a stop to all this, Ruska will become even more overrun with the very monsters you're worried about. Splitting up is the most logical choice."

"I think it's stupid," Coal said, as if his position were not already abundantly clear.

"It's not ideal," Noswen agreed, "but I think it's what we need to do. What do the rest of you think?"

Yurzu and Jatiri had thus far been sitting quietly on the couch, listening to Coal and Lop bicker. The bat shrugged and said that he would do whatever the group thought was best.

Jatiri said, "I agree with both of you. I think it's wildly unsafe, but I also don't think we really have a choice. We're just in a bad situation and we'll have to deal with it."

They all then looked to Biror, who shrugged and said nothing, which they took to mean he was taking Yurzu's position on the matter.

I do not like the plan, said Zsoz. None of them had been expecting the slime to respond, which made Coal feel slightly guilty. Of course Zsoz would have an opinion. **My function in the group is to safely store the artifacts. I am one being. If the group divides into two, I cannot become two beings. Therefore, I will have to remain with one group, while the**

other obtains an artifact that cannot then be safely stored within me.

"That's a solid point," said Coal.

"Nonsense," Biror said. "I can hold a rock just as well as the slime can."

These are not rocks. They are ancient, powerful, magical artifacts.

"It was analogy, slime. It will not be a problem. Let us dine."

I do not eat.

"Biror's right," Lop said. "I admit, I'm a little uncomfortable about what you're saying, Zsoz, but in the end I think it would be fine. It's easier for a person to protect one artifact than having to juggle six, which is why we needed you."

I do not juggle.

"I think majority rules on this one," said Noswen. "We're gonna split up. Sorry, Coal. You too, Zsoz."

Coal understood the points they were making, and deep down he did agree with them, but breaking apart into smaller groups still felt unsafe to him. Now that he'd lost the argument, though, he had to ensure he did not end up in whatever group Lop went with. Having even less of a buffer between them would be a recipe for disaster.

Yurzu then amended, "Maybe we should meet in Toothshadow instead of the Palace. We could meet at my house there, maybe. It's much more neutral ground. If the group without Lop shows up at the Palace first, they might run into trouble getting in."

"That could be true," Noswen nodded. "I agree. Let's go with Toothshadow as the meetup spot. It's not far from the Palace, so it won't make a big difference time-wise."

"And who's going where?" Yurzu then asked.

"Good question," said Noswen. "I already had some thoughts on this, too. Obviously, especially now that you've also said you know where the city is, I think you should go for the hoof, Biror. You know the Mudlands better than anyone else."

The boar nodded. "This is true."

Then Noswen turned to Yurzu. "I think it'd make sense for you to go for the beak," she said. The young bat blinked in surprise. "You know Buatang, right?"

He nodded. Coal had never heard him speak the language of the flyers, but it wasn't a stretch to believe he knew it.

"On the off-chance Ranatt Waraspoke or any other birds in Moonoshk only speak Buatang, we need someone there who can translate."

Suddenly Fennigha's stories sprang to mind, and Coal asked, "Why do the macaws speak Buatang like the bats and other flyers if they're not from Ruska? Don't they have their own language?"

Everyone stared at him, including Yurzu.

"I don't know what you're talking about," Noswen said.

Lop looked annoyed by the question. Jatiri was confused.

"You are talking a load of shit," said Biror.

They quickly moved on, putting his question out of their minds.

"I'll go with you, of course," Noswen said to Yurzu with a smile.

You two would be ineffective in protecting the beak, said Zsoz bluntly. **I will accompany you to Moonoshk so that I may store the beak once it is obtained.**

"You didn't quite have to put it that way, but I was going to say the same thing," the raccoon nodded. "I definitely think you should come with us."

The slime and Lop were inseparable, so Coal anticipated the man would be joining that expedition.

And sure enough, the orangutan then said, "I'll go to Moonoshk as well. As Zsoz so rudely put it, you two are not the best fighters in the bunch. In case things go sideways, you'll need someone who can fight."

"I think we'd both feel a lot safer with you around," Noswen confessed. "The other group will have Biror, anyway. He can pack as good a wallop as anybody."

"This is true," Biror repeated.

Guess I'm going to the Mudlands, Coal thought. A part of him was excited for the opportunity to see a place he truly knew very little about. Having Biror as the tour guide, though, was unideal.

But at least he'd be with Jatiri. She and Yurzu were his best friends among the group, so he was glad to be with at least one of them.

"So Lop, Zsoz, Yurzu, and myself will head east to Moonoshk and grab the obsidian beak," said Noswen, "while Biror, Coal, and Jatiri go into the Mudlands to find the jade hoof."

"This sounds like a good plan," Biror said, rising from his chair. He loudly clapped his meaty hands together. "Let us dine!"

Once more, everyone ignored the man. Jatiri asked, "When are we leaving?"

"Tomorrow," Lop answered. It was the answer Coal was both expecting yet dreading. "There is no time to waste. The Dirt King requires our service. All of Ruska does, in fact."

All of them begrudgingly accepted this as the best course of action. Coal could sense that everyone was as worn out as he was, so he felt mildly better knowing that they commiserated with him.

"I know it'll be pretty late, but you two should definitely check out the hot springs after dinner. I think it'll be refreshing and prepare you for all the bullshit that tomorrow will bring," he suggested to Noswen and Jatiri.

The women shared a look and grinned, agreeing to the idea.

They were starting to discuss the hot springs again, and Biror grumbled something in Ronog before storming across the room and out the door, slamming it behind him.

The rest of them stared at the door for a few seconds before bursting into laughter, Lop and Zsoz excluded.

"I think Biror is a bit grumpy, if you can believe it," Jatiri joked.

"Baby needs his bottle," Noswen laughed. "I'm hungry too, though. Let's hurry and catch up to him." She stood and started toward the door, followed by Yurzu.

Coal quickly skipped through the room behind them, his stomach allying with Biror as it gurgled incessantly.

"Let us dine!" he declared.

THE NEXT MORNING, THEY stood in their two separate groups outside the inn to say their farewells.

Coal's group would be staying near the western side of Ruska, heading north up the Lunsk River and eventually venturing into the Mudlands where they would find the city of Vuntagonyeo. Noswen's group would have to head east, through the Innards and toward the Houndspine. They would then travel over the massive bridge and navigate the forest on the other side to reach Moonoshk.

Their journey across the Houndspine would grant them many more opportunities to sleep in beds and eat at restaurants, which Coal was immensely jealous of. All he could envision for himself was trudging through mud, the soles of his shoes slapping against the wet ground.

Coal stepped forward and embraced Yurzu in a tight hug. "Don't let Lop ruin the rest of your vacation," he joked, patting the bat on the back.

"I won't," Yurzu giggled. They pulled apart and Yurzu said, "Don't let Biror ruin yours."

"He'll try his damnedest, I'm sure. Hey, when we get to your place in Toothshadow, how's about we settle that bet?"

"Hmm?" Yurzu blinked at him, confused.

"Don't act like you forgot!" Coal chided him playfully. "You're just trying to back out because you know it's an impossible task. But you said you could prepare tree bark in a way that I would find delicious."

"Oh!" said Yurzu. He laughed. "Of course."

"I'm granting you the advantage of cooking in your own home, so I'm expecting greatness."

"Sounds like a plan," the bat grinned.

Coal then said a quick goodbye to Noswen, and an even quicker one to Lop. Zsoz was affixed to the man's shoulder, ready for the voyage ahead.

With everyone's farewells in order, they took off to find the final two artifacts. Closer to the end than the beginning. Soon it would all be behind them.

13

A S IT TURNED OUT, Coal had to thank the Valohir or whatever god was listening that their mission had taken on a newfound urgency, because it meant that walking was no longer the best option.

His group had been given funds to book passage on a riverboat heading north up the Lunsk River. It would be at least a week of travel, cutting them across the span of Ruska in far less time than it'd take for them to walk the same length. It was a boat route that Biror was familiar with, and he informed them that it should conclude at the grand city of Jink'rel on the outskirts of the Mudlands.

And all the while, Coal could lounge in his room, reading *A Popular Bargain*.

Or stand out on the deck, gazing at the water, watching the fish swim by.

Or gorge himself on the free food provided at all hours of the day.

He was absolutely giddy with anticipation as he, Jatiri, and Biror made their way north through the Innards in search of a town called Bottado, where they would be boarding the boat. There was some cheeriness to Coal's gait with the knowledge that his walking days would soon be over.

It was a hot day in the Innards, even with the canopy blocking out most of the sun's harsh heat. They were nearing the end of Highmonth, the peak of summer. Soon they'd enter Redmonth; the heat would still be nearly unbearable, but at least it would be winding down in preparation for the cooler winds of Drymonth.

Huh, he thought. *My birthday is soon.*

The thought had not occurred to him until just then. Last Redmonth, he had still been on the run from Palace Stingers and hadn't had the chance to celebrate his birthday. He tried to recall what it was he'd done that day. Was he even in a town? Or was he stuck in the middle of a forest somewhere, sleeping in the dirt?

It was hard to know. Much of that year was a blur in his mind, all the memories running together messily like a painting left in the rain.

He wondered where he would be this year. Without knowing how long each leg of their journey would take, it was difficult to be sure. Maybe he would be in the heart of the Mudlands. Or perhaps this wild quest would culminate with their magical powers combining at the foot of the Houndstooth while presenting him with a neatly-wrapped gift.

Coal chuckled at the notion of Lop and Biror being forced to shop for a birthday present for him.

Before they set off that morning, Coal and Jatiri had spoken in private and decided they should try to get to know Biror a bit more. If they worked on their rapport with him, it could help ease the journey along. They wanted to avoid any awkwardness or bad blood, especially when they finally reached the Mudlands and were totally out of their element.

Stepping over a mushy, larvae-ridden log, Jatiri took a deep breath and asked Biror, "How do you know about this boat? Do you ride it often?" During their talk that morning, they both realized they knew nothing at all about the boar's past.

Biror huffed, as he usually did before speaking to any of them. It was a sound nestled somewhere between irritation and amusement. Like he was preparing himself to talk to a dumb child. "Yes, I ride often," he said, stomping through the underbrush. "For work, it is good. Much faster than walking or wagons."

"What was your job, before all this?"

He laughed. "We do not need to speak of my job. We do not need to speak so…how do you say? *Frivolous*? We do not need to speak so frivolous."

"I was just wondering," said Jatiri, slightly hurt.

Biror huffed again. This time it definitely sounded amused. "We are doing a job together. That is all. We must do the job, and when the job is over, we will go away from each other. All we need to know is each other's names. Even that I am not sure is necessary, but it is polite."

Coal almost laughed, hearing the gruff man talk about politeness. If the demeanor he'd adopted was what he considered being polite, Coal did not want to see him being rude.

Plus, he could not recall a time the boar had actually used his name. Did he even know that much about him?

"That is how the boars work. We get it done, and that is it. No fuss. No frivolous."

"So you're trying to tell me you never knew *anything* about anyone you've ever worked with?" Jatiri asked him, unconvinced.

"What I know is that they can kill geigexes and hold a rockblade steady. That is all I need to know, and so it is all I know."

In his limited research about the Mudlands, Coal had read a little bit about rockblades. They were a specialty of the boars. Originally, they were blades fully carved out of rock, though nowadays it was no more than a name. What made a blade a rockblade was its serrated edge, the jagged points irregular, carved according to each forger's unique pattern. The hilts were typically made of smooth, polished rock, in keeping with the blade's name.

Rockblades were no longer used very often. In fact, their most common use was—

"You're a mantis runner," Coal blurted out.

Biror did not respond, nor did he stop walking. He simply huffed again, this time in irritation.

Which Coal took to mean he was right. He grinned.

"What's a mantis runner?" Jatiri asked.

Living such a secluded life, it made sense that she would be unaware of the practice. It had also been outlawed for at least a decade.

Apparently Biror was not going to answer the question, so Coal took it upon himself. "They track down mantises and saw off the spines on their arms," he explained. Mantises were usually just as big as spiders, but could grow to be easily twice their size. There were only two types of insects in Ruska that were larger: the beetles that traversed the Houndsvein, and snails.

"What for?"

"The spines are used for all sorts of things. Some people believe that if they're heated and then ground up, the powder is a powerful cure-all. But they're mostly used to create luxury goods. Sculptures, jewelry, piano keys. It's mostly among the boars, but sometimes the items are shipped off to other parts of the country and sold at a high price. It's risky, though. It's been illegal for a long while now."

Coal was walking behind Jatiri, so he could not see the expression on her face, but it took her a few moments to process what he was saying. Biror was still choosing to stay out of the conversation.

"Why is it illegal?" she asked.

"Well, it used to involve killing the mantises," said Coal. "So that was a big part of it. Their population was rapidly declining. A new method was developed, though, that involved sedating them and sawing off the spines instead, but that usually leads to death, too. Not always, but those spines are what the mantises use to catch their prey. Without them, a lot of times they starve."

"That's awful!"

"It's not great," Coal agreed. "They're usually found hiding up in trees, near geigex colonies. I don't know how the two are connected. Oh, and a lot of times mantis nymphs are collected, killed, and made into a jelly that is considered a delicacy. Which is also highly illegal and therefore valuable."

"Biror!" Jatiri gasped. "Why would you do that?"

Finally, Biror responded. "I did not say I do that."

"You didn't say you didn't, either," Coal pointed out.

"I say nothing."

If Biror had been a mantis runner (which Coal was now sure he was), taking a boat from the Mudlands down to the Innards and back would indeed be the easiest and fastest way to obtain their product. Mantises could be found all throughout the wooded areas of Ruska. The Mudlands were definitely not an environment suitable for the bugs, and the land to the east of it was grasslands for miles and miles. One of the few such places in the valley. The boars' best bet to hunt for mantises would be to take a boat south to the Innards.

They weren't going to get a solid confirmation from Biror, but the lack of denial and the nuggets of information he'd dropped were enough to convince Coal.

"Well, now that we know *your* unfortunate job, don't you want to know what we did before we got wrapped up in this?" Jatiri then asked.

"No," said Biror.

"I was a doctor," Jatiri said anyway.

"I know this."

"I was a librarian," Coal added.

"I do not care about this."

Soon they stopped for lunch, which Biror ate in silence while Coal and Jatiri chatted. They made earnest attempts to loop him into the conversation, but he was resistant. He wanted to be left alone. Eventually, they gave up.

As they packed up their stuff to continue on their way (after an admittedly disappointing meal consisting of only fruit and bread), Biror informed them that he estimated the town was only an hour or two away.

"How could you possibly know that?" Coal asked. "Everything looks the same here. Is your blight the ability to sense water?"

It was true. All around them was nothing but trees and bushes and other unidentifiable plants. Unidentifiable to Coal, in any case. He did not see any way for Biror to know where they were with any sort of precision.

"No," Biror said. "Look, little fox. Use your eyes."

He pointed skyward. Coal followed his finger, but could not see what he was referring to. All he could see was the leafy canopy.

"What?" he asked.

"There is shadow," Biror said, still pointing. "Do you see it? Those leaves are darker. The sun does not hit them."

"So what does that mean?"

"It means that we are beneath the Ferryman's Stone."

"The hell is that?"

"It's a large stone structure that starts near the river and curves out over the forest," Jatiri answered. She may not know a lot about Ruska as a whole, but she was well-versed in the Innards.

Now he was intrigued. He had never traveled through western Ruska, so he had never heard of such a structure. He had already put away his stuff, so he walked over to a nearby tree, kicked off his boots, and scurried up its trunk.

At the top, he peered out over the leaves. Sure enough, a massive piece of stone was jutting out over the forest. There was some weathering on its surface, but he could tell that it was not a natural structure. The curve of it was too perfect. Sharp stone spikes sprouted on its underside, and just beyond it, Coal could see a small township on the edge of the Lunsk River.

Biror was right. Judging by the distance, it should take two hours tops for them to reach Battado.

He carefully made his way back down the trunk. Reunited with his companions, he asked, "Who made it? What's the point of it?"

Jatiri shrugged, and Biror didn't have an answer for him either.

So that was that.

When they continued walking, Coal said, "My birthday's next month."

"When?" asked Jatiri.

"The third." With a smirk, he then said, "Hey, Biror. When's your birthday?"

"You must be making a joke," said the man with a grunt.

Coal and Jatiri laughed.

AS BIROR PREDICTED, THEY came upon Battado a couple hours of strained conversation later.

Surprisingly, despite how reluctant he was to engage in their discussions, Biror at least did not seem annoyed or resentful toward them for trying to include him.

Battado was a small fishing village, one that Coal knew nothing about. Its homes were modestly built from wood, and there was an enormous watermill on the edge of town that could be seen from any point. The building stood two stories tall with a striking red roof, and the massive wooden wheel attached to it rotated hypnotically with the river's gentle flow.

A merchant's wagon was parked near the entrance to the village. Several men were unloading crates and barrels off of it, each one marked with symbols that meant nothing to Coal.

There was a dock stretching out onto the river, with a small hut stationed beside it. Biror told them that was where they'd buy tickets for the riverboat, and so they set off for it. On their way through town, Biror explained that there were four or five riverboats in rotation, all owned by the same company.

Given the boar's prior experience, Coal and Jatiri stepped aside and let Biror handle booking the tickets. He quickly grew irritated with the man's "incessant" questions, which were simple and reasonable, such as "How many people are in your party?" and "How many rooms do you want?" and "How much luggage do you have?" and other things of that nature. But once they moved past that, they acquired three tickets for the next ship departing. It was a vessel called the *Sister's Diatribe* and it would be leaving in roughly an hour.

While they waited, Biror opted to stay near the dock, but Coal wanted to take some of the Dirt King's tups and buy himself a tasty snack. Something to supplement the meager meal he'd eaten a couple hours earlier. Jatiri didn't want anything, but she wanted to keep him company.

There were no vending machines anywhere, but he found a bakery selling jonweks and eagerly bought three of the delicious, deep-fried delights. They didn't hold a candle to the ones he'd bought from the kind old marten woman in Vinnag, but they were pretty good. A touch spicier than he would have liked, but he still relished the warmth and flavors.

They sat outside the bakery at a flimsy metal table that wobbled every time they placed their elbows on it. Many laughs were shared as they discussed their failed attempts to get Biror to open up about himself.

Coal still couldn't believe the man was a mantis runner. Well, he *could* believe it, but it was still shocking. While it was true that Coal was a fugitive, in his heart he believed it was unjust. Biror, however, was a legitimate criminal.

The hour passed quickly, and they returned to the dock where Biror was waiting for them. A line had already formed, and the three tacked themselves onto the end.

At the end of the dock was the *Sister's Diatribe*. It towered three tiers high, with a murky green hull and rooftop. There were bright red stripes painted all along each tier, distinctly separating each one. The waterwheel at the ship's bow was a matching red. The rest of the boat was painted a brilliant white that shone in the sun reflecting off the water. Coal could not look directly at it for more than a couple seconds without hurting his eyes. Painted on the sides of the second tier, as well as on the front so that it hung proudly above the waterwheel, was the ship's name in blocky capital letters.

"Welcome aboard the *Sister's Diatribe!*" a jolly frog called from the head of the line. He was dressed in a baggy, ill-fitting suit, white with red pinstripes. He was like a mini version of the ship. "Step right up! Please have your tickets ready!"

The line moved fast, and it was no time at all before the trio was handing the frog their tickets. They ascended the ramp onto the ship, and Coal's body began tingling with excitement.

He had never been on a boat before, and the *Sister's Diatribe* was more extravagant than he ever would've guessed.

The thing was massive and could comfortably fit a hundred people. From the looks of it, they were going to be at full capacity. Having never lived near such a massive river like the Lunsk, Coal had no idea riverboat cruises were such a big tourist attraction. He had never thought of a boat being more than a mode of transportation, so he couldn't fathom what sorts of things this one could fill three floors with.

Luckily for him, a nearby rabbit dressed in the same suit as the frog approached them with a manic grin on his face. "Hello, travelers!" he greeted them. "Have you ever joined us on one of our fantastic voyages before? Would you care for the rundown?"

Coal saw that Biror was about to decline the man's offer, so he blurted out, "Yes, we're new! Please tell us!" He chuckled at the boar's subsequent grimace.

"Faaaaaantastic!" said the rabbit with a tiny hop. "Well, as you may or may not know, the *Sister's Diatribe* is part of Pancho's Paradise, Ruska's number one fleet of riverboats. Our beautiful ship—one of the largest in the kingdom, I might add—is full of amazing amenities for our guests.

"Every spacious room aboard the *Sister's Diatribe*, as well as every ship in Pancho's Paradise, has its own private balcony for you to sit on and enjoy the fresh river air as we roll on down the Lunsk. And inside the rooms are everything you could want: large beds, silky sheets, writing desks for the scholarly among us, private bathrooms—and room service enters each day to tidy up for you while you enjoy the ship's many pleasures!

"When you're ready to step outside, take in the fresh air on our top deck, with its breathtaking views and open exercise areas. If exercise isn't your thing, though, there's plenty of room to kick back and take in some sun! The deck is also equipped with an open bar and a menu of specialty cocktails, all handcrafted by Pancho himself. My favorite's the Sidekick Roundup. It packs quite a punch!

"On the second floor, you'll find the library. Pancho keeps it stocked with the latest bestsellers, so you never have to feel like you're missing out while you're on board. Of course we have all the classics, as well! There's plenty of places to sit in the library if you want to get away from the Highmonth heat and crack open a rollicking tale.

"The first floor is home to our gorgeous dining room, where meals are served any time, day or night. Are you an early riser, wanting your breakfast at four in the morning? Or do you get wrapped up in your activities and find yourself not coming down to dinner until close to midnight? None of it is a problem for our top-of-the-line chefs, who have curated a delectable menu cooked only with the freshest vegetables and most flavorful spices in all of Ruska. If you're just wanting to pop down for a snack rather than a full meal, there is also a buffet that is constantly being refreshed!

"Oh, and did I mention that on either side of the boat, at each level, there is a spacious lounge with panoramic views of the river and the scenery beyond? Our lounges are outfitted with plenty of chairs and sofas, as well as hosting a small drink and snack bar so that you don't have to worry about traversing the boat in order to relax to your full potential. Many of our guests spend their entire day in a lounge! If you look closely, you might spot me there, too! Ha!

"And when you're ready to wind down and relax for the evening, you can pull up a chair and watch the sunset on our bow terrace. The *Sister's Diatribe* truly has it all, and that's the Pancho Promise!"

Coal had lost his breath just listening to the man gab. He glanced over at Biror, who looked as if his eyes were about to roll back into his skull and fall out of his head. Jatiri was endlessly amused by this, and Coal cracked another smile. He briefly wondered if the "Pancho Promise" meant anything at all to anyone in the kingdom besides this rabbit standing before him.

The idea of Biror and his fellow mantis runners enduring these speeches and spending time relaxing on these riverboats was incredibly funny to him. He pictured Biror sprawled out on the sundeck and almost laughed.

Taking some time to read in the library sounded great to him, though. That was much more appealing than sitting on the sundeck or exercising. He was on this boat specifically to *not* move his body.

"That sounds lovely," Jatiri finally said, much to the rabbit's delight. His face split into an even wider smile.

"I'm so very excited to be here," said Coal. He was playing it up a bit to humor the rabbit, but it wasn't a lie. Like his time in the hot springs, this would be a good opportunity to escape the troubles of the world and his life for a few days before trudging through the Mudlands.

His mind went back to Marl, who he assumed was probably still on his trail. Garna Nomak was not the type of man to give up easily. Hopefully the wolverine was far behind, though, and would be left even farther once the boat pushed off.

"Please show us our room," said Biror, shoving his ticket in the cheery man's face.

"Sure thing!" The rabbit took a look at the number written on the stiff piece of paper and then said, "Right this way!"

He led them through the crowds of people milling about and brought them deep within the boat's first floor of rooms, where he soon came to a halt in front of a door with the number 37 scrawled across the entire length of it.

"Room 37! One of our best," said the rabbit with a wink. "Is there anything else I can do for you at this time?"

"No," said Biror before Coal or Jatiri could butt in.

"Great! Let me or any of the other staff know if you need anything at all. Enjoy your stay!" And with that, he disappeared down the hallway.

"I need a drink," said Biror as he shoved open the door to their suite.

The room was amazing. It reminded Coal of the one he'd stayed in at the Longowosk Hotel in Soponunga. Much like that room, this was one he very clearly would never have been able to afford on his own. He had Garna Nomak and the Dirt King to thank for his brief stints in the lap of luxury.

There were four small closed-off areas in the enormous room, each one with its own gigantic bed, side table, and lamp. Coal picked one of the two beds that was closer to the balcony and threw himself onto it. Jatiri took the other, while Biror was closest to the door.

"What should we do first?" Coal asked, his face muffled by the pillow he was nuzzling into.

"What?" said Jatiri.

He turned over onto his back and repeated himself. Then, before either of them could reply, he asked Biror, "Is the buffet already open? Or is that not until we actually depart?" The three jonweks he'd eaten were settling nicely in his stomach, and he was not hungry at all, but one of his favorite activities was eating free food.

"The buffet opens half an hour after the boat leaves the dock," said Biror. "I, too, would like to go to the buffet."

"Wow," said Coal. "Does that mean you want to hang out with me?"

"No. This means I want to go to the buffet."

"I think you want to hang out with me, Biror!" Coal said with a sing-song lilt in his voice.

"You are gravely mistaken," said the boar.

"You two are becoming such fast friends!" said Jatiri, egging them on. She giggled lightly.

"You, as well, are gravely mistaken," Biror told her.

"There's no reason to be embarrassed," said Coal. "It's very sweet that you want to be best friends with us."

Biror sighed. "It seems I, too, made a grave mistake, and mine was that I came on this trip with you."

Coal guffawed.

When he regained his composure, he hopped up off the bed and slid open the door to step out onto their private balcony. Fresh air wafted up from the river below as it beat against the ship's hull. The scent soothed him. He closed his eyes and took it in, as well as the warmth of the sun soaking into his fur.

For a few seconds, he thought that a trip on one of the Pancho's Paradise ships would be pretty fun to do with Ilio once all this Houndstooth madness concluded. He didn't want to give up the Jaq Yul trip either, though.

Why not both?

I could get used to this, he thought.

He opened his eyes and watched the other people file onto the boat from Battado's dock.

And soon after that, they were on the move.

14

COAL WAS HAVING A fucking great time on the
riverboat.

They had already spent two full days aboard the
Sister's Diatribe and were now coming up on lunchtime again.
The first day, Coal and Biror had indulged in the ship's exten-
sive buffet, piling their plates so high they rivaled the Houndstooth. For the rest of his meals, Coal had taken a keen interest
in the kitchen's more limited but extremely delicious menu
(which he learned changed every day). These meals were com-
plemented by frequent stops at the buffet in between whatever
leisure activities he was doing.

There was just so much food, and Coal wanted all of it.

Most other customers were behaving the exact same way,
so Coal did not feel gluttonous. Well, he *did* feel gluttonous,
but he at least did not feel he was out of line.

Biror, for instance, was packing in more than double what Coal was. The latter would have loved to taste that many different items, but the boar's stomach was much more resilient than his own. He knew that if he matched Biror potato for potato, he would find himself either vomiting overboard or dead in the bathroom.

His feelings on the boar were mixed ever since deducing the man's previous occupation as a mantis runner. Part of him didn't want to judge the Biror too harshly; he had no idea if there were certain circumstances that led him to the practice, something that gave him no other realistic option. And Zank, his childhood best friend, had ended up as a criminal working in Vinnag's underbelly, doing who knew what for the anteater Garna Nomak. Coal had never thought less of Zank for that. Should he have?

No matter what, though, he had to work with Biror for at least a few more weeks, if not months. So even if they would not be friends, Coal wanted to be on good terms with him.

Which was why, for the third day in a row, they were getting lunch together.

Coal always invited himself and was astonished that Biror never put up any resistance. Maybe the boar accepted that there was no escaping him while they were stuck on a boat together.

They were standing in their suite, getting ready to leave for the dining room. Jatiri was nowhere to be found, but Coal knew that at this time of day she could usually be found either up on the sundeck or in one of the boat's six lounges, laid up and enjoying a drink.

Lunch was usually eaten with Biror, and then for dinner Coal would eat with Jatiri, with some relaxation in the library in between. He had made steady progress in *A Popular Bargain*. The flowery prose was still slowing his pace, but he was enjoying the story and characters.

He followed Biror out the cabin door and asked, "Menu or buffet today, you think?"

"I will be eating the buffet," said Biror. "These people, they do not understand…food needs sauce. When there is sauce, it must be swimming. I will put my own sauce today."

Coal personally was not quite so into sauce, but checking out today's buffet offerings sounded like a good idea to him.

They wound their way through the deck's pretty yet monotonous halls, passing by all the similarly huge passenger rooms. Biror had made several attempts to smoke a cigarette on their walk to the dining room, but was admonished by the boat's staff every time. He no longer bothered trying. Adorning the walls were countless paintings of a gray-haired bear performing various tasks that Coal had come to assume was Pancho, the owner of this fleet of ships.

And then they came to the dining hall, Coal and Biror's favorite room on the *Sister's Diatribe*.

The dining room was less than half full, given the pair's predilection for eating lunch early. The floor was covered in red tile, the same color as the stripes on the boat's exterior. Also matching the boat were the walls, which were painted with alternating white and green diamond patterns. The tables were all oval-shaped, some able to accommodate up to six people while others were more intimate and seated one or two. Past the sea of tables and chairs was the long, white-clothed buffet table.

Their love. Their beauty.

They hurried toward it with greedy anticipation.

As Coal looked down the table, it seemed like it was a mile long, covered with warming trays filled to the brim with various bugs and vegetables. All of them were completely full and steam was visibly rising from every tray. They had just been refilled minutes ago. A thing of beauty. At the far end were desserts, which Biror never touched. Coal always satisfied his sweet tooth at the end of these meals, though.

He grabbed his first plate, still slightly wet from being washed in the kitchen, and started down the table. He knew that if he went behind Biror, the man would be doing his best to clear out each tray and he'd be left with the scraps.

Over the course of his tumultuous year, Coal had spent every day uncertain whether he'd have something to eat. Oftentimes all he could afford was some bread and, if he was lucky, a bit of cheese. Even when he rooted himself in a town for a week doing odd jobs, it was a struggle to get by. So he wanted to take advantage of this opportunity while it lasted. Biror had mentioned that they had probably five or six more days left on their ride, depending on the strength of the river's flow.

Coal packed his plate with anything that seemed even mildly appealing to him. He had waspballs soaked in a brown gravy, a vegetable medley tossed in a spicy cream sauce, roasted potatoes, beetles poached in butter, and plenty of bread rolls.

That was enough for round one.

He picked out a two-person table and seated himself. He immediately went for the buttered beetles, which were incredibly light and juicy. They practically popped in his mouth.

Biror sat across from him. True to his word, it looked as if he had foolishly spooned soup onto his plate, considering how much extra sauce he had poured over everything. All of it combined into one big, wet mixture that was unappealing to Coal, but Biror seemed excited about it. The only thing the man ever showed any sort of enthusiasm for was food.

Like during their previous meals, they did not say much to each other at first, instead focusing on shoveling as much food into their mouths as they could fit. Once they returned to the table with their second plates (which was mostly new foods for Coal, though he had grabbed a few more beetles), Coal initiated a conversation.

"So, the mantis runner thing," he said, getting straight to the point.

Biror rolled his eyes and crunched down on a crispy piece of fried kale. "I will not speak of this," he said. "You do not need knowledge of my past."

"But you *were* a mantis runner?"

"What I was or what I wasn't, this is irrelevant to you."

"Not if we're working together. I want to know the people I'm spending my time with."

"You want to make sure none of us is a crazy person."

"Put it that way, sure."

"Maybe I am crazy. Maybe I am mantis runner. Does it matter?"

"…yes, that's what I'm saying."

"It does not matter."

"Well, okay, then."

"You must go with me to Mudlands whether or not I am mantis runner, yes? You cannot kick me off the team and replace me with one of these bumblers," he said, gesturing at the other passengers currently dining. "So why do you care what the answer is? The answer will change nothing."

"It'll change what I think about you."

"What do you think of me now?"

"That you're kind of an asshole. That you don't want to have anything to do with any of us."

"Your thought is correct. Why that is not good enough for you? If I tell you I am mantis runner, then you will think 'Oh, he is a bad guy. He kills mantises. He is piece of shit.' You gain nothing from this."

"Maybe not. But isn't it better to know the truth? I don't see how you could be okay spending months and months with people who you don't know anything about."

"I do not care about your past, and I do not care what you think of mine." He maneuvered two waspballs onto his spoon, smothered in gravy, and shoved them into his mouth. Brown sauce dribbled down his chin.

Coal sighed. "If you don't care what I think of you, why not just tell me the truth? You're avoiding it like you're ashamed, or something. I think you *do* care."

"You think that because you are a fool. I avoid because it is none of your concern. When this is over, I will return to my life, and you will return to yours. We do not see each other again. The life you return to does not matter to me. All that matters to me is the life that I return to."

Coal decided to try a different approach. He was determined to learn something—anything—about this man today.

"If you care so little about any of us and about this mission, then why are you still here? Why haven't you snuck off in the night?"

"Because the mission must be done."

"But you don't care about it. You've called it 'nonsense' several times."

"I do not care about these artifacts, but I must help find them. You are Flesh Eater, yes? You understand this."

Coal ate another beetle, cocking his eyebrow. "What do you mean?" he asked.

"We all know laws about Flesh Eaters. And the ape was not happy about you, this was plain to see. His mind is clouded by the Dirt King's words. If you are Flesh Eater, then you are doing this so that they do not lock you up, yes? We all have assurances from the Dirt King. I am thinking that is yours."

"It is," Coal nodded. "If we've all got assurances, then what's yours?"

The boar grinned. There was still a bit of sauce on his chin. "I know what you are doing, little fox."

"Humor me. It must be something pretty big, if it's convincing you to stay with the group and carry out a bunch of tasks that you think are nonsense. It has to be something on the same level as my Flesh Eater status being revoked, I bet. You don't seem like the type to do it just for the promise of a fancy house, or something."

"Perhaps I am doing it for the tups. Would not a man who is mantis runner be concerned with money?"

"I don't think so. This mission is too big a commitment to just wring a payday out of it. Maybe you're a Flesh Eater, too."

Biror shook his head. "I know many who are. In the Mudlands, we still practice the old ways. We have no cares for the Dirt King or his foolish rules, and the Palace has no cares for us in the mud. They do not come to watch us. We are out of their sight and out of their mind. But I am not a Flesh Eater. I do not fault you for being one, though, little fox."

"If it's not that, then maybe it's some other crime. Something that only the Dirt King can help you with. Isn't the punishment for mantis running pretty severe? There's a ban on poaching them, since their population is so low…" He thought for a second, trying to remember. Then he had it. "The punishment is execution," he said. "I think you were going to be executed."

Biror laughed, spraying spittle and gobs of food onto the table between them. "You are a clever fox," he said.

"I'm right?"

"If that ape and bat did not find me in the prison, I would be dead now. This is true. This is why I stay. When we finish, I will return to my life and forget all of you."

The image of Yurzu entering a prison was hard to believe. The poor guy must have been terrified.

"Lop promised you your sentence would be cleared away if you helped with this?"

"Yes. They find me three weeks before I was to be killed. If I find these artifacts for the Dirt King, they will forget about me. Clean slate."

"Are you gonna go straight back to mantis running?"

Biror grinned. "Nice try, little fox." He took another bite of kale, the last thing on his plate. He then pushed his chair back, the legs scraping noisily against the floor, and stood to fetch his third plate of food.

"HOW WAS YOUR DAY?" Jatiri asked him when they met up that evening for dinner. A stark contrast from Biror, who would sooner face a hundred men in close quarters combat than ask someone how their day was.

She and Coal spoke about how they'd spent their third day on the *Sister's Diatribe*. After his strange but enlightening lunch with Biror, Coal had spent a couple hours cooped up in the ship's library. He read a chapter of the book Ilio had gifted him before wandering around, inspecting the library's offerings.

They didn't carry the stuff he usually enjoyed. He tried to find Ilio's favorite books, the *Masters of Mud*, but could not find any volumes from the lengthy series. And in spite of their claim to have all the latest bestsellers, he did not see *A Popular Bargain* anywhere. Though maybe it was not a bestseller.

Jatiri, as he had guessed, spent most of her day on the second deck's starboard lounge. When asked why she chose the second deck, Jatiri shrugged and said it just seemed fun at the time. There, she downed numerous cocktails and sustained herself on bar snacks throughout the day. She was definitely ready for a real meal now.

Their meal together was much less barbaric than the one he'd shared with Biror earlier in the day. They ordered from the daily menu, which had two appetizer options, four entrees, and sadly a single dessert. One of the appetizers was a flatbread sprinkled with herbs and oil, so they ordered one of those to share. Then Coal ordered a bowl of black bean soup, something hearty but still far lighter than the heavy meal he'd consumed for lunch. Jatiri opted for a salad full of crisp, fresh vegetables and shredded cheese. Neither of them thought the dessert offering sounded good.

Conversation was light and jovial, and afterwards they decided to take a walk out on the top deck together.

The bow terrace was filled with people contentedly watching the sunset. The ship's red waterwheel chugged along happily, spraying a light shower of water onto the deck, which the children loved to run around in while their parents stood back and conversed or watched the pretty views passing them by.

Right now, they were passing through a particularly flat area of Ruska. On either side of the river was grasslands, with only a few errant hills in the distance. There were no towns to be seen, but far away on the port side, Coal could just barely make out a farm.

Coal had filled Jatiri in on what Biror told him over lunch, but something about the man's words gnawed at him still. He turned it over in his head for a few minutes while they silently watched the world go by.

"Don't you think it's too big a coincidence that we all found each other?" he asked Jatiri.

The saola looked away from the setting sun, frowning in thought. "What do you mean?"

"I mean that out of all the thousands or millions of people in Ruska, don't you think it's very convenient that the only six people with blights in the entire kingdom somehow found each other?"

Jatiri shrugged.

"That doesn't seem insanely coincidental to you?"

"I guess so," she finally said.

He went on. "I mean, Biror was locked up in a prison cell when Lop and Yurzu were out searching for the others. I guess maybe the Dirt King ordered Lop to search prisons, but what if he hadn't considered that? Biror wasn't just walking around somewhere for them to stumble upon."

"But the Dirt King *did* consider it."

"Sure, but what if they hadn't arrived for another month because he was locked up farther south and it took them longer to get there? Biror said that he was three weeks from the chopping block. If we truly were the only six people who could do this, and he got executed, then what? Ruska's just fucked and the world ends?"

"I don't know," Jatiri said softly.

"The idea bothered me back when Noswen and Yurzu first explained it all, but I haven't had a second to just sit and think since then. But it makes no sense, right? First, that only six people in the entire kingdom would be afflicted with this, and second, that we would all find each other."

Jatiri mulled over what he was saying for a few moments. Then, "You think there are more Blighted than just us?"

That was where his mind was going, but he hadn't yet formulated the thought. "Maybe? I think it's possible," he said. "It's stupid to think that we're *chosen ones* or something. And if we're born with this in us already, what are the chances that we'd all still be alive when the time came to save the Houndstooth? What if one of the six died, like, forty years ago from old age?" His mind was running wild now, and he couldn't stop the thoughts from spilling out of his mouth. "What's the probability that every time this has happened, the *only* six people who could stop it all found each other? Especially if one of them wasn't a tracker or whatever the hell Yurzu is that made it easier to find us?"

He stopped to catch his breath. Jatiri was nodding along to everything he was saying.

"I guess that all makes sense," she said. She looked back out over the ship's railing. The farm was drifting farther away from them as the seconds passed.

Coal did not really have a point to all this. It had been distantly bothering him for the past week and a half, and hearing how close Biror was to not even being alive today had brought it back to the forefront of his mind.

Jatiri said, "It doesn't really matter, though, right?" A surprising refrain from his talk with Biror. "The six of us have blights, and we found each other. So we need to do what needs to be done, coincidence or not. Yeah?"

"Yeah," he nodded. That was hard to argue against.

She smiled. "Let's just be thankful for that, then. That we found each other and that things are going to be okay."

Coal sighed and leaned his elbows on the railing. "If there really are other people out there who could do this, I sort of wish they'd been found instead of me." Then something else occurred to him. "If we're *not* the only ones, though, why would the Dirt King say we are? What's the point of that?"

"Maybe to motivate us so that we don't give up the cause and decide someone else can deal with it. You *did* just say that you wish someone else was saddled with this instead of you."

"Yeah, maybe." It still nagged at him, though.

"But whether or not there are others, we're the ones here. We're the ones doing it. And it's what needs to be done. So we'll do it."

Coal had the fleeting thought that she sounded a little like Lop in that moment, blindly following whatever it was the Dirt King pronounced. Doing what everyone else did in the past simply because it was what had always been done.

He wasn't sure what else to say just then, so he watched the farm disappear from view as the ship sauntered up the Lunsk River.

15

YURZU YAWNED. HE SAT up in his tiny, rickety bed and raised a hand to block the sun from his eyes. It burst through the curtainless window, seeping into every inch of the room.

It was their second day on the Houndspine, the massive bridge that reached into the sky over the Innards, connecting north and south Ruska. Up there, the sun was relentless in the mornings. And in the afternoons. And a little in the evenings.

The moon was breathtaking at night, though. It was so big, Yurzu felt like he could reach out and touch it. Run his fingers along the grooves of its craggy surface.

Their traversal through the Innards on their way to the entrance of the Houndspine had been peaceful. Not even the occasional wildlife sighting. After the tribulations they had to face in Nitulo, Yurzu appreciated getting a break. A week where he did not constantly feel like his life was in danger.

They knew they would be on the Houndspine for several days, which meant multiple nights spent sleeping in inns. Lop, ever the dutiful Palace servant, was trying his best to conserve the Dirt King's funds; as a result, for their first night they had stayed in the cheapest spot the orangutan could find. Every room was cramped and dirty and could only accommodate a single person, so they had to book three rooms (with Zsoz resting on Lop's ceiling). When Noswen pointed out it would've cost the same to get one shared room in a nicer place, Lop grumbled and sulked away.

Yurzu hadn't unpacked any of his belongings the night before. He crawled out of bed, grabbed some fresh clothes from his bag, and slipped them on. Then he slung the bag over his shoulders and stepped out of the room into the narrow hallway.

Noswen and Lop's rooms were across the hall from his and both their doors hung open, as per the innkeeper's instructions for checking out. Yurzu left his ajar and walked down the hall to the lobby.

His companions were seated by a large blue leaded glass window. They were chatting animatedly about something, but ceased their conversation as Yurzu approached. Zsoz was stuck to the underside of the table, nearly brushing against their legs.

"Morning, kid," Noswen greeted him. Lop nodded in his direction.

"Hi," said Yurzu. "Is something wrong?"

Noswen shook her head.

They were engaging in an argument about Coal Ereness, Zsoz said beneath them.

Lop nodded, unashamed, while Noswen rolled her eyes.

"Is something wrong with Coal?" Yurzu asked.

Noswen opened her mouth to speak, but Lop beat her to the punch. "The man is a criminal. What *isn't* wrong with him?"

"He's fine," Noswen groaned. "We've been around him longer than you have, and even you've seen that he's just a normal guy. Relax."

"I like him," said Yurzu.

Lop's wrinkly eyes widened at the admission. "If I had it my way, he would've been hauled off to the nearest Flesh Eater encampment the moment I found out what he is. It's despicable that we must count him among our ranks."

"Well, tough shit. He's one of the six. He's just like you, pal," Noswen smirked, knowing it would set Lop off.

And it was successful. "An outrageous claim!" the man balked.

Coal is a fox. Lop is an orangutan.

"Besides," said Noswen, "I told him that the Dirt King would erase his record at the end of all this. That's the whole reason he agreed to it. Other than the fact that, you know, he had to agree no matter what."

"Outrageous," Lop muttered again. He tugged at his beard irritably.

Yurzu failed to understand why Lop had such an issue with Coal. The man openly admitted to being a Flesh Eater, but also said that it was a complicated situation. A misunderstanding. After getting to know him more, Yurzu was willing to give him the benefit of the doubt. And not to mention, Biror was literally a convicted criminal who they met locked in a prison cell. Yet Lop did not butt heads with him any more than the rest of the group did.

He thought about Fennigha's words in the Nitulo hot springs, calling orangutans willfully ignorant. Obeying the

192 • *Travis M. Riddle*

Dirt King without question. Seeing Lop instilled with such unfounded hatred for Coal simply for being marked as a Flesh Eater, it was easy to agree with the old tiger.

Fed up with the topic of Coal, Lop rose from his seat. "Let's go," he said with a grimace. "Lots of ground to cover today."

Zsoz plopped down to the floor, its gelatinous body jiggling with the impact. The four artifacts the group had acquired hung suspended perfectly still within the slime. It then made its way up Lop's back and came to rest on the man's shoulder.

They left the inn and emerged onto the Houndspine.

It was an impressive structure. The bridge stretched for miles and miles across central Ruska. Yurzu couldn't fathom how long it actually was, and he did not want to think about it anyway, knowing they would have to walk across the entire thing. He wasn't sure what it was constructed from, but it was held aloft both by pillars and by thick, sturdy trees in the Innards. Long ago, that had resulted in geigexes climbing the trees to sneak their way onto the Houndspine and cause a bit of trouble, but that became less of an issue over time as the animal population declined.

The Houndspine was like a city unto itself. When it was first built, it had acted solely as an enormous bridge with a few inns and shops dotting its length, but in the intervening years it had rapidly grown in density. Now each side of the bridge was lined with structures of varying heights, with the middle of the bridge serving as the walkway. There were even stretches that acted as neighborhoods, solely residential.

At first it was beyond Yurzu why someone would want to live on the bridge, but after spending only a day walking it, he came to see the appeal. It had all the same amenities as a typical city, with the addition of amazing views of the kingdom. It was a thrill standing out on one of the designated overlooks and peering at the forests and rivers below. It made his quaint cottage in Toothshadow seem so insignificant.

His home had a garden, though. One big thing he would miss if he lived on the Houndspine was the lack of vegetation. No trees, no grass, no flowers except in vases. Just stone all around. That was not a life he wished to live.

The group wandered through the street, milling past throngs of people. Yurzu had quickly learned the Houndspine was eternally crowded. Between the people who were passing through and those who called it their home, there was always somebody to bump into.

With his blight, navigating such a crowded place was troublesome. There were loads of people with illnesses big and small, ranging anywhere from a short-lived stomach virus to a chronic condition. Yurzu's senses were always banging against his skull, trying to point out every single person who was sick. Walking through crowds was dizzying. After so many years, he had gotten a handle on it and could lessen the impact, but the first few moments every morning when they walked out onto the street were overwhelming.

Lop led the way with Zsoz bouncing along on his shoulder. The bulky orangutan cut a path through the crowd, clearing the way so that they would not be trampled by his mass. Noswen and Yurzu scurried behind him. They were like blades of grass and he was a towering tree.

Noswen glanced over her shoulder at Yurzu and said, "Hey, keep up."

He nodded and picked up his pace, slowing as he came to her side.

"I am so glad to be back on a straight fucking path," she said to him after a minute. "What a relief it is to only have one way to go. No nagging doubts about whether you picked the right direction or not. Here, if you go backwards, that's the wrong direction. Easy to remember."

Yurzu looked out at the edge of the bridge. He could not see past any of the buildings, only stone and sky in his vision, but he was thinking about the forest.

He and Lop had found Noswen in her treetop village just before traveling along the Houndspine for the first time months ago. Their methodology for tracking down the other Blighted was fairly rudimentary, sticking their noses into every town they passed on their way south, where they knew the deer antler was being displayed in Vuela's museum. They wouldn't be far from her home once they reached the other end of the bridge now. It was more westerly than they needed to go to reach Moonoshk, though. Her village was essentially located in the center of the kingdom, while Moonoshk was in the far east, by the mountains.

She lived in Holluwak, a village nestled among the treetops that was connected to two other townships: Vil's Branch and Baoa. Yurzu learned from Noswen that the three villages were closely interconnected and governed by the same political group. Her husband, Gose, was a part of that group, so their family was fairly wealthy and powerful within the community. Noswen and he had gotten married at a young age, and she had never needed to work.

When they met Noswen, as usual Gose was out at the office and she was at home with the kids. The children had never met a boar before and were fascinated by Biror, who very clearly wanted to be left alone but did not object to their prodding questions. Eventually, though, when they were distracted by lunchtime, he slipped out of the house and waited for the group in a bar.

"Have you heard anything I've been saying?" Noswen asked, stirring Yurzu from his remembrance.

"No," he confessed. He often found himself lost in his thoughts. His parents had loved to make the "You're talking too much!" joke when he had been silent for a long period of time. He stopped finding it funny long before the hundredth time he heard it, but nowadays he missed even that annoying constant.

Noswen chuckled. "You're just like Dena, I swear." Dena was the oldest of her six children, and she had often told Yurzu he reminded her of her daughter. He did not know whether he should be embarrassed being twenty-five years old and regularly compared to a fourteen-year-old. "I was saying that tomorrow, we'll be passing over Jatiri's village, I think."

"Oh, yeah," Yurzu said with a nod. It was hard to picture himself living in the Innards too. While the Houndspine had too little greenery, he thought there might be a bit too much in the Innards. His home in Toothshadow was perfect.

Up ahead, Lop briskly shuffled past a deer who was uninterested in him, but seemed to think Noswen and Yurzu were good marks. The man approached them with a toothy grin and a glimmer in his eyes. In each hand he grasped a rolled-up parchment, with an open sack slung over his shoulder that was filled with similar papers.

"Hello, hello!" he boomed.

"Not interested," Noswen dismissed him without a thought. She didn't even break her stride to speak to the salesman. He followed along, walking backwards into the crowd, trusting that they would part for him.

"Ahh, but you are, ma'am! You just don't know it yet! Take a look here, take a look." The deer unfurled both the parchments at once, revealing detailed maps of both north and south Ruska. "Which way are you going, ma'am? Either way, I've got you covered. I do, I do."

"You can see which way I'm going. I'm walking that way."

The deer knew when a sale was hopeless, so he took a step forward and began walking alongside Yurzu instead. "Hey, pal," he said with a wink. "I've got just what you need right here. Whether you're goin' north or south, up or down, left or right, Kokomanu's maps are what'll get you there. I'm Kokomanu, by the way." Another sly wink.

"No thanks," said Yurzu, taking his cue from Noswen.

Kokomanu knew what was going on. "Don't let her spoil your interest!" said the man. "Let the maps speak for themselves. Here, take a look." He shoved the southern Ruska map in Yurzu's face.

It was a beautifully rendered map, there was no denying that. Each line was hand-drawn, with explicit details sketched throughout. There were numbers written on various points of the map, with a legend on its side that was filled with Kokomanu's personal notes about them.

Expansive apple orchard! Juicy, crisp, and delicious. Open to the public. Perfect date spot or just a pretty place to stop and grab a snack! said #8.

Home of the best lajnoss I've ever eaten! said #22.

I once got mugged here! said #49.

MOTHER PIG • 197

"You spelled 'Soponunga' wrong," said Yurzu with a giggle.

"What's that, pal?"

"You spelled it S-O-P-A-N-U-N-G-A. It's not supposed to be an A, it's an O."

"It's Soponung*a*, my friend, not Soponung*o*! Kokomanu's maps are one hundred percent accurate, guaranteed. More than one hundred, actually! As you can see here, I've marked over eighty points of interest gathered in my expansive travels. That's quality you simply won't get from your boring old store-bought map. Nope!"

Noswen came to a halt and grabbed the deer by the shoulder. "Would you leave him the fuck alone, please? We don't need your maps."

"A foul mouth on such a beauty!" Kokomanu gasped.

"I'm about to hit you in *your* mouth."

Yurzu grinned. Noswen might not be the best in a fight against a monster like Ghoresn, but she was more than willing to put idiots like Kokomanu in their place.

The deer rolled his maps back up and held his hands in the air, surrendering. "Fine, fine. Kokomanu knows when he isn't wanted. Your loss, you're lost! That's what I say!" He then disappeared into the crowd in search of a paying customer.

To Yurzu, Noswen said, "You need to be more aggressive with them. Guys like that don't want to take no for an answer. They look at people like us and think we're stupid, that we'll just believe anything they say and want to throw our tups at them for blessing us with the opportunity to buy whatever they're shilling."

It wasn't like he was planning on buying one of the man's maps, but he did find it difficult to wriggle out of situations like that. "Thanks," he told Noswen.

Kokomanu had not been the first person trying to hawk their wares at them on the Houndspine. Three others had tried the day before; one was selling flowers, one had flasks of water, and the last proclaimed his specialty powders would help "even the fattest of men shed fifty pounds." Yurzu thought it safe to assume the deer would also not be the last.

They continued along the Houndspine, dodging passersby. While they walked, Yurzu peered into windows. The further along they went, the more repeated types of items he saw in storefronts, which was to be expected given how long the bridge was.

In all honesty, it was somewhat exhausting walking through this city that felt endless. It was rare to find a break in the buildings, a piece of the bridge undisturbed.

But shortly after lunch, they came to such a place. Scattered along the length of the Houndspine were spots designated as official overlooks. They were large circular platforms that hung out over one side of the bridge. The areas were adorned with benches, potted plants, and guardrails so that people could get right up to the side and peer out over the land.

On each of these platforms was a painting of a rugged black bear wearing a proud expression on her face. Lop had previously explained this woman was Constaine Ladent, the first person put in charge of the Houndspine once it was clear it was expanding beyond being a simple bridge. It was she who saw the need to preserve some pieces of the walkway, to keep the spirit of the Houndspine alive. Some parts of it were to be dedicated to the kingdom's natural beauty.

In stark contrast to Constaine Ladent's intentions, the areas across from these pavilions was always congested with vendors selling food and souvenirs. Additionally, there were always street performers set up with tip jars, soliciting money from people trying to enjoy the view. Many saw the overlooks as the best moneymaking spots, and they weren't necessarily wrong.

"Can we take a look?" Yurzu asked, pointing at the pavilion on their left.

Noswen nodded without bothering to ask Lop. "We're stopping," she called out to him.

He turned and lumbered after them oafishly.

Yurzu was the first to step foot on the pavilion, which was packed with other people. A few feet away, a spindly rabbit sat cross-legged on the ground just below Constaine's painted neck, his tail brushing against her fur. Propped up on his legs was a guitar, and he strummed a jaunty tune while singing along.

The lyrics were familiar, but Yurzu couldn't place the song. He bobbed his head along to the rhythm without realizing, and the rabbit grinned at him and sang louder. Quietly, so that no one else could hear, Yurzu hummed along to the melody.

Noswen stopped beside Yurzu and enjoyed the music with him. A few others had gathered as well, some clapping to the beat (or at least trying to). Lop stood behind them, and Yurzu thought he faintly heard Zsoz say something, but the slime's vibrations weren't audible over the rabbit's voice.

The musician strummed the final chord with a wide smile, letting it ring out in the fresh open air. It was muddled by the chatter of others who were not paying attention to the performance.

Yurzu clapped giddily. He still couldn't remember the name of the song, but he loved it all the same. He stepped forward and placed a handful of tups in the man's jar and received thanks in exchange.

Their group stepped beyond the rabbit, who broke into another catchy song. There were two other performers on the overlook. A frog had set up a low table with five cups and a metal ball, which he hid under one of the cups to play a game with a person for a nominal fee. It was another in a long line of things Yurzu did not understand the appeal of, but the frog had a short queue of people waiting for their chance to best him.

The other person was a bat with a tall stack of parchment, a ton of different paints, and an easel. She was currently painting a depiction of the land just below the guardrail behind her. There were a few paintings propped up around her with prices attached, but she also had a sign that proclaimed she could paint one's portrait in fifteen minutes or less.

He'd never had a painting done of him before, nor owned a painting at all, and it seemed neat. But Yurzu knew Lop would be opposed to wasting time on that, and probably none of them wanted to lug it around for the remainder of their journey. He took a moment to admire the woman's artwork, yearning to take a piece with him. Right then, he made a vow to buy some art for his home when he returned to Toothshadow.

Yurzu walked over to the guardrail and leaned out, looking at the treetops below. He breathed in deep and smiled contentedly out at Ruska. For as far as he could see, it was forest. Far in the distance, he could make out the Lunsk River winding through the valley, but for the most part it was green, rustling leaves. In a few short months, they would start to turn orange and yellow and red, and Yurzu imagined how beautiful that sight would be.

It was such a privilege to see the kingdom from this angle, looking down and seeing it in all its glory. Despite all the trouble the kingdom was currently going through, Yurzu thought it was a gorgeous place, and he loved living there.

There were a few spots where smoke from towns and factories rose into the air. He turned to ask Noswen if she knew whether any were billowing up from Jatiri's hometown, but the raccoon wasn't there. Yurzu craned his neck further and saw she was seated on a bench, writing something in a plain red notebook.

He walked over and sat beside her. "What's that?" he asked.

She spared him a quick glance before looking back down at her paper. "Just writing to my kits," she replied.

"Is there a place to mail that here?" he asked. Zsoz was the only slime he could recall seeing up on the bridge thus far.

Noswen shook her head. "I'm just..." She was flustered, not having anticipated explaining this. Yurzu felt guilty, thinking he should get up and leave her alone, but she went on. "It's not a letter. More like a story. But nowhere near the level of a real, normal writer. I'm writing down stuff about the journey so that I don't forget any of it. Even the small stuff like this. Most of my kits are too young right now—all of them are, really, except for Dena—but eventually, I'd like to tell them about all this. This wild fucking journey their mom went on. When the time comes, I don't want to miss a single thing." She grinned, then said, "I think they'll love the part about the shy, quiet bat knocking out the big-ass wolverine with some sleeping powder."

Yurzu laughed, thinking about the sound that wolverine made when he plummeted to the ground.

Lop was over at a vending machine with Zsoz, picking out a snack. He cantered over to them holding a steamed bun wrapped in plastic. It crinkled as he unsheathed it and gulped half of it down in a single bite.

Spitting crumbs everywhere, the orangutan said, "Are you ready to go yet?" He was not one to stop and appreciate scenery. Zsoz was motionless on his shoulder.

Noswen scribbled one more thing down and closed her notebook. "I'm good," she said, but turned to Yurzu for his answer. He had been the one who requested to stop, after all.

He looked at them both, then said, "Just one more minute."

They nodded. Lop was annoyed, but accepting. Yurzu returned to the guardrail, standing near a family of frogs. The father was holding up his son so that he could see the forest.

"Wow!" the kid declared, pointing a stubby green finger out at the expanse of trees.

Yurzu smiled and took one more look at the kingdom.

16

A S THEY CONTINUED ACROSS the Houndspine over the course of the week, Yurzu learned
that it was a far larger city than he realized. Not only
had every available inch of real estate on the bridge been gob-
bled up, but some areas *underneath* were dedicated to different
shops and restaurants as well.

The day before, they had eaten dinner in a restaurant that
was built suspended from the bottom of the bridge. To reach
it, they descended a staircase that protruded from the side of
the Houndspine and curved underneath it. Down there, the restaurant jutted out from the bottom of the bridge like a growth.
Yurzu had seen other staircases leading under the bridge since
then, but their group had ignored them in spite of the enticing
mysteries they presented. He wanted to know what lay beneath
their feet.

It had been another day of endless walking, pushing
through crowds and dodging persistent salesmen. There hadn't

been any street performers to break up the monotony either, much to Yurzu's disappointment. Half their day was spent trudging through one of the residential stretches, so while they did not have to deal with salesmen or crowds, the sights were much less interesting. Children playing in the street, homeowners tending to small plants hanging from their windows, others up on their roofs patching things up.

Every neighborhood on the Houndspine had its own distinct architectural style, but every home within each neighborhood had the exact same layout. Long rows of the same building repeating over and over. It was as if they were caught in a loop, passing by the same building for what felt like hours.

A signpost designated this neighborhood as Dalwood. They had walked through a few residential areas on the Houndspine already, but this was by far the most boring. The houses in Dalwood were squat and square, one story tall, built with red brick and gray tiled roofs. Each one had its own fenced-off area in the front with a short gate to offer its resident a modicum of privacy. Yurzu found the houses to be exceptionally ugly. He would not want to live in Dalwood.

"Could I even fit in one of these houses?" Lop wondered aloud. "They're so tiny, I could pick one up and throw it over the side of the bridge. These things are Zsoz-sized."

Slimes do not live in homes, said Zsoz from his perch on the man's shoulder. **We do not require shelter, and we do not have the slightest sense for interior design. These houses are indeed very small, however.**

When they reached the end of Dalwood, it was like waking from a dream. The buildings finally varied and had some character to them again.

They ate dinner at a restaurant just outside the neighborhood that served dishes which were a fusion of southern and mountain cuisines. Chefs in the mountains liked to cook saucy, stew-type meals. In the south, they largely preferred using bold, sweat-inducing spices in their preparation of any entrée. The combination at this restaurant resulted in incredibly spicy, creamy vegetable dishes. Yurzu ate a delicious bowl of cauliflower florets with wilted spinach and diced onions in a spicy tomato cream sauce.

Lop landed on what was by far the most traditional dish on the menu: a vegetable medley floating in thick, brown broth. The stewiest of stews. Yurzu chuckled at how accurate Coal had been in his assessment of the man's tastes.

The sun was starting to set by the time their meal concluded, and Noswen declared they should stop for the day. Lop wanted to continue on, but begrudgingly went to find a place for them to stay. He had since relented to booking higher quality rooms for them all to share.

While he handled that, Yurzu and Noswen decided to explore the area. This time of day was Yurzu's favorite, when he could simply relax and enjoy exploring without feeling pressure to move on as quickly as possible. It was always a treat when they stopped for the night.

In their immediate vicinity were a handful of things that caught Yurzu's eye: a flower shop, a small grocery store, and a sign next to some stairs that read CONSTAINE'S WILD RIDE. The latter especially intrigued him.

But first, he headed toward the market while Noswen rested on a bench to write in her notebook.

It was a little shop with only about ten shelves, more of a specialty store than somewhere one would actually go for their weekly groceries. The proprietor was a beaver who greeted Yurzu warmly as he entered. "Anything I can help you find?" the man inquired.

"Just looking around," said Yurzu.

He browsed the shop for ten or fifteen minutes, beaming at the artisanal products it offered. He couldn't help but wonder what the process of importing all this stuff to the middle of the Houndspine entailed. Obviously no one was planting crops up there. He did not feel comfortable asking the shopkeeper, though.

There was a shelf dedicated to pickles, which naturally caught his eye. He grabbed a jar of pickled sweet peppers. They were bright shades of yellow and red, sliced thin and floating in a clear liquid. Granules of pepper and garlic could be seen floating around. Yurzu liked that.

After how much time he'd spent in the store, he felt obligated to make a purchase, so he brought the pickles to the counter and slid the necessary tups over to the beaver. He then stepped outside and joined Noswen on her bench.

He unlidded the jar with a satisfying *pop!* and offered Noswen a pepper, but she declined.

Yurzu bit into it himself, savoring the crisp crunch. The pepper was as sweet as he'd expected, but there was a surprising mild heat to it as well. The maker had incorporated slightly more garlic into the liquid than Yurzu would have, but it was still tasty.

There was no avoiding it. He simply *had* to eat five more peppers.

He sat there munching and crunching with delight while Noswen wrote down the day's events for her children. After a minute, he asked if she would watch over his jar of pickles.

"I guess so," she said. "Where are you going?"

Yurzu pointed at the alluring sign advertising some sort of ride. "I want to see what that is."

The raccoon looked up from her notebook to read the sign. "A ride? Yuck. No thank you. Go enjoy yourself, though. And be careful." She promptly returned to her writing.

Yurzu scooted himself off the bench (after ensuring the jar was secured safely and would not fall onto the ground and shatter) then scurried over to the staircase leading underneath the Houndspine.

Below, he was amazed to discover practically a whole other street.

Rows of buildings hung from the bottom of the bridge like long, rectangular stalactites. Flat stone extended out from their bases, creating pathways for people to walk on. This hanging street stretched on for miles in the direction from which they had come. It must have extended all the way back to a staircase Yurzu had seen before entering Dalwood. There were even more restaurants, shops, clubs, and even some apartments down here.

Yurzu's mouth hung open in awe, taking it all in. He was entranced by the craftsmanship of it. His brain could not fathom how one would go about constructing this place.

What he came to see, though, was Constaine's Wild Ride, and it could not be missed.

Dangling from the Houndspine was an enormous white stone swing suspended by rigid chains that latched onto the bottom of the bridge. The swing had three tiered rows that could each seat fifteen people. Scrawled in purple, curly script on the back of the swing was the name of the ride. It hung at the edge of the understreet, with a narrow platform jutting out to reach it. A bear stood at a table at the edge of the platform, collecting entry fees from people taking a ride on the massive swing. They eagerly filed onto the swing and strapped themselves into the seats. After a couple minutes, it was filled up. The bear seemed to then be shouting something at the riders, which they responded to in turn.

The bear motioned to some unseen person, and the swing began to move. It was slow at first, but as it gained momentum it reached higher and higher into the air. The riders onboard screamed with excitement and fear at every movement, some of them laughing manically. After around two minutes, the swing slowed to a stop, and the bear ushered everyone back down the platform to make way for the next riders.

"Whoa…" Yurzu couldn't help but mutter.

His only thought was: *I gotta ride this thing.*

It didn't matter what the cost was or that Lop was trying to save the Dirt King's money. He was going to take a spin on Constaine's Wild Ride.

He raced over to the end of the line and waited patiently. It took a few more rides, all of which he watched with giddy anticipation, before he reached the front. He paid the bear and filed onto the swing.

The next available seat was in the middle row, just past the center. Almost the perfect seat, in his opinion. He settled in next to a couple, two deer, one of whom looked petrified.

"I hate you," she said to her boyfriend.

"No you don't," he laughed. "You're gonna have a great time."

"I'm going to throw up and wipe it all on you. You're going to regret this." She clasped her hands together tightly and was visibly trembling.

Yurzu chuckled at the woman. There were plenty of things he was scared of in the world, but a ride like this did not rank among them. There were always lots of rides at the annual Rechando Festival in Banak Tor, and in all the years he attended, they were easily his favorite part. That had been his primary complaint about the Soponunga Spiderback Showdown festival: the lack of fun rides.

He strapped himself into the seat a little tighter than was comfortable, just to be safe. The last thing he wanted was to be flung off the Houndspine into the Innards. The nervous woman beside him noticed what he'd done and adjusted her straps accordingly, gasping for breath before loosening them a smidge.

Yurzu watched the rest of the seats fill up. To his left, he looked at the lucky person who'd gotten the exact middle seat and a pang of jealousy shot through him. The entry fee hadn't been too high; perhaps he could ride again and try to get in the middle. All he had to do was count the people in line and place himself at the right spot...

As he was formulating his plan and waiting for the ride to commence, he peered out at the understreet to watch people going about their business.

Far across from the swing, an overlook was jutting out from the understreet (an under-overlook?). There weren't too many people on it, but he spied a crew of martens performing a dance for some onlookers. At this distance, he of course could not hear the music, but their moves were entertaining. Elsewhere, he saw a wolverine shouting to someone before storming off into a building—all Yurzu could make out on its sign was a bottle, so it could have been either a bar or an apothecary. A few buildings down was a family stepping out of an inn; Yurzu liked to think they were going out to get dinner together. He imagined shouting a recommendation for the fusion restaurant above and the family being able to magically hear him over the huge distance.

The last person buckled into their seat and the bear roared, "All aboard! Are you folks ready for Constaine's Wild Ride?"

"*Yes!*" everyone cheered, Yurzu included. He chuckled with glee. Only the woman beside him remained silent and motionless, steeling herself for what was to come.

"Are you wild enough?"

"*Yes!*"

"Well, let's go, then!"

The bear waved his arms at the operator and the swing started to rock back and forth.

Before they had barely started to move, the deer was murmuring to herself, "Oh shit, shit—shit on all this, fuck—"

Yurzu ignored her dismay and basked in the breeze hitting his face. His stomach did flips as they swung higher and higher into the air. When they swung forward, he was sure they were going to collide with the bottom of the Houndspine. When they went back and his body pressed against the seat's straps, he could see them all tumbling out of the ride into the forest below. That terror fueled the exhilaration inside him and he cackled giddily, kicking his feet.

Before he knew it, the swing slowed. A couple minutes had passed, but they had flown by in an instant. As the swing returned to its stationary position, the bear called out to them, "Welcome back! Constaine Ladent sure does know how to entertain her guests, don't she?" They all cheered in response.

Yurzu sighed. The ride was over too soon. According to the deer woman, however, that was a blessed thing.

"You didn't throw up! Wasn't that fun?" her boyfriend said cheerily.

"No. Hell no. No, no, no. Awful. No." She threw the straps off her and edged past Yurzu and shuffled down the rest of the row to the exit before even waiting for everyone else to disembark.

Yurzu followed behind the rest of his row back onto the platform and returned to the understreet. The other riders dispersed, but he remained near the line, considering another ride.

Without fail, Lop always spent the evenings cooped up in their room with Zsoz. He said it was so that he could protect the artifacts alongside the slime in case anyone was planning to attack them, but Yurzu suspected the man was simply a bore. He wasn't even reading books or doing anything up there, just sitting around aimlessly. Noswen would be preoccupied for a while yet with her notebook. Maybe she would even give one of those pickled peppers a try while he was gone. He knew she liked to indulge in a post-dinner snack most nights.

So he would still be on his own for a while.

This was the best possible spot for them to stop for the night. Yurzu counted up the tups Lop had given him for the day and determined that, if he so desired, he could hop on Constaine's Wild Ride another four times.

He so desired.

With a mischievous grin, Yurzu commenced counting the eager riders waiting in line so that he could attach himself to the end at the perfect time. He would get his center seat on the next go around. The other three times, he would let fate decide for him.

Some people shot him an odd look as he walked down the line counting them. He was trying to be discreet, but perhaps his enthusiasm was betraying him. It was difficult to find it within himself to care, though.

A magnificent evening awaited.

17

THREE MORE DAYS HAD passed aboard the *Sister's Diatribe*. The captain of the ship, a tall, lean fox named Captain Lev, informed everyone that they would be arriving at their destination in two days. The captain always donned a jolly, boisterous tone when addressing his passengers. It seemed that part of the employee handbook when signing up for Pancho's Promise was adopting the same personality.

Coal was still bothered by the thoughts he'd expressed to Jatiri a few nights prior, but he decided not to bring them up again. In the end, she was right. They were the six people already on this quest, so what did it matter if they weren't actually the only Blighted in Ruska?

Plus, he needed the Dirt King's favor to erase his record. So did Biror. Probably everyone in the group had something in their past they needed the kingdom's immortal ruler to fix.

As the days and meals passed, the relationship between Coal and Biror did not warm at all. The boar was utterly uninterested in forging a bond, and Coal had to admit he was caring less and less too. He was growing more put off by the man's past as a mantis runner. And on top of that, if he did not want to put forth the effort to be friendly, why should Coal?

The trio was keeping up their regular routines on the riverboat, including Coal's lunches with Biror. Even if they would never be friends, it felt good to have someone to over-indulge with. Somehow it made him feel less guilty. He knew Jatiri was not the type of person to attack a buffet with him.

It was now mid-afternoon, and Coal had just spent two hours in the library after eating lunch. He was close to the halfway mark in *A Popular Bargain*, which he had slipped into his jacket pocket while he wandered around the library like usual.

The same few people who were always present were there again today. A young deer mother and her child always spent the afternoons in the library, with her reading children's stories to the kid while they both acted them out with toys. Then there was the old, portly beaver, who nestled himself into the same exact armchair every day and took a nap. The last regular who Coal always saw was a macaw, no more than ten years old, who devoured a new book every afternoon. He would browse the shelves (usually the newer releases), pick out something that interested him, then find himself a quiet place to sit and read it cover to cover. Coal used to do the same when he was his age.

Coal smiled at the macaw as he passed him by, though the kid was too engrossed in today's novel to notice him. It was titled *A Dark and Gorgeous Thing*, sporting a striking abstract orange and yellow cover.

For the first few days on the boat, Coal had foolishly wasted time trundling back and forth through the halls, unable to track down the staircase leading to the other decks, but by now he was well-acquainted with the ship's layout. He made his way through the pristine hallways, passing by a two-person cleaning crew standing in the doorway of a passenger cabin, squabbling over some disagreement between them. They did not deign to put up the same cheery illusion that every other employee did as Coal slipped past them, which he appreciated.

He traveled up the spiraling staircase past the second deck and emerged on the top deck, where the sun beat down on him. He reflexively squinted his eyes in the light before they readjusted.

The stairs spat him out in the middle of the ship, near the third deck's port lounge. Coal headed toward the back of the boat, onto the sundeck where he knew there would be an after-lunch exercise class underway.

It was a pleasantly warm day. If he had come out here after eating the frankly enormous meal he'd had for lunch, he would have passed out instantly. He would still be napping now, hours later.

In fact, that was what many people out on the boat's six lounges were doing. He had not spent much time in any of the lounges, but he was sure Jatiri was over there at that very moment.

Coal was just starting to think about how nice a nap sounded when the ship suddenly began tilting to the right. *Starboard,* he mentally corrected himself.

This was no time for semantics, though.

He did not know a ton about boats, but Coal knew at the very least that the boat should not be tilting.

A few children fell over with the abrupt shift, and their parents were hoisting them back to their feet while others were shouting their distress and confusion. The unfortunate souls who had been exercising under the instruction of a muscular tiger had all tipped over onto their asses, just like the children. The instructor was cheering them on to stand back up, trying to turn it into part of the experience.

The ship was still tilting, though. Panic was beginning to spread throughout the deck. People were scrambling out of their chairs while bottles at the bar were rolling off the countertop and shattering on the wood paneling. Some passengers were racing toward the stairs, seeking shelter in their cabins. As if they would be safer there when the boat capsized.

Coal stayed rooted in place, staring at the side of the ship that was slowly tipping toward the water.

A long, slimy green tentacle slithered over the railing onto the sundeck. It puckered itself to the floor, and the appendage was at least eight or ten feet in diameter, coming to a clawed tip that punctured the deck like a grappling hook.

The boat tipped even further in that direction as a second tentacle sidled up and lodged itself in the deck.

Those who still remained topside screamed in terror. The boat pitched further on its side, threatening to flip over and drown them all.

The exercise instructor was screaming and scrambling over his students, desperately trying to reach the stairs leading down into the boat. He lost his footing and careened over the side, splashing into the Lunsk. Others soon unwillingly followed him.

Coal rushed to the port side of the ship and grabbed hold of the railing as it pushed skyward. He looked back down and saw more people being flung into the river, as well as the disturbing sight of the creature's face.

The two tentacles protruded from the sides of a round head that was all maw. The entire head was an open mouth, lined with hundreds, if not thousands, of tiny, razor-sharp teeth all around the opening. A thick, fleshy tongue lashed out, sometimes slapping against the teeth and poking itself, spraying blood as it whipped around. Unlike the soft flesh of the tentacles, the beast's head appeared covered in a hard shell.

Coal watched with horror as some of the passengers missed the river and instead fell into the monster's mouth, bypassing all the teeth and tongue, and simply disappeared into the abject darkness.

What happened next was possibly worse. It was difficult for Coal to definitively rank such horrifying things, though. It was all bad.

From the depths of the creature's mouth, three other ghastly things were suddenly spat onto the deck. As the mucus-y sacs landed with a wet *splotch*! on the wood, the monster's claws unhooked from the boat and slid back into the water, returning the *Sister's Diatribe* to its appropriate angle.

For a second, Coal was hopeful that the sacs would contain the passengers who had just fallen inside the beast and that they were being returned safely, but he also knew that was absurd.

The sacs burst open almost simultaneously, revealing more monsters within. They sloughed off the viscous white substance encasing them and looked around, absorbing their surroundings.

They were all identical in both appearance and size. They had faces like fishes, with thin lips and bulbous, stupid eyes on either side of their head. Similarly, their bodies were covered in glistening scales, and there were small fins on the sides of their torsos.

That was where the similarities ended, though. Like every other Houndstooth-infected monster Coal had faced, there was something distinctly wrong about the things' flesh. Some of the scales were already clattering to the deck, popped off the body by rapidly-growing pustules that continued increasing in size until they exploded into gunk.

The not-fishes' bodies were long and slender, and standing at full height they would tower as tall as Lop if not slightly higher. They stood slouched, though, their bodies slithering through the air as if riding the river's current. They stood on a single foot that resembled a ventem's hoof, though greatly engorged.

Coal was now standing upright again, though he still clung to the port-side railing. Those who had not fallen overboard were now screaming about the not-fishes and trying to get below deck.

The sudden movements attracted the not-fishes' attention. Each one focused on a specific target and made its move.

They did not comically hop on their lone hoof, which Coal was silently hoping for, but rather dove forward, crashing their heads onto the deck. But then they kept rolling forward, clasping their hoof in their mouth, rolling along the length of their body like a slimy, disgusting wheel.

Somehow they could still see or sense when their target moved, because their precision was impeccable. They followed closely at a remarkable speed. When each one reached the person it was after, it leapt straight from its roll, lunging through the air and biting down on the person's neck, coiling itself around their body.

Coal took a second to lament the loss of the vacation he had been so deeply enjoying before he raced toward the staircase like everyone else.

He rushed past one of the not-fishes, which was still busy gnawing on a deer's face. Coal wanted to help, but he had no weapons and very little fighting experience. He also did not want his face to be eaten.

"Fox!"

Coal was halfway to the stairs, with two not-fishes still between him and his destination, when the call came. He turned and saw Biror standing on the deck, his fingers furled into fists.

The boar charged forward, tackling the not-fish tangled around the deer to the ground. Sadly, the man was already dead, and the monster was enjoying feasting upon him.

It hissed at Biror's interruption of its meal. Biror lifted a fist into the air and brought it down hard on the creature, slamming its head into the deck and crushing its skull in a damp *crack*. Bone, blood, scales, and slime spattered across the wood and Biror's knuckles.

Biror stood and Coal stared at him wide-eyed.

"You take this one and I take this one," Biror said, pointing at the respective not-fishes to which he was referring.

"No!" Coal sputtered, but his words were either left ignored or unheard as Biror shot past him.

Coal swerved on his heel and watched as Biror brought another of the monsters to the ground. He ripped it from the person's face, who was still alive, but badly mangled. Coal wished Noswen was with them to help the man. Magic was the only thing that could save him at this point.

The other not-fish, the one that Coal was supposed to be beating to a pulp, unfurled itself from its prey. The person dropped to the floor in a tattered heap. Their face was ripped to shreds, bits of skin and hair dangling from their bloodied white skull.

The monster stood at its full height, readying itself to pounce onto Biror. The boar was totally unaware, preoccupied with bashing the other one to bits.

"They are like baby!" said Biror with too much joy. "Worthless and weak. Even you can kill, little fox."

Coal was about to yell out a warning, but it was too late. The not-fish leapt forward, latching onto Biror's shoulder. He roared in pain, swinging his arm back and forth to dislodge the creature.

"You stupid fuck!" Biror shouted. Coal did not know if he was speaking to the monster or to Coal.

It jostled Coal out of his stupor. He ran forward and grabbed the last remaining not-fish's lower body, yanking with all his might to pull it off of Biror. He began punching the thing's hoof for good measure, but it was unclear whether that was doing any real harm.

The not-fish let go of Biror's shoulder, leaving some nasty puncture wounds and sending Coal flying backward toward the ship's railing. He landed with a heavy thud, his hands still wrapped around the not-fish, which was now rearing up on him instead.

But Biror was a much better and faster ally in battle, and he quickly set himself upon the monster. He punched its head right out of the air, sending it crashing onto the deck. The boar then lifted a foot and brought it down onto the not-fish's head with a satisfying crunch.

Coal loosed the monster's limp body and stood on shaky legs before Biror. The man looked unbelievably agitated, and blood dripped from the holes in his shoulder.

"Sorry," Coal apologized. "What was that thing?"

"How should I know?"

"Fair enough. Where's Jatiri? Is she okay?"

Biror did not have time to respond before the boat started to tilt again. Both men swore loudly and turned to face the colossal tentacles hooking into the deck.

By now, everyone who had previously been topside was either below deck, in the river, in the monster, or dead on the deck. Those in the latter group, however, were now tumbling down toward the creature and crashing into the water. Only Coal and Biror remained in place on the sundeck.

"How do we kill this thing?" Coal asked. It was not what he wanted to do, not by any stretch, but it seemed inevitable.

"You ask many questions," said Biror, tensing his body for the coming fight. He said nothing else.

"Shouldn't you have your gun?" Coal asked, adjusting his footing as the boat shifted.

Biror did the same, then said, "It is in the room. No time. Unless you would like me to leave you here alone while I get it."

Coal would not like that.

The monster revealed its gaping maw again, and Coal felt a sudden rush of air pulling him toward the starboard railing. It was trying to suck them in.

They both held on tight to the port rail, watching as the beast's tongue whipped around, cutting itself on its own teeth.

Biror pointed at one of the tentacles. "See the spot?" he asked.

Coal followed the man's finger and saw a lighter splotch on top of the tentacle. It was nearly the same color as the rest of its skin, but there was a slight change in the hue.

And then it blinked.

"An eye," Coal said.

Biror nodded.

"We should attack those."

Another nod. Then, "There are two. One for each of us. If you do not fuck it up again."

"What do we do?"

"Gouge it. Bite it. Fuck it, if you want. I care not, little fox. As long as it is ruined."

The monster spat out five more mucus sacs onto the deck, which landed with a splatter. In a few moments, it would recede back into the river. Their window was closing.

Biror recognized this fact as well. *"Go!"* he bellowed.

They both let go of the railing and careened down the tilted sundeck. Biror was doing so in a controlled sprint, while Coal felt as if he were losing himself running down a hill and would soon trip over himself, earning another "stupid fuck" from Biror.

They weaved between the not-fishes, which were now bursting from their sacs and taking in their new world. Halfway down the deck, Biror sprung forward and wrapped his limbs around the left-side tentacle, which was starting to lift up off the ship.

Coal attempted to be just as graceful, but he instead collided with one of the not-fish that stumbled into his path and he flew through the air, smashing into the starboard railing a few feet away from his assigned tentacle.

The limb had unhooked itself from the deck and was lifting into the air. Coal stood and, panicking, hopped up and slammed his back into one of the tentacle's suckers. He effectively got stuck to the tentacle as it lifted higher into the air, and he started flailing his body, trying to un-stick himself.

He didn't know what he'd been thinking. He was on the underside of the tentacle, far out of reach of the eye he was meant to be gouging out or fucking.

You truly are a stupid fuck, he berated himself.

Biror was yelling something incoherent from his own tentacle, but he was drowned out by Coal being suddenly plunged underwater.

He closed his eyes and thrashed against the tentacle, unsure if the monster even knew he was there. The thing's sucker was immensely powerful, and he could not feel himself budging at all. Soon, he would drown.

Drowning was not how he had envisioned himself dying.

He began to writhe even more ferociously, kicking and hitting the tentacle, but the sucker would not loosen its grip on him. His movements were slowed by the water, and panic rose in his chest being unable to see while his lungs quickly ran out of air.

His thoughts drifted to Ilio. Musings on what the man might be doing at that precise moment.

Sleeping. Reading. Taking in the summertime air on a nice walk through the city streets.

Coal's chest tightened and he stopped struggling against the tentacle. The movements were useless and were only making him run out of air faster. He briefly opened his eyes, but all he could see was the hull of the *Sister's Diatribe* in front of him. The corpse of a not-fish drifted slowly through his vision toward the bottom of the river.

His instincts kicked in as he ran out of air and his body surged with panic. Despite himself, he began beating against the tentacle again, but to no avail.

Suddenly blinding light assaulted his eyes and air filled his lungs. The monster had shot its tentacle out of the water and began waving Coal's battered body in the air.

He looked down and saw Biror standing on the deck, gazing up at him, dumbfounded. The boar yelled something else that Coal couldn't hear.

The monster's other tentacle, the one that Biror had likely injured, rose high into the air as well and came swiftly crashing down on the riverboat's deck, breaking off the tip of the boat and sending wood splintering into the air and splashing into the river.

Biror had narrowly ducked out of the way of the tentacle's wrath, but a small piece of wood pierced his leg. Coal looked on helplessly, stuck to the monster's limb in the sky.

It occurred to him that if the monster attacked the boat in a similar fashion with the tentacle he was currently attached to, that would be exceptionally bad news for his personal health.

"Help me!" he screamed fruitlessly to Biror below.

The boar was busy removing the wood from his leg. When he finished, with a small amount of blood spurting from the wound, he looked back up at Coal and scrunched up his face.

A second later, Biror had to dodge another blow from the monster, which tore its claw across the sundeck. It then quickly lashed out again, breaking off more of the boat.

The *Sister's Diatribe* began taking on water.

It was sinking fast.

"Shit," Coal muttered to himself. That seemed to be all he could ever do in a battle.

The monster reared back the tentacle that Coal was stuck to, readying it to strike the ship. Coal was bracing himself for impact, knowing now that this would be his ultimate fate rather than drowning.

As the tentacle swung forward, though, the force with which it moved flung Coal off the sucker, sending him flying completely over the doomed vessel and crashing into the water on the other side.

He breached the water's surface, fighting against the current and heading toward the river's edge. If monsters such as that lived within the depths of the Lunsk, he wanted out of the river immediately.

By the time he was able to make it back onto dry land, both the monster and the *Sister's Diatribe* were out of sight.

He had been sent downriver, back in the direction from which they'd come, putting himself even farther from the Mudlands and hopelessly separated from his companions.

Biror would be alright. The man was resilient and resourceful. Coal could not say the same of the riverboat's other hundred passengers and crew. His heart sank at the thought of their bodies littering the riverbed.

And all throughout the fight, he'd been unaware of Jatiri's whereabouts. He hoped she'd survived.

Coal pulled himself up onto the grass and brought himself into the forest, putting some space between himself and the Lunsk in case one of the not-fishes decided to make an appearance. He traveled as far inland as he could manage, which he doubted was very far at all, before collapsing on a bed of dead leaves and wilting flowers.

There, alone and in an unfamiliar forest, he finally got his nap.

18

I T WAS MIDDAY AND the heat was starting to get
to Lop. It wasn't bothering Yurzu too much, and Noswen
had not voiced any complaints, but it had to be unbearable for the orangutan if even *he* wanted to take a break from
their quest.

"I need a drink," he declared, stopping in the middle of the
walkway. They just so happened to be passing by a bar, which
he nodded toward. "Five minutes, then we'll get going again."

"Fine by me," said Noswen. Yurzu agreed.

They entered the establishment, which was a cheerier joint
than Yurzu was anticipating. In his mind, all bars were dimly
lit and patronized by ruffians. He had little to no experience
with bars or alcohol. But this place was full of vibrant colors,
polished furniture, and patrons of all sorts laughing and
cheersing their glasses.

The group approached the bar with Lop leading the pack.
He slapped his large hands onto the counter and hummed in

thought. Zsoz crawled down from his shoulder and planted itself on the floor.

While Lop pondered what he was in the mood for, Noswen told the bartender, "Glass of longwine, please." The lizard nodded and hurried to fetch her drink.

By the time the man returned and slid the glass over to Noswen, Lop was ready to order. "One beer."

"That's what it took you so long to think of?" Noswen gibed.

"What kind of beer?" the lizard asked.

Lop had him read off a list of the brands they served and chose the last one mentioned. Yurzu was clueless as to how anyone could remember the differences between so many of them based solely on random brand names.

The lizard nodded then turned to Yurzu. "Anything for you, bud?"

They were already here. Yurzu decided to be spontaneous and said, "Same as him."

Lop and Noswen were both visibly shocked. He had always declined alcohol for as long as they'd known him.

"You ever had that before?" Lop asked him. "It's definitely an acquired taste."

"Not that kind specifically," said Yurzu. He'd had a few alcoholic beverages before, only ever finding the mildest enjoyment in sweet cocktails, but even those he did not order often. Every type of beer he'd tried in the past tasted awful to him, so he did not know what compelled him to copy Lop's order.

"You're gonna fucking hate it," Noswen said before taking a sip of her longwine. She moved the glass from her lips and there was a faint purple stain on her fur. She wiped it away with the back of her hand.

He would soon find out. The lizard returned with two glasses of whatever beer Lop had ordered and placed them down on the bar, sloshing the amber liquid around. A bit dribbled down the side of the frosted glass.

Lop wrapped his long fingers around the glass, ignoring the handle, and chugged half the beer in one ravenous gulp. He slammed it back down and loosed a satisfied sigh.

"*Ahhhh.* Exactly what I needed today."

Yurzu picked up his drink and took a tentative sip. The second the beer hit his tongue, he regretted his decision. It tasted sour, bitter, and earthy. The last combination he would ever want to consume.

"Bad," he said, returning the glass to the counter. "Bad." Noswen and Lop both laughed at him.

"I'll take it, if you don't want it," said the orangutan.

"It's yours."

"Want some of my wine?" Noswen asked him, still giggling at his plight.

"No, thanks," Yurzu replied. Whenever the bartender returned to their side of the bar, he would request a glass of water instead. It was time to admit defeat after so many failed attempts. Beer was not for him.

Lop downed the rest of his beer then turned his attention to Yurzu's abandoned glass. Noswen was less than halfway through her wine.

There then came a booming voice from the entryway. "Lop, you bastard!"

All of them turned to see who the voice belonged to. A thick-bodied macaw was approaching them, donned in all-black, form-fitting clothing that was stark against his colorful feathers. The man clucked his beak and Lop stood to meet him, wrapping each other in a rough hug.

Lop pulled away and said, "Fetts! What are you doing out here?"

The macaw, Fetts, clapped Lop on the shoulders. "Out here doing my job, obviously. What are you doing, you fat fuck?"

The men laughed heartily at the insult. Yurzu stared blankly at them and looked to Noswen. She shrugged.

"I'm doing the same," said Lop. "Official business. Top secret, though. Can't really speak on it."

"I understand," said Fetts. "Who're these chuckleheads you're drinkin' with?" he then asked, gesturing toward the rest of them by the bar.

Lop returned to his companions. "This is Noswen, this here's Yurzu, and that's Zsoz," he said, introducing everyone in kind. Then, "This here's Fetts. He's an old friend from the Palace. He's a Pincer now. Ain't that right, Fetts?"

"That's right," the bird nodded. He sidled up to the bar and awaited the lizard. "I put my time in at the Palace and worked my way up to Pincer status. Unlike Lop here, who I guess is runnin' errands for the King like some little bitch boy." He laughed at himself.

"Your friend is very charming," said Noswen dryly.

"Like I said, it's secret stuff, but we're definitely not running errands," Lop laughed, ignoring the raccoon.

It's not far off, though, Yurzu thought.

Fetts looked down at Zsoz and squinted his beady eyes, trying to ascertain what the slime was holding. In response, Zsoz solidified his body to make it murkier. The macaw quickly lost interest.

"Well, whatever you're doin', it can't be anywhere near as fun as what I get to do," said Fetts. *"Hey, can I get a fuckin' drink already?"* he shouted to the bartender. The man hurried over and took his order.

"And you do what, exactly?" asked Noswen. There was once again a ring of purple around her thin lips.

"I'm a Palace Pincer!" Fetts repeated. "I'm out here huntin' down criminals. Sendin' 'em where they need to go."

"Doing great work," Lop chimed in.

"That's right. I've got a few assigned to me right now, some lower-risk individuals, which is why I'm on my own. Don't even need a partner, though, really. But it's typically protocol, so I like to go for the ones they say are less danger-ous, that way I can work alone. I need my space, y'know?"

Yurzu thought it more likely that no one wanted to work with this man, but he refrained from saying so. Noswen might not suppress the urge, though, especially with a glass of long-wine in her.

"Who've you got in your sights?" Lop asked.

Fetts puffed his cheeks. "Can't name names, of course, but the dude's hiding out somewhere in the middle of the Hound-spine. I should reach him tomorrow, but finding him is a whole other story. He's a grisp dealer up here. Not the head of any operation, more like a mid-level guy, but I've gotta take him in. Might lead us to the manufacturer. That'd be a great one to be assigned to, but I bet it'd require a partner, so fuck all that."

"Of course. Other people are a disease," said Noswen.

"Exactly," Fetts concurred, entirely missing her sarcasm.

Lop asked him, "You ever round up any Flesh Eaters?"

Yurzu's stomach dropped. Why would Lop bring up Flesh Eaters to a man from the Palace, totally unprompted? What was the point? Was he about to put his friend on Coal's trail? *If you wanna find one, head to Vuntagonyeo!*

Fetts shook his brightly-colored head. "Nah, but that'd be a lot of fun. I'm itchin' to be promoted to a Stinger, to be totally honest with you."

"I don't blame you," said Lop. He did not see Noswen roll her eyes.

"I've been to Talanap, though," Fetts continued. "Can't talk about it, but man, that place is fucked. I'd love to throw a couple of those nasty cannibal fucks in there. Nothin' would satisfy me more."

Yurzu stared anxiously at Lop, unsure of what the orangutan was going to say. He had completely forgotten about asking the bartender for some water.

Lop grinned at his awful friend. "I hope you can get one someday," he said. "Maybe I can be there to see it!"

Noswen groaned and forcefully set her glass down on the countertop. There were still a few sips of wine remaining, but she stormed out of the bar.

The macaw watched her go with an amused expression. "What's her problem?" he laughed.

"She can get a little prickly," Lop said. "We had better get going, though. We were just stopping for a couple minutes. Back to our secret business now."

"Fair enough. It was good to see you, you dumb bastard," said Fetts, wrapping Lop in another hug. They patted each other on the back.

Yurzu and Zsoz followed Lop outside, where the slime then resumed his position on the man's shoulder. They found Noswen pacing nearby.

"What's wrong?" Lop asked her.

She stopped and stared at him, mouth agape. "Are you shitting me?" she asked. Lop shrugged. "What was that shit in there?"

"About the Flesh Eaters?"

"Yes, about the Flesh Eaters!"

Lop furrowed his brow. "What exactly is your problem?"

"That was just…" Noswen huffed and puffed, fuming. Trying to grasp the right words. "That was repugnant," she finally said. "Your *friend* is one of the nastiest men I've ever met." The word "friend" dripped with malice.

"Fetts is a good man. A good soldier of the Palace."

"He's a dickhead. The way he was talking about his job was disgusting. And the fact that you were agreeing with him, laughing like dumbshits about throwing people into prisons, was disgusting too. I know we don't totally see eye-to-eye, but I thought better of you. I really did."

"Excuse me? That could've gone in a much different direction."

Noswen glared at him. "The fuck is that supposed to mean?"

"It means that Coal's lucky I didn't spill his secret. Fetts would be more than happy to scamper over to the Mudlands and bring him in. That would get him the promotion he's after, I bet. Or I could send a letter to the Palace any time and have ten Stingers on his ass."

"For fuck's sake. Are we really having this argument again? What is wrong with you?" she snarled. "Coal has done *nothing* to you. He's been completely decent, even when you haven't deserved it. You keep giving him shit and he just takes it."

"He's a Flesh Eater," said Lop. It was a definitive statement. In his eyes, there was no argument that could be made.

"He's a good person," Noswen retorted. "But I guess you're too fucking stupid and I need to remind you that he saved your ass back in Nitulo. When Ghoresn was smashing your arms up, he didn't let you get killed despite how shitty you'd treated him."

"Biror is the one who killed Ghoresn."

"Oh, fuck off. He did it with Coal's help. If Coal was locked away in prison, you'd be dead in the dirt and the whole kingdom would be fucked."

"A good deed does not erase a bad one," Lop growled.

"And one mistake doesn't define a person's entire life."

"He's a Flesh Eater. Someone doesn't become a Flesh Eater *by mistake*."

"None of us know what happened," Yurzu interrupted. They both turned to look at him, but he didn't know what else to say. He fumbled around, trying to reach a point. "We don't know his story. We don't really know anyone else's story but our own. I don't know why Biror was in jail. I don't know what Noswen's life was like before this. I don't know what you did in the Palace," he said to Lop. "You shouldn't judge him so harshly. It's not right. I've only ever seen him do good, and he's always been kind to me. I think he's a good person, until he proves otherwise."

Noswen nodded. Lop was still unconvinced.

The orangutan had no rebuttal. He turned away from them and continued down the Houndspine in silence.

"Good job, kid," said Noswen. She gripped Yurzu's shoulder and smiled. "I'm proud of you for standing up to his shit."

They followed Lop through the crowd.

THE HOUNDSPINE WAS THE tallest structure in all of Ruska. Its construction took place hundreds of years prior, using methodology and technology that the Dirt King helped develop. Every technological marvel in Ruska could be attributed in some way, big or small, to the Dirt King.

Being up so high, Yurzu daydreamed about flying over the Yuluj Mountains and leaving the valley behind. Going beyond Ruska to the unknown lands outside, places that hadn't been seen by a Ruskan in centuries. Places like Zawraht, if it truly existed as Fennigha the tiger claimed.

He imagined unfurling his wings, beating them harder and harder as he ascended, letting the wind carry him along on its currents. Cresting the mountain's peaks, touching the clouds.

Once, he had read that the higher you go, the harder it was to breathe, but in his fantasy he was doing just fine. In his mind, he settled in on the tip top of a craggy, unexplored mountain and peered out into Zawraht.

What does Zawraht look like? he wondered.

The possibilities were endless. No one had ever written about the country (or at least he was unaware of anyone doing so), so it could be one giant swamp, for all he knew. A massive Mudlands. Maybe that was why the tigers, orangutans, and macaws had moved to Ruska instead, because they did not like the climate. In the same vein, maybe it was perpetually covered in snow. In Ruska, they got snow during Fakemonth and it generally lasted until Newmonth. That was always Yurzu's least favorite time of year. He couldn't stand the cold. Or perhaps Zawraht was completely covered in sand. He had read fantasy books with worlds like that before, and they sounded fascinating. Maybe it was like Fennigha said: tiger storytellers from Zawraht passed along their tales through the years, and eventually it resulted in some random author taking bits and pieces from those folktales and incorporating them into their book.

He decided that in today's imagining, Zawraht would be a country of sand. So he was perched on the ledge of a mountain, peering down at the dull yellow sands of Zawraht, keeping a lookout for the colossi that roamed the kingdom. He pictured a spiraling tower bursting through the earth and piercing the sky. An orbcrafter lived there.

Orbcrafters were something Yurzu dreamed up eleven years prior, when he was fourteen. They created glass orbs of varying sizes. Some could fit in the palm of a hand, while others were the size of rooms. The orbs were instilled with magic that let a person see into other worlds that were like their own, but with minor changes. Or sometimes big changes. It all depended on the world you were looking in on. With the smaller orbs, one could only watch what was unfolding. If you came upon a bigger orb, you could actually enter it and experience the alternate world firsthand.

In his fantasy, Yurzu leapt from the mountaintop and swooped down through the sky, smiling at the wind whipping his face. In real life, the highest he'd ever flown was only up onto his roof when he needed to patch a hole after a storm or perform some other maintenance. Even that small exertion tired him out, but as he flew through Zawraht toward the orbcrafter's tower, there was no weariness whatsoever. He could fly for days.

He flew through an open window near the top of the tower. Inside he found the orbcrafter, a wrinkly old tiger, fiddling with a massive orb.

It easily took up half the room. At the moment it was opaque, its surface a smooth, gleaming green with crackles of blue shooting across its surface like lightning. As Yurzu placed his palm on the orb, it shifted from green to pink. Bolts of blue converged on his hand, extending outward and inter-connecting like a spiderweb.

The orbcrafter explained that he had been getting it ready for Yurzu. He could enter it whenever he was ready.

Yurzu passed through the surface of the orb. It was solid most times, but when a person entered, it turned into a gel that they could slip through. It encased his body, dampening his clothes and fur. His movements were lethargic, strange, dreamlike. Orbcrafters said this was meant to represent slip-ping into another world.

The world inside the orb was nearly identical to their own. Yurzu was back in his home in Toothshadow. It was a small cottage, with two bedrooms, a modest kitchen, and a lounge area where his parents had set up some comfortable chairs and shelves filled with records. Music took up most of the shelf space; only a few books joined the thin paper sleeves.

Yurzu sat down in his chair. It was the smallest one, plush and pink, shaped like an egg with a piece scooped out to sit in. His chair was also the one nearest the window, because as a child he enjoyed watching his parents in the garden outside.

While he sat in the chair now, his father Zanhu rifled through the record collection on the shelf. Zanhu had often said he wanted to display his records in a prettier way, so that all the gorgeous artwork on their covers could be admired, but he owned too many. In the real world, Zanhu had yet to come to a solution before he died.

Zanhu finally settled on an album. It was called *Wispland*, by the band Zoj. He removed the record from its sleeve and placed it on the player. Soon melodies from the world of Wispland were drifting through their small, cozy home.

Yurzu laughed at his father shaking his tiny hips next to the record player. Zanhu told him he'd never have moves this good, and Yurzu laughed even harder. He looked out the window to his left and saw his mother was finishing up in the garden and heading toward the door.

Muneer walked inside and grinned at the sight of her husband's dancing. She told him he was embarrassing himself, to which he took great offense. He said that if she was so confident in her own moves, then she should come and show them off.

The challenge was accepted. Muneer sauntered over to Zanhu, stepping in time to the rhythm of the song. When she reached him, they locked hands and swayed together.

They looked to their son, who was still nestled into his chair. He could stay in this spot forever, relishing the warmth of the sun that trickled through the window.

Both his parents urged him to get up and join them. It pained him to abandon the comfort of his spot in the house, but he did want to dance with them.

He hopped out of the chair and boogied over to his parents. They both laughed heartily at his little steps and shakes of the hips. He grinned and flailed his arms in the air, getting lost in the music.

As the song faded away, so too did the world the orb had generated. First it was the sounds, then the colors, then the objects, then the house. Only Yurzu and his parents remained. And then they were gone, too.

Yurzu came out of the orb dripping with clear, viscous gel. He looked to the ancient orbcrafter and asked if the worlds inside the orbs were real or just a fabrication.

"They are real while you are in them. Beyond that, does it make a difference what my answer is?"

Yurzu shook his head. It didn't.

19

THE FIRST THING COAL did once he'd recovered a bit was remove his copy of *A Popular Bargain* from his jacket pocket and set it on a rock to dry out in the sun. The pages were warped, but thankfully none of the ink had run, and it seemed like a few hours in the warm open air would do it some good.

One of the big things that irked him was that somehow his bookmark had gotten dislodged, so now he would have to seek out his place in the book again.

The rest of his possessions were back in his cabin on the *Sister's Diatribe*, which was probably now sunk to the bottom of the Lunsk River. Being picked over by those strange not-fishes.

He had floated downriver quite a way, but given his condition at the time, he could not be sure precisely how far he drifted. All he knew was that he needed to head north along the river, and eventually he would reach the town they were planning to disembark at. Though he quickly realized he did not remember which town that was, because he had been relying on Biror's prior knowledge to guide them. He did not think it necessary to fully grasp the plan, which made him feel like a humongous moron right about now.

Still, heading north was what he had to work with, so once his book was sufficiently dried off and he felt at least somewhat rested, he set off.

Now, a day later, he was still wandering the woods without any sign of civilization. Yet again surrounded by nothing but foliage. An annoyingly familiar sight.

Last night he had gone hungry, subsisting on the enormous meal he'd eaten aboard the riverboat for lunch, but his stomach was reminding him now that he needed some food. Shortly after waking he stumbled upon a blackberry bush, which he'd stripped of its berries. They were jostling around in his pocket, waiting until he was actually hungry to consume them. He grabbed a couple and popped them into his mouth. They burst with a delightfully tart sweetness as he chewed.

The Lunsk was to his left, and he thought it wise to stick close to the river in case he came upon any survivors of the wreck. There was the slight risk of encountering the river beasts that put him in this position, but he could easily retreat into the forest. He didn't figure the not-fishes could survive for long out of water.

That assumption was based on normal fish, so maybe it was a foolish assumption to make. Who knew how the Houndstooth's infection was altering their physiology. Their transformation was a lot more extreme than that of the not-ventems and not-retnos, which were mostly the same as their regular counterparts, just…grosser. Melting away, falling apart.

Coal did not find anything on the banks of the river, though. He did not know if that was good or bad. It would be nice to have some companionship, especially if it was Jatiri (and Biror too, he begrudgingly admitted, though more out of necessity than real desire), but finding a corpse washed up would be awful. He wished everyone survived the attack, but that beast was pretty relentless. He wasn't sure how likely that was.

As the sun began to set and the day drew to a close, Coal veered farther into the forest, away from the Lunsk. He was paranoid about sleeping near the river and having not-fishes slink out of the water, coiling around him as he slept.

His vision was adjusting to the dark, suddenly allowing him to spy an unusual form between the trees in the distance.

Is that a house? he wondered.

It made little sense for a house to be in this random spot in the woods, though maybe it was just someone who wanted to be isolated. During their journey through the Innards they had encountered several standalone homes, after all. Coal could not relate, but maybe this person would be his ticket to a meal and directions toward the nearest town. Or at least some indication of how far he was from it.

Coal hurried toward the structure, tripping over a few exposed tree roots in the process. As he approached, his heart sank.

It was indeed a lone house, two stories tall, constructed primarily from stone. There was a small shed and some fencing around it; at some point, Coal was sure it was a cute, quaint little place. But now, half the upper walls had crumbled to pieces and lay scattered around the perimeter of the bottom floor, leaving the second story exposed to the elements. From where he stood, he could see bookshelves fallen over and some sort of fabric was hanging down, flapping lazily in the breeze. Thick layers of fuzzy moss covered most of the structure, creeping inside on the upper story. A tree had fallen over as well, its trunk blocking the front door of the home, though the bark appeared soft, the trunk rotten. It could be easily stomped into the ground if he wanted to access the building.

Clearly the house was abandoned. No one had been living here for quite some time. If they had, they were deranged. There would be no hot meal or townward directions for him tonight.

The top floor was ruined, but at the very least he could make his way into the bottom one and perhaps feel slightly more secure while he slept. Finding shelter was rarely a bad thing.

Coal trudged through the underbrush toward the dilapidated building, his mood deflated. A minute ago he had such hope, and now it was already dashed.

He noticed an easily accessible window nearby and decided to enter through there rather than mess with the rotted tree trunk. He found a rock and threw it through the glass, wincing at the sound of it shattering. He then grabbed a stick and used it to smash up the remaining bits of jagged glass so that he would not puncture himself while climbing through.

Inside, the place was just as messy and run-down as what little he'd seen of the upstairs. What furniture remained was falling apart with neglect, and somehow grass and flowers were infiltrating the building through various cracks in the floor and walls. It was being overrun by the forest outside. In the kitchen, ceramic plates and cups were smashed on the ground, leaving little traps for unsuspecting feet.

It certainly wasn't the Longowosk Hotel, but it would do for a night.

Coal set his book down on a side table near the couch and slipped his jacket off, tossing it onto the floor. There were no clean surfaces, so it did not particularly matter where his jacket ended up. The ground was just as good as any table or chair.

Coal walked through the house, inspecting each room one by one. For reasons unbeknownst to even himself, he had been thinking that maybe there was a not-horribly-run-down bedroom somewhere, but every room was as decrepit as the last.

The first floor consisted of the living room, kitchen, and an office. The latter held several dusty, rotted bookshelves, many of which had fallen apart over the years, sending books tumbling to litter the ground. There was no chair behind the desk, and one of its drawers hung slightly open. Coal pulled it out the rest of the way, but it was empty. There were scratches on its bottom, as if someone had yanked something out of it at some point.

He then wandered over to the stairs, which did not look like they would pass an inspection. Every step was covered in a thick layer of moss, almost like carpet. The railing had loosened and fallen behind the couch below, ripping into it along its backside.

There were portraits hung on the wall, which Coal stopped to take a closer look at as he ascended. The family that lived here had consisted of two deer men and two young daughters, a fox and a hedgehog, neither older than ten. Each had their own individual portrait, flanking one large family portrait. The two deer smiled proudly next to their daughters, each man placing a hand on one of their shoulders.

Were they still that young when this house had been abandoned? Or were they already grown? Coal could not help but
wonder what happened to the four of them.

Upstairs, past the portraits (which were now creeping him
out), things were much worse. With the roof and walls torn off,
most of the furniture had slowly deteriorated in the heat and
rain. There were two bedrooms, presumably one for the parents and one for the kids. Many of their possessions still remained, including toys and books and clothes and countless
other objects.

In the parents' room, Coal found what appeared to be a
handwritten note left on the dresser. It had been ravaged by the
weather, most of it disintegrated. What remained of the mes-
sage was either faded or bleeding across the tattered bits of
paper. It was entirely illegible.

There was a chill, so Coal decided to head back downstairs
where at least there were four walls to shield him from the
wind. Sifting through this family's belongings was also de-
pressing him and making him feel uneasy, so he wanted to just
lay down and forget about it. If he could focus, maybe he
would read a chapter of his book.

He then heard a thump from outside the bedroom. Something landing heavily on the stone.

The only animal that could reasonably reach these heights
was a geigex. But were geigexes even in this part of the forest?
Maybe it was just another book falling off a shelf.

Coal took a cautious step out of the bedroom and discovered something worse than a geigex. Vastly worse than a book.

It was seven feet tall and made entirely of light green metal.
Coal had never encountered a machine like this before, one
that was so person-like. All he'd ever seen were devices that

made coffee, or elevators, or other such things. But this one had a distinct face, one that was long and curved like a crescent moon, with bright shining blue eyes lit up like lightbulbs. Its torso was V-shaped, narrowing to two tall, skinny legs. The arms were long and gangly as well, drooping nearly to the thing's knees. Its joints were connected by some sort of black substance. In the middle of its chest was what appeared to be an empty housing unit, a big gaping rectangle, the edges of which were crusted with a dark, congealed orange substance not dissimilar to a slime's body.

The machine man was covered in scrapes and rust and other signs of age, making it seem hundreds if not thousands of years old. Parts of its body were chipped, and it was missing two fingers on its right hand. Cracks shot across its chest like lightning bolts from the empty rectangular hole in its center. It whirred and creaked with every stiff movement.

Coal froze in fear, staring at it from the bedroom doorway. There was nowhere to run, and the thing looked like it could overpower him without breaking a sweat. Not that it could sweat. If it could, that would be an odd feature.

There was a collection of tiny holes, no bigger than pinpricks, in the spot on its face where a normal person would have a mouth. From the holes came clear as day, "Hello." Its voice was tinny and quiet. "Can you hear me? It has been many years since I used my voice."

Coal nodded slowly, still unable to speak.

"I will adjust my volume," the machine man said anyway, the sentence getting louder with each word. "How is that?" it then asked.

"Better," Coal croaked.

"Good. My name is Horace," it said.

It said? He said? Coal did not know what was appropriate. This was an unprecedented conversation.

While he was internally debating how to refer to the machine, it asked him, "What is your name?" The voice was calm and pleasant, but did not fluctuate like a real person's. It remained monotone.

"Coal," he answered.

"You are a fox, yes?"

"Yes."

"It has been many years since I have met a fox. Or met anyone at all. Welcome to my home."

The machine man—Horace—seemed friendly enough. Coal did not trust him completely, but his fear was gradually giving way to mere confusion.

Horace must regularly enter and exit the house through the exposed upper level, since the downstairs door was blocked and he could definitely not fit through a window if he tried.

They stared at each other for a few moments, and Coal had the brief thought that the machine might have abruptly died. Or was *broken* the correct term? Shut down?

But then Horace sprang into motion, heading down the stairs without another word. His metal feet clanked against the bits of stone that were not shielded by moss.

Coal had no choice but to follow the machine downstairs. When he reached the bottom of the staircase, he saw Horace standing by the couch, looking at the window Coal had destroyed.

"You broke my window?" he asked.

"Sorry," said Coal. "I didn't think anyone lived here."

Horace looked from the window down to the novel and jacket that were now resting on his table and floor, respectively. "These are yours?"

"Yes."

"Okay."

Horace then entered the kitchen, ceramic crunching underfoot. He stared out the window into the darkness. Coal could distantly hear cicadas and crickets battling over nighttime soundscape dominance.

"What brings you to my home?" Horace then asked, turning and exiting the kitchen. He walked through the living room, toward the couch. The rounded tip of his head nearly scraped against the ceiling. He had to hunch slightly to navigate the house.

Coal was still standing idly by the stairs, watching this bizarre machine man traipse around. "I'm just making my way through the forest," he answered.

Horace picked up *A Popular Bargain* and examined its front for a second before turning it over to read the back cover copy. "It's been a long time since I saw a new book," he said. Without pupils, it was impossible to tell if he was still reading the blurb. But then he set the book back down and said, "That one does not appeal to me."

Sorry, Ilio. The metal man thinks you're bad at picking out books, Coal thought, amused. Though, really, it reflected more on his own taste in books than Ilio's ability to choose them.

"You can sit," said Horace, looking over at the frozen Coal. "You are welcome here. I would like you to stay."

Horace didn't seem like a threat to him, but if they were attacked by any blightbeasts, he could surely put up a decent fight. Coal took a step closer to the machine and sat down in an armchair (missing an arm) near him.

"You are a peculiar fox," said Horace. "Foxes are typically orange and white, are they not? I might be wrong. As I said, it has been many years since I last met a fox. But I have a painting of one on the staircase. That is how I remember what foxes usually look like. Perhaps you saw it."

"I did," said Coal, uneasily. Suddenly the thought occurred to him that maybe the machine man was indeed a threat. What had happened to the family that lived here?

"I am sorry. I did not mean to imply that you look strange. I must find my manners again. They have been buried deep for many years. It has been so long since I've talked to anyone, you see."

"That's alright," said Coal.

"I have been quite alone here."

Horace shifted in his seat, leaning his metallic back against the mushy cushions of the couch.

"What happened to that family?" Coal asked, testing the waters. "The one on the staircase." If Horace had something to do with their disappearance, he doubted the machine man would say so, but he wanted to see what answer he provided.

The bulbs of Horace's eyes flickered, as if he had blinked. "I do not know," he replied. "This house was empty when I discovered it. It has been a nice refuge for me." Without absolutely any change in his tone of voice, Coal could not deduce whether the machine might possibly be lying or not. The "blinking" was unexpected, though.

"I see," said Coal.

"It is most unfortunate. I have been alone for quite some time. Did I already mention that?"

"Yes."

"My apologies. It is so hard to remember what I've said, since I have not said anything in many years. Because I have been alone. My memory is fading, I think. I used to have brothers, but I cannot remember their faces. The sound of their voices is lost to me, lost to time. Is that not the most heartbreaking thing you have ever heard of? Forgetting one's own kin? It is the most heartbreaking thing I have ever heard of, and it is happening to me. Has already happened to me. I fear that when you are gone, I will forget you, as well. My memory is fading, I think."

"You had brothers?" Coal asked, befuddled. "Do you mean there were other machines like you?"

"Of course," said Horace with a nod. "Why would there not be? There must be. Must have been. Oh, dear."

"What happened to them?"

Horace slouched. Based on his body language, Coal knew the machine man would be frowning if he had a mouth with which to frown.

"They are all dead, I must assume," he said. "I am the last of my kin, and I cannot even remember them fully. They are in my mind, but each of them is shrouded in a fog. They are clouds of mist, walking through my memories, gesturing wildly and speaking to me, though their voices are distorted and unpleasant to the ear. I have few memories of them, but what remains are corrupted. Do you know what it is like to have a corrupted memory?"

He knew Horace meant something else, but the memory of Coal and his father Von in that collapsed library certainly felt corrupted to him. So he nodded.

"That is unfortunate," said Horace. He sat up straighter and looked down at the ground. "I am sorry to bring down the mood. It's not polite to do when you have company. It's just been so long since I have had any company, I have forgotten my manners. They have been buried deep. I am trying to dig them up, but I am missing some fingers, you see, and it makes digging harder and more laborious. It puts added strain on my other fingers, the ones that are still around to dig. I lost the two fingers in an accident, I think, but I cannot remember it. I fear I am already forgetting you. What is your name, again?"

"Coal."

"Coal. I will try to commit this to memory, but I know I will not. You must forgive me. Most things I cannot remember, but I can remember that I cannot remember. Is that not the most heartbreaking thing you have ever heard of? One remembering their lack of remembrance?"

"It is," said Coal. He did not know how to react to Horace's multitude of existential crises.

Horace stood and took a single step toward Coal. The machine man towered over him, and Coal sagged back into his chair. Those solid blue eyes stared down at him from the green crescent-shaped head. Somehow the machine's lack of breathing was what intimidated him the most. Horace simply stood there, completely silent and still, looking at him.

Then Horace said, "There is something about you. I don't know what it is."

"Okay," Coal muttered.

"I like you, Colt."

"Thanks." He did not correct the machine's slip-up.

Horace walked back into the kitchen, crushing more broken plates with his metal feet, and stared blankly out the window.

Coal watched him standing there, completely motionless, for a full two minutes before he turned around again.

"It is starting to rain," he declared.

Coal flicked his ears, listening harder, and did in fact hear the pattering of rainfall outside. He then looked over to the window he'd broken and saw raindrops falling, a scant few blown in by the wind picking up and starting to form a small puddle on the ground.

"The rain is bad for my health. I will have to avoid the window you broke."

"Sorry," Coal apologized again.

"It's quite alright. It will never be fixed, because I lack both the tools and the knowledge of how to accomplish such a task. It is why my home is in such a state of disrepair, as you may have noticed."

"I did. Sorry."

"It's quite alright. You are welcome to stay the night. I do not know your destination, but it is not close, because this house is not close to anything. There is something about you. Nandara is the closest town, but you would not make it there until the middle of the night at the soonest, and the rain would make it quite a miserable trek, I would think. I don't know what it is about you. You are welcome to stay the night, though. I would be happy to have you as a guest. Can you believe you would be my first houseguest?"

Coal could believe that, but he did not say so.

Something was wrong with Horace, but Coal did not want to venture out into the cold rain and spend an awful night curled up next to a tree getting his clothes soaking wet. Putting up with the machine man's eccentricities was far more appealing, given the choice.

"I would appreciate that," Coal told him. "I don't wanna ruin my book in the rain, after all," he said playfully.

"That's true," Horace nodded, returning to the couch. He gave the novel another once-over then said, "It does not seem like a very good book, though." He picked it up and flipped it over to read the back cover blurb a second time. After setting it back down, he said, "This does not appeal to me. Not in the slightest. It has been eighteen years since I have read a new book, but I believe that if I tried to read this one, I would throw it against a tree before I finished. Did I mention that already?"

"Not the tree part, no."

"Well, the tree part is the most important part. Yes, I believe I would throw this book against a tree in either rage or frustration or sadness due to the first new book I read in eighteen years being something unenjoyable. Sometimes when an overwhelming sadness grips you, you must throw something at a tree."

"I understand."

Horace nodded. "I knew you would, Coat. There is something about you."

20

ORACE AND COAL SPENT another hour or so having dizzying circular conversations before Coal told the machine that he was exhausted and ready to get some rest.

Since Horace did not require sleep, he sacrificed the couch for his guest. As Coal got himself as comfortable as he could (which was no easy feat given the condition of the furniture), he wondered what Horace would do all night while he slept. It seemed Horace regularly gazed out his kitchen window; would he do that for six to eight hours? Did the machine man possess night vision like himself? Better than himself, even?

Coal rested his head on one of the couch's flat throw pillows and clamped his eyes shut, turning his body to face the back of the couch, away from Horace. Not that he was trying to obscure himself from the machine man, though that was a nice bonus. He never liked facing out toward the open world when laying on a couch. There was something more snug about facing the back cushions. More cozy. And right now, he needed all the coziness he could muster.

"Enjoy your sleep, Code," said Horace from a few feet away.

"Thanks, Horace." He had given up trying to get the machine to correctly remember his name.

As he lay there, his thoughts drifted back to those of Horace's potential night vision.

Was such technology possible way back when Horace was created? Probably so, considering that Coal didn't even know technology existed to create a functioning machine man *today*, let alone whenever the hell Horace was brought into existence.

To what end were Horace and his alleged brothers created? What had he been doing all these countless years? Wandering Ruska, keeping himself secret, losing his mind, seeking out abandoned homes?

Or making *them abandoned,* he couldn't stop himself from thinking. A chill ran down his spine with the image of the staircase's family portrait.

He pushed the disturbing thought from his mind. With his back turned to the machine man, he had to put some trust in him. He did trust him. They had partaken in a long, amiable chat. Horace was a bit eccentric, but ultimately harmless.

The rainfall pattering against the stone building soothed him. His heartbeat slowed as he listened. It was only then that he realized how on-edge he'd been the entire day. Probably ever since the shipwreck.

While he dozed, he attempted to concoct a plan for the following day. He would leave the fascinating machine behind and continue north, presumably toward the town Horace had mentioned, Nandara.

Nandara, Nandara, he thought, wracking his brain.

It sounded somewhat familiar. Was that where they were planning to disembark? Was that the name Biror had said when he told them their route?

Had the boar even informed them what the route was in the first place? It would not be out of character for him to keep that to himself, and Coal was too wrapped up in enjoying the ship to bother asking. Now, separated from his companions, he cursed himself for being so blissfully ignorant. If he knew for certain where they were all going, they could meet there and continue on their merry way.

But Nandara was the only lead he had at the moment, so that was what he'd pursue.

He forced himself to stop thinking about it, because it was starting to make his heart race. Instead, he concentrated on the raindrops and calmed himself down, willing his mind to empty itself of any thoughts.

Soon, he was asleep, and the rain continued to fall.

AN UNDETERMINED AMOUNT OF time had passed when Coal abruptly awoke, unable to breathe.

Horace was towering over him, his cold metal fingers wrapped around Coal's throat, throttling him.

A thought flittered through Coal's mind: *Well, I was wrong.*

The machine man's unchanging eyes made it all the more unsettling as Coal looked up at his blank expression. The blue bulbs flickered wildly, and his tinny voice screeched, nearly into distortion: *"You touched it! You touched it!"*

Coal did not have the first clue as to what the fuck Horace was talking about. He struggled underneath the heavy metal of Horace's body, kneeing him in the chest. Sometimes his knee missed and went through the open rectangle in the middle of the machine's torso, at which point its edges suddenly spurted globs of orange goo that then fell onto Coal's stomach.

He tried speaking, but Horace's grip tightened and choked the air from his lungs. Coal continued thrashing, and accidentally stuck his leg completely through the rectangular hole.

More orange gunk shot out, this time encasing his leg, which stuck out through Horace's backside. The rectangle had entirely filled with the orange substance and hardened, much like a slime could, locking Coal's leg into place.

Surprised by what had happened, Horace suddenly let go of Coal's throat and leaned back, looking down at his own chest.

"It has been so long..." the machine man uttered, his voice soft. Then, the volume of his words increased as if he were angry, though there was no other indication in his tone. "Stop!" he shouted. "This is not right!"

Horace stood, bringing Coal's leg up with him. Coal slid off the couch and knocked his head against the hard floor. His lower body was held aloft by Horace, who was now smacking against Coal's leg, seemingly in an attempt to dislodge it. He took a few steps across the room, dragging Coal's head on the floor behind him.

Outside, the storm was raging. It had worsened considerably since Coal had fallen asleep, and there was now a large puddle underneath the window he'd broken.

Finally able to speak, Coal yelled, *"What the fuck are you doing?"*

Horace was too preoccupied with the leg jutting through his torso. He stopped moving, standing perfectly still. The goo loosened, dribbling onto the floor and freeing Coal, sending his ass crashing to the ground in the puddle of orange.

With that out of the way, Horace addressed him again. "You touched it," he said.

"I don't know what you're talking about," said Coal. "Look, this is a misunderstanding. Let's just calm—"

"You touched it!" Horace roared again, the volume of his voice louder than it had ever been before. The words were distorted, crackling, manic. Quieter, he said, "I need it. I need to protect it. You understand, don't you, Cone? I know you do. I know you do. I know you do." He took a few steps forward, and with each one Coal scrambled backward on his hands and feet. "I knew there was something about you. I knew. I said it. I said it, didn't I? I think I said it. You touched it. I know that you touched it, and I need it, and I need to protect it. I need it. You understand."

Coal had backed up all the way to the opposite wall. His head bumped against the stone, nowhere else to go, while Horace still crept toward him, babbling about whatever it was he'd supposedly done.

"I've been asleep," Coal said. "I didn't touch anything. Just calm down. I don't know what you're talking about." His voice wavered as the machine's shadow loomed over him.

"That simply isn't true," said Horace. "You touched it. I can sense that you touched it. It is part of who I am. I know. I have to know. That is why I am the way that I am. I need it, and I need you to give it to me. So that I can protect it. You understand. I know you do."

Horace's babbling was growing tiresome and it was becoming more and more obvious that there was no reasoning with him anymore. Coal needed to get out of there, storm or no.

But he did not react quickly enough to Horace's next move. The machine's hands shot forward, his pipe-like arms as fast as they were long. He grabbed Coal by the shoulders, pulling him up to stand on his feet.

Horace brought his crescent-shaped head only a few inches from Coal's. If the machine could breathe, Coal would be able to feel it on his face. Taste it in his mouth.

"Where is it?" Horace asked him.

"Where is what?" Coal wriggled in his iron grip.

"These games are not fun. I do not play games. I have never played a game in my life, and I am very old, so that should tell you how little patience I have for games. You touched it, Cove, and I know that you did, because I can feel that you did. I can feel it."

Thunder cracked outside and Coal could hear the rain pounding harder against the stone, against the glass just to the right of his head.

Which gave him an idea.

He could barely maneuver his arm with Horace gripping his shoulder, but he managed to lift it and slam his fist into the window.

Nothing happened, and Horace said "What are—" before Coal tried again and the glass shattered.

A great gust of wind blew and sent raindrops flying into the house. Horace loosed Coal and leapt backward to avoid the sudden assault, stumbling away toward the safety of the kitchen.

"The rain is bad for my health!" Horace screamed.

Coal stood near the safety of the window, letting the rain soak into his fur, while he calculated his next move. Horace would not approach him while he stood there, so he had a second to think things over.

The window he'd just broken was smaller than the other, too small for him to feasibly climb through.

That would have been too easy.

It's never easy, he thought with a defeated sigh.

"Please come over here," said Horace. "Let's do what needs to be done. We can make it quick, and we can make it easy. The easy way is often the best way. When given the choice between the easy way or the hard way, it is better to choose the easy way, in my opinion. You know that. You understand. And I know that you have what I need. I need it. I need to protect it. Please. It will be so easy. I can feel it inside you. Let me just look. Is it in your chest, too? Let me just look. It will be easy. Please come over here."

The machine took a few cautious steps forward. Horace was standing between Coal and the window through which he'd originally entered, the one that he knew could fit him. So that wasn't an option.

Horace was steadily growing closer. Coal needed to think faster.

To his right were the stairs.

It seemed so obvious now that he was looking at them.

Almost all of the upper level was exposed to the storm. Horace could not go up there without severely damaging himself.

There wasn't much distance between Horace and the staircase, so he might catch him, but it still seemed like Coal's best option.

He went for it.

Coal darted forward and Horace instantly knew what was going on, shouting out his dismay.

He slipped past the machine and was halfway up the stairs when Horace reached his long arm forward and grabbed him by the ankle, yanking him down. Coal fruitlessly clawed at the walls for purchase, but all he did was knock the family portrait down, sending its frame clattering onto the stone.

Coal fell with a similarly brutal impact, smashing his snout against the mossy step. Horace started to drag him down the stairs, leaving behind a thin trail of blood from Coal's nose.

Without time for thought, Coal grabbed the framed painting and twisted his body to slam it on Horace's head.

Horace did not react, continuing to pull Coal down the steps, totally unhurt by the action.

The frame had broken into pieces, the painting itself torn on the tip of Horace's head. Coal now held two edges of the frame, one in each hand, and held them both out into Horace's rectangle.

Like before, the machine man's goo spurted out to encase the newly-detected objects, immediately solidifying to hold them in place.

This was not acceptable to Horace, who said "No!" again and reflexively let go of Coal, stumbling backward to address the unwanted objects piercing his torso.

"Not right," Horace uttered. "No, no. Not right."

The slimy substance in his chest unsolidified and the sides of the frame fell uselessly to the ground, bouncing the rest of the way down the steps.

But Coal was already bounding up the staircase on all fours while Horace was distracted.

The second story was being battered by the storm, which pleased Coal greatly. It beat against the floor, the walls, the shelves, ruining books and clothes and rugs and everything else. He raced out into the open area, letting the ice cold rain pelt his fur while he stood, warily watching the staircase.

Horace peeked his head up, still covered in the area at the top of the staircase. He did not come all the way up, though, so as to avoid the wind blowing any rain onto him.

"Please come over here," Horace pleaded again. "The rain is bad for my health. I cannot go over there. You know that, Rove."

Coal nodded. He did indeed know that.

He took a moment to relish the rain soaking into his clothes, into his fur. It chilled him to the bone, but rain had never felt so good.

There was nothing left to say to Horace. Coal turned his back on the machine and approached the edge of the building, looking down at the grass below. After his horrific attempt at a falling roll in the spiderback race during his encounter with the geigexes, he did not trust himself to jump down without injuring himself. That was not an inconvenience he needed right now.

There were several trees in proximity to the house, though. Coal chose one, took a few steps back to get a running start, and dashed forward, leaping off the stone.

He slipped, but the tree was close enough for it to not matter. His nails dug into the bark, but he could not get a good grip without the help of his feet, which were covered by his boots. He swiftly slid down the trunk, leaving behind scratch marks along the length of the tree, and came to a stop at its base.

Looking up at the second story, there was no sign of Horace. The machine was not going to risk the rain, not even for whatever he desired from him.

Coal then realized he was standing just outside the kitchen. He looked ahead and, sure enough, Horace was staring at him through the window. His crescent moon head was pressed against the glass, his fingers splayed on either side of it, staring straight at the fox who got away.

Coal had the impulse to say, "Bye, Horace," but he did not want to be dramatic like one of his mystery novels.

Which made him realize that his copy of *A Popular Bargain* was still sitting on Horace's side table, and his jacket was left on the floor. He let out a defeated "Fuck," and sighed deeply.

Ilio's first gift to him, and he had lost it in the home of a deranged, ancient machine man.

There was no way to retrieve it, and no use mourning its loss right now. He needed to first get far, far away from Horace's home so that the machine could not track him down after the rain stopped. Finding some alternative shelter to shield himself from the rain would be ideal, too, but he wasn't going to be picky at this point.

Coal found the Lunsk then ran, following it upriver for a solid half hour before slowing to a walk. The rain had not let up even the tiniest bit. He was feeling confident in the distance he put between himself and Horace.

264 • *Travis M. Riddle*

Another thirty minutes of walking later, he came upon the wreckage of the *Sister's Diatribe.*

Part of it, anyway. The back portion of the riverboat that the monster had hacked off evidently washed up on the riverbank, its exposed inside facing down. Rain beat against the hull.

It saddened him seeing the ship there, looking so pathetic, devoid of all its previous pomp and grandiosity. There were no bodies anywhere around the boat. Just broken planks of wood, random bags, and other luggage strewn about.

Coal walked toward the boat, figuring if he could find a window or a hole to squeeze through, it could work as a place to shelter for the night while waiting for the storm to pass. Then he could set off in the morning in search of Biror and Jatiri, possibly in the town of Nandara.

It was closer to the river than he felt entirely comfortable with, fearing that a not-fish might make its way ashore, but he did not see what choice he had in the matter.

He quickly found an already-broken window and managed to just barely squeeze his body through, finding himself among a jumbled mess of furniture and decorations. After a light scrounging, he regrettably did not find any food or other helpful items. He settled in near an overturned table, positioning himself away from but within eyesight of the window, in case he had a visitor in the night.

Coal curled up on himself, shivering in the cold. His clothing and fur were completely soaked through, and he felt like his skeleton was chattering with every shiver. During his search, he had been unable to find anything resembling a blanket. He had also silently hoped to find his own belongings among this wreckage, but of course it was unlikely and in the end he did not. Again, it would have been too easy.

He lay there, curled up and miserably cold, thinking about his night.

Despite the rain, the cold, and the murderous machine man he'd barely escaped, what bothered him the most was losing Ilio's book. For some reason it made him feel immensely guilty, and he was not looking forward to admitting to the man that he'd lost his gift.

Granted, he had a pretty good excuse, but still. At least it would make for an interesting story when he saw Ilio again.

Coal closed his eyes and tried to go to sleep. This time, the rain was neither soothing nor reassuring to him. It beat against the ship's hull relentlessly. A constant reminder of what had happened. Horace filled his vision, and would not leave.

In his mind, the machine man repeated, over and over, "Please come over here. Let me look inside you."

21

HORACE SAID THAT NANDARA was only a few hours away. Coal woke the next morning in the wreckage of the *Sister's Diatribe* feeling groggy and morose. The only thing that even mildly brightened his mood was Horace's assurance that the town was not terribly far.

Although, the machine had clearly lost its mind, so maybe that simple fact could not be trusted either. Coal wondered if he was doomed to wander the forests of Ruska for eternity. More and more, that was what it felt like.

Nothing had come for him in the night. He walked through the overturned boat, trying to salvage anything that might come in handy, but there was nothing. Not even the tiniest morsel of food, soggy and half-eaten.

At that moment, Coal swore he would face one of the Faranap abominations again if it meant he could eat a buttered biscuit.

He exited the ship and breathed in some fresh air. The river was trickling behind him. The sound made his mouth dry. He smacked his lips and walked over to the river's edge, reaching his cupped hands down into it and bringing the cool water to his lips. Not quite as satisfying as a buttered biscuit, but it was refreshing.

There was a small splash, and he looked up to see a fin in the water. A curved back.

A school of not-fishes were swimming downriver, popping their backs out of the water's surface every so often. None noticed him, or if they did, they were uninterested. Still, he slowly retreated from the riverbank and returned to the relative safety of the forest.

He could still feel Horace's cold, cylindrical fingers wrapped around his neck. He rubbed it gently, trying to massage away the feeling. Sleep had not come easily to him. He dreamed of gazing with Ilio at the moon, which transformed into Horace's crescent-shaped head, and the machine man leapt down from the stars to terrorize them.

It was a cloudy, windy day in Ruska. Coal wished he still had his jacket. He hugged himself tight, rubbing his arms to generate some warmth.

His father, Von, would call days like these "biters." Without fail, every time he'd step outside and get a taste of the bitter winds blowing, he would rub his arms in the same fashion and say, "Yep, today's a biter."

In these small moments, Coal missed his father. They had not always seen eye to eye, and their relationship had been fairly strained, but there was love there.

Mostly, he regretted what he'd missed out on. The days he should have spent with him, the conversations he should have had. Coal had every opportunity in the world to know his father better, but he had not taken them. And now he couldn't. He would have to live with this hollow relationship, this half-vision of the man Von Ereness was. A man whose dreams and joys Coal knew nothing about. Only that he would say "Yep, today's a biter."

Coal then said it out loud. His voice was croaky. "Today's a biter." He felt corny doing it, but admittedly it did make him feel closer to his father. Right now, he would take even the smallest bit of companionship he could get.

His walk through the forest was uneventful. Like past days, he kept close to the river and followed along its winding path while keeping his distance from the bank. There was no wildlife whatsoever in the forest. Not even the distant skittering of an unseen animal.

A thought suddenly popped into his head. *I wonder what White Rose is doing.*

He was referring to the orb weaver spider he had let loose into the forest surrounding Soponunga a couple weeks prior, though for a second he did also wonder about the burlesque dancer from Vinnag after whom the spider was named.

This would be a much more pleasant journey if he was riding spiderback. He began trying out different whistle calls, pretending that one of them would instantly summon White Rose to his side. He toyed with a few different melodies, attempting to pinpoint which one perfectly encapsulated the spider's essence.

It was a good way to pass the time, but many hours of boredom passed after he settled on the right whistle. All he found to eat for lunch was some dirty mushrooms that he sniffed and deemed safe to eat, though he knew nothing about anything and had possibly poisoned himself. An hour after eating, he still felt fine (if not a bit peckish), so they must have been alright.

Coal was about to succumb to his most base desires and let out a frustrated scream when he noticed smoke drifting lazily into the air. Smoke meant one of two things: either there was a forest fire ahead that would maybe kill him, or he was close to Nandara and someone had a fire burning in their fireplace. He did not hear the roar of a wild flame, so he did not think it likely a forest fire was about to consume him. It had to be the town.

He rushed forward breathlessly, and soon the town came into view through the trees.

It was another small riverside town with a great turning waterwheel, similar to the one where they had boarded the riverboat. Cute, quaint buildings with thatched roofs along cobblestone roads. It was possibly the smallest village Coal had ever seen; he wasn't sure if he could even spot an inn anywhere. Just beyond the town, he could see a great deal of farmland and two barns. From his vantage point, he could not make out what any of the crops were, but the farm appeared to be flourishing. With so much of the valley apparently withering away, it was a reassuring sight.

He entered the village and approached the first person he saw, an old, cranky hedgehog who was tending to the flower garden in his front yard.

"Excuse me," said Coal. "Is this Nandara?"

The man looked at him with an irritated, scrunched-up face. His eyebrows were so furrowed they could nearly touch his wiggling snout.

"No," said the man. "This is Yandara. What's Nandara?"

"Oh. I don't know, I guess I was misinformed. A slip of the tongue."

"This ain't Nandara, kid. It's Yandara."

"I understand. Thank you."

"If you's lookin' fer Nandara, then keep lookin'! This ain't it."

"Thank you," Coal said again. He then hurried away before the hedgehog could continue to tell him this town was, in fact, called Yandara. Another failing of Horace's ancient mind. Coal was grateful that the machine was at least accurate about how far away the place was.

He didn't know where to look first. This was the first town he encountered on the river after the point where their boat had crashed, so he believed that if Biror and Jatiri were anywhere, it'd be here. He just hoped that they were waiting for him and had not moved on already.

Not wanting to bother the old hedgehog again, Coal asked the next person he ran into what the village's best restaurant was. She told him, and he headed there. If Biror was going to wait around in this tiny town, it would be at its highest quality restaurant, and it was already nearing dinnertime. Biror's dinnertime, anyway. The boar liked to consume his meals slightly earlier than most people.

Coal entered the modest establishment, a place called Breeze. Appropriate for the biting day they were having. There were maybe fifteen tables set up, most of which were full, much to Coal's surprise. The people of Yandara liked to eat early too, it seemed.

He scanned the tables, looking for—

Jatiri.

His heart lifted at the sight of her. He had always expected Biror would make it out of the ordeal just fine, given the man's resilience and stubbornness. But having not known where Jatiri was at the time of the attack, Coal spent the past few days questioning her fate.

Seeing her face was an incredible relief. Her dark brown fur, the streaks of white running along her jawline. He looked at her horns and noticed the one on the left side of her head was broken, now two or three inches shorter than the other and coming to a jagged edge.

She was sitting near the middle of the restaurant, tapping her index and middle fingers on the table, her extraordinary boredom evident. Staring down at her own hand, she had yet to spot him.

Coal took the chance to surprise her. He swiftly slipped between the chattering tables and seated himself across from her. She looked up and let out an audible gasp.

Without saying anything, she jumped up from her chair, nearly sending it tumbling to the floor. She ran around the table and wrapped her arms around him, enveloping him in a tight hug.

"Hey," he said casually, smirking.

Jatiri pulled away and stared at him, a smile breaking across her face. "When did you get here?" she asked, though with her inflection it sounded more like an exclamation.

"Just now. This was the first place I went. I figured it would be Biror I'd find here, honestly."

"That was a good guess," she said, taking her seat. "He'll be here soon. He's out looking for you, actually. He's been walking around the outskirts of town after dinner, trying to find you."

"After dinner? He already ate? It's early, even for him." Maybe the man had to eat earlier than everyone else no matter where he was. If the citizens of Yandara were eating now, he had to eat an hour earlier.

"Well, we got in a fight today, so he went out searching a bit early," Jatiri said.

"What was the fight about?"

"Nothing, really. Just him, I guess. He's an asshole, and he was annoying me."

"That sounds about right." Coal took a deep breath, smiled, and said, "I'm so glad to see you're okay. I had no idea what happened to you."

"Same here," she said. "Biror was doubtful, but I knew you'd show up eventually. He kept insisting we keep going, but I convinced him to wait it out a few more days."

"Little fox is at bottom of river. We can go," Coal said in his best Biror impression.

Jatiri laughed. "Exactly. Are you okay, though? Do you need me to help you with anything?"

Their group might be lacking Noswen's magical healing, but at least they had Jatiri's medical expertise.

Coal shook his head. "I'm a little banged up, but I'm okay. Nothing serious. Your horn, though…"

She touched a hand to it and sighed. "Yeah. That…did not feel good. When the ship was going down, I got tossed into some rocks and it broke off. I managed to make it onto dry land with some other people, though, and we made our way here. This place is small, but they have an herbalist I was able to get some painkillers from and I'm doing okay now."

"Did everyone survive the wreck?"

Jatiri shrugged. "There were a lot of survivors, I think, but I can't be sure about *everyone*. I was here for a day before Biror and some others showed up. Some people are still here, recovering, but a lot have already left. Another riverboat from the same fleet docked, but none of the people from our boat wanted to get on it after that experience. Not even the employees."

"I won't be riding down the river any time soon either," said Coal. He probably wouldn't have the opportunity to anyway, but still. He wanted his stance known.

They shared their riverboat attack stories. Jatiri had heard most of what Coal had to offer from Biror's retelling, though the man had somehow left out the part about Coal being attached to the monster's massive sucker. Biror had also left out any imagery of the creature at all, leading Jatiri to believe no one had seen it, so she was both astonished and horrified by Coal's description.

As for her side of things, she had been inside the boat when it started tilting, and once alarms started blaring she knew she might have to abandon ship. When she was running to reach either a lounge or deck to see what was transpiring (and jump off into the water if need be), she noticed how many people were panicking, and so she started helping them to the few lifeboats available on the bow terrace while Coal and Biror were on the opposite side of the ship tangling with the notfishes. She was still in the process of assisting people when the monster launched its big attack, the one that broke the boat apart, and that was when Jatiri was flung overboard onto the rocks, along with many other passengers.

274 • Travis M. Riddle

Coal admired her tenacity. She had surely done more good on that ship than he had with his feeble attempts to subdue the monsters.

By the time they finished telling their tales, Biror showed up and expressed no amazement whatsoever at Coal's presence. In fact, it was quite the opposite, and the man seemed annoyed that Coal was here the entire time while he was out traipsing through the woods.

After exchanging curt greetings, Biror simply said, "I have a hunger." Peeking out from his shirt was a bandage wrapped around his shoulder where he'd been bitten by the not-fish.

They ordered some food, and while they waited, Biror needlessly informed Coal that his performance up on the sundeck was pathetic. Coal was well aware of this, and he told the boar so, but Biror still acted as if he was providing him with new information.

Coal then told them how he'd spent his past couple days. The story of Horace enraptured Jatiri, who asked many questions throughout its telling, but once again, Biror was unimpressed.

"It was…a machine, but alive?" Jatiri asked yet again. She still could not believe what he'd said.

Coal nodded. "It had a distinct personality and was responding to me and everything. It was…well, it was partially very cool, but also very scary. I thought the robots that Palace Stingers rode around in were intimidating, but the fact that this thing could think and act on its own was…I don't know, *eerie.*" An involuntary shiver ran down his spine.

"What do you think it was made for?" said Jatiri. Coal didn't know what to say, so she went on. "Every machine is built for a purpose, right? I doubt whoever made it did so just for fun."

"'Whoever made it.' The Dirt King made it. Right?"

"I mean, probably. Very few people have access to the same technology as him. Especially so long ago, if it's truly as old as you said it looks. But why make it?"

Coal shrugged. He genuinely did not have the faintest clue.

"You scared it with water?" Biror suddenly asked. "If it is scared of water, it is not a threat. Water is something that babies are scared of. Not men of might."

"The motherfucker was super tall and super strong and also super out of his mind. I'd like to see you fight him," Coal shot back.

"I would crush him easily. I would not need any water, either. This I can assure you."

Their food arrived shortly and conversation turned from the past to their future plans. Biror was eager to move on, to get this whole chapter of his life behind him. While Lop's insistence on forging ahead was due to his blind devotion to the Dirt King, Biror's was due to sheer desire for efficiency, and they had lost several days already.

"This is not where we were supposed to be," Biror started.

Coal did find it suspicious that he was able to reach the town in the same number of days it was meant to take the much-faster boat to reach it. This must not be the place after all. They had to still be a few days out from wherever they were planning to disembark.

"If we were in the right town, we could easily book passage to the Mudlands. Now this is not possible, and it will take many more days to reach this town. More than many days. I know Yandara, and there are no entrances to the Houndsvein near, so that is not an option to us."

"That's fine by me," said Jatiri around a mouthful of salad. "I can't say I feel too comfortable about the amount of monsters the Houndstooth is pumping out anyway. I'm not sure the Houndsvein is the best travel route anymore." Coal nodded his agreement.

Biror nodded as well. "Yes, it is probably bad down there. Everywhere is bad now. But some are less bad than others. This is my plan: we follow the Snail Tracks."

Coal blinked. He looked to Jatiri, who appeared just as lost as he was.

"What are the Snail Tracks?" he asked, inviting the boar's further frustrations.

"Foolish fox. Dumb of mind and weak of body."

"Fuck off," Coal said, tired of Biror's attitude. Though he hated to admit that the boar was not entirely incorrect in his assessment.

The jab made Biror grin. He said, "It is migration season for the snails. Summer is ending, so they are going north into the Mudlands, where they will hibernate. They will begin their slumber in Deadmonth. It takes them long time to reach there, so they leave now."

Coal knew very little about snails, so this was the first he'd heard about them hibernating. He was not going to admit that out loud, though, and have Biror call him an idiot again.

"There is no bridge nearby, so we will pay someone to take us across the river. On the other side, I will find the Snail Tracks, and we will follow them to the Mudlands. The snails are intelligent beasts. If we follow them, we will reach the

Mudlands faster than going north and booking passage. This is the truth."

"Funny that following snails is our fastest option," said Coal. Jatiri chuckled, but Biror was characteristically unamused.

"The Snail Tracks will lead to the heart of the Mudlands," Biror continued. "The beasts hibernate far past Vuntagonyeo, in a place we call *Opotch Nekriplo*. But they will be going in right direction. If we catch up to them and follow them for a time, I can bring us the rest of the way. I know the Mudlands."

He sounded confident, and Coal believed him.

"This is the plan," Biror then said. It was not up for negotiation or collaboration.

That was fine by them. Neither Coal nor Jatiri put up any argument and they both said that the idea sounded good. Neither of them knew anything about the Mudlands, so if Biror thought this was their best bet, then it probably was.

Jatiri's concern was whether there would be anywhere for them to stop and rest along the Tracks, and Biror said there would not be. The snails migrated through uninhabited areas, far from any towns. They would be spending their nights under the stars. Coal was not looking forward to another week or two of wretched walking.

They agreed to get some good rest that night, then wake in the morning and buy whatever supplies they needed that could be found in this small town. Biror wanted to depart across the river no later than mid-morning. After the recent rains, he did not want to further risk losing the tracks.

With dinner finished and exhaustion overtaking him, Coal was ready for bed even though the moon had yet to rise. Jatiri made fun of him for that, and so he agreed to go on a short walk with her first.

"I am truly sick of walking," he told her as they left the village and entered the surrounding forest.

"So am I," Jatiri laughed. "But it feels kind of good too, doesn't it? Getting your body moving, stretching a bit. Feels healthy!"

"My body feels like it's a broken pot being held together by thick globs of spit. So no, moving it does not feel good."

"Hmm."

"What?"

"It seems like you're confirming Biror's claims that you are weak of body…" she teased.

"Wow. Maybe you can fuck off too!"

She laughed at him. "Don't be rude," she said. "And come on, pick up the pace!"

22

AFTER MORE THAN A full week of walking the Houndspine, they were finally nearing its end. The structure was beginning to ramp downward at a shallow incline, and no longer was sky all that they could see. It was still far off, but up ahead, white stone relented to green grass. At the base of the bridge, where the city ended, was a small park. There was a pond filled with colorful, glittering fishes, a couple vending machines, and equipment for children to play on. Beyond that lay more of Ruska's forests.

If they were to travel west from there, they could eventually reach Noswen's village of Holluwak. Suspended in the trees, connected to the sister villages of Vil's Branch and Baoa. The latter was famous for its spiced rum, which Yurzu had no plans to taste.

They were heading east, though. Toward the Yuluj Mountains. Moonoshk was built in the treetops just like Noswen's triad of villages, but it was a much larger city. It was built by

280 • *Travis M. Riddle*

the woodpeckers, owls, and macaws, who wanted to live close to the mountains.

Something about their culture kept them close to the Yuluj mountain range, but Yurzu was not sure what it was. He was not even particularly well-educated in his own cultural history, let alone that of others. His tribe's historical territory was the Yagos cave system in the northeast, but his parents had never taught him much about it. They were farmers in Toothshadow; what did they need Yagos for?

The plan today was to reach the end of the Houndspine, stay in an inn for one more night, then wake up feeling refreshed and set off into the forest. Lop was vehemently against this plan, but Noswen had not been holding back since their argument outside the bar. She told him that if she had the opportunity to spend one more night in a real bed, she was going to. The fire in her eyes convinced Lop that he should not press the issue.

Yurzu was not holding a grudge like Noswen. He still wholeheartedly disagreed with the orangutan's attitude, but he did not want any tension amongst the group. Their job was hard enough already without introducing friction between them. He had said his piece, made his stance known. Now he just wanted to move on. Preferably without any further conflict.

Zsoz remained unperturbed by anything that had happened. The slime continued riding on Lop's shoulder, making its bizarre stray remarks. Yurzu wasn't sure whether that was the slime's personality and it didn't care about the fight at all, or if it was silently taking Lop's side in the conflict. No matter what, it had made it perfectly clear that its primary concern was bringing the artifacts safely back to the Palace.

Noswen and Yurzu made idle conversation while they walked. Lop was only a few feet ahead, but with the sounds of the crowds on either side of them, the man couldn't hear what they were talking about.

"This part of the story is gonna be the most boring when I tell it to my kits," said Noswen. "Walking across a bridge for a week isn't exactly what you think of when you hear about an epic journey, huh?"

"No," Yurzu chuckled. "Maybe you can exaggerate a bit. You can say that we got into a big fight with that Fetts guy. You threw him across the bar right in the middle of the conversation."

"He crashed through a table, broke a bunch of glasses."

"Got beer all over himself."

"Made Lop cry because I boo-booed his friend."

They both laughed.

"I can't imagine Lop crying," said Yurzu.

"Me neither. He thinks he's too much of a manly man to cry. He'd never admit that he's ever cried before in his life. That's why I have to make him do it in my story."

"He would hate that."

"Exactly."

After a pause, Yurzu said, "I bet I know how to make him cry."

Noswen grinned madly. "Oh, yeah?"

"Yeah. Hide Zsoz, then tell him they went missing."

"Brilliant!" she guffawed. "One question, though. Just to clarify."

"Mm?"

"Is he crying over *Zsoz* being gone, or his precious King's artifacts?"

Yurzu laughed. That was a fair question.

A constant headache dulled Yurzu's mind for the entire week they'd been on the Houndspine, and it was only getting worse as they approached its end. He recalled feeling groggy and disoriented like this the first time they traveled the Houndspine, when they were heading south toward Soponunga. It was at its worst when they had gone through the upcoming park, but he never understood why.

There was one person nearby who stood out to him, though. A weary moose who had to be somewhere in his fifties sat slumped on a bench. His clothes hung loose on his frame, bits of the fabric torn and tattered. Dirt caked his trousers. His breathing was ragged.

As they grew nearer to him, Yurzu's head pounded insistently. Everyone else was passing by the man without a second glance. Maybe Yurzu could only tell what bad shape the man was in due to his innate magic. Or maybe everyone else simply didn't care.

Yurzu poked Noswen, then pointed at the moose.

"What?" she asked.

"He's hurt."

"Didn't you say you've been feeling like a ton of people are hurt or sick all week?"

Yurzu nodded. "That's why I know he's even worse. He's the only person I can feel right now."

Noswen looked at the man, then back to Yurzu. "You wanna stop," she said.

Another nod.

"I don't think there's anything we can do for him."

"But we can try."

She sighed and yelled to Lop, "Hey, hold on a minute."

The orangutan shot a confused look over his shoulder and watched them approach the old moose. He followed behind, with Zsoz swaying gently on his shoulder like a bulbous second head.

Before they reached the man, Lop asked, "Who is this?"

"Don't know," said Noswen. "Yurzu says he's sick."

Lop grunted. The implication was *so what*?

Yurzu could feel the man's sickness as they approached the bench. It wrapped itself around his brain, squeezing. Tightening. The sensation was not as intense as the times he'd first met each of the Blighted, but it was similarly unpleasant.

Despite it being Yurzu's idea, Noswen took the lead. Yurzu liked that about her. "Hi," she said to the old man.

His eyes fluttered open and he breathed out noisily. "Hello," he said.

"Sorry to bother you. We just thought you might need some help. Are you alright?"

The moose smiled but said nothing. His eyelids shuttered closed again. His chest heaved steadily.

"Sir? What's your name?" Noswen asked.

"Barnba," he answered with a sigh.

"I'm Noswen. This is Yurzu, Lop, and Zsoz. Do you need us to help you? Is there somewhere we can help you get to? Any medicine we can fetch?"

Knowing what Noswen was capable of with her magic, it was amusing hearing her speak of medicine. But she could not exactly strut down the street healing people of all their ailments.

"No, I'm okay," said Barnba. "Thank you, though. I'm just tired from my travels, that's all." His hairy face sagged with wrinkles.

There was clearly more at work here than simple fatigue, but Yurzu couldn't say that. He needed to pry without casting suspicion on themselves.

"Where did you come from?" he asked.

It took Barnba a few moments to formulate his thoughts. Every answer was delayed. He said, "I came from Varoosh. My...my daughter lives there. I went to visit her. She just got married last Leafmonth."

"Congratulations," said Noswen before shooting a look at both Yurzu and Lop. They were all thinking the same thing. Varoosh was eastward, in the direction they were headed.

Maybe this man was just sick, but maybe something had happened to him. If they were heading into the same area he'd come from, they needed to be sure something calamitous did not await them.

"I assure you, I'm okay," said Barnba. "I have always had trouble breathing, even in my youth. And in my old age, it has only gotten worse. The doctor gave me some medicine before my trip, but even with that, a single day's travel takes a lot out of me. Especially in the dead forest. I simply need to rest."

That could explain what Yurzu was sensing. In a way, it was a relief to hear this man was already sick and that it probably wasn't caused by something in the forest. But the same question on his mind was on the tip of Noswen's tongue.

"What is the dead forest?" she asked.

Barnba looked at all their faces. His long, brown face was scrunched up, perplexed. "You are not from the east," he said.

They all shook their heads. None of them came from the area, and they had not traveled through it on their journey until now.

"The forest between the Houndspine and the mountains is dying," Barnba told them. "It has been for many months, now. Long before my daughter's marriage."

"Do you know how long, exactly?" Noswen asked.

With Barnba's delay, it was Zsoz who answered. **Reports of the forest's failing condition first started to come in during Cheermonth of last year. When tests were conducted on the soil and the foliage, however, it was estimated that the decay began two years prior. It has been a slow but steady process.**

"Not that slow," said the moose. "It's bad out there. It's not right."

Noswen turned to Lop, the man who had worked in the Palace. "Did you know about this?" she demanded.

The orangutan took a brief moment before answering. "…I have heard rumors," he said.

"Rumors? The slime seemed to have the full fucking rundown of it, but you want me to believe you've only heard rumors?"

Lop struggled to respond.

Noswen turned back to Barnba and placed a hand on his shoulder. "Thank you," she said. "I hope you feel better soon. Sorry to have bothered you."

She gripped the moose's shoulder, and Yurzu could actively feel the severity of his ailment lessen. He didn't know what Noswen was doing, but it was working.

"No bother at all," said Barnba. "I'm feeling better already. I'll be good to go soon."

They then stepped away from the bench and slipped into a narrow alley between buildings, secluding themselves from the crowd.

"What did you do to him?" Yurzu asked.

"Nothing specific. Nothing useful either, probably. Just pushed some good energy into him. Maybe it'll help, maybe not." Then she scowled at Lop. "We're heading into a dead, fucked up forest, and you weren't gonna give us any warning at all? What is wrong with you?"

"I wasn't lying!" Lop said. "I have only heard rumors about the state of the forest. I haven't seen it myself."

"You're allowed to spread rumors. That's what they're for, really."

The Dirt King initiated his rejuvenation plan six months ago.

"Six months," Noswen laughed dryly. "This shit's been going on for two years, and he only started trying to fix it six months ago. Sounds about right."

"Do you think an undertaking that large is easy to plan and deploy?" Lop snarled. "The Dirt King works tirelessly on this and countless other problems throughout the valley. In case you've forgotten, the Houndstooth is leaking infection."

"Yeah, and don't you think that's maybe related to *the forest dying*?" Noswen half-shouted. She lowered her voice and said, "And don't give me that shit about him worrying over the Houndstooth and the artifacts. We're the ones out here risking our lives for them. I'd like to see the Dirt King's ancient, crumbly ass fight whatever Ghoresn turned into."

"Do not call the Dirt King crumbly. He is strong. He leads this country with strength and brilliance."

"Yeah, sure. I bet that thousand-year-old motherfucker is falling apart at the seams."

"He is doing his best to provide for Ruska, just as he has done for thousands of years. The kingdom has never fallen into turmoil before, and it won't now."

There was no point in arguing about the Dirt King. Yurzu asked, "What's wrong with the forest?"

Lop locked eyes with him and sighed. "I do not know for sure," he said. "All I am aware of is that the forest is rotting away and its wildlife is dying."

Noswen glared at Zsoz. "Is that really it?" she asked the slime.

As always, the slime's tone was impassive. **To my knowledge, that is the extent of the damage. Much of the grass has already died, and the trees are rotting. Any wildlife that did not leave died of starvation. This includes a great number of the retno population, as well as the cask population.**

They took a second to process the information.

"That doesn't sound too bad," said Yurzu. "Not for us, I mean," he amended, seeing the look on their faces. "It's terrible for the forest and the animals, of course, but it doesn't sound *dangerous*. Right?"

Noswen had to agree. "Some dead grass isn't gonna kill us," she nodded.

"That is why I did not think it to be a concern," said Lop.

"No, you're still a dipshit for not saying anything," she told him. "You should've said something, if only for us to not be blindsided and distraught and shit when we discover the forest rotting away. We had to hear it from some old guy on a bench." Yurzu nodded his agreement.

Lop frowned. "Okay. You're right. I am sorry."

I am sorry too, Zsoz echoed. **It is difficult for me to know what I am supposed to say to people. I am trying to improve this aspect of myself. This conversation has been enlightening.**

"It's alright," Noswen told the slime. "Glad to hear you're working on yourself," she said dryly.

We should all strive for constant improvement. Contentedness may lead to disinterest, which may lead to ignorance. Ignorance is the seed that sows conflict throughout history and will be what continues to grow in our future if we are careless.

They were all taken aback by the slime's monologue.

"Very elegantly put," said Noswen.

Zsoz remained motionless on the orangutan's shoulder.

When it became obvious it was not going to say anything else, they left the alley and continued toward the northern end of the Houndspine. Toward the dead forest beyond.

23

PAST THE HOUNDSPINE WAS Lakilu Park, and beyond the park was Lakilu Forest. It only took half an hour wading into the forest before they saw signs of decay.

At first, it was small things. The grass was drier. The canopy was thinner, casting more sunlight down on them. Lop was quick to complain about the heat again, missing the canopy's shade.

They saw the signs only because they were expecting them; they would have been easy to miss otherwise. But Yurzu thought that, all things considered, the forest was in okay shape.

Then things got progressively worse. Fast.

The dry grass grew more and more brittle, crunching underfoot. Soon there was no grass at all, only dirt and detritus.

The canopy became entirely devoid of leaves. Naked, crooked branches clawed desperately toward the sun.

Light and heat bore down on them, bouncing back up off the dirt and making them even hotter. Lop complained even more and Noswen told him to quit whining. He grumpily sipped from his flask.

It made sense now why Yurzu's senses had been assaulted the first time he'd passed through Lakilu Park a few months earlier. The entirety of the dead forest nearby must have been muddling his mind.

As they trudged deeper into the forest, the trees darkened from brown to black. Yurzu had never seen anything like it. The sight conjured images of the Houndstooth with its black, jagged, unbreakable bark.

He reached out to one of the trees and gripped a piece of its bark. Unlike the Houndstooth's, it came away easily, like peeling the rind from an orange. He held it in his palm, gazing at it. Then he curled his fingers around it, squeezing, and it turned to mush. He unfurled his fist and stared down at the gloppy mess left behind.

"Gross," Noswen commented, watching the whole thing.

Yurzu flung the black slop onto the ground and wiped the residue on his pant leg. It left behind a faint black streak like a tiger stripe.

Not much time passed before all other vegetation was gone. No bushes, no flowers, nothing but dirt and rotting tree trunks. Every so often a branch would plummet to the earth and splatter in a wet burst.

"This is awful," Noswen muttered. "Two years of this…how have I not heard anything at all about it? It's not like Holluwak is far, in the scheme of things. We're practically neighbors."

"Maybe because no one lives out here," Yurzu suggested. "No one to spread the news, really."

"And it's not exactly a point of pride for the Dirt King," said Lop. Zsoz was on his shoulder again after an unsuccessful experiment with riding on his back, which nearly resulted in Lop toppling over.

"So he's just suppressing the information?"

Lop did not respond.

Yurzu said, "If he let more people know about it, maybe they could work together and figure out a way to help."

Noswen laughed flatly. "That's just it, kid. He doesn't want any outside help, does he? He's gotta solve it all on his own. And with all the wildlife dying left and right, how would it look if his forests start withering away too?"

She had a point. Lop's expression showed his annoyance at her disrespecting the Dirt King yet again, but he kept quiet.

"Well, when we get the artifacts to the Houndstooth, that'll fix everything. Right?" Yurzu said.

Neither of them responded at first. But then Noswen said, "I'm having trouble believing that bringing some old sculptures to the Houndstooth is going to instantly revitalize this whole forest." She jumped at the sudden sound of another branch falling and exploding in a gloppy spray.

"Why not?" asked Yurzu. "It's magic."

The raccoon shrugged. "Maybe you're right."

"He is," Lop chimed in. "The Dirt King knows what he's doing."

"Yeah, clearly," said Noswen, gesturing around at the dead forest. Lop said nothing but huffed in irritation.

Something about the forest suddenly occurred to Yurzu. It cast doubt on his own assertion that saving the Houndstooth would heal the forest.

"I don't sense the infection here," he said.

Noswen looked to him but did not break stride. "What do you mean?"

It was a minute difference, hard to discern, but when Yurzu sensed a regular sickness in someone such as Barnba, it was like a pounding in his head. An insistence. In contrast, when he could feel the Houndstooth's infection within his fellow Blighted or inside a monster like Ghoresn or other blightbeasts, it was more of a sharp pang.

An attack, he thought.

Yurzu had a headache ever since they stepped foot in the forest, and it had only gotten worse as they continued their trek. Sickness was all around them, in every tree. Every inch of soil. Something was wrong with the forest, and it was practically screaming for help in his head.

But he could not feel the Houndstooth's influence. The infection that was leaking out, kept at bay by the colossal tree's bark.

He tried explaining this to them as best he could. They had always been a bit fuzzy on the details of his blight, but he tried to be as clear as possible. When he finished, Lop asked, "What do you think that means, then?"

"Oh, come on," Noswen groaned. "Don't act like a moron. It's obvious what it means. The land isn't sick and dying because of whatever's coming out of the Houndstooth. It's sick and dying all on its own."

Lop's saggy face scrunched up in thought, trying to formulate a response. An explanation. He tugged anxiously at his scraggly beard. "Whatever the case may be, I am confident the Dirt King will deftly handle it. He always does."

"You are so fucking annoying," Noswen told him. "I'm gonna tug that beard off your fuckin' head. Yeah, I'm sure the Dirt King will handle it just as well as he handled the animal issue. He'll outlaw walking on grass so that we don't kill it. Don't worry, it'll all be fine."

"I am sorry if my outlook on life is more optimistic than yours," Lop shot back. "Not all of us are so cynical."

"Yeah, and some of us are just capable of thinking for ourselves."

Yurzu had not wanted his observation to devolve into yet another argument between them. His gut twisted every time they raised their voices at one another.

"Can you please not fight?" he begged. "We're all on the same team. We're all trying to help Ruska. Please don't argue."

He didn't see why every minor disagreement had to lead to a blowout. Things would be so much easier if they all got along. Why didn't they see that? It was dumb to fight.

"Sorry, kid," Noswen apologized.

Lop only grumbled incoherently. It would take something drastic happening for him to ever admit he'd done anything wrong.

The scenery became more grotesque as they progressed through the forest. The soft, black bark was sloughing off tree trunks. It dribbled into dark, viscous puddles at the base of the trees. The trees' inner layer sat exposed, their trunks a faded, yellowish white. It was prettier than the stark blackness of the other trees, but sadder, too. The dark substance pooled around the trunks, bubbling gently and seeping into the ground. The

294 • *Travis M. Riddle*

puddles expanded outward, combining with other puddles, creating a vast, shallow lake of darkness.

Every dull ache in Yurzu's head emanated from those puddles.

"We should avoid that," he told them. A useless remark, as nobody seemed eager to ruin their shoes by wading through the muck. He didn't really think they could get sick from touching the substance, but better to be cautious.

The puddles stretched out across most of the ground as they merged with each other, and they only became harder to sidestep as the group continued. There were narrow paths of dirt to follow, but those became mere splotches of ground every few feet. They leapt from each patch of land to the next, and Zsoz nearly fell from Lop's shoulder. Even those patches disappeared, though, and they had no choice but to walk through it.

Yurzu shuddered as they walked through the muck. The soles of his shoes stuck to the ground and came undone with a wet *smack!* with every step he took.

Noswen continued to express how disgusted and upset she was by the condition of the forest. Neither Yurzu nor Lop could disagree. Zsoz reminded them unnecessarily that the Dirt King had a rejuvenation plan in mind, but Yurzu was coming around to Noswen's side of the issue. It seemed too far gone.

What could the Dirt King realistically do to salvage the forest at this point?

The sound of their shoes puckering on the ground was a point of irritation for all of them. It punctuated every second that passed by, making the time seem to stretch on forever. One minute felt like one hour.

"I was happy about this group because we weren't going to the Mudlands," said Noswen. "I don't know if this is worse. It's equally fucking nasty, at least."

"I seem to recall you telling me to stop complaining," Lop said.

"You're right. So stop complaining about me complaining."

"How are we going to sleep in this?" Yurzu asked.

"Aw, fuck," Noswen sighed. "I hadn't even thought about that yet."

"Me neither," Lop admitted.

I can safely ascend one of the trees and keep myself away from the substance.

"Good for you," said Noswen.

Yes.

They spent the next half hour trying to come to a plan for making camp that night. They did not come to any reasonable solution.

The matter was still up for discussion when Yurzu came to a halt.

Noswen stopped as well and turned to him with an inquisitive look on her face. Lop bumbled forward, blissfully unaware. He only realized something was happening when Zsoz said, **The others have stopped moving.**

When it became clear Yurzu was not going to say anything, Noswen asked, "What's wrong?"

But he was trying to concentrate and did not respond to her question. That sharp, familiar jab was piercing his mind, breaking through the dull roar of the forest's rot.

Something nearby was infected by the Houndstooth.

Something small, it felt like. Small and unmoving.

"I…there's something near here that's sick," he said.

"No shit, kid."

"No, I mean like us. It feels like something the Houndstooth infected."

"Where?"

Yurzu focused on the source of the pain in his head. He thought he pinpointed the general direction of it and pointed with a stubby finger.

"Okay," Noswen nodded. She pointed her thumb the opposite way and said, "Let's go this way, then. Away from the monster."

He could get behind that idea. Lop was the only one amongst them who had any fighting experience. Yurzu still had some leftover powder he could blow on an attacker, but he wanted to avoid physical conflicts in addition to verbal ones.

"No," Lop disagreed. "Our duty is to Ruska. If there is a monster afoot, we should slay it. For the safety of others."

"My duty is not to Ruska," said Noswen. "I'm just a woman on a really shitty vacation."

"You are working for the Dirt King. Your duty is to Ruska." Lop then addressed Yurzu. "Lead us to the beast."

"No!" Noswen objected. "He's just a kid. You can't send him gallivanting into danger like that."

"He is not a kid!" Lop fired back. "He is an adult. He has faced worse before, have you not?"

Yurzu shrugged. He hated that they were fighting yet again, and this time over him. He could make his own decisions.

"I don't think it's very big," he said. "It doesn't feel like it. And I don't sense it moving, either."

"Ahh," said Lop. "It slumbers."

"Or it's just sitting around, not moving, because its brain is so fucked up," Noswen offered.

"In either case, it is excellent news for us. An easy kill, a swift victory for the kingdom. Lead the way, Yurzu."

Yurzu looked at Noswen. A deep scowl etched across her face. Her nose twitched, long whiskers wiggling. She believed he couldn't handle himself. Thought she knew what was best for him.

"It's over here," he said, and began walking.

The others followed close behind. By now, the lower halves of everyone's shoes were caked in a layer of thick grime.

Yurzu girded himself for a fight. If whatever they were nearing really was small, hopefully Lop could stretch his arms out and eliminate it with ease. No need to get himself or Noswen involved.

In the distance, past the copse of stripped trees, was a dim yellow glow.

Lantern light? Yurzu wondered. It didn't make sense, though. *A blightbeast wouldn't be carrying any light, and there are only six of us with the infection in them, so it can't be a person. Unless it's someone like Ghoresn, who got turned into a blightbeast...*

He apprehensively slipped through the trees and laid eyes on the light source. He held his breath.

It was not a blightbeast.

It was a plant.

Small and bulbous, almost like a mushroom, but with a wider stem. Its surface was yellow and it gave off a soothing glow. There were also green pustules protruding all over it.

298 • *Travis M. Riddle*

They were mildly translucent, and Yurzu could see thin liquid resting inside.

It grew out from the pitch black substance on the ground, its pleasant glow reflecting on the shimmering surface of the sludge. It looked surreal with its vibrant glow set against the unyielding darkness.

The plant reminded him of Ghoresn. She had been covered in similar abscesses, and she leaked yellow and green gunk during their battle.

Everyone else was on the same page. "That definitely looks Houndstoothish," said Noswen.

Yurzu was glad that it wasn't a monster, but he was left confused by the thing. He'd never before felt the infection in a plant. Only monsters and people. It was peculiar.

Lop's left arm bubbled and morphed into a sharpened blade. It began to stretch toward the plant, but Noswen yelped at him to stop.

"What's the issue?" he asked. "You didn't want to fight a monster, and we don't have to. This is perfect. We can cut the plant from the earth and do Ruska a service without any danger."

"First of all, you don't know if there's any danger. What if you slice through it and there's something inside that burns your hand? If you even call that a hand still." She pointed at the sword on the end of his elongated limb.

"You're sure this is the source?" Lop then asked Yurzu. His blade still hovered in the air a few feet from the plant. "There is not a creature lying in wait somewhere?"

Yurzu nodded. There was no doubt in his mind that this was the thing infected by the Houndstooth. The pain from the plant grew sharper the closer he came to it, but he was able to wrestle it down like he did with his companions. Its power was not nearly as overbearing as theirs anyway.

"We should...I don't know, investigate it first or something, right?" said Noswen.

"What is the point?" Lop asked. "Our mission is to eliminate this infection from the valley."

"We've never seen anything like this before. That makes it worth not immediately leaping to 'destroy it with reckless abandon.'"

"This is not reckless abandon. This is our mission. Our duty."

"Yeah, yeah, the fucking duty."

Our mission is to retrieve the six artifacts from across Ruska and safely return them to the Houndstooth, said Zsoz.

"Thank you. Exactly," Lop said.

"That didn't sound like total agreement with you," Noswen pointed out. "It actually sounded to me like our slime buddy thinks you should leave it the hell alone and get on with your life."

"Absolutely not! I cannot leave this to spread throughout the forest."

"The forest can't get much worse," Yurzu muttered.

"We must excise the plant," Lop said, ignoring him.

Noswen suppressed a scream. "Just—give it a second, okay?"

She started creeping toward the plant, past Lop's blade-hand that he still held aloft.

"What happened to not knowing if it's dangerous?" the orangutan asked her.

"I'm just looking at it," she said.

"To what end?"

"I don't fucking know!" she snapped. "I'm just trying not to introduce more death into the world, okay? Calm down!"

"*You* are the one shouting at *me*!"

Noswen swore at him and continued forward.

Yurzu's skin tingled with nervous anticipation. Lop seemed to admit defeat by retracting his arm to its normal length and shifting the blade into a hand.

"Careful…" Yurzu whispered, not even loud enough for the raccoon to hear him. Just saying it to say it.

Noswen kneeled down a foot or so away from the glowing plant. She leaned her head closer, cocking it to the side.

"I don't—"

Before she could finish her sentence, the plant began to glow brighter. It shone bright as a lightbulb now, and the pustules all over it began to squirm in ecstasy.

"Get back!" Lop cried.

But she wasn't fast enough. The boils popped, spraying her with their thin green liquid. It splattered onto her face, into her eyes and mouth. It soaked into her fur.

She fell backward, planting her ass in the black tar that had dripped off the trees. She kicked her legs and flailed her arms, scooting away from the plant.

A ragged cough pushed itself from her lungs. She instinctively reached to her throat, rubbing black slime on her fur. She hacked and spit and soon collapsed.

Lop and Yurzu raced toward her body laying prone near the plant. All of its pustules had burst and were now nothing more than saggy, wrinkly bits of flesh dangling pitifully from it.

They hadn't even reached Noswen before she sat up again. Whatever knocked her out, it had only been for a couple seconds. She looked around, dazed. As if she didn't know where she was.

"Wow," she breathed as they crouched beside her.

A sudden bolt of pain shot through Yurzu's brain. He clutched his head and had to stand, taking a few steps back from the woman. The pain was overwhelming. It was like the first time they'd met.

He then realized he was no longer getting any sort of feeling from the plant, though its glow had returned to its original brightness. It wasn't dead, but it was no longer assaulting him.

Its energy had transferred to Noswen.

They looked at each other. Both knew that the other had come to the same conclusion.

"You can feel it, can't you?" Noswen asked him.

He nodded.

Lop tried to catch up. "What are you talking about? Feel what?"

They both ignored him for the moment.

"Do you feel okay?" Yurzu asked. "Do you feel sick or hurt or anything?"

Noswen shook her head. "I feel great. Well, maybe *great* is stretching it, but I feel good. Normal. Not bad at all. I just feel...I don't know how to describe it. It's different."

Lop glared at the plant a few feet away. "I told you we should have destroyed it!"

"No," said Noswen, rising. Blackness dripped from her clothes. All trace of the green liquid was absent from her face. As if she had absorbed it into her. "It...the thing gave me a new power."

Lop stared at her. His expression was as blank as Zsoz's. "What do you mean?"

"I think I was pretty clear," she said. "It gave me another ability. New magic."

"What kind of magic?"

"I don't know. But I can feel it." She nodded toward Yurzu. "He can feel it too."

Lop looked to Yurzu but immediately swung back around to Noswen. "This is nonsense," the man said. "It's impossible."

"I bet you thought possessing any magic at all was impossible until you accidentally turned your hand into a hole for you to fuck."

Yurzu winced.

"Do not be crass," said Lop. "We were born with these abilities. A side effect of the Houndstooth leaking. You cannot get one from a *plant*."

"How can you think you know the rules of this shit?" Noswen demanded. "You don't know how *any* of it works. Neither do I. Maybe it's part of the natural world. How else do you explain a plant springing up in the middle of nowhere with magic in it?"

"You're speaking nonsense," Lop repeated.

"Maybe. But my point stands. We don't know how this shit actually works. All I know is that there's some kind of new magic in me. Yurzu knows it too."

Lop was coming around, but he still had his suspicions. "If what you're saying is true, do you still have your old ability? Can you heal?"

"I think so. We can test it, though. Cut your belly open and we'll see if I can patch it back up."

That would be unwise.

"Thank you, Zsoz," said Lop. To Yurzu, he said, "I trust your ability. It has yet to fail us. If you can detect new magic within her, then I believe you."

"I do," Yurzu confirmed.

The orangutan sighed. He then said, "Well, we still need to get to Moonoshk. And we must figure out how we shall sleep in this decrepit forest. Let us continue." He marched in the direction they were headed before being sidetracked by the plant.

Yurzu and Noswen trailed several feet behind him. The raccoon leaned over to Yurzu and whispered, "You know what I hope my new power is?"

"Hmm?"

"I hope it lets me shut orangutans up. I should give it a shot." She hurried ahead and shouted, "Hey, Lop!"

24

LAKILU FOREST WAS DOING a little better as
they pressed onward. It seemed the worst of the rot
was concentrated in the middle of the forest and currently in the process of spreading outward. A short bit of traveling later, the black gunk was receding and they began to find
healthier trees.

Some were still dying, though. Yurzu poked a tree's bark
with his fingernail and it slipped right in, smooth as slicing
butter. By no means was the forest okay, but at least they were
clear of the worst of it.

Noswen had yet to figure out the new magic power she'd
been gifted a few hours earlier. She tried to turn herself invisible like Jatiri to no avail. There were a few times when she
wanted to stretch her arms out several feet long and slap Lop,
but that didn't work either. She joked that next she would have
to eat someone to see if she got the same power as Coal, which
Lop did not find funny.

The conflict brewing between them was making Yurzu anxious.

None of the Blighted held any preconceived notions about what the group was. Nobody, Yurzu included, believed that they were automatically great pals just because they had been lumped together by destiny. They had a job to do, and that was it. Personalities clashed, and that was fine. But they tried their best to get along, for the most part. Biror had gotten on everybody's nerves, but no one had been outright hostile toward Lop before.

Not until Coal joined the group.

That could be attributed to Lop's own behavior, though, Yurzu conceded. Maybe these frustrations with Lop had always simmered underneath the surface and only now were they boiling over for Noswen. He was being more outspoken, so she was finally lashing out.

At least we're almost done, he thought. *We won't have to bother each other anymore. We can all go home and forget this ever happened.*

That somewhat pained him. He had come to think of Noswen and Coal as friends, but it would make sense if they did not want to speak with him anymore after all this business concluded. It had been a rough few months and they would all be glad to put it behind them.

The canopy was thin in this part of the forest. Above them, the sky was darkening. The moon had begun its ascent, and soon stars would dot the canvas.

"We should find somewhere to set up camp soon," said Lop.

No one disagreed. They were relieved to no longer be surrounded by a lake of melted black bark.

306 • *Travis M. Riddle*

They soon came upon a small pond devoid of any life. No plant fronds stuck out and no fish swam beneath its surface.

Everyone's flasks were at least half-empty, so it would be useful to fill them up again now, as well as in the morning.

"This seems as good a spot as any," Lop declared. He sat himself near the pond's edge and Zsoz crawled down his back onto the dry grass.

Noswen moved past the pond and pressed her thumb against the trees nearby. They were all soft, and she came away with thin black liquid dripping from her finger. "All the trees around here are dying," she said. "Are we sure that water's safe to drink?"

Lop shrugged. "It might be our only choice."

"I'd rather go thirsty than shit my brains out all the way to Moonoshk," said Noswen. "I've been rationing my water just fine."

"How does it seem to you?" Lop asked Yurzu.

He concentrated on the pond water. It was difficult to discern among the vast sickness surrounding them. He couldn't tell whether he was actually picking up on the pond or just the trees near it. It might even be the dirt around it or beneath the surface.

"I'm not sure," he answered.

Lop mulled it over for a second, then said, "It's probably fine." He unscrewed the cap of his flask and was about to fill it up when Noswen interrupted him.

"If you want to be the one to test it, that's fine by me. But if you mix that water with what's already in your flask and it ends up making you sick, then you're screwed until we get out of the forest. I know I'm not sharing mine with you."

It was a fair point. Lop put his flask away and instead morphed his hand into the shape of a shallow cup and dipped it into the water. He filled it to the brim.

"Nasty," Noswen shuddered.

Lop was bringing the sloshing, hairy hand-cup to his lips when a shot rang out.

Behind Lop's head, a tree trunk burst in an explosion of goop. With the softness of the rotting tree, the bullet had gone completely through it and left behind a huge hole. Black ichor dripped inside the gap.

The three of them instinctively ducked down and scurried into the relative safety of the trees. Although clearly the trunks would not protect them from any bullets.

Yurzu was small enough to position himself fully behind a nearby tree trunk, but Lop would not be so lucky. Yurzu glanced around the trunk and saw Zsoz had been left behind near the pond.

"Zsoz! Safeguard yourself!" Lop called to the slime.

The slime's body instantly hardened and it fastened itself to the ground. No one would be able to dislodge the slime from its current position.

Whoever was behind the attack still hadn't made themselves known. Yurzu peered out into the trees but could not spot any bodies.

More gunfire. Two shots in quick succession. One hit a tree to Yurzu's left, while the other pierced the ground somewhere between Lop and Noswen. Multiple shooters.

Another shot. Were there three? Just two?

Yurzu wasn't sure. His heart beat against his small chest. He panted heavily. It felt like his body was being wrapped in fabric, tightening around him, tightening, tightening, he couldn't breathe, couldn't move—

The tree directly beside the one he stood behind burst. Some of the black bark sprayed onto the right side of his face. He wiped it away and tried to think of what he should do.

They know where I am. They must.

He had to move. But if he did they would probably fire on him.

At least in the fight with Ghoresn, he could see the thing that wanted to kill them. And it couldn't kill him from however many feet away.

Yurzu reached out with his blight, trying to sense any of the people that were shooting at them. Maybe if one of them was sick, he could keep track of their movements. But either they were out of his range or were all perfectly healthy.

Once more, Yurzu was useless.

Zsoz sat motionless by the pond and no one was making a move for the slime. They needed to get out of there, but Zsoz and the artifacts could not be left behind.

Suddenly one of Lop's arms lunged forward, stretching across the expanse between him and Zsoz. A few bullets whizzed through the air, but all missed. The man's limb wrapped around Zsoz, who unsolidified and allowed itself to be yanked from the ground.

Another bullet fired as Lop retracted his arm, and the orangutan roared in pain as its pierced his flesh. Zsoz appeared to be uninjured, but blood drops stained the grass.

Lop placed Zsoz on his shoulder and unwound his arm from the slime. He made eye contact with Yurzu and jerked his head back. *Run.* Then he did the same to Noswen.

Just as Yurzu darted from the tree trunk, it exploded in a spray of black, staining the other side of his face. It blended in with the dark shade of his fur, but it felt thick and heavy dripping down the side of him. Now he wanted to jump into the pond to wash himself clean.

He followed the reddish-orange blur of Lop's lumbering form tearing through the woods. Far to his left was Noswen, who would soon overtake Lop with her speed.

Gunfire rang through the air as tree bark burst all around them, littering the forest floor. Lop was leaving behind a thin trail of blood. When he realized this, he slapped a hand to the gunshot wound to stop it. He would need Noswen to heal the wound soon.

This wasn't sustainable. The forest was bare. There was nowhere to hide. Yet they could not get close enough to their pursuers to fight back.

Yurzu rummaged through his mind in an attempt to deduce who might be after them, but he came up short. Maybe a bitter resident of Nitulo, enacting revenge for Ghoresn's death? Or was Fetts after them now for some reason? He didn't know.

More and more rotten trees were decimated as the unknown people tried and failed to shoot them.

Up ahead, Yurzu saw Noswen lose her footing and fall forward, slamming her nose into the hard ground. Lop veered toward her and helped her back up.

As they ran, the gunshots grew less frequent and more inaccurate. Was it possible their pursuers were losing track of them? They were at an advantage, being able to run without bothering to stop and aim. At a certain point, whenever a gunshot did crack through the air and impact with a tree, the bullet did not shoot straight through. The trunks were growing stronger.

Yurzu's legs were already aching, but he knew they could not stop. Not down here, where the people would eventually easily find them.

He then noticed the canopy thickening as the minutes went on. The leaves overhead effectively obscured the branches. This part of the forest was much healthier. Almost normal, even.

His companions ran beside him, and he called to them, "We can hide in the trees!"

Hopefully their attackers could not see them well from this distance. It was a risk, but one they might have to take. They wouldn't be able to run forever, and so far there had been no places to hide on the ground.

Noswen and Lop both glanced upward at the canopy. Lop especially looked displeased with the idea, but they both relented.

The orangutan's arms stretched upward and wrapped around the branches. He hoisted himself and Zsoz into the air, disappearing among the leaves. Yurzu strained to see the man; if even Lop was hidden up there, he and Noswen should be fine. They only had to hope that the shooters could not see them going into the tree.

Noswen climbed up the trunk. Her boots gave her a bit of trouble, but she managed to make it up there with Lop. Yurzu slipped his jacket off and unfurled his wings, easily flapping upward and nestling himself beside them.

They all sat with bated breath. Listening for the shooters.

Several minutes passed before they heard faint footsteps. Someone was finally coming. Yurzu was confident that if the people knew they were up there, they would have already been shot by now. No reason to get so close.

Soon the footsteps were right underneath them, but nobody made a move to get a better look at whoever was down there. The slightest rustle of the leaves would give their position away.

Yurzu glanced down and could not make out anything through the leaves. He caught glimpses of bodies through some gaps, but that was all. He couldn't even be sure how many there were.

His body tensed. He wrapped his fingers around the branches, his nails digging into the mercifully solid bark. His body faintly trembled and he held his breath, not wanting to make a sound.

Suddenly one of them fired their gun, and Yurzu had to stop himself from shrieking in alarm. But they had not fired at them. It was a warning shot straight ahead. Something to scare them.

And it worked.

A couple more shots rang out. They were obviously aiming at nothing, so maybe the group had lost track of them long ago. Yurzu felt some mild relief at that.

But only mild. These were still people with guns searching for them.

"They's gone," said someone below.

The voice was totally unfamiliar to Yurzu. He looked to his companions, who both shrugged. He bit his lower lip with worry and listened more intently. He was determined to figure out who this was, though part of him knew it was hopeless.

There came no response except for a growl, to which the first voice said, "Where they at, then? Cause I don't see 'em. That's fer sure."

Someone laughed, though it sounded more like a tired grunt than anything with real joy in it. Yurzu could not tell who the hollow laugh belonged to.

One of them fired their gun again. Yurzu clapped a hand to his mouth to stop himself from yelping.

The four sat in silence, waiting for the people below to continue their conversation. Or offer any sort of indication as to who they were, why they were in pursuit. But no explanation came, and it was another few seconds before a new voice spoke.

"C'mon," he said.

It was gruff, but too brief for Yurzu to latch onto any characteristics beyond that. The man had barely pushed it out of his mouth, more akin to a growl than a recognizable word.

"Fine," first unknown person groaned.

With that, their footsteps started up again, continuing onward into the forest. Every so often, it was punctuated with random gunfire. Their footfalls eventually receded into silence, and after a while the gunshots could no longer be heard either.

Just to be safe, the group remained in the treetop for another half hour. When they were confident that the shooters were gone and not coming back, they gingerly made their way back down to the ground.

First things first, Noswen inspected Lop's wound. The bullet had gone straight through his arm, leaving behind a nasty, bloody hole in its wake, with bits of skin dangling and muscle exposed inside. Blood rushed from it, but Lop swore he did not feel woozy or weak.

Somehow, Yurzu had forgotten the man even got shot. He couldn't fathom how he'd silently endured it for so long up in the tree.

Noswen placed her index fingers in each side of the hole, cringing as she did so. Lop suppressed a yelp, but had to clamp his eyes shut and bite his lip. Noswen's magic coursed through her and into Lop, and she slowly extracted her fingers from the wound, which filled with a dark red substance pouring from her fingertips. It stuck to the ends of her fingers as she pulled them out of the wound, then suddenly snapped free and smacked into Lop's arm.

"That's that," the raccoon said.

"What a horrific feeling," Lop muttered, examining his arm. The dark red splotch was already lightening to match his skin tone. It would probably take a few days for his hair to grow back.

"If it makes you feel any better, you handled it a lot better than Coal did," she told him with a smirk.

He ignored the remark. Apparently he did not even want to entertain jokes about Coal. He asked, "Do either of you know what happened back there? Who was that?"

Yurzu shook his head.

"No," Noswen replied.

I do not know, Zsoz said as well. **What I know is that we were fired upon by three distinct attackers. Two were using rifles, while one only had a handgun of some sort. The person speaking was a rabbit.**

They all stared at the slime.

"How do you know all that?" Lop asked it.

It was obvious, was it not?

No one was going to dispute the slime's claims. It sounded accurate, as far as they could tell.

"Only one was a rabbit?" Lop clarified.

I know that the person speaking was a rabbit. I do not know about the other two. Perhaps they were the only rabbit, or perhaps all three of them were rabbits. I cannot be sure.

"Well, whatever the case," said Noswen, "it won't do us any good standing around gabbing about it. We should get a move on before they decide to double back."

Lop nodded and said, "I'm no longer sure it's wise to make camp." He looked up at the forest canopy, at the leaves shifting in a light, cool breeze. "It is far from ideal, but we should keep moving. I believe there are some towns on the outskirts of the Lakilu Forest. Is that right, Zsoz?"

I do not know. I am not a repository of information. I am simply a slime. I am a courier of goods. I carry mail and other objects from—

"Yes, okay," Noswen interrupted before the slime dove into a long, winding, unnecessary explanation of its job. "I don't know if there are any towns nearby to stop in, and I'm tired as all hell after that, but I think it might be best to sleep outside after all. Chances are those guys will be seeking out shelter too, so we do not want to end up in the same inn as them. We'll just have to make the best of it out here. How are you feeling?" she asked Yurzu.

"I'm okay," he answered. His heart was still racing, but his headache was fading. Now it was only the dull awareness of the forest's decay and Noswen and Lop's blights. That much he could handle.

Noswen crouched beside Zsoz and examined the slime's innards, making sure all the artifacts were accounted for. She stood and said, "What a shitty day. Let's keep it going."

25

AFTER SEVERAL DAYS OF traveling along the Snail Tracks, the group had still not encountered even a single snail, much to Coal's disappointment. As they continued along the Tracks, the tall, sturdy trees that Coal was used to seeing throughout Ruska gradually gave way to those with wide bases, gnarled trunks, and white wisps hanging from their crooked branches like ghosts in old children's tales. Coal had not seen trees such as these before, but Biror said they were common in the Mudlands.

The ground changed, too. More and more grass faded away, leaving them with nothing but dirt to trod on, until eventually that started to soften and they were constantly plodding through mud.

Coal was thankful for his thick-soled boots, but Jatiri was displeased with this development. Her shoes were a lot flatter and thinner, and she worried that the moistness would soak through to her feet. The first day they started walking through the mud, she made a minor complaint—mostly joking—and Biror said grumpily, "What did you expect when you heard *Mudlands*, hmm?"

Every morning now, Biror woke with flecks of mud on his tusks and Coal made fun of him for it, which never failed to get a rise out of the boar. Biror was such a jerk, it felt good to start the day off by antagonizing him a little.

On their fifth day of travel, Biror announced that they were officially in the Mudlands territory.

Their feet squelched in the mud as they continued deeper into the Mudlands. The canopy here was thinner, with the trees' bizarre wispy branches, so the sun was beating down on them more than it usually did. Now Coal was glad to be missing his jacket. If the rain came back, it'd be a different story, but for now it felt nice.

A backpack was strapped to his back, carrying a few pieces of new clothing and some food. All three of them had to purchase some new supplies back in Yandara, but the selection in the tiny village was pitiful. The only good food they could find that would last them the whole trip without going bad were dried, salted mealworms and some dehydrated vegetable chips. They got some fresh fruit as well, but all of it was eaten within the first two days, and Coal was already sick of the overly-salted worms and chips. His stomach was growling, but the thought of eating that stuff again already was unappealing and he fought against the urge.

Aside from that, the only other things they'd thought to buy were some medical supplies in case Jatiri needed to administer any medicine or tend to wounds. She said the village's selection was bare, but that she was able to obtain the essentials.

They had still not seen a snail, but the creatures' tracks were highly evident on the ground and easy to follow. The tracks were dug into the mud with the slow, steady movement of the giant snails. Each track was roughly five feet wide, and Biror told them the smallest snails were around ten feet tall. The adults, the oldest among them, could be easily twice that size. They were by far the largest creatures in all of Ruska.

The largest *natural* creatures, anyway, taking the enormous blightbeast in the river into account.

Based on what he was seeing, and factoring in some overlap in the tracks, Biror estimated they were currently following a pack of five or six snails.

"The snails, they produce a mucus, you see," Biror said, stooping down to show them some of the remnants left behind. A limp cigarette dangled from his mouth, its tip glowing bright orange. "Back when we start, it was dried up. There is not much left here, but you see it is wet still. It is a sign we are getting close to them. We are catching up." He wiped the gunk off on his trousers. "The mucus is used in the Mudlands for many things. There is much more closer to the snails, and it is simple to scoop up and collect in a jar. Some people mix it with other shit, I do not know what, to make adhesive. But some people can make into delicious jelly for pastries. It is good for many things. What is the word for this?"

"Versatile?" Jatiri suggested.

"Yes. *Versatile.*"

"I'm not sure I'd want to eat something that is also used as glue," said Coal. He was excited to hear they were getting close to the snails, though.

"The mucus is very delicious when a lot of sugar is in it. And it is very sticky in all situations. That is efficiency. That is the way of the boars."

"If you say so."

"I do." He took a drag from his cigarette.

Coal did not know much else about the way of the boars. They were a solitary group of people, with very few of them venturing out of the Mudlands. He'd once heard that boars who did not live in the Mudlands were those exiled for unspeakable crimes, but he wasn't sure if there was any truth to that or if it was some stupid myth perpetuated by people who knew nothing about the boars' culture.

Everyone knew the boars wanted to be left alone, so many steered clear of the Mudlands entirely. Coal wasn't even sure if anyone other than boars lived anywhere within the territory. He hadn't seen much of it yet, but so far it was not a place he was interested in moving to. It was also hard to imagine any macaws or woodpeckers or other flyers wanting to live there.

Maybe that was why Ilio was so fond of his *Masters of Mud* book series; it offered him a glimpse of a world that he was otherwise wholly unfamiliar with.

He grinned, imagining telling Ilio all about this place. The woodpecker would be thrilled. And jealous.

Coal soaked in everything around him. He did not want to miss a single detail. He wanted Ilio to be able to see it vividly. To be there with him. He was eager to tell Ilio about this place.

THE FOLLOWING DAY, COAL asked, "What are the Mudlands like?" He did not expect to get much out of Biror, and conversations with him were generally unpleasant (to put it nicely), but this was his chance to learn about the territory.

"What do you mean, little fox?"

"I don't know. I just don't know anything about it. Do you?" The question was directed toward Jatiri. The saola shook her head.

"There is much to the Mudlands. Your question is foolish."

"Fuck me. Okay, tell me *anything* about the Mudlands. I didn't mean to explain their whole history and all their shit to me. What is Vuntagonyeo like? Is that easier?"

Biror mulled over the question for a few moments. Then he nodded and said, "Vuntagonyeo is the biggest city in the Mudlands. It is smaller than most other cities, though. The boars have nothing to prove. We do not need our buildings to touch the sky. We do not need to stretch out as far as possible. This is not our way."

There were many different cities and villages in the Mudlands, but the territory took up a relatively small portion of land in the valley, so it made sense that they would not have built places that rivaled Vinnag or Muta Par.

"Vuntagonyeo is the home of the boar matriarch, our Mother Pig. She leads our people. Not your Dirt King." With the venom in his voice, Coal was surprised the man did not spit after saying the name. "Mother Pig lives deep within the chambers of Vetch Kaya at the center of the city. She does not leave there, not for anything. Most are not allowed to enter Vetch Kaya. This is sacred place, you understand? But I think to find our hoof, we will have to go in. I have never met Mother Pig before. It will be a great honor for me, and for you, as well."

Coal had never heard of Mother Pig. Apparently neither had Jatiri, because she asked, "Is Mother Pig immortal, like the Dirt King?"

"Of course not," said Biror with a huff. "The legacy of our matriarchs is not poisoned with such foolishness. Our people have always been led by a matriarch, ever since the boars first recede into the Mudlands. The first Mother Pig, her name was lost to time. When she becomes the Mother, her name is erased from all records, and she is simply Mother Pig. When she reach the end of her life, she choose a new Mother. I do not know the process of this. It is a secret kept within Vetch Kaya, far from my eyes and ears. When the new Mother is chosen, her name is lost, and she enters Vetch Kaya. This is how it is. This is how it always has been."

"So as far as you know, your ruler is just chosen through some random process with criteria you have no idea about?" said Coal. "Does that not bother you, not knowing what's looked for in your leader? Having no say?"

"No, foolish fox. It does not bother me. I trust Mother Pig to make the correct choice, for the good of the boars. This is better than one man ruling all of Ruska, yes? Your never-dying Dirt King?"

Coal shrugged. He hadn't put much thought into it before. The Dirt King had always existed, and he always would exist. Like Biror clumsily said: this is how it always has been.

"So once a woman becomes Mother Pig, she's just ushered into Vetch Kaya and stays there for the rest of her life? What does she do in there?" Jatiri asked.

"I have not entered Vetch Kaya. I do not know its happenings. It is not my place to question what Mother Pig does within these walls."

They continued their trek through the swamps with little conversation. Biror was unsurprisingly reluctant to talk to them at all, let alone about the Mudlands.

There was a half hour break to eat lunch, which only took about five minutes since all they had were the mealworms and chips. But everyone seemed in need of a short rest, though Biror would never admit it.

After lunch, they resumed following the trail. Biror led the group while Coal and Jatiri hung back a few feet, chatting about nothing of note.

The mucus remnants in the Snail Tracks were getting thicker. Coal made a point to avoid them, and laughed at Jatiri as she got her foot stuck in a particularly viscous puddle that she hadn't noticed.

"Quiet, fox," said Biror before *shh*ing him. He lowered his voice and said, "Look. We are upon the snails."

Biror pointed ahead, and Coal realized what he had originally thought to be boulders far ahead (*Why would there be boulders here? And why would they be that color?* he then asked himself) were actually the snails' shells.

And the shells were gigantic. There were six of them, as Biror had predicted. Huge, curved, all beautiful shades of brown streaked with yellow, white, and black, depending on the snail. The shells towered above them, at least half the height of most surrounding trees. The snails were currently drawn into their homes.

"They must rest once every hour or so," Biror explained. "The migration, it is tiring for them."

Coal wanted them to emerge from their shells. He wanted to see the beasts in motion.

The trio grew nearer to the collection of massive shells, all huddled near each other. Without hesitating, Coal placed a palm on one of them. It was a darker shade of brown than the others, with ripples of black lines skating across its surface. It was rougher than he expected as he ran his fingertips along it. Warmer, too.

"Are they gonna wake up soon?" he asked.

"I do not know," said Biror.

He then circled around to the front of the pack, then ventured a little farther, never taking his eyes off the ground. When he returned, he looked somewhat irked. More so than he usually did.

"We are still in an unfamiliar area, and I do not see tracks from other snails. We are not yet close to Vuntagonyeo. We will need to wait for these to wake and follow them. Their instincts are better than mine. They will show us the way."

"Won't that take a while? Aren't they pretty slow?" said Jatiri. She was standing a few feet back from the shells, not as interested in them as Coal. Perhaps even disgusted, after getting her foot stuck in their slime.

"Yes," said Biror, "but it is what we must do. Becoming their companions will be slow, but it is better than wandering the Mudlands with no sense of direction. This is the plan."

Coal had no intention of arguing. He was excited to hang out with some snails. They were the only thing that could make this slog through the swamp entertaining.

While they waited for the snails to wake up from their nap, Jatiri and Coal asked Biror more questions about the Mudlands.

"Are you from Vuntagonyeo?" Jatiri wanted to know.

"I am from Dasna. I have been to Vuntagonyeo many times for work. It is better than Dasna."

"Why don't you move there?"

"Not all things are possible," Biror grunted. "Some of us are responsible for more than our own desires. I must care for my brother in Dasna. Kofa is very ill and cannot care for himself. His medicine is very expensive, and I need to be staying in Dasna for him."

"I'm sorry to hear that," said Jatiri.

Coal too felt a pang of sympathy for the boar. It must have been unimaginably hard for him being thrown into jail with the sentence he received, and on top of it knowing he was leaving behind a sick brother.

"Who's with Kofa now?" Jatiri asked, voicing the same question Coal had. If he were the one to ask it, the boar would call him a foolish fox and tell him to shut up. With Jatiri asking, there was the smallest chance he would actually open up to them.

Biror said nothing for a minute, just watching the dozing snails. Coal tried to read the expression on his face, but it was unchanged. He was unwilling to show them even the slightest vulnerability.

"I do not know," Biror finally said. "I was on a job when they arrest me. I was taken to the prison and sentenced and then the ape and bat find me. I have not been home in a long time."

Coal didn't know what to say. He stared at Biror, trying to figure out something comforting he could offer the boar without being utterly rejected. Comfort and consolation were not of interest to the man.

"...I'm sorry," Jatiri said again. "Are we going to be passing Dasna? Could we stop there?"

Biror shook his head, still refusing to look at either of them. "Dasna is in the northern part of the Mudlands. It is past Vuntagonyeo. We will not be near it."

Jatiri appeared as if she was going to say more, her mouth hanging open, but there came a sudden rumbling from behind them, and they looked to see the snails starting to emerge from their shells.

They all stood and took a few steps back, though Biror assured them the creatures were docile and would not mind their presence at all.

Coal grinned goofily as he watched the snails coming out of their shells.

Their bodies were huge and hulking, each of them fifteen or twenty feet long tip to tip. Their soft, gushy bodies were light tan in color, and they looked almost scaly—though *bubbly* might be the better word. There were deep ridges in their skin, and Coal felt an uncontrollable urge to run his fingers through the labyrinthine maze of their flesh. As they extended to their full length, antennae emerged from the tops of their heads, weaving through the air as if in search of something.

The snail whose shell Coal had been touching earlier was the only one that wasn't tan; its skin was rather a murky green, like dirty water. All of their bodies, though, had an identical sheen to them. Eternally wet. Their shells raised higher into the air. Coal loved riding spiderback, but he imagined riding atop a snail's shell would be great fun, too. He gazed in awe of the creatures.

The pack wasted no time in setting off again. Their pace was slow, to be sure, but not quite as lethargic as Coal would have guessed. They were so serene, drifting through the Mudlands without a sound.

"Let us go," Biror said, following after the snails. He was evidently done talking about his brother and the notion of making a stop in Dasna. He was fixed on completing their mission. That would be the most efficient way to return to caring for his brother, after all.

Coal giggled at the sight of the tracks the snails left behind, pushing up tiny mounds of mud on either side of their bodies, the trails shining with fresh mucus. He couldn't wait to tell Ilio about this. The man's novels were sure to be filled with descriptions of snails, and Coal wanted to brag about seeing them in person.

Once more, Biror was leading the trio, though still keeping a respectful distance from the animals they were following. This time, Jatiri was sure to avoid the slime as she walked.

They would be slowly following the snails for quite a while, though, and Coal wanted to keep things interesting. He bent down and scooped up a handful of mucus, cringing at the feel of it in his palm. Some of it dripped between his fingers, plopping into the mud at his feet.

He then reared his arm back and swung, flinging the glob of goo at Jatiri's back. It landed with a wet *splat*!

"What the fuck?" she shouted, the first time Coal had ever heard the woman use such profane language. She spun around on her heel to confront him, but slipped, and planted her ass in the cold, damp mud.

Coal just about died laughing.

26

THE NOVELTY OF THROWING mucus-balls at Jatiri grew old quick, which she was probably thankful for.

They had been following the snail pack for a couple days now. Each night they would make camp near the creatures, already drawn into their shells, and in the morning they'd wake up to find them gone. It was never an issue catching up, however.

Coal liked to stick close to the greener-skinned snail. He felt a kinship with it. He knew what it was like to be one of the few among your kind that looked different. In his head, he named the snail Lub. He did not tell Jatiri this, and he definitely did not tell Biror.

The saola was futilely prying for more information about Biror's brother, a topic which Coal was staying far away from. Biror gave her nothing to work with, refusing to answer any questions she had or accept any of her sympathies. It was easy to see the man regretted revealing what little he already had.

All Biror would talk about was how far into the Mudlands they were, whether or not he recognized anything yet (so far, no), and wanting to eat something besides dry mealworms and salty vegetable chips. With that last part, Coal could agree.

Every time the snails stopped to rest, they would stop too. Biror would take the opportunity to scout ahead, see if they were close enough to Vuntagonyeo for them to break off from the pack without getting lost. Given the lack of any identifying landmarks, Coal had no idea what exactly the man was using to determine their location.

Coal was settling in next to Lub's shell and Biror was preparing to wander away when Coal asked, "Why have we not seen any towns? Or any people at all?" It had been around a week of travel through the territory and the only signs of life they'd seen were the six snails they were traveling with. They hadn't even spotted any other migrating snails.

"I told you already the snails avoid towns," said Biror, still walking away. Then, "The towns of the Mudlands are dense-packed. There is not a lot of solid ground to build on, so a lot of villages are close to each other. We have only been traveling on the outskirts. The snails do not go through the towns. This would be mayhem."

"If we're not gonna be passing by anything, how will you know when we're close enough to the city?"

"I will know, and that is all that matters."

The more vague his answers, the more you could tell Biror was unwilling to speak to you, so Coal dropped it. He was curious about whatever methods the man was using, but not enough to force a conversation out of him.

When Biror was gone, Jatiri said, "We need to go to Dasna."

Coal sighed. "You think?"

She nodded, sitting down next to him and leaning against Lub's black-streaked shell. The tip of her unbroken horn knocked against the snail's shell, but the other came up short. Yesterday, Coal had asked her if it was going to grow back. She said that eventually it would, but it would take many months.

"Biror needs to see his brother. I'm afraid we'll find the worst has happened already, but maybe there was a friend or family member who stepped in to take care of him in Biror's absence. Either way, he needs to get to Dasna to know the situation."

He wasn't the boar's biggest fan, but Coal knew if he were in the man's position, he'd be itching to go check on things. "You're probably right," he admitted. "Like he said, though, it's a ways past Vuntagonyeo. I think it's probably smarter if we grab the jade hoof first and then stop by on our way north to the Houndstooth. Whatever happened with his brother, it happened months ago. A few extra days isn't gonna make a difference."

"Okay," said Jatiri. "That's true."

Coal then said, "Him having a brother is weird, right? Isn't it weird to think that he has any family at all?" Jatiri chuckled, and he went on. "The impression I get of him is that he just popped into existence somewhere, already pissed off about coming into existence."

A couple minutes later, Biror came hurrying back to the group.

330 • Travis M. Riddle

Jatiri stood and said, "We were talking, and we think we should go to Dasna after we get the hoof so that you can check on your brother."

Biror waved her words out of the air and said, "This is fine, whatever you say. We have bigger worries on our plate right now."

Coal pushed himself up off the ground and almost made a joke about being hungry, but not hungry enough for a plate full of worries. He was able to suppress the urge.

"What's going on?" Jatiri asked. It was not common for Biror to be so flustered. Something up ahead had rattled him.

He looked at the resting snails a moment before addressing Jatiri and Coal. "I found two snail carcass. They were torn up pretty bad. There was not much left of the flesh, and even the shells were cracked. One was completely smashed. It takes a lot of strength to do this."

"What's strong enough out here to destroy a snail shell?" Coal asked. Snails were so huge, he did not want to imagine the creature that took them down.

"There is nothing," said Biror, running a hand over his scalp. There was some mud on his tusks again, and even a little on his crooked snout, but Coal did not think it was the appropriate time to crack a joke about it. Biror continued, "That is one of the reasons why they hibernate in the Mudlands. The conditions are better here for them, yes, but also there are no predators out searching for them."

"So you think it's a blightbeast," Coal said.

Biror nodded gravely. "It is all that makes sense." He looked at the sleeping snails again and said, "We need to kill whatever it is. Not only for our own safety, but for theirs. They are our guides to Vuntagonyeo. Come, look."

They followed Biror out to where he had found the dead snails.

The scene was more unsettling than Coal was anticipating. To see such big, majestic creatures struck down filled him with both sadness and fear.

The nearest was half-eaten. Its mushy corpse was stretched out, with chunks bitten out of its side. Bits of pale, stringy flesh trailed out from the opening in its shell, with other pieces scattered around, sinking into the mud. There was a withering antenna near Coal's feet. The shell was cracked and chipped in several places, but it was left mostly intact.

Beyond that one, though, the other snail had been obliterated by whatever monster preyed upon them.

For starters, the shell was no longer a shell. It lay shattered in the mud, broken into a handful of large pieces and a ton of tiny shards. All that remained of the snail was globs of tan jelly either stuck to some of the bits of shell or tossed around in the mud. There was no discernible body left.

"How can we kill something that did this?" Jatiri asked softly. "It has to be something huge and powerful, right? Do we even stand a chance?"

"It does not matter. It must be done," Biror declared.

"You don't even have a gun anymore," Coal pointed out. "It sank with the ship."

"I do not need a gun to kill, little fox. My hands are up to the task, I tell you true."

"It seems like a very big task for some very small hands."

"My hands are not small."

"Comparatively speaking, I mean. I don't think you're gonna be able to punch this thing to death."

"We will see."

The boar was too confident in his own abilities. Jatiri wasn't a fighter, and Coal wasn't much of one either. He would feel a lot better about killing this monster if he had a firearm.

Biror kneeled down close to the ground and inspected the area around the two carcasses. "The tracks are fresh," he said after a minute of silence. "It might be near. We will go to it."

"Wait," Coal objected. "I don't think any of us is ready for a fight."

"Ready or not, little fox, the fight comes. Better to catch it unaware than to be caught ourselves, no? We shall kill it while our snails rest, and then we will continue."

"That's a very optimistic goal," said Jatiri.

"Yes," Biror nodded, not detecting any of her trepidation.

He then stood and set off, following the monster's tracks. Once again, Coal was not going to question him about his methods. Jatiri and Coal exchanged a nervous look, then hurried after him.

"I don't understand what it is we're actually going to do," said Coal.

"Shut the fuck up," Biror responded, his voice a harsh whisper. "It will hear."

Coal rolled his eyes and continued following.

It was only a few minutes before they heard a crunching noise up ahead. Biror hushed them again, even though nobody was talking, and a dazzling array of colors came into view amongst the dangling wisps of trees in the distance.

Whatever it was, they had found it. As was customary before every fight, Coal's stomach was knotting and he felt bile rising in his throat. He was never going to grow accustomed to this lifestyle.

They crept slowly toward the monster, which was still producing sounds that Coal didn't understand. It was like glass breaking.

The creature then came into clearer focus.

It was a blighted snail.

The rainbow of colors was its shell, which now had spiky protrusions sticking out all over and was a swirling blend of green, yellow, black, pink, and blue. It would be beautiful if the beast it was attached to wasn't so horrifying.

It had the same gushy body with the bubbly skin texture of a normal snail, but its skin was pitch black. Rather than two antennae, its head was covered in a mass of them, varying in length, all tangled up in each other, some hanging down off the side. A mouth hung open dumbly, drool dribbling from its maw, exposing six large, sharp fangs, but no other teeth. The other end of its body curved into a spiked tail, which lashed angrily in the air and dripped with mucus. Unlike a normal snail, it stood on two meaty legs, thick as tree trunks.

It was stomping on pieces of shell. Another dead snail. It was pounding its feet into the carcass, breaking apart the shell and beating the poor creature's flesh into pulp.

This is bad, Coal thought.

"This is bad," he said aloud, so that everyone else would know.

"It is distracted," said Biror, balling his fists. "We kill it now."

He did not wait for agreement from the others, nor wait to formulate a plan. Instead, he charged forward at the blightsnail.

"Fuck," Coal whispered, running after him.

Their feet slapped against the mud as they ran, kicking up the brown muck with every quickening step. The blightsnail had a shitload of eyes, but Coal wondered if it had any ears with which to hear their loud approach.

He couldn't collaborate with Biror, but Coal tried to concoct a plan in his head as they ran.

Is he gonna try to punch it until it dies? Can we tear off all the eyes? Would that kill it? Do we have to remove the shell? Is there a weak spot inside the shell?

He knew nothing about the anatomy of snails, and his fists were not killing machines like Biror's. Nothing seemed feasible.

At least it only has six teeth, he thought in an effort to comfort himself. It almost worked.

Biror leapt onto the swinging tail, grabbing the attention of the blightsnail. It turned, flinging Biror around with it, of course, and only saw Coal standing there stupidly.

The blightsnail roared—or, at least, it opened its mouth as if roaring, but no sound came out. A few seconds later, as its mouth was already closing, a sudden earsplitting shriek cut through the air, debilitating Coal. He dropped to his knees, sinking into the mud, grasping at his pointed ears.

There was a dull ringing in his head as he stared down at his knees. He could no longer hear anything.

He could sense a vibration in the ground, but he looked up too late to see that the monster was running toward him. He had been unable to hear its footfalls. It headbutted him and he violently flew backward toward Jatiri, though he had no clue where the saola had disappeared to. Hopefully she was well-hidden.

The blightsnail was still chasing after him, so he stood shakily to his feet and tried to compose himself.

He was never going to catch a break. He was always going to be tired, and his body was always going to ache. It was high time he accepted that.

Biror was still swinging around on the creature's lashing tail, scooting his way up toward the long, curved spikes on its end.

With a gun, Coal was still mostly useless, so without one he was less than useless. He was a liability, really. The best way he could ever contribute to a brawl was as a distraction while more competent people beat down their attackers.

He assumed Biror had a plan in mind, so he would do his best to keep the monster occupied while it was carried out.

Coal rushed to the left, clearing out of the blightsnail's path. The monster ran forcefully into a tree, but all it took was a few stumbling steps backward and a shake of the head to recover from the blow.

It turned to face Coal, ignoring whatever was happening on its tail. Coal was already running in the opposite direction, aiming for the mess it had made with the other snail's corpse.

He couldn't arm himself with a gun or even a dagger, but the sharp edge of a broken shell might be the next best thing. By the time he was close enough to the monster to attack, it might already be too late, but at least it'd give him a fighting chance. No matter how small the chance.

Coal came to a sliding stop at the carcass, digging through the broken bits of shell until he found a piece roughly the length of his arm with a nasty, jagged tip. It could undoubtedly do some damage.

And soon he'd have the chance to try it out.

The blightsnail was already almost upon him. For only having two stubby legs, the bastard was fast.

He ducked out of its way again. Apparently the thing only had one move, which was to headbutt. Coal could imagine it knocking over an unsuspecting snail then proceeding to kick and beat at it while it lay helplessly on its side, smashing apart its shell and body.

"Fuck you," he muttered, holding out his shell blade as the blightsnail passed.

It sliced through the monster's leg with ease, but then it whacked against the shell. The force with which it hit the shell knocked it from Coal's hands and it fell splattering into the mud. Coal scrambled to retrieve it before the creature could launch another attack.

By now, Biror had made his way to the tip of its tail and had grabbed hold of one of the spikes. His whole arm shook fiercely, muscles bulging, as he pulled on the spike. It then broke free of the blightsnail's tail, and Biror let himself fall to the muddy ground. He held the makeshift weapon aloft with pride.

"Mine was easier to get," Coal said, holding up his piece of shell.

"Go fuck yourself, I think," said Biror. Coal could just barely make out the words, with the world still mostly muffled in his ears.

He watched Biror rush toward the blightsnail, weapon in hand. The boar grinned manically, eager for bloodshed.

Coal ran too, trailing shortly behind Biror. Those were his two roles in a fight: distraction and backup.

The blightsnail seemed mostly unbothered by the cut in its leg and the spike missing from its tail. Green ooze pumped from the fresh, deep wound. The antennae atop its head were now thrashing as wildly as its tail, getting even more wrapped up in each other. It was a wonder the thing could keep track of the two of them.

Biror reached the beast and it snapped at him, which he deftly dodged, impaling his spike right beside the wound Coal had created before swiftly extracting it again.

The blightsnail loosed another bizarre, delayed roar, ruining Coal's hearing again just as it was getting back to normal. He screamed in pain. Being so much closer to it this time, he nearly passed out. He managed to stay on his two feet, but his legs were wobbly.

Coal saw Biror's mouth open wide in a battle cry, but he could not hear it in the slightest. He knew the boar's shoes were smacking wetly in the mud, but he couldn't hear that, either. Just a dizzying ringing in his head. Biror seemed unmoved by the aural assault.

The creature launched its body to the side, slamming its colorful shell into Biror and sending him flying into the muck. It then refocused on Coal and charged ahead.

Coal was still shaky from the beast's roar, his head pounding and his vision swimming. Before he knew it, the blightsnail was upon him. This time he did not have the capacity to dodge in time and was knocked backward by the thing's massive head.

He collapsed into the mud, sending up a spray of brown. There was a sudden white hot, blinding pain in his left leg. Stars burst in his vision and he smacked his head back down into the dirt, arching his back, hitting his fists into the ground.

It took a few seconds, but when he finally mustered the strength to look down at his leg, he saw—

Well, it was what he didn't see.

His left foot was gone.

The blightsnail before him wasn't even chewing on it, and it wasn't spat out anywhere nearby. It had swallowed the appendage whole.

Blood gushed from the wound, mixing into the dark mud. Coal screamed at the sight, but he couldn't even hear himself. The scream was just a pounding in his head, a tightening in his chest.

Astonishingly, Biror then hopped up onto the monster, using the wound Coal had made as a foothold. Coal shuddered looking at the man's foot disappear into the blightsnail's leg, being caked in green gunk. His vision began to blur as he watched the spectacle.

Biror looked over his shoulder and yelled something, grinning widely, but Coal could not hear it. Based on the expression on Biror's face, he pretended the man had said, "I'm having a wonderful time!"

He could not relate.

The blightsnail was utterly uninterested in Coal now and was trying to shake off this new parasite clinging to its body. The two were colorful blurs in Coal's weakening vision, growing more and more amorphous as the seconds ticked by. For a second, it looked like the Biror blob was going to be flung aside, but he held on tight to the lip of the snail blob's shell and was not bucked off.

Coal's hearing was gradually returning, and he could faintly hear Biror screaming like a madman in Ronog as he started stabbing the spike up and underneath the blightsnail's colorful shell.

They both had the same idea. Maybe there was a weak spot under there after all. Coal distantly felt accomplished, even though he was not accomplishing anything. He lay in the mud, bleeding out, too hurt to do anything and unknowing of what needed to be done anyway.

He blinked, trying to clear his vision, but it didn't work. His breathing was becoming ragged, and the tightness in his chest was not lessening at all. He sat on the ground, wheezing, clutching a dirty hand to his chest.

Another shriek, and Coal's hearing was gone again.

He could barely make out what was going on, but he thought he saw the blightsnail tripping over itself, disoriented by the pain Biror was inflicting on it. It fell onto its side, mouth opening and closing like it was gasping for air.

The whitish blob that was Biror climbed down off the creature and yelled something incoherent at Coal.

Coal pointed to his ears and shrugged before hacking up a cough. He didn't know if the boar had even noticed his severe lack of foot.

The boar surged toward him, coming into startling focus as he neared Coal, grabbing the shell blade from his hands and racing back to the blightsnail. He then got to work slicing into the monster's neck, sliding the shard back and forth like a craftsman sawing wood. The blightsnail's green and yellow ichor mixed with blood spurted from the gash, spraying onto Biror's face, but he did not care. Its legs kicked helplessly and its tail bashed against the ground, showering their surroundings with specks of mud.

Coal stared wide-eyed at the display. Sharp pain and heat coursed through his leg. His eyelids fluttered, and he had to force himself to remain conscious. He wasn't sure how much longer he would last, though. He looked down at the stump spurting blood and wanted to scream, if only he'd had enough power in his voice.

Biror was halfway through the thing's neck when its movements finally slowed, then ceased. Regardless, he kept going.

Coal's hearing returned before Biror was finished, and he winced at the squishy, wet sound of the sharp shell cutting through the monster's meaty flesh.

After another minute or two, the blightsnail's head separated from its body. Biror stood and gave it a solid kick, though it was too heavy to do much more than lazily roll over an inch or two.

Biror turned to face Coal, panting heavily. He walked over to where Coal lay, and as he shifted from a blob into a person, Coal saw the smirk on his face. In addition to the previous mud, his tusks were now dripping with the blightsnail's luminescent blood. Biror dropped the shell onto the ground.

"You see now what my hands can do," he said. Then, realizing, "You have no foot, little fox. What happened to you?"

Coal stared wide-eyed at the man looming over him. "The fucking snail ate it!" he shouted, slurring half his words. "What, you think I *misplaced* it?"

"Do not cry, little fox. Is okay."

Out from behind a tree many feet away, Jatiri called out, "Is it dead?"

"It is dead!" Biror confirmed. "My hands throttled the life from its pathetic body."

"Doesn't count," Coal said. He wanted to give Biror a hard time about using tools, but he was too exhausted. His breathing was rapid and he could hardly form words.

Jatiri made her way over to them, saying, "I'm sorry. I just…I couldn't do anything. And when it screamed, I just—"

Then she saw Coal's stump and shrieked. She rushed to his side, kneeling down into the mud and inspecting the wound. "Hold his leg up," she instructed Biror.

The boar grunted but did as he was told. He elevated Coal's leg into the air with a gasp of pain from Coal.

Coal was thankful that he couldn't see how much the stump was actually bleeding, but he risked a glance down, and the sight of his foot being gone made him dizzy. Intense pain coursed through his leg and his vision blackened for a second. He placed his head back down in the mud and stared into the sky, grateful that Jatiri was there to take care of things.

Using their water supply, she quickly cleaned the wound and then grabbed a clean shirt from her pack. She wrapped it tightly around his leg just above the ankle. The pressure somewhat pained him, but it was a strange relief, as well. Coal fought against the heavy blanket of sleepiness draping itself over him.

"Keep his leg up," Jatiri told Biror. Her voice sounded like it was miles away. She scooted over to Coal's head and asked him something, but he couldn't hear her. He mumbled nonsense, and she said, "How are you feeling?"

"Bad," he managed to say.

"Do you feel like you're going to pass out?"

He nodded his head. It sloshed in the mud.

She looked him over for a second then said, "Being able to answer questions is good. So is being conscious. You're probably going into shock, though. Try to stay awake." She glanced back down at the leg and whispered, "Shit." She said something else, something about bleeding, maybe, but the words were hard for Coal to decipher. What he made out was, "...fully stops, we'll cover it up. I have tinctures I can use to sterilize some cloth. That should stave off any infection." She swiveled her head, looking around the area. "I don't see it anywhere..." she muttered.

"Should we burn the wound?" asked Biror, still holding Coal's leg aloft. "You can use my lighter. Burn away the bad."

"No, I don't think we'll need to cauterize it. The bleeding has already slowed a bit. And your lighter wouldn't be enough, anyway."

The trio sat there, waiting for Coal's bleeding to slow to a stop. Jatiri was constantly talking to him, trying to engage with him to keep him conscious. After a while, the bleeding had mostly stopped, and they decided they should get back to their pack of snails in case the creatures had woken up and continued their pilgrimage.

With all the blood loss, though, Coal was in no condition to move on his own. His head was still swimming and he couldn't make out anything more than a few feet ahead of him. One positive was that his breathing had slowed back to a normal pace, but still he was lightheaded and beyond tired.

Biror and Jatiri hoisted Coal to his feet (foot?), making him even more lightheaded. They carried him over to the snails, which were still asleep. Thankfully all six were still accounted for.

Jatiri then further patched them both up. She administered a powdered concoction for them to place on their tongues that she said should help ease their aches. It wouldn't heal anything, but it would make the pain more tolerable. Coal thanked her profusely, though he couldn't be sure any of his words were intelligible. The medicine did dull the pain in his leg somewhat, but there was still heat around his ankle. She gave him some water and he gulped it down greedily.

She proceeded to sterilize some cloth and wrap it around his stump. While she worked, Coal slumped down on the ground next to Lub. Deep breath in, deep breath out. Trying not to fixate on the fact that he no longer had his left foot.

Even Biror finally admitted that he needed to take a few minutes to rest, and the man quickly dozed off with a cigarette in his mouth, leaning his head against one of the gently rocking shells.

Coal closed his eyes, feeling Jatiri messing with his leg but unable to keep himself awake for even a second longer. Darkness came swiftly, and he was rocked to sleep by the snail's breathing.

27

COAL ALREADY THOUGHT ALL the walking
he had to do was the worst thing in the world, and
now that sentiment was doubled by the loss of his
foot. Tripled. No, quadrupled, at the very least.

Thankfully, Jatiri was a good doctor. He would have maybe
preferred Noswen's more instantaneous and magical wound
care, but Jatiri was doing a fine job keeping him healthy. And,
on second thought, he did not want to experience re-growing
a foot or whatever it is Noswen would have done to him.

For the rest of their trek through the Mudlands, Jatiri routinely checked his wound while the snails stopped to rest. On
occasion, she would swap out the old dressing with some fresh
bandages. During the process she would rub some sort of clear
gel or paste on the stump, which she explained was supposed
to ease the pain and prevent infection. Coal did not know what
the substance was, and he did not particularly care, as long as
it worked.

It also quickly became apparent that it was unsustainable having him lean on someone to walk the entire rest of the way to Vuntagonyeo, and they could not get him up onto one of the snails' shells for a free ride, so they had to improvise. Biror retrieved some thick, durable branches from surrounding trees and fashioned them into makeshift crutches. They dug uncomfortably into Coal's armpits, but they did make getting around easier.

The pain in his leg receded with each passing day. Jatiri's gel was working wonders. Perhaps it was just as good as any magic Noswen had in her arsenal.

Coal felt more useless than ever before, though. He was a burden. He told himself that this was not merely his opinion; it was fact. He could see it in Biror's face. In Jatiri's, too, though she hid it well, and she would never admit it out loud. Most likely not even to herself, either, but Coal could tell. It was in her movements as she unwrapped his bandages. In the sighs, both heavy and light.

That was the first of three things that kept him up at night. Knowing that he was actively making others' lives harder simply by being there. By existing. If he left, life would be easier for them. Life would be considerably more difficult for him, but that was neither here nor there.

The second thing was the pain. While it was improving every day, it still nagged at him. Especially at night, when there was nothing else to focus on but his missing foot. It was a heat traveling up his left leg, making him restless and uncomfortable. There was also an itch at the stump, one that Jatiri insisted he could not scratch, and it drove him mad.

The final thing was Ilio. Thoughts of Ilio had previously kept him up on many nights of this journey, but for much more enjoyable reasons. Now, however, he could not help beating himself up over how Ilio might react to seeing his injury. Would he be repulsed? Would he not want to touch him ever again? Coal knew he was being unreasonable, that Ilio was a kind man (the kindest he'd ever met, probably) and would not reject him over something so shallow. But their relationship—if it could be called that—was so new, so fragile, Coal could not wrangle that doubt and insecurity.

ONE DAY WHILE JATIRI was inspecting his wound, Coal said, "You know what might be the worst part of this?"

"What?" she asked, unwrapping the bandages. He did not know how many medical supplies she had left in her bag, but he could not imagine there were a lot. Yandara had not exactly been bountiful.

"Buying shoes is gonna be so annoying. You know? I'm gonna be forced to buy a pair and just throw one away. A complete waste of money."

"Maybe you can haggle," Jatiri grinned. "Get them to bring the price down, only buy the shoe for your right foot."

"Not a chance. Only the dumbest businessmen would agree to that. What would they do with the other shoe they'd end up with? Pray that some idiot with only a left foot wanders in after I leave? What are the chances of that?"

"Maybe you can manufacture such a scenario. Wherever you decide to live, orchestrate some accident—and it *does* need to look like an accident—that results in some other townsperson losing their foot." Her inspection done and gel applied, she began to rewrap his stump. "You'll have to be very careful to make sure they lose the opposite one that you lost, and also that they have the same size feet, but I think you could pull it off. You're resourceful."

"I think you're overestimating my resourcefulness. I couldn't even manage to keep my foot attached to my body, as you may recall."

"That's true. Your alternative is seeking out a town that already has a resident who's missing their right foot, who's experiencing the same shoe-buying woes as you. You two can make an arrangement, split the cost of a pair. As long as they have the same size feet."

"Now you're making sense!"

A COUPLE DAYS LATER, when he was already in a sour mood, one of Coal's crutches got stuck in the mud while he was walking and he plummeted face-first into the wet muck.

He rolled onto his back, spit mud out of his mouth, and yelled, *"Fuck!"* He let go of the branches and slammed his fists on the ground, splashing more mud onto himself.

Jatiri stood by and let him release his anger, but Biror felt the need to comment.

"Calm yourself, little fox," he said.

"Fuck yourself, big boar," Coal replied.

"Tantrums are for the little babies."

"Biror—" Jatiri started.

"Not helpful," Coal spat. "I'm fucking sick of these fucking *things.*" He smacked the branches in the mud for emphasis on the last word.

Despite how much he'd improved over the past couple days, sometimes he still screwed up with the crutches and the frustration overwhelmed him. He knew deep down that he'd be alright, that he was doing okay, but he just needed to vent.

Biror took a step toward him and extended a hand to pull him up. Coal took a deep breath, then reached his hand out and accepted the man's help.

"We are nearing the city," Biror said as Coal propped himself up on the muddied branches. "Vuntagonyeo has the best clayworkers in the kingdom. I tell you true. Your troubles will be soon behind you."

Coal did not follow. "What, am I gonna buy a vase and put some pretty flowers in it to cheer myself up?"

Biror shook his head and clucked his tongue. "Once again, you reveal yourself as stupid. In the Mudlands, our claymakers do not only make *vase* and *pot* and *bowl*. We treat the clay with respect. We use it for many things. They will make you a foot from it, so do not worry."

Coal laughed. Jatiri appeared unsure whether Biror was attempting to make a joke or not.

"You want me to walk around with a clay foot?"

The boar nodded. "Mudlands clay is strong. Stronger than the rest of the world. It will not break. We do not have need for the Dirt King's…what is the word? Mechanicals? I do not know. But the boars, we get along fine with our clay limbs."

"Easy to say for someone who still has all their appendages."

"Yes, because I am not idiot who gets my foot bitten off by a snail."

"Fuck you."

"Fuck you. You will have clay foot."

JATIRI UNAVOIDABLY NOTICED HOW much Coal was struggling with his new situation. The crutches were working okay, but they hurt his armpits and were often difficult to dislodge from the mud. He winced with every step, from either the branches digging into his body or the hot pain in his leg. Or both.

While they were waiting for the snail pack to rest, she approached him and kneeled down to say, "I know the past few days have been rough for you."

He didn't have a response. Her statement was obvious. He was feeling too irritable after the day's walk to say anything.

So she went on. "I figure that if you're struggling to learn something, I will too." She offered him a smile. "I don't want you to feel like you're alone in this."

Coal tried to smile back. "Thanks," he said. "What are you gonna do? Hop around like you lost a foot too?"

She laughed and shook her head. "No. Something a bit more useful. I think it's about time I try to get a handle on this invisibility thing of mine."

His brows perked up at that. "Oh, yeah?" Back in Sadatso, she had been able to make her hands and forearms disappear, but that was the extent of her power.

"Yeah. What use am I if I can only make my fingers vanish, right? What if we need to covertly infiltrate some place in Vuntagonyeo to steal the jade hoof?"

"You cannot steal from the boars," Biror chimed in. "They will crush you."

Jatiri rolled her eyes at the boar completely missing her joke. To Coal, she said, "Anyway, how's that sound? Want to help me out?"

"I don't know how I could, but sure," he replied.

"Alright. Let's head over here, so we don't bother Biror more." She stood and started walking away from the pack of snails.

Coal struggled to his feet, placing his makeshift crutches underneath his armpits and following after her. As they wandered away, Biror of course lit up a cigarette.

While he walked, Coal was extra careful about his placement of the branches in the mud. Trying to not be too hasty. If he was cautious and took his time, he could ensure they wouldn't get stuck, and he could walk smoothly. He needed to be patient. That was all.

Jatiri came to a stop a few feet ahead and turned around, watching and waiting for him with a kind smile. When he reached her, she said, "Okay. Here we go."

She held up her hands, exactly as she had the first time she demonstrated her power to him. He looked at the blue-inked tattoo on her palm, the fenté bowl.

"What does fenté taste like?" he asked as her fingertips began to shimmer out of view.

Her palm was half gone when she said, "It's very syrupy. Both the taste and texture. It's thick and sticky and sweet. It really coats the throat, in a pleasant way."

"I'd never even heard of it before you told me about your tattoo."

"It's not really made outside of saola communities, and those communities are shrinking. That's why our people put such an emphasis on community and heritage. We have to constantly keep our traditions alive so that they're not lost forever. My tattoo reminds me of that." As she said it, the tattoo disappeared.

"That sounds...kind of exhausting," Coal said. He hoped it wasn't offensive.

"It kind of is," Jatiri confessed. "But it's important. If we don't do it, then that's the end. Our traditions are as much a part of us and our history as anything else. We don't want to lose ourselves."

Her forearms were now invisible, and her brow furrowed in concentration.

Coal wanted to coach her somehow, but this was as foreign to him as it was to her. Probably even more so. He couldn't imagine what it felt like to turn yourself invisible.

Then her upper right arm started to disappear too. Coal almost yelped in celebration, but kept quiet so she could focus. The other arm followed suit, and soon she appeared to have no arms at all.

But they reappeared in an instant and she let out a gasp, panting as she doubled over.

"You okay?" Coal asked her.

"Yeah," she said. "It's just super tiring, is all. I don't know how I'm supposed to do that to my entire body at once, if I can barely manage my arms."

Coal took a tentative step forward. "What's it like?"

Still panting, she looked up at him. "It's...hmm. It's weird. You have to basically think about the body part not existing anymore. Truly believe it. Believe that it's not there, yet know that it is. Does that make sense? I feel like it doesn't."

Coal could not totally follow, but he nodded. "How did you even discover you could do this?" he asked.

"I first did it when I was a kid," she said. "I was really young, out playing by myself while my parents worked. I was at a small lake near Kilutsk, one that is admittedly quite murky. I was just messing around, putting my hands in the water, and when I did it I started to think about my hands being gone. I couldn't see them under the water, so I started to think that they didn't exist. Just using my imagination. But then when I yanked them out, they actually were gone."

"Shit. That must've scared the hell out of you."

"Oh, yeah, I screamed at the top of my lungs. They reappeared instantly, but it was the scariest thing to ever happen to me. I didn't go back to that lake for a month."

"But then you got curious, I'm guessing."

She giggled and nodded. "I wondered if the lake had made them disappear. So I went back and put them under, but nothing happened. It was a few months of messing around before it finally happened again, and I somehow made the connection. Then I was able to do it whenever I wanted, which was not very often."

"Have you ever tried it on something other than your hands?" he asked.

"Not yet. I've never done much with it at all until the others tracked me down, honestly. And since then I've just been focusing on the hands, trying to make it cover my body from there."

She stood upright, her breathing under control, and closed her eyes. Coal waited to see if anything vanished.

After a few seconds, he noticed it. Her unbroken horn started to dissipate, its tip receding until it was the same length as the one broken in the boat crash.

"You're doing it!" he told her.

When her eyes shot open, the horn reappeared. "Really?"

He nodded, grinning excitedly.

Jatiri closed her eyes again and Coal watched as the horn gradually disappeared completely. Now only the broken horn jutted from her head. She opened one eye, then the other.

"Still gone?"

"Still gone."

She beamed. But the smile was quickly wiped from her face as she held up her palms again. Her face scrunched up in concentration.

The horn was still gone, and her fingers began to vanish from her hand. Coal kept a close eye on both, making sure the horn didn't so much as flicker into existence for the briefest of moments.

Soon both her hands were gone and the horn was still missing. She tried to continue down her wrists and up her arms, but it was too much. Everything popped back into place as she exhaled deeply.

"That was amazing!" Coal exclaimed.

Her chest heaved as she caught her breath. "*Wow*, that was tough."

"Don't push yourself too hard," Coal told her, finally coming up with some halfway decent advice. "Rest a bit before you try again."

Jatiri nodded. "How about this: while I take a break, you do some laps around me. Get a better feel for those things."

"That sounds awful."

"I know, but your situation's not changing, so..."

She was right. He just didn't want to admit it. Some practice would do him good, though. And there wasn't much pain in his leg at the moment, so it was an ideal time to do it.

Jatiri squatted down, keeping her clothes hovering a few inches from the mud, while Coal began to walk in wide circles around her. When one of his crutches got stuck in the mud, he paused to wiggle it free rather than force himself onward like he usually did (which only ever resulted in him falling over, dirtying and angering himself).

They went on like this for another half hour, alternating between Jatiri turning herself invisible and Coal walking on his crutches. Biror then came over to observe, staring blankly at them.

Jatiri was successfully making her left arm and both horns invisible simultaneously when Biror said, "The snails are waking."

"Okay," Coal said. "We'll be there in a second." Jatiri had maintained her concentration and kept the body parts invisible even when Biror spoke.

The boar nodded and turned to head back toward the snails. "Do not delay," he said as he walked away. "You are not as quick as you once were, little fox."

"I think I'm still faster than a snail," Coal snapped back.

Biror laughed. "I would not be so sure."

Coal turned back to Jatiri, who was fully visible again and clearly worn out by all the practice. He was too; his arms ached, and he was dreading continuing their trek. Part of him regretted not getting even a little bit of rest, but he had enjoyed his time with Jatiri. Plus, he felt like he had actually accomplished something, even if it was minor. They both had.

"Great job today," she said to him as they returned to the pack.

"Me? How about you over there making yourself disappear. I'm jealous! Soon you'll be able to avoid Biror and Lop any time you want." They both chuckled. "You're the one doin' great."

"Thank you. You shouldn't sell yourself short, though. This is a huge adjustment, and you're handling it very well. It might not feel that way, sometimes, but you are. I'm proud of you. I'm sorry it happened, truly, but I'm proud of how you're dealing with it."

Her words almost made Coal's eyes well up, which caught him off-guard. What she said was true: he did *not* feel like he was handling things well. Hearing her outside perspective put him at ease.

"Thanks," he said softly.

She patted him on the back as they walked.

"Hey," he said playfully, "don't knock me off-balance, now."

They laughed and continued on.

It was only later that night, when he was settling in to sleep, that Coal realized it was his birthday.

28

SEVERAL DAYS LATER, DEEP into the night, the group found a natural trench in the ground, one that was deep and surrounded by wide trees. Lop decided it would be a good place to stop and rest for a couple hours. He would take first watch while Noswen and Yurzu got some sleep.

There had been absolutely no sign of the attackers since their narrow escape, but it was better to be cautious.

The orangutan positioned himself at the top of the trench. He was wearing his usual outfit: overalls and no shirt. Despite being a large man, his dark, reddish-orange hair along with the dark fabric of his clothes helped him disappear into the night. Zsoz wanted to sit up there with him, but Lop declined. Instead, the slime was stuck to the wall of the trench just beneath where he sat. It was a strange reversed image of how they usually sat back at the Sadatso inn.

Noswen wasn't sleeping yet, instead taking the opportunity to write in her notebook.

"The chapter about the fight the other day is gonna make a really good story," Yurzu said. His voice was quiet in the dark.

Noswen looked up at him and smiled. "Less fighting and more fleeing, really," she whispered back.

Yurzu listened to the gentle sounds of her scribbling for a minute or two. That and the chirruping of insects was all he could hear.

"Does your family know about your healing?" He asked. He didn't know where the question came from.

"My husband does," Noswen answered. "The kits...well, I've healed them when they needed it, but I think most of them are too young to understand even if I explained it to them. Right now, if I heal them, they think nothing of it and go about with their day playing and running around. Dena is old enough to wonder, but she hasn't asked me about it. I think it makes her uneasy." She sighed at that and continued writing in her notebook.

Yurzu then asked something that had been on his mind ever since Lop recruited him so many months ago. "Do you think that we're gonna keep our powers?"

There was a lull before she replied. "Why wouldn't we?"

"I dunno. The Dirt King says we're supposed to channel our magic into the artifacts to seal the Houndstooth, right? Maybe that removes the blight from our bodies."

Noswen pondered this for a moment. "Maybe that's true," she said. "We'll find out soon, I guess."

Yurzu was curled up against one of the dirt walls. Stringy plants jutted out from the dirt, hanging over his head and drifting in the slight breeze. He reached up to touch a leaf. His fingernail flicked against the pointed tip of the star-shaped leaf and he sighed.

They had entered Redmonth a few days prior. After that would be Drymonth, which meant that he was coming up on the twelfth anniversary of his parents' death.

He was fourteen years old when it happened. Two months before he was to turn fifteen.

Yurzu had experienced frequent headaches all his life, but in Toothshadow, the population was small and his family did not venture out often. He was usually cooped up at home, which was what he preferred. It was always his father Vanhu who left to go sell the family's products to stores around town or closer to the Palace. It was only when Yurzu went on errands with his mother, or when they went out to eat somewhere, that his senses were assaulted.

His parents tried to find cures for what was bothering him, but nothing ever worked. As he grew older, he learned how to tolerate the pain and stopped complaining about it to his parents. He knew there was no way to fix it, and he did not want them to worry over him. They assumed the problem had fixed itself.

When he was twelve, he went out on a walk by himself one day. The town was full of winding forest trails, and he was wandering down a shadowy path when he felt the onset of a pounding headache.

It hurt more and more as he continued down the path. In the distance he saw a man leaned over in the underbrush, hacking up a lung. Yurzu's headache was at its peak when he approached the man and asked, "Are you okay?"

The man coughed a few more times, spitting out globs of saliva mixed with blood onto the dirt path.

"Yes, yes, don't worry about me," said the man. He was a marten with short brown fur and a tan chest. His ears drooped as he coughed some more.

Yurzu accepted his words at face value and continued his way through the forest. As he grew further from the man, his headache went away. That was when it dawned on him.

He took a few steps back in the direction of the sick marten, and the headache returned.

Then some steps away, and once more it receded.

He thought he had to be imagining it. Of course he was. It didn't make any sense.

But he carried out his experiment for another minute or two, and every time he retreated from the man, his headache went away.

It was a foolish notion, but one that he couldn't ignore. He tried to recall whether he was near visibly sick people each time these headaches came on, but he couldn't remember for sure.

Yurzu returned to the man. The pounding in his head dizzied him. It felt like his skull was going to split open.

"Let me help you back to town," said Yurzu.

The marten sighed and thanked him, reluctantly accepting his aid.

Yurzu nearly passed out on his way back to Toothshadow with the man, but finally they reached the village's small clinic. He brought the man inside, and the pain in his head increased tenfold the moment he stepped into the building.

He was convinced now. For some reason, he could sense when people were sick. It wasn't clear what ailment they suffered; all he could tell was that there was something wrong with them.

The marten thanked him again, and Yurzu left. By the time he got home, he felt completely fine.

Two years passed with Yurzu nurturing his secret. He continued to test it out, and there was no denying what he was capable of.

Telling his parents was out of the question, though. Perhaps part of them might feel relief knowing there was an explanation for their son's headaches, but at what cost? The explanation would probably scare them more than the headaches did in the first place.

So Yurzu kept his power to himself.

Back then, he never thought of it as a blight. He didn't understand why he possessed this ability, but from what he knew, no one else could do it. That delighted him.

He was special.

But still, he did nothing of value with the power.

Even when he encountered someone who was sick but showed no symptoms, he did not inform them that they should go see a doctor. He just continued on his way, minding his own business. The thought of approaching someone, speaking to a stranger, terrified him.

A decade past, now, he regretted that. Sometimes he tossed and turned in the night, torn up over how many people he might have saved if only he hadn't been afraid to speak to them.

When he was fourteen, though, he was at home by himself slicing vegetables for his parents. He was cutting cucumbers into spears and placing them into empty glass jars. Earlier that morning, he had cut some into rounds. Those were still sitting in jars nearby, awaiting the pickling liquid.

His parents entered the house, calling out a greeting to him. He wasn't sure where they had been, but they'd instructed him to prepare vegetables while they were gone, so that was what he did. He loved contributing to the business.

Yurzu opened his mouth to say hello, but it hung open and no sound came out. There was a sudden pounding of his head. One that had not been there seconds before. It only started when his parents entered the house.

"Yurzu?" his mother Muneer said with a tinge of worry. She walked into the kitchen and found him standing there, mouth agape and knife in hand. "Is everything okay?"

He blinked and turned to look at her. Everything appeared to be perfectly normal. Her fur had a healthy sheen, there was no redness around her eyes, her nose wasn't runny. There were no symptoms of any type of illness at all.

"Everything's fine," he then said.

Muneer smiled at him. "How are things going in here?" She stepped into the kitchen and placed a hand on his back. His head throbbed savagely, but he maintained a neutral expression. He tried to sport a smile for his mother.

"They're going fine," he answered. He nodded toward the filled jars on the other end of the counter. "Lots done already."

"Wow, I am very impressed!" she beamed. "You can take a break, if you want. Dad and I can finish this up." There was still a hefty pile of cucumbers as well as carrots left to cut.

Yurzu shook his head. "I want to help," he said.

"I'll join you, then."

They stood side by side cutting vegetables together. Yurzu's head was killing him, but he couldn't find it within himself to tell his mother that. He wanted to spend the time with her.

But he also couldn't find it within himself to tell her that he felt something. Felt something was wrong with her. He was worried about what her reaction might be. How she might think of him. She probably wouldn't even believe him, would just think he was imagining things. He was still a kid, and kids had active imaginations. An easy explanation.

The headache worsened when his father came into the kitchen. Something was wrong with him too. Luckily for Yurzu's head, the man was only saying hello before trundling off into the garden.

Yurzu told himself that the feeling would probably go away in a day or two. His parents seemed fine. Nothing was seriously wrong. They were probably just about to get a cold or something. There was no need to fret.

A week later, though, his headaches hadn't subsided. The only time he got any peace was when he went on walks by himself or when his parents were out of the house.

A week after that, he still hadn't said anything to them. He just kept wishing the feeling would go away, that his parents would be okay. They simply *had* to be. They were still not acting sick at all. Whatever he was feeling inside them, it must not be of much concern.

But then a knock came at the door while he was home alone, napping in his plush chair. His heart raced as he jolted from his slumber. Another knock came, and he hurried to the front door.

When he opened it, he discovered Doz Wabba on the other side. Doz was an old family friend of his parents', a kind bat with a hunched back and a clipped ear. She had walked with a knotty wooden cane for as long as Yurzu had known her.

"Hi, Yurzu," she greeted him.

"Hi," he said. "My parents aren't home."

"I know, dear," she said with a frown. "They're out here, just on the other side of the garden."

Yurzu peered around the doorframe and saw that his parents were indeed standing across the garden, far from the door. He waved to them and they waved back, but he was confused.

Doz said, "Your parents asked me to watch over you for a few days. The doctor says they're sick, and they don't want you to catch what they've got."

His heart skipped a beat. "Are they okay?" he asked. "Is it really bad?"

"They're okay," Doz assured him.

He leaned around the corner to look at them again. They did still appear to be normal. Muneer wiped at her nose. Was it runny? Was that a symptom? Did they have fevers?

None of them knew he'd been sensing the illness for the past two weeks. "What if I'm already sick?" he asked.

"We'll take you to the doctor to get you checked out," the woman said. "Go grab your things and we'll take them to my house. Then we'll go see the doctor, just to be safe. Okay?"

"Okay," Yurzu nodded, not sure what else to say.

He retreated into his bedroom and gathered what few possessions he wanted to bring with him. When he returned to the front door, Doz offered him a warm smile.

"All ready?"

Yurzu nodded.

He stepped out of the house and turned to face his parents across the garden.

"It'll just be a few days!" his father called to him. "We love you!"

"Love you," Yurzu said back.

Those few days in Doz's house stretched into a week, then to two weeks, and then the woman came to him with sorrow etched into her face.

Before she even said the words, Yurzu knew what they were. Before the woman could open her mouth, tears were streaming down his face. Staining his puffy cheeks.

Doz explained to him what had happened, but her words were drowned out by a buzzing in his ears. He just kept thinking about that day chopping vegetables with his mother in the kitchen. The day he knew but did not tell them.

The funeral was a few days later. They had a traditional flyer's funeral, which involved cremating the bodies and placing the ashes in a large urn with some of the deceased's most prized possessions. The urn was then cast off a mountain's peak. It took over a week to travel from Toothshadow to the mountains in the east, but Yurzu knew it was what his parents would've wanted.

Many of the townspeople showed up. They all knew Vanhu and Muneer. Everyone loved their food. A great number of people approached Yurzu afterwards and told him how much his parents would be missed. All he could bring himself to do was nod in response.

He rode back to Toothshadow with Doz. She offered him a place in her home, but he declined. His parents had left everything to him, and he wanted to remain in his home. She told him that any time he needed anything at all, she would be there for him. He thanked her.

The house felt barren without his parents. It was too quiet. Too still. For a few days, Yurzu didn't even leave the living room. It was the first room when one entered the house, and he was too afraid to venture deeper into the home. So he remained curled up on his chair.

When he finally mustered up the courage to walk around the house, the first thing he did was clean the kitchen. Then he went to his bedroom and slept for several hours.

His parents' room remained untouched. It was twice the size of his own, but he didn't feel right invading their space. The room was still theirs. He stayed in his childhood bedroom. Even a decade later when Lop came across him, he was still sleeping in his old bedroom.

He got by for a few months with the tups his parents left him. The only time he ever interacted with another person was when he went out to buy food. Always something pre-prepared, nothing he had to cook himself. He wasn't up to the task.

Part of him believed this would be his life now. Waking up in the morning, shuffling from his bedroom to his chair in the living room and laying in it all day. Sometimes getting up to go buy a meal. Staggering back into his room to sleep for the night.

Eventually he started listening to his father's records, which livened the days up a bit. He became intimately familiar with all his father's favorite musicians. His father's all-time favorite album was *Wispland* by Zoj. It soon became Yurzu's as well.

One day, he glanced out the window from his chair and noticed the garden was dying.

He had no idea how much time had passed since the funeral. How much time he'd wasted inside that house. But seeing the garden wilting away, decaying, knocked him out of his daze.

That garden meant everything to his parents. He couldn't let it die off. If he did, that would truly be the end of them. The end of everything they'd worked toward in their lives.

Yurzu forced himself out of the chair and went outside. He approached the garden with no small amount of trepidation. He kneeled down and placed his hands in the soil. His fingernails were overgrown and they dug into the dirt.

He looked up and stared at the spot where he'd last seen his parents. Where they had stood far from him, not wanting to infect him with whatever illness they had. One last act of love.

Starting that day, he got to work reviving the garden. He employed every piece of knowledge his parents had instilled in him. It took a lot of time and effort, but eventually it was thriving again.

Picking his first harvest was the proudest day of his life. He carried an armful of cucumbers into the house and dropped them on the countertop, where he began to slice them into both rounds and spears.

He knew all of his parents' pickling liquid recipes by heart. While he was working on the garden, waiting for it to be ready, he had been memorizing the recipes they left behind. He no longer needed to consult the tiny notebook in the kitchen drawer.

Over the years, though, every couple months he would take it out again just to read their words. Relish the swoops of their letters. Run his fingers over the dried ink on the pages. It was like they were speaking to him again.

Yurzu thought about the recipe book while he lay in the trench, staring up at the star-shaped leaf poking out from the dirt. A few feet away, he could still hear Noswen scribbling in her notebook. Writing the story of their journey for her children.

He wondered if one day they would obsess over their mother's notebook the same way he did his parents' recipe book.

The book was one of the few things he'd brought from home. He sat up and pulled it out of his bag, wiping off the plain front cover. It had been a few months since he looked over it. Sometimes it made him too sad. It made him feel connected with his parents, which was a joyous thing, but there was still some sadness to it.

He opened it to the first page, the most basic recipe in the book. Their best seller. He began to read.

29

MOONOSHK WAS BUILT IN the thick-canopied treetops of the Lakilu Forest. The city was originally constructed from wood, like other treetop towns such as the triad of Vil's Branch, Holluwak, and Baoa. But in the intervening decades, the birds who called Moonoshk home innovated and rebuilt the city over time. They used new technology from the Palace, with a generous grant from the Dirt King, as well as those of their own invention. Now the city was a metallic red, its buildings and bridges high in the air, latched onto the sides of massive tree trunks and held aloft by technology Yurzu had no hope of ever understanding. All the buildings were cylindrical, varying in height and width. Series of tubes (some clear, some opaque) connected each of them, and to reach the city one had to ride an elevator inside a large clear tube. There were a few open-air metal decks spread throughout the city as well as balconies on the buildings. A wide bridge spanned the length between

Moonoshk and the nearby Yuluj mountaintops. At the base of the trees that held up the city were several squat buildings, factories that manufactured a good portion of the kingdom's tech.

But their arrival after such a long journey was not as jovial as they expected. At the moment, the city was in chaos.

It was hard to tell at first since so much of Moonoshk was contained in its interconnected series of tubes, but when looking at the clear glass ones, Yurzu could see people tangling with some sort of blightbeast. He couldn't make out many details at this distance, but there were a great number of them. People outnumbered the blightbeasts three to one, but they were having a rough time handling the monsters.

Yurzu squinted and saw that the tops of some of the tubes were cracked, broken open. The creatures must have come from the treetops and beat against the tubes until they could get inside.

Surely if they had accessed the tubes, they were running amok in the city proper as well. From where they stood below Moonoshk, Yurzu could only spot perhaps ten or fifteen of the things inside tubes or on the decks, but there was no telling how many there were in total.

People were screaming out on the open decks, dodging the beasts' attacks. Some were leaping off and flying away, coming to land safely on the ground before fleeing toward the mountains.

The elevator that brought visitors in and out of the city was clearly nonfunctional. They could see the elevator inside the tube, stuck halfway up, with people trapped on board. A family of rabbits huddled close together, while a macaw and lynx peered anxiously through the glass. At the base, the doors were clamped tightly shut.

"What in the hell is going on?" Lop muttered, staring up at the city. It was mid-day, and they were all looking forward to a hefty lunch after spending so much time on the road.

This did not figure into their arrival plans.

"Can you tell what those are?" Yurzu asked them.

"Doesn't matter," said Noswen. "The elevator's out. We need to figure out a way to get up there and help." She turned to her companions and said, "I can climb the trees. Do your arms stretch that far?"

The orangutan nodded. "It will be close, I think, but I should be able to manage."

Noswen nodded. "Good. Then let's get up there and do what we can. You kill shit while I help get people to safety."

The only time Yurzu had seen the woman so fired up was when they mounted their hacklemesh weavers for the spider-back race in Soponunga. Retrieving these artifacts was good motivation for her.

I will stay on the ground, said Zsoz. **While you fight, I will affix myself to the side of a tree trunk high off the ground. Up there, I should be out of the way and safe.**

"I think the blightbeasts are coming from the treetops," Yurzu said.

Lop looked up at Moonoshk and nodded. "That makes sense," he said. He removed the slime from his shoulder and placed it on the ground. "You should…shit, I don't know." He glanced around, trying to find a good spot for Zsoz to lay low.

"We don't really have time to debate this," Noswen said.

Yurzu pointed at the busted elevator. "Maybe behind that?" he offered. It was as secure a place as any, given the circumstances.

I will solidify and secure myself to the ground hidden behind the elevator that leads to Moonoshk City. With that, Zsoz took off, leaving behind a thin trail of goo in its wake.

"Yurzu, go with Zsoz," said Noswen.

"What? Why?" It had been a long time since he'd had reason to really fly, but Yurzu thought he could do it. He could at least reach the lowest tube or deck then make his way up higher from there. He did not need to stay here, hiding away.

"It's too dangerous!"

It was time to go. The people of Moonoshk needed their help.

Noswen kicked off her shoes and darted to the tree nearest the elevator, scrambling up its side with haste. Lop wasn't far behind her, stretching his arms out toward the city. He wrapped them around a particularly thick branch, like a rope, and began to shorten them again, pulling himself into the air.

On the ground, Yurzu stood frozen.

Maybe Noswen was right. He couldn't do this. Lop and Noswen were far braver than him. Far more skilled. They could handle the situation just fine. They didn't need him. He could stay here.

Yurzu watched Zsoz sliding through the grass toward its hiding place. Perhaps he should join the slime after all. Cower behind the elevator until the situation was under control.

People need your help, he told himself. *You can help them. You just have to do it.*

There were so many people he might have helped in Tooth-shadow if he had not been so afraid to. His parents included.

You have to help them.

He threw his bag onto the grass and rifled through it. He grabbed all his baggies of sleeping and killing powders. His pockets bulged, one type of powder in each. He possessed enough self-awareness to know that he could not fend off these monsters with his bare hands, so he needed to work with what he had.

Yurzu tossed his jacket to the ground beside his bag and unfurled his wings. He took a couple steps back, got a running start, and flew into the air.

It was rough at first, but he found the current and rode it skyward into the city. He came to a shaky landing on top of a connective tube, one of the glass ones with a jagged hole on its top where a blightbeast had broken in.

His plan was to continue upward and stick close to Noswen, despite her inevitable protests, but someone needed help here.

Below his feet, through the thick pane of glass, a macaw was fearfully swiping and kicking at an encroaching blightbeast. She was backed up against the door at the end of the hall, which Yurzu presumed must be locked. They were the only two bodies in the tube, though. An easy first target for Yurzu.

Hopefully.

His head was roaring in pain being near so many blightbeasts, but he tried his best to shake it off and focus on the task at hand. He had gotten a lot of practice ignoring the sensation after spending so much time with the other Blighted.

He scrambled through the hole the blightbeast had created, scratching his arm on the sharp glass as he fell through. He landed with a thud behind the monster, which turned around to investigate the curious sound.

The monster was about half Yurzu's height. Its body was long, like a centipede, with even more legs. The legs were thin as strands of hair, and there were thousands upon thousands of them keeping the creature upright. Two appendages protruded from its back, each one ending in long, hooked blades. Those had to be what it used to shatter the glass tubes. Its skin was a sickly yellow and perfectly smooth. The thing's face had eight small, beady black eyes set atop a circular mouth that seemingly could not close. It clicked irritably at the sight of Yurzu.

It scuttled toward him, utterly uninterested in the macaw now.

Yurzu walked backwards away from it, hoping he would not bump into another monster behind him. He fumbled in his pocket as he walked, already forgetting which one contained which powder. His mind was too focused on the creature attacking him to think about whether his hand was touching a leather or velvet bag.

He yanked a bag from a pocket and shot his hand into it, grabbing a healthy portion of the grainy powder inside. His eyes did not tear away from the blightbeast for even a second.

"Cover yourself!" he shouted to the macaw on the other side of the monster. The powder might not travel that far on the air, but he wanted to be sure the woman was prepared.

The blightbeast was only a few feet away now.

Yurzu opened his palm, with no time to check which powder he was holding. He blew and showered the monster in yellow powder. The killing powder.

This stuff was used to kill pests on his crops, and this monster was definitely an oversized pest.

It blasted into the creature's face, entering its open mouth hole and stinging its many eyes. The blightbeast halted its advance, crouching closer to the floor and blinking erratically to cleanse its eyes of the substance. It made no sound as the powder worked its way down the throat. After a few seconds, the creature collapsed in a heap on the red metal floor.

The macaw looked from the corpse to Yurzu and gasped, "Vyru above! Thank you!" She turned and pounded on the door behind her. "Let me in! It's dead! There's nothing out here! Come on!"

The door opened a crack, with a suspicious eye peering out, then it swung open fully and the macaw ducked inside. A woodpecker stood there and motioned for Yurzu to follow.

"It's safe in here," the woman said. "We've been locked away the entire time. Come."

Yurzu shook his head. He had no time to explain and simply turned to exit out the other end of the hall.

He found himself on the second floor of a massive building four stories tall. It appeared to be an office of some kind, filled with desks and cabinets and papers. The floor of each level was semi-translucent and he could see the outlines of people and monsters going all the way up. It was dizzying. He looked down and saw more people fighting the same blightbeasts.

There was a single creature on his level, with no one but himself there to stop it. He had brought along his green sleeping powder as a precaution, but now that he had a second to think, he did not find it likely the residents of Moonoshk would be appreciative of these monsters dozing around their city. Best to stick to the yellow powder.

The blightbeast surged toward him, and Yurzu stood his ground. He grabbed another handful of powder and waited for the creature to reach him. When it was only a couple feet away, he blew on the powder and leapt out of the way of the monster's attack.

It stumbled around, shaking its whole body as if trying to dry itself off. Then, like the previous one, it fell to the floor with a *thunk*.

Yurzu looked around and realized there were no stairs anywhere. He then spotted a glass rectangle that went from floor to ceiling, connecting each level of the building. He ran over to it and pressed a button, waiting for the platform to descend.

When it reached him, he hopped on and rode it to the next floor up. He exited out onto the third floor and discovered the people there had killed all the blightbeasts. The monsters lay scattered across the floor, bleeding from multiple gunshot wounds.

People pushed past Yurzu and stuffed themselves into the elevator. Before the door closed, he hurried onto it with them. Together they ascended to the fourth floor. Yurzu felt uncomfortable, shoved between a bunch of strangers.

The elevator dinged and they all rushed out. Yurzu tripped over himself and the others ran ahead, firing wildly at the monsters attacking their friends.

Yurzu pushed himself up off the ground and took a step forward but immediately slipped on a streak of blood. He tumbled onto his back and saw a pair of blightbeasts clinging to the ceiling, staring down at the proceedings below.

"Up there!" he shouted, still laying on the ground.

He couldn't see who, but apparently someone heeded his warning because suddenly the monsters were riddled with bullets. They careened to the floor below and splattered with the impact.

An owl appeared in Yurzu's vision and extended a helping hand. Yurzu grabbed it and the man hoisted him to his feet.

"Good eye," said the owl. He held a pistol in his other hand.

"Thanks."

The owl dug into his pocket and pulled out a bottle of Noctgone. He popped it open with his thumb, letting the lid clatter to the ground. Then he kicked it back, dry swallowed the pill, and extended the bottle to Yurzu. "Need any? Got two more."

Yurzu shook his head. The owl shrugged and downed the rest of the pills then threw the bottle at the wall.

Looking around more, it seemed the top floor of the building was actually its lobby. There was a doorway leading outside, which everyone was running toward now that the monsters were dead. Yurzu followed the owl and the others.

The tube they entered was opaque. Metal curved all around them with no view of the forest outside. Part of the ceiling was dented where a blightbeast must have tried penetrating it. Whatever metal they had used to build Moonoshk was strong, though.

Yurzu brought up the rear as the group—ten or fifteen people, give or take—filed through the connective tube. There was a sudden shift beneath their feet, a groaning of metal. Then a loud clank and heavy thuds above.

More dents.

Everyone rushed forward just as the tube started to tilt downward. The monsters were attempting to dislodge it entirely if they could not penetrate it.

People ran through the open doorway at the end of the tube, but there were still six of them left when it detached from the rest of the city.

It swung downward, sending people flying out the open end that they had been moving toward. Yurzu plummeted through the air, losing some of his powder bags in the process.

When he was clear of the tube, he flapped his wings again and took to the sky. The others followed suit, although one among them had been a hedgehog who plunged toward the ground. A macaw tried to save them, but was too late.

In the air, Yurzu saw what had broken the tube.

It was the same as the rest of the blightbeasts, but easily ten times bigger. The thing was nearly the size of some of Moonoshk's buildings. It had large pores in its side, and Yurzu was terrified to see one of the smaller blightbeasts ushering out of one such hole.

As long as the mother was breathing, there would be an endless supply of blightbeasts to fight. Yurzu's powder was no match against such a massive creature, so he had to hope that Lop or the city's residents could take it down. He would stay focused on its offspring.

Yurzu came to a rough landing atop the office building he'd just exited. He watched the blightmother clamber over buildings, pounding into them with the claws on its back. A few other tubes had collapsed onto the forest floor, some crashing into the factories.

The owl from before perched beside him. "We should go to Wrestrep's Watch," the man said. "Lots there." He took a moment to reload his gun. Yurzu stared at the firearm for a second before speaking.

"I don't know what that is," he said.

"Oh," the owl blinked. "Not from the city?"

A shake of the head.

"Okay. Well, thanks for helpin' out. I'm Gogg."

"Yurzu."

Gogg finished tinkering with his gun and grinned. "Are you feeling up to flying?" Yurzu nodded, so Gogg said, "Good.

Follow me, then." He took off, and Yurzu followed close behind.

They flew around to the other side of the city. It seemed like Gogg was heading toward one of the decks, and Yurzu hoped they would be landing soon because his arms were killing him. He had never flown so much before. There was never any reason to.

The deck ahead of them was littered with corpses, and not those of blightbeasts. Many of the monsters skittered around the metal deck, going from body to body, planting their mouths on their unfortunate victims. When they pulled away, they left behind gaping, bloody holes where the meat had been sucked away.

It was not a place Yurzu wanted to go.

But Gogg came to a landing on the deck, so Yurzu did too. His arms were sore and the whole situation was starting to get to him. He suppressed a full sob, but a few teardrops raced down his cheek. He wiped them away with the back of his hand before Gogg saw.

Two of the blightbeasts noticed their arrival and lunged toward them. Gogg shot them both in the head. This got the attention of the other six, though, and they all converged on Gogg and Yurzu.

Gogg started firing, and Yurzu ran to the two nearest him. He extracted more powder from the leather bag and blew it at the monsters. They stumbled around for a second before collapsing. One had staggered over to the edge of the deck and fell off it.

His new ally had taken down three of his own, which left one more. It jumped onto Gogg's back while the owl was dealing with his third monster, sending his face smashing into the metal plate flooring.

Blood rushed from his face and he struggled to push the thing off him. Its stringy legs covered his back, wiggling in ecstasy, slithering underneath his shirt and into his pockets and anywhere else they could go.

Yurzu couldn't use his powder on it without risking Gogg ingesting some. Even using the sleeping powder would be too risky; he couldn't leave the man sleeping up on this deck in the middle of this mayhem.

So he tackled the creature, sending them both tumbling intertwined across the deck. It clicked at him as they rolled toward the edge and wrapped its legs around his small body.

He tried to push it off himself, but his legs weren't powerful enough. The thing's grip was too tight.

Thankfully they came to a stop a good distance away from the edge of the deck, but the monster was still viciously swiping at him with its claws. They scratched Yurzu's back, but none of the gashes were deep.

There then came the pounding of footsteps, and suddenly Gogg was beating his fists into the monster's head. It let go of Yurzu and crawled away but was quickly put down by a blast from Gogg's gun. The shot rang out and Yurzu clutched his hands to his ears.

Gogg helped him to his feet again and asked if he was alright. Yurzu confirmed, though again he wanted to be down near the elevator waiting things out with Zsoz. For the first time in his life, he wished he was a slime instead of a bat.

The owl clutched a hand to his chest. "Fuck me!" he sputtered. "Maybe I shouldn'ta took so much Noctgone, huh? My heart's beating like a drum!"

Having a frantic heartbeat didn't seem to bother the man much, though. He laughed emphatically and glanced around the deck. There were pathways looping around the tree trunk, but Yurzu did not know where they went.

He wanted to know where Noswen and Lop were, whether they were doing okay. There was no scurrying raccoon anywhere he could see, nor a stretchy orangutan, so he had to hope they were taking care of themselves. Yurzu trusted that Lop could take down the blightmother, with the help of some gunmen. Maybe he was making his way toward the monster. It seemed like the type of challenge Lop savored.

"What'd you do to those things?" Gogg then asked. "I saw you throw some shit on them."

"It's a powder that kills insects," Yurzu explained.

Gogg laughed. "Amazing! These are some nasty fuckin' insects, eh? Good work, pal." He pointed at one of the walkways, which led into another opaque tube. "Let's head through there. That'll take us to Bramble Plaza."

Yurzu didn't have any better ideas. He figured he might as well continue following the man.

They ran into the tube, which was empty but for the bodies of two blightbeasts. Yurzu was glad to see whoever they were attacking had gotten away.

He and Gogg hopped over the corpses blocking the pathway and went through the other door onto a huge platform encircling the largest tree in Moonoshk. The circular platform wrapped all the way around the massive trunk and had a few vendor stalls set up, though only a handful of them still stood proudly. The rest were battered or completely torn apart, with bits of wood scattered across the plaza.

There were bodies everywhere. Mostly blightbeasts, but more than a few people too. Yurzu shuddered.

"Fuck," Gogg muttered at the scene.

Yurzu tore his gaze from the corpses. He was going to cry again if he kept looking. He wanted this all to end. In the distance, he could hear the blightmother lumbering through the treetops. Screams pierced the air.

Blightbeasts crawled along the enormous tree trunk before them. People ran past, retreating into the relative safety of buildings. Gogg broke from his stupor and raised his arm to fire on the monsters. They fell from the tree, smashing their heads against the metal plating. Some tumbled across the platform, leaving trails of blood.

Somebody nearby shouted for help.

While Gogg killed blightbeasts, Yurzu sought out the caller. They yelled again, and Yurzu found them knocked down underneath a dead blightbeast.

"Help," the man begged. He was a macaw with a cracked beak. His words were weak.

Yurzu helped shove the blightbeast off the man and discovered his left leg had been crushed in the scuffle. Shards of bone poked through his bloody pants. The man sobbed at the sight of his own ruined leg.

It took all of Yurzu's willpower not to vomit. He swallowed and said, "Where can I take you? Where is safe?"

The man was too distraught. He just cried. Big wracking sobs.

"I'll be right back," Yurzu told him. "Don't worry." He raced over to Gogg, who was still firing on blightbeasts. They were endless. He tapped the owl on the shoulder and said, "Someone needs our help."

Gogg didn't question him. He followed Yurzu over to the injured macaw.

"Where can we take him?" Yurzu asked. The man needed to leave Bramble Plaza as soon as possible. He winced again seeing the man's broken beak.

Gogg considered only for a second before answering. "The Fingrass Hotel might be safe," he said. "Nothing had gotten in when I was there, and they were working on barricading the doors and windows. It might be too late, but maybe there's a way for us to get him inside. Not very far, either."

Together they lifted the man up and propped him on their shoulders. They slowly made their way across the plaza and through another bloodied glass tube before reaching the hotel.

They set the man down and Gogg proceeded to slam his fist on the door. "Hey!" he shouted. "Open up! Got someone hurt here!"

"Fuck off!" came a muffled cry from inside.

"You fuck off!" Gogg yelled in retort. "This man needs your help! Open the fucking door!" His knocks became punches.

"Stop it!" the person inside shouted. When the owl refused to cease his pounding, the person finally relented and opened the door.

It screeched against the floor and could only open up a foot or two. The door pressed against a pile of furniture just on the other side.

"I can only open it this much," said the begrudging man. He was a hedgehog sporting a deep scowl.

"You're an asshole," Gogg told him, but then began helping the macaw through the entryway.

It was a tight fit and the man had to suck in his gut, but he made it through to the other side. The hedgehog slammed the door shut without another word, not even offering them refuge.

"Baswat," Gogg grumbled. The word essentially meant "bitch" in Buatang.

Gogg turned around and his eyebrows shot up in alarm. He raised his pistol, practically placing it on Yurzu's shoulder before pulling the trigger.

Yurzu screamed and twirled, falling to the floor of the tube. As he landed, he saw a blightbeast collapse to the ground behind him with a bullet lodged in its cheek. Gogg fired again and blasted its skull open, sending bits of brain flying onto the walls.

"Sorry, sorry," Gogg said, kneeling down. "No time to warn you. Your ears okay?"

His words were muffled, but Yurzu could faintly make them out. He nodded and stood.

Gogg reloaded his gun, then led the way back out to Bramble Plaza. There, he shot at more blightbeasts crawling along the tree trunk as well as a few that had leapt onto the platform.

Past him, Yurzu could see the blightmother.

A ton of people were shooting at the creature, and he could see Lop's hulking form in the fray. He wasn't stretching out his arms, since that would be exceptionally obvious to onlookers, but it appeared his hands were blades. That, at least, he could play off as having been holding swords and was simply misconstrued at a distance. If anyone even bothered to notice or question it, that is. Yurzu suspected everyone was too busy trying to stay alive and kill the things destroying their city.

Gogg spotted the massive monster too. Seeing everybody else fighting it seemingly left him feeling antsy.

"That way!" he declared. He then lifted into the air and flew toward the raging battle.

Yurzu considered that the end of their partnership. He knew there were only two possible outcomes of himself joining the fight: either he would get in everybody else's way, or the blightmother would stomp him to death.

Neither was appealing.

The trunk that Bramble Plaza looped around was still crawling with blightbeasts. He knew he could not take them all on now that he lacked Gogg's trigger finger, so he needed to get out of there. Surely there was someone else nearby who he could help. Someone who was only tangling with one or two of the monsters.

That was more his speed. That much he could handle with his powder.

He took a deep breath and flapped his wings, taking off in search of people who needed him.

30

COAL NEVER FELT SUCH relief as he did when they finally reached Vuntagonyeo.

The trio had broken off from the snails two days prior, leaving the beasts to continue making their way to Opotch Nekriplo for their hibernation. To Coal, the prospect of laying down and sleeping for six months sounded blissful.

It had been almost two weeks now since his accidental amputation, and Jatiri said he was recovering nicely. But she also said that it would probably be a minimum of two more weeks before he was fully healed, if not longer. The news was disheartening, but there was nothing he could do about it.

A short clay wall surrounded the city. Given its height, it seemed to be more for appearance rather than protection. Coal could scale it with ease, even after taking his lack of foot into account. There was a gap in the wall wide enough for two wagons to fit through, but Coal could not imagine any wagons making it through the muddy terrain all the way here. It made him wonder what method they used to import or export goods, but such things were beyond his understanding (and interest). Etched into the side of the clay wall was the city's name, and underneath was a phrase in Ronog that Jatiri asked about and Biror told them translated to: Birthed From the Kiln's Flame.

Just like my foot, Coal thought dourly.

They entered the city.

Vuntagonyeo was just as filthy as the rest of the Mudlands, though it did have stone streets for them to walk on, which Coal appreciated with his crutches.

True to Biror's word, the city did indeed make much more use out of clay than simple vases and pots. Every building was constructed with clay bricks. There were some typical rectangular buildings, but others incorporated smooth, curved walls into their architecture. Biror said that these places, with the more complex construction, were public buildings such as libraries, inns, and the like. He went on to explain that no one in Vuntagonyeo owned their own home; rather, the city consisted of several buildings filled with connected living spaces. He insisted they were not called apartments, despite Coal saying they sounded exactly like apartments. In Vuntagonyeo, the structures were called *blotskas*. When Coal asked if "blotska" was just the Ronog translation of "apartment," Biror told him to shut up.

Every building radiated out from an enormous clay dome in the center of the city, which Coal presumed was Vetch Kaya. The home of Mother Pig. The dome had one single door on its front, which Biror informed them was only ever unlocked when a city official entered or exited. Carved onto the dome was a circle with several thick strands emanating out from it, swirling and wrapping themselves all around the dome. When Jatiri asked if it was meant to depict the sun, Biror said no, but did not elaborate any further.

Boars and frogs milled about the city streets. None offered the group any friendly salutations.

A frog sat cross-legged on the ground beside the entrance to a small grocery store. He had a clay bowl in front of him with a few measly tups inside. The man was caked in grime and had sad, sunken eyes.

"Ignore him," said Biror unprompted, noticing Coal looking at the man. "He is trash. That is why he sits on the street like trash."

Coal glared at the boar and stopped walking. Shifting most of his weight onto one crutch, he fished in his pocket for some spare tups. Without him asking, Jatiri took the money from him and offered it to the frog.

The man smiled warmly and thanked her. His voice was a low rasp.

"Foolish," Biror grunted.

They then sat Coal down on a nearby clay bench while Biror lit a cigarette and spoke.

"There are three things we must do," he began, blowing smoke out through his mouth and nostrils. "We must book rooms at an inn, we must arrange a meeting with Mother Pig, and we must obtain a clay foot for little fox. I will do the first two, and you will do the last one." He nodded toward both Coal and Jatiri.

"Given how secretive you said Mother Pig is, do you think we'll be able to speak with her?" Jatiri asked.

"I said I will handle this. All you must do is get a foot. The easy task falls to you. I will bring you to the claymaker, and then I will leave. This is the plan." He took another drag from his cigarette. Coal watched the tip of it brighten then fade.

They both knew there was no use arguing with Biror, who was the authority on all matters in the Mudlands and had essentially proclaimed himself to be their leader while in the territory.

"I don't think getting a prosthetic yet is the best idea," Jatiri then said.

Coal blinked. He hadn't expected that. "Why not?" he asked.

She sighed. "You're not fully recovered yet. I'm worried that having something pressing up against the wound might prevent it from healing or incite an infection."

"You worry much," said Biror. "Little fox's leg is fine. Mudlands clay is strong and will make him better than before. You will be glad you lost your foot, I tell you true."

Coal wasn't sure he'd go that far, but he found himself agreeing with the boar. "You've said every day that my leg was doing well," he pointed out to Jatiri.

"Yes, and it is. But I think you should hold off."

He didn't want to discount her opinion, but he was so tired of the crutches. He wanted to be able to walk on his own. No matter how much Jatiri denied it, he still felt like a burden to them. A nuisance. He wanted this.

So that was that.

"Is there some way we can give it some extra padding or something so that it doesn't affect the healing process?" Coal asked Jatiri.

She shrugged. "Maybe." Her tone was unconvincing.

Coal thought for another second before speaking. "We'll keep an eye on it, how about that?" he offered as a concession.

"I'll get the prosthetic, but we can still make sure everything's healing alright."

Jatiri frowned. "I mean, that should be the plan regardless…"

"Sure, sure. I just mean that if things start taking a bad turn, I'll remove the prosthetic. But if they don't, then hey, all the better."

The saola was clearly not thrilled with this compromise, but she agreed to it anyway. She could probably guess he wasn't going to budge.

Jatiri convinced Biror to give Coal a few more minutes of rest before they continued down the stone street to the claymaker. The boar agreed, mostly because it gave him time to smoke a second cigarette.

As they walked, Biror pointed to a tall building on their left. He told them it was the inn where he'd be renting rooms and that they should find him there once business with the claymaker concluded. The inn, called the Naked Moon, was beautifully built with swooping red clay walls and ornamental designs etched into the trim.

The claymaker, by contrast, operated in a plain, squat square building with a flat roof that had a long chimney sprouting from it.

Inside, they found an old boar woman hunched over a table, shaping clay into a figurine. It was not any animal that Coal recognized, and had to be something from her imagination. Three completed, similarly odd figures sat proudly on the other end of the table. The woman was short and fat, with curved, yellowed tusks jutting from her mouth. She wore a loose-fitting blue smock that was streaked with red from wiping her fingers off on it. She stepped away from her figurine to address them.

The woman greeted them in Ronog, which Biror responded to, and she switched to the common tongue. "How I can help you?" she asked in an even stronger Mudlands accent than Biror's.

Without the simplest farewell, Biror ducked out of the shop to attend to his own self-appointed errands.

"Uhh…" Coal did not know how to start. He held up his leg and showed the old woman his bandaged stump. "I need a foot," he said, feeling massively stupid as the words left his mouth.

The claymaker was unfazed by this. It was as if someone wandered into her shop every other day asking for a clay foot. She nodded and grabbed the four figurines she'd been shaping, then smashed them all together into one big lump of red clay. She shuffled away and returned moments later with a few tools. There were some differently-sized blades, a stone roller, a thick needle, and a ruler.

First she set to measuring his remaining foot, as well as the empty space where his lost foot was meant to be. Where his new, clay foot would reside. Whatever measurements she obtained, she did not write them down. Coal hoped she still had a good memory and that he was not going to end up with a massive clomper down there.

She then wet her hands before touching the clay, moistening it, making it more malleable. It only took a couple minutes for her to mold the lump into roughly the same shape as Coal's real foot, though slightly larger to take into account the extra padding usually provided by footwear.

"How much is this going to cost?" Coal asked the boar.

"Pah," she grumbled, waving her hand at him. "No speaking while work."

Coal and Jatiri respected her wishes and observed her craft in silence.

After completing the initial mold by hand, which already looked remarkably good to Coal, she then started to scrape off the rough edges and more finely-tune the curves and lines with her blades. It was fascinating watching her work, taking what was once a dull brownish-red lump and turning it into something recognizable and real.

"This is insane," Coal muttered as this woman made him a foot. "My foot is gone and I'm going to have a clay one instead."

"Yeah," Jatiri whispered. "Maybe now you'll complain less about your feet hurting, though."

Coal chuckled, and the claymaker shushed them again.

He didn't know how much time had passed when she finally finished sculpting the foot. She used the needle to poke a hole in either side of it, which she told them would be where the strap attached. The claymaker stepped away from the table and placed her hands on her hips, admiring her own handiwork.

"It looks great," said Coal. "How long will it take to cook?" Using the word "cook" in reference to his future foot was odd.

"Not ready for cook," said the woman. "Needs dry. Will crack. Bad."

Coal knew nothing about claymaking, so he had foolishly assumed he'd be walking out of there on his brand new foot. "How long does it need to dry?" he asked.

"Two weeks."

"Two weeks?"

"Two weeks," the woman repeated, bobbing her head up and down. "Maybe more. Wet air. Clay needs dry."

"That would give your wound more time to heal," Jatiri pointed out. "That wouldn't be the worst thing in the world."

"True, but that's just...so long."

He didn't even know if they were still going to be in Vuntagonyeo in two weeks. Time was not exactly on their side.

Coal sighed. "Is there any way to...speed it up?" he asked, unsure if that was even a possibility. A second ago he hadn't known clay needed to dry at all, let alone for two weeks.

The woman grumbled before responding. "I candle," she said. "One night. Not so good. Not pure."

He did not know what it meant to candle, but getting something tomorrow sounded a lot better than in two weeks. Jatiri's point about giving it more time to heal was understandable, but he was getting sick of these crutches. And waiting for the clay foot to dry wouldn't do him any good if they departed for the Houndstooth (or the whole kingdom was destroyed) before it was ready.

To the claymaker, he asked, "It can be ready tomorrow?"

The woman was disgruntled, but she nodded. "Evening," she said.

"Thank you." He once again asked how many tups he owed for her work, but she said he could pay tomorrow when he picked up the prosthesis, since she was still worried that it might crack while cooking in the kiln.

With that settled, Coal and Jatiri headed back to the inn that Biror had pointed out earlier. They entered the Naked Moon with Coal feeling somewhat deflated, not only about his situation in general but also specifically for having to use his crutches for another day.

"I haven't seen a single person in this city with a clay limb, by the way," Coal said as they sat themselves in the lobby to await Biror. "I think he might've been fucking with me. He's gonna laugh his ass off when he sees me bumbling around with a clay foot, I just know it."

It was close to an hour before Biror showed up at the inn. His brow raised slightly at the sight of them in the lobby. He approached and asked, "Why are you not in your rooms?"

"We didn't know we had rooms," said Jatiri.

"I told you I was coming to get us rooms. Of course you have rooms."

"Well, we didn't know we were supposed to talk to the receptionist or something. We were just waiting for you."

"How would you two get by without me?" Biror asked with total sincerity. "Even when you had both foot, you were a mess. Come. We all have our own room. For privacy."

"Wait," Jatiri said, and Biror turned back around to face them again. "What's going on with Vetch Kaya? Are we allowed in?"

Biror looked at her like she was an idiot for asking such a question. "Of course we are allowed in," he answered.

"You said most people aren't allowed in," Coal reminded him.

"Vetch Kaya is not forbidden place. It is sacred place," said Biror in a tone that suggested he was speaking to children. "Many have no reason to enter, and so they do not. I explain our need to the city officials, and we will be allowed inside in two days. This is the earliest Mother Pig is available for meet with us."

"Simple as that?" said Coal. "What'd you tell them? What's our reason for meeting her?"

Biror rolled his eyes. "I already tell you I will handle this, and I did. You do not need to know more, little fox. All you had to do was get a foot, and I can see clear you could not even do so simple a task as get a foot. Pathetic."

"My foot is candling," Coal spat back, sounding much more authoritative than he felt.

"What does that even mean?" Biror asked, calling his bluff.

Coal fumbled his words for a second before saying, "I'll have the damn foot tomorrow. I'll have it in time for our meeting so Mother Pig can be super impressed with it, okay?"

"Mother Pig will not be impressed by a clay foot."

"I was making a joke."

"You are not funny."

"So you've told me."

"I am unamused by you, little fox."

"I get it."

Biror showed them to their respective rooms. Coal threw himself down on the bed without even really looking at his lodgings, letting his branch-crutches clatter to the floor.

He let out a deep sigh into the pillow, his warm breath enveloping his face. His foot itched. No, not his foot—the stump where his foot used to be. He kicked his legs in frustration, and a jolt of pain shot through his left leg.

He balled his hands into fists and began to cry. Soon, he was sobbing.

It was the first time he'd been alone since the accident. The first time he finally let all his frustration and sadness and fear out.

He flipped over and stared up at the clay ceiling. The back of his head sank into the pillow, damp with his tears. Heat ran up his leg, replacing the itch. He thought about his new clay foot cooking in the kiln, and imagined the rest of his body in there with it. Flames licking at his cheeks, singing the fur on his arms. Heating him up too quickly, his body cracking, shattering into pieces.

31

MORNING CAME AS IT always did: bright and unwelcoming.

Coal had gone to bed without any dinner, so he awoke with a pit in his stomach that was in desperate need of filling. He sat up and hung his legs over the side of the bed, the sole of his foot slapping onto the cold clay floor. The gap between his stump and the floor seemed unimaginably large. An immense void.

His crutches lay pitifully on the floor beside him. Thick, twisted gray branches. It was a wonder his armpits weren't filled with splinters every day. He picked them up one by one and headed downstairs.

Jatiri was in the lobby. She claimed she wasn't waiting for him, but Coal didn't believe her. She was aware of how frustrated he'd been and probably wanted to keep him company. Try to cheer him up.

Today she was wearing clothes she had picked up in Yandara after losing all her belongings in the shipwreck. The outfit was not her style at all: a pink blouse with a high collar around the neck and some ill-fitting, wrinkly white pants dirtied with mud from their long trip through the wilderness. Even while shopping she had complained that the pants were going to be ruined, but that style was all she could find in her size, aside from some skirts that she did not want to wear day in and day out.

They got breakfast together at a restaurant attached to the inn, unappetizingly called the Naked Plate to match the inn's (also unappetizing) name. It was not the best meal he'd ever eaten, but far from the worst, and his hunger led him to ordering multiple plates of food regardless.

And then it was just a matter of waiting.

Waiting for Mother Pig to be available the following day, and waiting for his clay foot to be ready.

Part of him wanted to take some time and explore Vuntagonyeo, but it was too much of a hassle on his crutches. Getting to the city in the mud was a huge pain in the ass, and Coal was in no mood to put himself through those annoyances again, getting his branches stuck in the muck. There were some stone paths, sure, but they couldn't cover the entire city.

So he and Jatiri returned to the inn and hung out in the lobby. There was a bar, which was already open, much to Coal's surprise. Knowing Biror, though, it should not have come as a shock to him that boars would be ready to drink as soon as they woke up. That was not typically Coal's style, but he saw no better way to make the time go by. Jatiri did not want to partake, saying it was too early for even a light glass of longwine, but that she would accompany him.

They sidled up to the bar, which was being manned by a boar who was even bigger and bulkier than Biror. Both of his tusks were missing, and he wore a permanent scowl. Coal leaned his branches against the countertop as he sat on a stool.

Just one look at them told the man they were not fluent in Ronog. "What drink would you like?" he croaked. His throat sounded tattered.

Coal took a moment to read the board of specials scribbled in chalk on the wall behind the bartender, but a lot of it was written in Ronog, so he gave up. "What do you recommend?" he asked the man.

The bartender rolled his eyes and Coal instantly regretted the question. "King's Pillow," the boar replied.

For a second, Coal considered not asking what the cocktail consisted of so as to not further annoy the man, but he had to, so he did.

"Two shot of hotchket mixed with tonic."

Coal had heard of hotchket, a specialty liqueur from the Mudlands, but had never tried it before. He knew it was thick and syrupy, but was unsure of its flavor.

No better place to try it than its home, he thought with a shrug.

"Sure," he said.

The boar nodded and started mixing the drink.

"Have you tried hotchket before?" Jatiri asked Coal while the bartender worked.

"No, have you?"

She giggled. "Yes. It's popular in the Innards, since tradesmen from the Mudlands travel up and down the Lunsk River a lot. It's one of their bigger exports, I believe. My dad is a big fan of it and usually has a bottle somewhere in his house."

"How's it taste?"

Jatiri widened her eyes and made her mouth small, shrugging her shoulders, acting as if she had no idea what he meant by the question.

The bartender then returned with his drink, the King's Pillow. It was in a tall, frosty glass that was cool to the touch. The cocktail was a dark brown color, almost like the mud outside. It was thinned a bit by the tonic water, which was a relief. Jatiri watched with anticipation as he took a sip.

Out of politeness and common decency he did not spit it all over the table. The hotchket was all at once herbaceous, fruity, earthy, and bitter, with a tinge of what he could only describe as a rotten sweetness. Cutting it with the bubbly tonic did not make things any better, either.

Coal did not know what sort of face he was making, but apparently it did not shy away from his feelings. Jatiri was laughing beside him, and he was thankful that the bartender had already walked away and was not witnessing his reaction.

"What the hell is this?" he whispered to Jatiri.

"It's bad, huh?"

"How could you not warn me about this?"

"You didn't ask before you ordered! It was too late." The saola was still giggling at his misfortune.

"This man should be arrested for selling such a drink. This is their biggest export? How?"

"People like it," she shrugged.

Coal could not fathom tasting the bizarre blend of flavors and finding pleasure in it. Then a horrid realization dawned on him.

"I have a full glass of this," he said.

"Yes, you do."

"I can't just *not* drink it…"

"That would be rude."

"And ordering a different drink would be rude too."

"If you want a different drink, order a different drink."

"I can't. It's too awkward. I'd feel so bad and so stupid and I would be wasting their supplies, even though this stuff should be poured into a sewer anyway."

"The choice is yours."

He chose to consume the drink, little by little.

It took a very long time. The more time passed and the deeper he got into the glass, the worse it tasted. He was still drinking it long after the frostiness of the glass wore off and the cocktail began to warm up. Every sip was like kicking back a shot of runny vomit.

Much of the day was spent in the Naked Moon's lobby. Coal appreciated Jatiri loafing about with him.

At one point, after making sure no one else was around, Jatiri nudged him and lifted her leg into the air.

"Hey, who am I?" she asked him.

He stared, and after a moment, her foot vanished and she waved the stump of her leg around in the air, giggling to herself.

"Very funny," he said with a grin.

"I thought so."

They never did see Biror, who had to be out in the city running his own errands, of which Coal did not give a shit about. He was growing sick of the boar.

Eventually, it was finally time to check in on the claymaker.

"Do you want me to go with you?" Jatiri asked him. They had gotten lunch at the Naked Plate but were back in the lobby hanging out and chatting.

Coal considered her offer, but he felt like spending a little time by himself, which he explained to her. She said she understood, and he set off.

It was easy enough to stick to the stone paths on his way to the claymaker's lodge. The sun had just barely begun to set, so he hoped this was sufficiently "evening" enough for the woman. He was anxious to get rid of the branches. He wanted to cast them into the mud, let them sink into the earth, gone and forgotten.

He had some difficulty opening and getting through the doorway, but once inside, the claymaker greeted him with a cheery "Pah!" At least, it sounded cheery to him.

"Is it ready?" he asked.

The woman nodded and scuttled into a back room to retrieve it for him. She returned a minute later, proudly holding it in her hand. It was a dull reddish-brown color, sculpted into the same general shape as his foot, though slightly larger. It was not overly detailed or realistic, but there were some interesting flourishes carved into the piece.

"No crack," the woman said with a toothy grin.

"Excellent!" Coal beamed. He was still having some doubts about Biror's claim that Mudlands clay was stronger than clay found elsewhere in the kingdom. "It won't break?" he asked. If a boar could walk around putting their pressure and weight on a clay limb, then Coal would probably be fine, but he had to be sure.

402 • *Travis M. Riddle*

In response, the claymaker hurled his foot at the wall. It bounced off and landed with a harsh thud on the ground, but was undamaged. Not even the tiniest surface-level crack.

"Wow."

"Good clay," she said. He nodded in agreement. "Not as long-last, but strong."

The woman hunched over to retrieve the clay appendage for him and set it down on her table next to some more figurines she'd molded after forming the old ones into his foot.

"What are those?" he asked her, pointing at the tiny clay creatures. Some still had a wet sheen to them.

"My monsters," the woman answered. "Come from my head." She tapped her forehead. "I create them. I tell my granddaughter stories and she plays."

Coal smiled. "That sounds very nice," he said. He wondered how many monsters the woman had dreamed up over the years to entertain her granddaughter, and her own children before that.

"I got you strap," the claymaker then said, hurrying into the back room again. When she reemerged, she was holding some straps the same color as the dried clay. She then got to work attaching the straps to the holes she had poked in either side of the foot with a small bolt.

The claymaker motioned for him to take a seat on a nearby stool, and he obeyed.

"Come, come," she said, and he held his leg out for her.

She gingerly placed the foot at the end of his stump, pressing it softly against the bandages. Then she fastened the straps around his leg, making sure it was a tight fit and would not slip off while he walked.

When she was done, she stepped away and told him to try walking.

Coal stood shakily. There was a bit of uncomfortable pressure in his stump, but he was sure that would go away once it was fully healed. Jatiri still expressed concern over not waiting until the wound was completely recovered, but when she checked it earlier that day, she said it was looking fairly good. Fairly good was enough for him right now.

He took a cautious step forward, and smiled wide when he did not fall flat on his face.

The clay foot clunked pleasantly on the hard ground. He walked in circles around the claymaker's shop, and the woman clapped in delight as he did so.

It was a bit unsteady as he walked back over to the claymaker, and so they took a second to readjust and tighten the strap a bit. That seemed to do the trick.

"Thank you so much," he said, wrapping the woman in a hug. She patted him on the back, speaking to him in Ronog.

"Strong, but not last long," the claymaker reiterated. "Dry and cook too fast. Will need a new."

"I understand," he nodded. In truth, he was interested in seeing what sort of technology was available elsewhere in Ruska—Soponunga's Mayor Bontrug with the robotic spider he rode around in flashed in his mind—but this clay foot would suffice for now.

He paid the claymaker the tups she was owed and gave her another tight hug. The woman chuckled heartily as she slapped him on the back. When she pulled away, she pointed at the gnarled branches he'd leaned against the wall and said, "Take."

Coal bid her farewell, taking one last look at the figurines on the table before he shuffled out the door with the branches in tow.

He was a bit unsteady on his feet, but it felt amazing being able to walk again without the crutches. Even after the clay-maker's showy display, he had felt uneasy and anticipated the clay appendage shattering with every apprehensive step he took.

The first thing Coal did was march out of Vuntagonyeo and toss the branches back out into the wild. They did not dramatically recede into the muck like he had daydreamed, but he was glad to be rid of them all the same. It might contradict his promise to Jatiri that he would use the crutches again if his wound took a turn for the worse, but in that moment, he didn't care. He wanted to be rid of the things.

His pace was much slower than everyone else's as he walked the city's stone streets, trying to learn how to keep his balance on this strange new appendage. It was exciting being able to move around easily and explore Vuntagonyeo a little more, though. He thought about holding Ilio's hand as they walked around, admiring the architecture and trying out the local cuisine (although he was disappointed by the lack of street vendors he'd seen thus far).

As he passed by Vetch Kaya, Coal grinned at how jealous of him Ilio would be if he knew where he was. Ilio could probably point to different parts of the city and explain the detailed history of them to him, after how much he'd read of his *Masters of Mud* historical fiction series. The books probably weren't totally accurate, but he had to know more about the Mudlands than Coal did.

That gave Coal a sudden idea. This was the first big city he'd been in since the shipwreck. It probably had a bookstore somewhere. Maybe he could replace his copy of *A Popular Bargain*. He felt terrible about losing the gift Ilio had given him.

Worst of all, he had lost it to a machine man who had stated multiple times that the book was unappealing to him.

It took a while to track down a bookshop, but Coal savored the opportunity to continue testing out his new appendage. He entered with a light ringing of a bell above the doorway, and a woman welcomed him with a kind hello.

The shop was small, with a limited selection, so his hopes were not high that he'd find the book. Regardless, it was a fun way to spend his evening. He missed being surrounded by books. Looking at their spines lining the shelves, varying in width and color and texture like a rectangular rainbow, filled him with glee.

Coal wandered around the tiny shop for several minutes, hunting for the mystery section, before coming to the conclusion that there wasn't one. He sighed. Someday, maybe, he would find out the answers to *A Popular Bargain*'s mysteries. At the point he'd gotten to, he still could not guess at all where the narrative was headed. Unfortunately, Ilio's prediction about it being simple enough for him to solve was proven wrong.

"Can I help you find anything?" the shopkeeper asked, suddenly appearing from around the corner of the shelf he was browsing.

"No, thank you," he said with a smile. But then, "Actually, do you carry the *Masters of Mud* series?"

The woman nodded. "Of course! They are some of our best-selling books."

She showed him to where the books were displayed, and Coal had to stop his mouth from hanging open when he saw that the series had an entire shelf dedicated to it. It was still beyond Coal how anyone could enjoy historical fiction, which was always incredibly drab every time he attempted to read it, but there was something for everyone's tastes.

"Enjoy!" the shopkeeper said, leaving him to attend to another customer who had just entered.

Coal scanned the shelf as well as his mind, trying to recall what Ilio had told him about the series while they walked around Soponunga. How many volumes had he already read before? Five? Five sounded right.

Every book's clothbound spine was a slightly different shade of brown, which Coal thought was a little on the nose considering the series' title. Each one also had a gold foil stamp declaring which number in the series it was, ranging from 1 to 8.

"There are eight of these fuckin' things?" Coal muttered to himself, running a finger along the spines.

He picked up a copy of book eight, which was titled *The Afterparty*. Its cover was adorned with an illustration of a boar in profile, cloaked in shadow, holding a dagger to his chest.

"Even the titles are boring as hell," he whispered, flipping the book open to a random page. He absentmindedly read a few sentences before shutting it and returning the book to its place on the shelf.

He may have lost Ilio's gift to him, but Coal thought it might be nice to return the favor the next time they were able to see each other.

Was it really the fifth book that he said was the last he read? Coal could not recall. That seemed right, but he could also vaguely remember Ilio saying he was two behind. So had he read number six? Or was he mistaken about how many books in the series were already released?

He could debate the issue with himself all night; he had to pick a book and buy it. He yanked book six from the shelf, its shade of brown more like tree bark than the dark richness of hotchket, and read its title: *Denya's Crossing*.

Coal shrugged and grabbed books seven and eight as well. He was spending the Dirt King's money, so he might as well buy them all to be safe. No harm.

With his bag of books slung over his shoulder, Coal headed back to the inn. His stomach was starting to growl, demanding dinner from somewhere besides the Naked Plate. He tripped two or three times on his way back, but quickly regained his footing and continued on. He was quite pleased with how fast he'd taken to the prosthetic so far.

Voices roared through the air, growing louder as he approached the inn. Soon Biror came into view, standing outside arguing with another boar. As Coal came nearer, he was able to make out the conversation. He stopped short of the inn and listened from down the street, hopefully out of Biror's view.

"You're full of shit, Nurot," said the stranger. He pointed an accusatory finger mere inches from Biror's face, who looked like he was about to bite it off.

"You are one to talk of shit," said Biror. "Go back to your home and eat the shit-pie your husband made you for dinner."

"Don't badmouth my husband's cooking."

"Your husband is the worst cook in all of Vuntagonyeo. Everybody knows this, even you," Biror smirked.

The man was becoming more irate, but decided to move past the jab at his husband. "You knew what would happen when you showed up here. You need to pay."

"You are aware of my situation. You will get the tups when you get the tups. Until then, I suggest you back the fuck up and get your fat finger out of my face."

"Or what? You gonna beat me like you did your brother? Get a fuckin' grip. You can't touch us." The man lowered his furry brown finger, but spit on the ground by Biror's feet. "Get us the fucking money. I don't give a good shit about you being in prison or wherever it is you claim you disappeared to, and neither does Heppek."

The man stepped away, and Biror did not have a retort. He watched the man depart, pushing past Coal, who now walked toward the inn.

"I see you have your clay foot," said Biror in lieu of a greeting.

"Yeah," Coal said. "It's weird, but it works for now."

"The Mudlands have the best clay in the world. Trust me, it will serve you well."

"Okay," Coal said. Then he asked, against his better judgment, "What was that about?"

Biror crossed his arms. "It does not concern you, little fox."

"It kind of does," said Coal. "Some guy's threatening you. If you're in danger, that means Jatiri and I are in danger too. We need to be aware of everything that's going on."

"Lampet? That man is no threat to me," Biror scoffed. "He is worthless and weak, like you. Do not worry about him."

Coal frowned and crossed his arms, a mirror image of Biror.

"What did he mean by what he said about Kofa?"

"He meant nothing. He is a fool, like you."

"Cut the shit," growled Coal. "He said something about you beating your brother."

Biror took a step toward him, looming over him, trying to be intimidating. It was working, but Coal wasn't going to let that show on his face. He glared up at the boar, whose tusks were too clean to ridicule.

"You really want to know, little fox?" he said, his breath wafting into Coal's nose, sour and stale. "I tell you true, that my brother is sick and I must care for him. But I am the one who put my brother in his bed. I am the reason he cannot walk and sometimes cannot breathe. He angered me, and I showed him that anger. I did not hold back. Your family must know your truest self, and he knew me that day." Biror's eyes narrowed to slits. He breathed out hard through his crooked nose. "You have asked questions of me for weeks now. You try to get to know me. If you press me further on this, you will finally know me like my brother knows me."

Coal couldn't let the man know how much his words rattled him. He was not going to be pushed around by him anymore.

"You know what?" said Coal. "Fuck your secrets and fuck your threats and most of all, fuck you."

It was not as elegant or frightening a speech as Biror's, but it effectively got his point across.

He went on, the words gripping him. "I thought you were an asshole when we found out you're a mantis runner, and then I felt kinda bad when we learned about your brother. I thought it was a 'heart of gold' situation, a guy doing bad things for a good reason. But it turns out my instinct was right, and you're just an asshole. Plain and simple."

Biror swung his fist.

Coal ducked and miraculously dodged the blow, then slammed his own fist into Biror's gut before he himself even realized what he was doing.

The boar guffawed. He then picked Coal up by the shoulders and kneed him in the stomach. Coal sputtered, all the air knocked out of his lungs. Biror then tossed him away like a sack of garbage. He landed with a wet smack in the mud.

By the time Coal managed to prop himself up, Biror was gone. Whether he withdrew to the inn or wandered off into the city, Coal did not know.

He stood with a groan and checked his clay foot. It was unharmed, and the strap had not even come loose. He was once again impressed by the claymaker's impeccable craftsmanship.

There were many groans and sighs as he wiped away as much of the mud from his clothes as he could. He then entered the inn and went to his room to set down his bag of books and change his clothes before finding Jatiri for dinner.

Coal peeked into the bag to inspect the books and was relieved to find no mud had snuck its way inside to ruin their covers or pages. They were still pristine. If Biror had damaged his gift for Ilio, he would have *really* been pissed.

He slipped off his shirt, wincing with soreness from the throw, and set to cleaning himself.

32

BIROR WAS, UNDERSTANDABLY, NOT invited to dinner. Coal and Jatiri got together and were recommended by the inn staff a restaurant nearby called Bubble & Gorge. They laughed after hearing the name, and Coal commented to Jatiri that the boars certainly had a style when it came to naming their establishments.

"Maybe it sounds much more elegant in Ronog?" Jatiri proposed. "It could be the translations that are giving these places their strangeness."

Bubble & Gorge was past the dome at Vuntagonyeo's center, which they would be entering the next day. Coal was eager to put all of the Mudlands behind him. His journey over the past few weeks was as fraught as his relationship with Biror, who he was also quite ready to ditch. He did not foresee himself keeping in touch with the man when all this was over.

The restaurant was a long, squat building that curved in its middle. Coal was briefly reminded of Horace's crescent-shaped head, but cast that image aside. He wouldn't let it ruin his meal.

They were eating fairly early, so they were seated quickly. Bubble & Gorge was decorated with ornately-sculpted white clay trim along the blue-painted walls, which was the first time Coal had seen a wall actually painted in this city. That simple fact led him to assume that this was a fine dining establishment.

Once more, he was excited to spend the Dirt King's money.

There were also plants potted in long clay troughs that hung from the ceiling. Their fronds were thin and trailed down like wisps of hair, almost far enough to brush lightly against one's head as they walked through the dining room.

With the restaurant so empty, so devoid of chatter, Coal was acutely aware of the *clack*ing of his foot on the floor as he walked. Clay against clay. It was annoying him, so it was probably bothering others as well. It wasn't a problem that would go away by replacing it with a mechanical foot, though. Just something new for him to live with.

The menu confirmed that Bubble & Gorge was a fancy place. It was filled with various pasta dishes, a cuisine that Coal was not expecting to find in the Mudlands. Importing the necessary ingredients must have been an ordeal. Pasta was still somewhat of a luxury, but it was definitely more common in other parts of Ruska, so maybe that was why the person back at the hotel had recommended this place to them; a guess that the visitors might be craving the taste of familiar foods.

Coal's eyes drifted across the page to the dishes' cost and let out a low laugh at the tups listed there.

"I'm glad we've got the Dirt King's wallet," he said.

"Me too," nodded Jatiri. She was still wearing her uncharacteristic pink blouse. "His funds aren't limitless, though. Even if it feels that way sometimes."

"Of course they are," said Coal. "What's the point of being king if you can't make as much money as you want for yourself?"

"You have a very rudimentary understanding of economics, I'm guessing?"

"*Less than* rudimentary, I'd say!"

Jatiri laughed. "I am not surprised."

Per Jatiri's suggestion, they skipped appetizers and went straight to ordering entrees. Coal was looking forward to a three-course meal, but if Jatiri said they should cool it a little on the spending, he would follow her advice. He figured his stupid foot had set them back; an unplanned expenditure.

And speaking of, Jatiri asked him, "How's the foot feel?"

He didn't know how to answer that. "It's weird," he started. "I can, like…still feel my old foot there, my real foot. But then when I touch this one, obviously I don't feel anything, so it's just like I have two there? I don't know how to explain. It's bizarre. Kind of uncomfortable."

"Does it hurt to walk on? I'm concerned about you applying pressure on your leg too soon."

"Nah, no pain. I can hardly feel it, really. There's a lot of padding between me and it. Just the same itching that's always been there. Does that ever go away?"

Jatiri frowned. "It usually does, but…it can take a couple years, sometimes. In rare cases, it never goes away."

Annoying clacking and a forever itch. Wonderful things to adjust to.

"I'm happy to hear it's not hurting you, but all the same, I'd like to take a look at it after dinner," Jatiri said.

"Alright," said Coal. Then, "Hey, look at us. All three meals together today."

"Is that odd?" she asked. "We're traveling together, after all."

"I guess that's true."

"No Biror at any of them, though."

"Biror's…" Coal trailed off, not sure what to say. With the look Jatiri was giving him now, though, he knew he needed to continue. She deserved to know, anyway. "He's maybe not the best guy."

"I think all of us knew that long ago," Jatiri chuckled.

"Sure, but—he attacked me, like, half an hour ago."

Jatiri's eyes just about popped from her skull. "What? Why?"

Coal sighed. "When I got back to the inn, I overheard him arguing with some guy who he owes money. While they were fighting, the guy mentioned something about Biror hitting him like he hit his brother. I confronted Biror about it, and he said that he's the reason his brother's constantly in need of care. They got into a fight and Biror beat the shit out of him, I guess. Now he's laid up in a bed and can't do anything for himself." After a pause, he said, "It must have been a pretty brutal beating, if he's in that sort of condition."

He watched Jatiri process this information. She was silent for almost a full minute, tapping her fingers on the table, looking down at her nails worriedly.

"That's vile. How could he do that to his own family?" she murmured.

Coal shrugged.

"And then he hit you just for asking about it?"

"Well, after asking, I essentially told him to eat shit. And it was more of a 'kneeing me in the gut and throwing me across the street' sort of thing rather than a punch."

Jatiri was taken aback. "He's…" She was at a loss. "He's more dangerous than we knew."

Coal nodded. "For a while, I thought his shitty attitude was just for show and that maybe deep down he *did* like us, but, uh…that is no longer my stance."

"There's no way for us to trust him."

"I think we can," Coal disagreed. "I think he's been perfectly honest about wanting to fulfill this mission and then get back to Dasna. I don't think we have to worry about him abandoning us or letting us die, because he knows that would result in failure, and he needs this thing to be a success. But I don't think there's any point in trying to cozy up to him, no."

"I definitely don't want to now," said Jatiri. "I can't imagine doing that to your own brother."

"I can't either. Not that I have one to imaginarily do this to anyway, but still. It's awful."

"No brothers or sisters?"

"Nope," said Coal. "Just me and my father. How about you?"

"I have three sisters," she said with a grin.

"Wow. Where do you fit into the ranking there?"

"What does that even mean? Which sister is best? Me, of course. Number one."

"Okay, yeah, that was a stupid way to phrase that. I meant age-wise. Are you the oldest? The baby?"

"I'm…second baby?" Jatiri chuckled. "Yola is the youngest, then it's me. Then Venet, then Suo is the oldest."

"Second baby, but the most accomplished, I'm sure. They must all be jealous of your doctorly-ness."

"Venet and Suo are doctors too."

"Well, shit."

"Yola is the one who diverged."

"How many doctors does one town need? How big are your towns out there in the wilds of the Innards?"

"They're not that big! Venet and Suo moved away to other villages. It's actually been more than a year since I've seen either of them." Her smile faded. "It's been tough, now that I know what's going on in the kingdom. I don't know if they're okay or not. The rest of my family was still fine when I left, but...that was months ago, so I don't know about them, either."

Coal frowned. In a way, he was lucky that he only had himself to worry about when it came to whatever was going on with the Houndstooth. He hadn't stopped to consider what his companions were going through, leaving family behind.

"I'm sorry," he said. "I know that's not helpful to hear, but I am. I hope you can get back to them really soon." After a beat, he tried to lighten the mood. "Which one of you is the best doctor, though? That's the ranking I'm interested in."

She smirked. "I already told you: I'm number one."

"Oh, naturally. I've seen the way you can wrap a foot. Or a lack of foot, rather."

"I'm the most skilled lack-of-foot-wrapper in the Innards. That's what I'm known for, actually."

"Wow, you don't say? I got incredibly lucky, then, being with you when I came into my own lack-of-foot."

They were laughing at this when their food came. Coal had ordered a bowl of thin, stringy noodles tossed in creamy tomato sauce with three waspballs thrown in. Jatiri would be eating little pasta shells stuffed with some type of cheese he hadn't heard of before, smothered in an herby green sauce.

As they began to eat, Jatiri asked him, "How are you feeling?"

The question surprised him. He felt like he had already answered it. "I'm fine," he said. "Just that itch. More irritating than painful."

"No," she shook her head. "I mean with everything. It's been a rough few weeks for everyone, but for you especially. Between the shipwreck, the machine man thing, and now your foot…"

"Oh," he said softly. He absently pushed one of the waspballs around with his fork. The trip from Nitulo to Vuntagonyeo had been such a whirlwind, he never had time to sit and reflect on it. No time to process. "I'm…well, 'fine' isn't really right, but I dunno. It's not out of the ordinary for the shitty year I've had," he said, wincing at his own admission. He'd never told Jatiri about what happened with his father, about his life on the run, and now was not the time. "Maybe I'm just used to it by now. As awful as that sounds," he laughed.

Now it was Jatiri's turn to say she was sorry. Then, "I'm sure things will turn around once we're all past this. Once the kingdom is in better shape."

He shrugged. "That's what I'm hoping. We'll see."

The waspballs were incredibly dry and bland. It was as if they were mocking his already meager optimism.

AN HOUR LATER, COAL was back in his room at the Naked Moon, lying in bed and flipping through book six of *Masters of Mud*, trying to latch onto anything at all that he found interesting so that he could discuss it with Ilio.

But it was impossible. The books were simply too boring. How could anyone enjoy these?

He amused himself by remembering how enthusiastic Ilio was about the books. It was cute knowing how much the man enjoyed these horrible, boring stories.

It was then that his window burst, sending glass shattering across the floor and bouncing off the walls.

Coal was too bewildered to move. The bed was thankfully not near the window so he was, for the moment, unscathed. He did not think that would prove to be the case for very long as a figure crawled through the broken window, skittering across the ceiling. Coal screamed in alarm.

The figure was dark, with a metallic sheen. Coal realized that whoever or whatever it was, it was wearing a mechanical suit. They dropped to the floor and turned to face him.

They were tall, imposing. A bobcat with clipped ears. He was wrapped in an exoskeleton, a mechanical suit akin to the HM-3 mechanical scorpions that had plagued Coal back in Vinnag what felt like a lifetime ago. The suit covered the man's whole body, only leaving bits and pieces of his fur exposed underneath. His head was covered by a bulky helmet with glass plating over his face. A lengthy robotic tail with a stinger flowed fluidly behind him.

It was an impressive piece of tech, and Coal had to assume it was the latest HM model from the Palace engineers. Something a lot more agile than the enormous, bulky HM-3s that had previously attacked him.

This man was undoubtedly a Palace Stinger.

And if a Stinger was still after him, that meant they wanted to imprison him. Or worse.

Why the fuck is a Stinger after me? he asked himself. He was on official Dirt King business now. They had no reason to capture him, and in fact, it was against the kingdom's best interests to do so.

Lop.

The thought embedded in his mind. The orangutan surely had something to do with this. He always had a bone to pick with Coal for being a Flesh Eater, some blinding loyalty to the Palace and its fucking rules. Coal could think of no other reason this Stinger would be after him than Lop reporting back to the Palace and claiming he was dangerous.

There was no more time to fume over what Lop may or may not have done. The Stinger lunged forward, arms outstretched.

Coal jumped off the bed, which the bobcat crashed into. The immense weight of his exoskeleton instantly crushed the bedframe. Wood splintered and the book resting on the sheets went flying into the wall.

If he ruins that book, I swear…

Coal scrambled away from the bed, impressed and scared by the HM-4's agility. The machinery looked far too bulky to maneuver with any amount of grace, but the bobcat was disproving that assumption.

With his new clay foot, however, Coal was not nearly so graceful. As he darted away from the bed, he immediately lost his balance and crashed to the ground. He rolled over onto his back.

The Stinger stood, his mechanical tail weaving through the air behind him.

"Don't resist," the man said through his shield of glass. "It's been a real bastard tracking you down. I'd appreciate wrapping this up quick-like."

"No, thank you," Coal sputtered. He stood and bolted for the door, but once more he wasn't thinking about his prosthetic and tripped. The man was upon him in seconds.

Rough metal fingers gripped Coal by the shoulders and forcefully tossed him backward, toward the window. He hit the floor and rolled a couple feet, letting out a pathetic yelp as shards of glass pierced his back and shoulders.

"This is the end of the road," the Stinger said, walking toward him. "Orders are to kill. I don't know what you did, but if they don't even want to lock you up, you must be a real sick fuck."

Why would there be orders to kill him? Coal did not understand what was going on at all. The whole kingdom needed him alive to save the Houndstooth.

"Has to be a mistake," he choked out, the words barely audible. The tumble had winded him.

He was laying on his back, with his head closest to the approaching man. His feet were pushed up against the wall, his knees bent. He kicked them out and sent himself sliding across the floor, more glass tearing into his shirt and back, and slammed his head into the man's legs.

His own head roared with pain as he hit the exoskeleton, but it was enough to offset the Stinger's balance and catch him by surprise. He went toppling forward, unfortunately landing on top of Coal, who let out a muffled scream of gibberish. That had not gone according to plan, although in retrospect he could not see how else it would've played out.

The rough landing set something off in the HM-4 suit, though, and the pointed tip of the man's tail opened and spat out a metal orb.

From where he lay, Coal could not see if it was a Fire or Lightning or Something Else Horrible orb—he could only hear the clatter of it bouncing along the floor—but no matter what, it was about to cause some massive issues for everybody.

The metal ball exploded in a barrage of flame. The force sent Coal and the Stinger flying back into the door, the weight of the man's suit causing them to crash through it into the hallway. Provided the size of the explosion, it had to have been a Fireball-M.

For some reason, Coal's first thought was that he was glad the tech developed by the Palace made it so that the fire did not spread and that his gifts for Ilio would be okay.

He was now no longer stuck underneath the massive bobcat, who had actually slammed into the wall and dented it, sending thin cracks skittering all the way to the ceiling. Coal stood and was about to make a run for the stairs when Jatiri and Biror both stepped out into the hall, as well as a few other random guests.

"Everyone get out!" Coal screeched.

The inn's guests stared in awe at the man embedded in the wall before scurrying back into their rooms to fetch their belongings and exit the building. Biror and Jatiri, meanwhile, surged forward.

But Coal ran toward them and said, "No, no, let's go!"

Biror stopped him, grasping him by the shoulders. Coal shuddered reflexively, given that when the boar did that earlier in the afternoon it had resulted in him being thrown carelessly like a bag of beans.

"Who is this man?" Biror asked.

"Asshole here to kill me," Coal said. The fastest explanation he could get out. The irony was not lost on him that mere hours before, he had berated Biror for not informing them of anyone who was out to get him. To be fair, though, Coal had thought the Stingers were called off once he joined the team.

Behind him, the bobcat started to rise, prying his suit from the clay wall.

"If he is here to kill, we must eliminate him," said Biror. "We cannot leave the city yet, and he will not leave either."

He was right, of course. Coal couldn't simply skip town like he always did in the past when a Palace Stinger showed up. They still had their meeting with Mother Pig the next day.

Biror produced a gun seemingly from thin air. Coal's eyes widened at the sight of the firearm.

The boar moved past Coal and fired a few blasts at the unsuspecting bobcat, who was still trying to get his bearings after the unexpected explosion. Bullets pinged off the suit without denting it, not even leaving the barest scratch. But Biror marched steadily onward and swung his empty fist just as the bobcat looked up. The boar's fist easily broke through the pane of glass protecting the Stinger, sending both the full power of his punch as well as bits of glass into the man's face.

The Stinger fell backward onto the floor, his nose crumpled and bleeding. Biror laughed. Shards of glass protruded from the bobcat's cheeks and chin, and the sight sent a pang of pain through Coal's back, reminding him that it was in a similar condition.

"You are done," Biror said, walking toward the man. He pointed the barrel of his gun at the bobcat's face.

But the Stinger kicked out at Biror's gut with his mechanical leg. The boar doubled over, wheezing.

The man stood, grabbed Biror by the head, and kneed him in the face. Biror collapsed to the floor.

"Fuck," Coal muttered. He turned to Jatiri and said, "You need to get out of here."

"But you—"

He didn't wait for her to finish protesting and simply shoved her toward the staircase.

She was stumbling down the stairs along with a few other guests when the Stinger bounded up the wall and onto the ceiling. The exoskeleton had tons of tiny protrusions that burrowed into the clay to keep the bobcat attached to the ceiling like an insect. From there, he launched another Fireball-M. The metal orb bounced along the floor, past Biror's unmoving body, coming to a halt at Coal's feet.

Coal panicked and grabbed the orb, then hurled it into his room. It was barely past the doorframe when it went off. He flew backward, rolling down the stairs, colliding with the unfortunate souls who were trying to flee.

The tangled mass of bodies came to a stop at the bottom of the stairs and woozily stood, limping away out of the Naked

Moon without another word to each other. Jatiri helped Coal to his feet, and he ushered her toward the front door.

"You need—"

"We'll be fine," Coal assured her, though he did not entirely believe it himself, now that Biror was incapacitated. "We need you safe, though, so you can patch up our stupid asses after. Okay?"

She nodded and reluctantly ran out the door onto the street.

Coal could hear the Stinger crawling around upstairs on the ceiling, nearing the staircase.

His mind raced with half-baked schemes. Nothing good had come to mind yet when another orb bounced jauntily down the steps.

How many of these does this fucker have? he asked himself, running to the opposite side of the lobby. There were a few awkward strides on his new foot before he could compose himself.

The Fireball exploded, its force damaging the walls with more cracks and blasting apart the stairs, sending debris scattering. Coal looked down at his clay foot and smiled at its sturdiness up to this point.

Coal ducked down near one of the fluffy chairs he and Jatiri had spent much of the day in. More dumb plans raced through his head, and only one seemed even slightly feasible.

He yanked the cushion off the chair and held it before him, slowly approaching the staircase.

The Stinger was descending, though not on the actual staircase. He was crawling on the walls, avoiding all the steps that were damaged by people frantically fleeing as well as his own Fireballs. His face scrunched into a grimace as he reached the lobby and discovered that his target was not yet dead. The protrusions from the exoskeleton suddenly clicked back into the suit and he dropped to his feet, rising threateningly.

"A pillow is not going to protect you," the man said. He grunted with amusement as he launched another Fireball-M.

Which was precisely what Coal had expected of him.

The cushion (*Not a pillow, you idiot,* Coal mentally corrected him) was not meant to be a shield for protection. Coal watched the arc of the metal orb, anticipated its trajectory, and ran forward a few steps to meet it.

He hit it with the large square cushion, sending it flying back toward the bobcat before the man could comprehend what had happened.

The Fireball-M exploded in the Stinger's face, sending him into a wall once again. When the smoke cleared, Coal saw that the fur on the man's face was singed.

Coal took a few cautious steps forward, but the Stinger was unmoving. "Biror?" he called.

There came a loud groan from upstairs, and Coal sighed with relief. The boar was a piece of shit, but they needed him. Not only for whatever absurd ritual they would have to do at the Houndstooth, but also because he was the only competent fighter among their group. Biror would not be caught dead attacking someone with a cushion.

A minute later, Biror came stumbling down the ruined steps, gripping his gun and nursing a bloody nose. He looked down at the unconscious bobcat and laughed mirthlessly.

"You did this, little fox?"

"Yeah."

"He is not dead."

"I didn't think so. I thought you could maybe handle that part."

"You want me to do your dirty work," he said with a huff. "Shameful. This man wants your blood, and you refuse yourself his."

"I don't want to kill him," Coal said resolutely.

"And yet you know he must be killed."

Coal did not respond. He stared stone-faced at the boar.

"Very well," said Biror. He holstered his gun and leaned down next to the Stinger. Then he grasped part of the protective glass shield that hadn't previously broken off, snapping it from its frame and swiping it across the bobcat's throat.

The man's eyes shot open and he grasped at his neck helplessly, gurgling as blood spurted from the wound. After a few seconds, he slouched limp against the damaged wall, leaning into the indentation he'd made.

Biror looked to Coal and said, "It is done. Why was this man after you?"

Coal stared at the dead bobcat, trying to process the last few minutes.

He looked to Biror and said, "I honestly don't know."

33

IT TOOK A FEW days for the city of Moonoshk to recover from the blightbeast attack. Of course the city was
still a far cry from its prime condition, but all things considered, it was remarkable that the technicians repaired so
much in so little time. They worked around the clock to ensure
every connecting tube was fixed and the entry elevator was
functional. Oftentimes this woke up Yurzu in the middle of the
night, with the sounds of construction ringing through the air.
A few times when he couldn't fall back asleep, he went outside
to watch the technicians at work.

Yurzu came out of the battle with only a few scratches and
bruises, which Noswen patched up without any trouble. Lop,
on the other hand, had sustained a sizeable gash across the
length of his back as well as a broken toe. The wound was
simple enough to heal, but he was hesitant to let Noswen fix
another broken bone given the pain he'd experienced with it

after the Ghoresn fight. Yurzu laughed at him suppressing a shout while Noswen worked on his toe.

In the end, the battle had lasted roughly another forty minutes. By then, Lop and the citizens had slain the blight-mother. The process involved Lop slicing off enough of the monster's legs for it to lose its footing and plunge to the ground below the city, where many then continued to fire upon it with their guns. The thing was too injured from the combination of the gunshots and the fall to get up again, so a collection of people flew down and fired into its head until it stopped moving. A few more of the smaller blightbeasts crawled out of its massive pores after that, but they were easy enough to contend with.

After that, it was simply a matter of marching through the city and eliminating any remaining blightbeasts. Some people sustained injuries still, but for the most part it was far less hectic.

When Moonoshk was clear of any more threats, the trio met up on the ground behind the elevator. Noswen was immensely displeased to learn that Yurzu had, in fact, entered the fray. She briefly yelled at him before wrapping him in a tight hug. Zsoz was waiting for them patiently, its body solidified and stuck firmly to the earth.

I heard a loud noise, the slime had said. **Is everything okay now?**

Yurzu was now laying in his bed in the Fingrass Hotel. Many bore witness to how much the group had contributed in defending the city from the monsters, so they had been provided with free rooms at the nicest hotel. Free room service included. The food wasn't spectacular, but it was free and better than plain nuts and berries, so Yurzu was indulging.

Early morning light poured in through the round window. There was a plate of half-eaten spiced jonweks with cream sauce sitting on his bedside table. They were a bit mushy and too spicy for him, but he liked the sauce. The person who took his order thought it was a strange choice for breakfast, but Yurzu didn't care. He was now digging through his bag, making note of what was left over.

He'd used almost all the killing powder that he originally brought with him from home. Merely two or three doses remained. There was probably a store in Moonoshk where he could restock on the necessary ingredients and grind them into a new batch.

Once they concluded their business here, they would be on their way to the Palace to seal the Houndstooth; it would still be wise to be prepared, though. They might encounter some more blightbeasts on their way north. It would still be a couple weeks before they reached the Dirt King's home.

Yurzu slid the near-empty leather pouch of yellow powder back into his bag. Next, he inspected the velvet pouch of sleeping powder, which was mostly full. There had not been many scenarios in which he needed to deploy it. He'd had a few restless nights at the start of this whole quest, and there was the wolverine chasing Coal who he had to knock out, but aside from that it went unused.

He pulled out the plain recipe book left behind by his parents. It was thankfully undamaged. He flipped through the pages, letting the scent of the old paper wash over him.

There then came a knock at his door. Yurzu placed the book on top of his sheets and hurried to answer. He swung the door open and Noswen stood on the other side, looking quite drained.

"I've been getting no fuckin' sleep," the raccoon groaned, stepping inside without an invitation. She plopped herself down on the bed, the shifting weight lightly bouncing the recipe book. "Those workers never stop."

"Things got pretty screwed up around here," said Yurzu. The Fingrass Hotel was one of the few buildings in the entire city that had sustained no damage.

"I wish we'd arrived a day later so we could've missed the excitement. Scratch that—a *week* later, so we could've also missed all the construction. We spent so many nights camping in the woods, I *needed* some good rest in a real bed. How was I sleeping better in the dirt than I am here?"

Yurzu chuckled. Noswen sat up and glanced at the book by her side. "What's this?" she asked, picking it up.

She began to flip through the pages. Yurzu said, "It's a recipe book."

"I can see that. Strange thing to bring on a trip like this."

His voice grew softer as he talked. The subject of his parents was not one he willingly spoke of very often.

"It belonged to my parents," he explained. "It's all of their recipes. Mostly for different pickling methods, but there are some meals in there, too."

"Ahh," she nodded. She was well aware of what had happened to his parents. She turned a page and smiled. "This one's called Yurzy's Yum."

"Oh, jeez."

"Your parents sold pickles with 'Yurzy's Yum' slapped on the label?" Noswen giggled.

"No, no," Yurzu shook his head. "They gave all the recipes silly names like that, just for their own amusement. Just for the book. That one was my favorite when I was little."

"Yurzy's favorite, but not Yurzu's?"

"It's still a favorite, I suppose."

Her eyes scanned the ingredient list. "So this one's on the sweeter side," she said. "What sort of stuff do you pickle with it?"

"Cucumbers and asparagus, mostly. I didn't like asparagus as a kid, but I would eat it if it was pickled with that."

"Little Yurzy," Noswen grinned. "Little Yurzy noshin' his asparagus. How cute."

Yurzu groaned amusedly. "Did you need something?" he asked, trying to steer away from the nickname.

Noswen closed the book and set it on the bed. "Yes, actually. They're ready to see us. Came knocking at my door ten minutes ago. Woke me up after I'd finally fallen asleep again. Really great. Don't these people sleep in?"

Most birds that Yurzu had met during their short time in Moonoshk (the owls excluded) were early risers. If it was a macaw coming to fetch Noswen, it made sense that the person assumed she'd already be awake at this hour.

Noswen was referring to the city's elected officials. She had tracked them down the other day, once things had cooled off from the monster attack. She requested a meeting with them, knowing that Ranatt Waraspoke was among their ranks, but they declined. They needed to focus on rebuilding the city first, which was reasonable. Noswen was told they would send someone to the hotel when they were ready for a meeting.

"They'll be ready for us in half an hour, so we should probably get moving. Are you good to go?"

Yurzu nodded. He was already washed up and dressed, having planned to go on a walk soon anyway.

"Great. Let's go grab Lop."

They locked Yurzu's room behind them and walked over to Lop's. The orangutan answered the door after a minute of Noswen pounding on it.

"What is wrong with you?" he demanded of her as he opened the door. "I was in the nude. I needed to dress myself before answering the door. I was calling out to you! I was being very clear that I would be a moment!"

"Didn't hear you. You still look nude to me anyway," she said, pointing at his exposed nipples underneath the straps of his overalls.

The man grimaced and asked, "What do you need?"

"City council's ready to talk to us. Time to get the beak and get out of here. We're almost done."

Lop's face lit up. "Oh!" he exclaimed. "Excellent. Let us go at once." He shuffled out of the room and locked his door. Zsoz was still inside, awaiting their return with the obsidian beak.

Walking through Moonoshk was like walking around a tin can. Everything was made of metal, granting every footstep a metallic clang. Navigating the closed-off tubes made Yurzu feel claustrophobic; it was a strangely huge relief to step out onto the decks or into glass-topped tubes he could see out of.

One thing the blightbeasts had destroyed that the city couldn't do anything about was the surrounding treetops. The monsters reached Moonoshk by climbing through the trees and had wreaked havoc on them. Tons of branches had snapped off and now littered the ground below the city, while others were stripped bare of their leaves.

While they walked through one of the windowed connecting tubes, Yurzu gazed out at naked branches swaying in the wind. Some scratched against the glass, though it produced no sound.

The place they were headed was a cylindrical building like all the rest in Moonoshk, but this one was much squatter and wider. It was affixed to the huge tree trunk at the city's epicenter, hovering above Bramble Plaza.

Being in the plaza reminded Yurzu that he had not seen Gogg ever since the blightbeast assault. He hoped the owl had made it through the fight, but he suspected he might never know for certain.

There was an elevator in the plaza that they rode up into a wide tube. In one direction, the tube branched into two pathways that led to other parts of the city, while the other direction would bring them to city hall. Navigating the city was wildly confusing. It was a technological marvel, but parts of it were too much for Yurzu's simple mind.

They entered the building and marched straight toward the reception desk. Noswen told the person about their appointment, and they were told to wait a few minutes in the lobby.

Noswen sat down in a chair while Lop paced nearby. Yurzu opted to walk around a little and check things out.

The lobby was huge and took up the whole width of the building. The far wall was lined with doors that he presumed led to the various offices and meeting rooms. There were several other people milling about, waiting for their appointments with the city's officials. Hung on the wall were portraits of mayors and councilmembers, most of which were birds of some kind—woodpeckers, macaws, owls. There were a handful of hedgehogs and a lone rabbit, but besides that, it appeared birds had been governing Moonoshk for a majority of its history.

Easily two or three times as large as any of the portraits was a symbol painted in the middle of the wall behind the reception desk. It was simple, but elegant. Two billowy clouds with a lightning bolt shooting out from between them. Every bird-established city had its own symbol, and this was Moonoshk's.

What Yurzu enjoyed most about the lobby was its greenery. Potted plants dangled from ropes attached to the ceiling. The pots were blue with white stripes painted across them, and the plants had long, winding fronds that burst outward from the dirt before curving downward and hanging far past the pot. They looked like water fountains, spouting streams of green water.

He was staring up at one of these plants when a macaw called to them. "Noswen Turam, please follow me."

They got together and followed the woman down a short hallway and into a small room at the end of it.

Inside waited two macaws, both men. One's feathers were a brilliant blue and green, while the other's were red and faded with age. They wore matching suits, dark blue with thin forest green ties. The men sat behind a long table in high-backed iron chairs that seemed immensely uncomfortable. The walls were bare and there was nothing else inside the room except for a single plant dangling from the ceiling.

Three similarly uncomfortable chairs were positioned on the opposite side of the table. Noswen took the seat in the middle, while Lop sat at her left and Yurzu her right.

Yurzu felt like he was at a group job interview. He shifted nervously in his chair.

"Hello," the older man greeted them. "My name is Vawkrus Fentere. City councilman."

"And I'm Nordris Mo," said the younger. "City councilman."

"Nice to meet you, councilmen," said Noswen. Yurzu could hear the mild derision in her voice, but it went undetected by the men. "I'm Noswen. This is Lop and Yurzu."

Both men nodded greetings to them. "What can we do for you today?" asked Vawkrus. He spoke with a heavy accent after likely growing up primarily speaking Buatang. Yurzu was glad that they didn't have to rely on his own knowledge of the language; it would have been fine, probably, but he was more than a bit rusty.

Lop answered before Noswen could. "Actually, we were hoping to meet with Ranatt Waraspoke. We were told she could be found here in Moonoshk. She is a councilwoman, yes?"

"She was," Vawkrus nodded. "And we did note that your request was to see Ms. Waraspoke. There is unfortunate news on that front."

"Oh?" said Noswen. "I hope all is well."

"It depends on your perspective, I suppose," Nordris said. "Ms. Waraspoke now flies on Vyru's Winds. She passed away some months ago."

All three of them deflated at the news.

Lop struggled to continue the conversation, so Noswen jumped back in. "We're very sorry to hear that." After a beat, "Maybe you can still assist us. I'm not sure. What we actually needed to speak with Ms. Waraspoke about was an object in her possession. Perhaps you've seen it before? It was a replication of a macaw beak, carved from obsidian."

The councilmen's faces brightened with recognition.

"Ahh, yes, we know of it," Vawkrus affirmed. "Ms. Waraspoke proudly displayed it on her desk. It was one of her favorite talking points. Her favorite piece of art she owned."

"Every time someone new came into her office, she would show it off," Nordris chimed in.

"Yes, yes," said Vawkrus. "But that is why the beak is no longer with us, I regret to say. Given how precious it was to her, the beak was placed in Ms. Waraspoke's funerary urn with her."

Noswen blinked. "What...does that mean?" she asked.

"It's a flyer custom," said Yurzu.

Vawkrus nodded. "The boy is right," said the old macaw. "In our culture, when one is sent to fly on Vyru's Winds, we place a few of their most prized possessions into an urn with their ashes and cast it over the mountainside."

Yurzu saw the swear word on the edge of Noswen's tongue. She bit her lower lip to stop the *f* from spilling out, let alone the rest of the word. He was grateful for her restraint.

Instead, she muttered, "I see."

The birds nodded in tandem.

Nordris said, "It was a beautiful ceremony, for what it's worth. All the councilmembers were in attendance. She had no family to speak of, so we paid for the service ourselves." He puffed his cheeks at this like it was a brag.

Lop sighed. "So the beak was thrown off a mountain."

"If you want to put it crassly, yes," said Vawkrus with a glare.

"Well..." Lop started but had no ending to the sentence. He was at a loss.

"I guess that's that, then," said Noswen.

There was nothing else to say to these men. The beak wasn't here. They no longer had a reason to stay.

"Sorry we couldn't be of more help," Nordris said. He pushed his chair back with a viciously loud scrape against the floor. "Thank you for stopping by." He held his hand out to shake, which each of them did before departing.

They returned to the lobby to regroup.

"What now?" asked Lop. The orangutan tugged at his scraggly orange beard and tapped his foot.

Noswen placed a hand to her forehead and sighed. "I hate to say this," she began, "but I have to. We're all in agreement, right? We have to go to the cemetery and find the beak."

Yurzu pipped involuntarily. The notion of entering such a sacred space and sifting through ashes to find the beak made him queasy. He thought about someone else stomping through his parents' ashes.

"I suppose so," said Lop. He sounded unsure too.

"I just don't see what other choice we have," Noswen said. "It's an awful thing to do, but we need the beak. Ruska needs us to get the beak. And that's where the beak is." She looked to Yurzu and asked, "Will that bother you?"

She was right, of course. They'd come all this way, traveled across Ruska and back. Five of the six artifacts were in their possession, assuming the other group hadn't hit any snags acquiring the jade hoof. It would be ludicrous to give up now.

So while it rubbed him the wrong way, he knew it was what needed to happen. For the sake of Ruska.

"I'm fine," he replied. "Like you said, we've got no other choice."

Lop then asked, "Do we know where the cemetery is?"

Noswen thought for a second then said, "There's that bridge leading into the mountains. That must be where they do it, right? Somewhere up there."

"Yeah," said Yurzu. "It'll probably be a bit higher up than that, but it's somewhere in those mountains. Nowhere else for it to be." Living so close to the mountains, it wouldn't make sense for Moonoshk's residents to travel elsewhere for their funeral ceremonies. Not like he had for his parents, since Toothshadow was so far from the mountains.

"I'm sure the area wouldn't be hard to find once we cross the bridge," Noswen said.

Yurzu agreed. Any markers up there would probably be written in Buatang, but he could easily read those and lead them to the resting grounds.

"I guess we're going to the cemetery, then," he said.

"Yep," Noswen nodded. "Wish we could've just grabbed the thing off her desk instead, but oh well. Sorry, Ms. Waraspoke."

34

SUFFICE TO SAY, COAL and the others had to seek lodging elsewhere after trashing the Naked Moon. The innkeeper was furious when he saw the destruction enacted upon his establishment, not to mention the bobcat corpse with its throat cloaked in dried blood. The man was screaming at them in raspy Ronog, so they had Biror speak to him to defuse the situation. Naturally, that resulted in them being kicked out altogether.

The next morning, they were on the other side of the city, waking up in an inn whose name Coal did not catch. It was smaller and also a bit drabber than the Naked Moon, if that was even possible. People of the Mudlands truly were uninterested in interior design.

One advantage this place had over the Naked Moon, though, was that it was nestled between a café and a pastry shop, the latter of which Coal was interested in perusing. Aromas from each floated through the air and into his room to wish him a pleasant morning.

He rolled out of bed and strapped his foot to his leg. It felt odd calling it *his foot*, especially in the context of attaching it to his leg, but he did not know how else to refer to the lump of clay. Calling it his foot certainly felt more natural than calling it a lump of clay.

Regardless, his lump of foot had made it through the scuffle the previous night without taking on any visible damage. When he had settled in to sleep, he had removed the appendage and looked all over its surface to find it remained in pristine condition. It was worth the claymaker's exorbitant price.

Maybe he would not need a mechanical replacement. When he thought about it, what value would it add to the experience of a foot? Would he be able to shoot steam from his toes, or something?

Coal exited his room and was locking the door behind him when Jatiri emerged from hers as well. "Hey," she said with a smile.

"Hey," he said back. "Breakfast?"

"I'm not hungry."

"I'm not either, but I want to eat. Know what I mean? I'm goin' down to that pastry shop, if you wanna join."

She declined. "I just wanna take a walk. Clear my head a little before we go to Vetch Kaya."

"Okay." He watched as she slipped past him and headed down the stairs, and he waited a few seconds before following.

Downstairs, Jatiri had already disappeared out the front door. But Biror was sitting around, flipping through some papers at a table. Strangely, there were also a few pieces of wood and a carving knife, though both seemed untouched at the moment while he was busy with his documents. Coal stepped toward the boar, an awkward knot already forming in his stomach.

"Hi," he said.

Biror glanced up without moving his head and quickly returned his gaze to the papers scattered messily before him. The area around his snout looked bruised from the Stinger kneeing him, and one of his tusks was chipped.

So that was as much of a "hello" as Coal was going to get. Undeterred, he asked, "How's your nose?"

"It is fine," said Biror curtly, not tearing away from his papers.

"When the hell did you get a gun, by the way?"

"I do not need to tell you all of my business. What I do with my time is none of your concern."

Coal sighed and said, "Well, thanks for helping last night. I know you probably didn't want to, so I appreciate it."

"It had to be done," said Biror with a cough. "Do not mistake my aid for affection, little fox."

"Trust me, I don't. But things would have turned out much worse, both for that inn and for myself, if you hadn't done something. So thanks."

Biror nodded, then asked, "Why does the Palace send a man after you?"

Coal shrugged. "You know I'm a Flesh Eater," he said, his voice low so that he wouldn't be overheard. "But when we sent word back to the Dirt King about me being the sixth and joining the team, I assumed he would've called off his men from going after anyone in the group. Even if he didn't know what I was specifically, I thought maybe…I dunno, just a plain

'Don't arrest or kill any of these people' order might've gone out."

"You have no other secrets hiding?"

"Nope. Just that one enormous, life-ruining one."

Biror considered his words and seemed to accept what he was saying. "Well, the man is dead now. But more will be coming, I say. It is good that we see Mother Pig today. We can leave Vuntagonyeo soon, if all is good."

"So that we can set off for the Palace as soon as possible. Exactly where all the people who evidently want me dead are," said Coal. "Sounds like a plan. When is our Vetch Kaya appointment?"

"In two hours."

Coal nodded, then tried scanning the pages Biror was reading over. It was all written in Ronog, which impeded his nosiness.

"What's all this?" he decided to ask.

True to his secretive self, Biror waved away his question and said, "None of your concern."

"Does it have to do with the guy who paid you a visit yesterday?"

"You would be wise to ask no more questions."

Coal did not want to get socked in the face, so he heeded the man's warning and stopped asking questions. While he was genuinely grateful for Biror's assistance the night before, he was not itching to spend more time than necessary with the man, so he departed from the inn without extending an invitation to the pastry shop.

He left Biror to his papers while he went and fetched his breakfast.

THE THREE MET OUTSIDE the inn when it was time to head over to Vetch Kaya. The giant dome was clearly visible from where they stood, but Biror wanted to lay out some ground rules before they walked over there.

"These are the most important people in Mudlands," he began. "You must show them respect at all times. They speak your language, but I will be the one talking to them. As a boar, this is what's right. You will speak to them only if they speak to you. Yes?"

Coal felt he was being condescended to, but he agreed for the sake of avoiding conflict. Jatiri nodded blankly.

"When we enter Vetch Kaya, we must remove our shoes. This will be especially easy for you, little fox, for you only have a single shoe." He said this with a smirk.

"You're very funny. This is all basic stuff so far, why are you explaining this to us? Let's just go over there."

"There is one more thing," said Biror. "In entry room, there is pit. Inside bottom of pit, there is a statue of the very first Mother Pig. We must make offering to this. I have made them for you."

He handed each of them a wooden token, hand-carved with a tusk on one side and some Ronog script on the other. Coal recalled the pieces of wood on Biror's table.

"What does this say?" Jatiri asked.

"How to say…'Soft graves cannot hold us back.' It is an old Mudlands saying. It means to be unafraid of death. The boars are powerful. We are the strong. You see?"

"Sure," said Jatiri.

Biror continued. "When you toss your token in the pit, you must not look inside at the statue. This is very important. It would mean great disrespect to the long line of Mother Pigs and all of Vetch Kaya to do this."

"How do you know about all this if you've never been inside?" Coal asked him. He ran his thumb over the bump of the tusk on his wooden token.

"How does one know anything about anything?" Biror snapped back. "You hear about it."

"Is there anything else?" Jatiri asked, flipping her token over and over again in her fingers.

"That is all. We will go now."

Together they marched down the street toward Vetch Kaya. It rose from the earth like a dark, rotting hill, one lousy with infection from the Houndstooth. As they grew closer to the dome, Coal got a better look at the strange tentacle-esque carvings swirling around the dome and could make out details etched into each one. Tiny stray marks peppered the tentacles, granting them a scaly texture. Whatever it was meant to represent, it was doubtlessly not the sun, like Jatiri had guessed. Coal was intrigued, but knew Biror would be unwilling to divulge any details. He also probably wouldn't get a chance to ask someone inside what it was, given the no-talking rule Biror had laid out.

They came to the entrance, the single door at the front of the dome. On it hung a clay mask depicting the melting face of a boar, which dripped down all the way to an iron knocker in the middle of the door. Biror grasped it in his hand and knocked loudly.

There came the sounds of something sliding, a mechanism moving, but the door remained still. Coal then noticed that real eyes were now peering through the eyeholes of the melted boar mask, their gaze piercing.

"Damanetch zab kee rut Vetch Kaya," said the person behind the door.

"Nomolots tahb Nurot Biror. Aba let mets," Biror replied. The bodiless eyes appraised all three of them for a few seconds before disappearing again. Moments later, there came the clicking of a lock, and the door drifted open lethargically.

They stepped inside.

Coal didn't know what he was expecting, but as it turned out, Vetch Kaya was just as devoid of character as every other place in Vuntagonyeo. He was thinking that maybe the most sacred building in all of the Mudlands might have a touch of flair to it, but if nothing else, the boars stuck to their principles.

They stepped past a tall boar woman dressed in dark red robes who closed the door behind them. Eyeing the two outsiders and rightly assuming they did not speak Ronog, she said, "Welcome to Vetch Kaya." She then stared at them expectantly.

Taking her facial expression as a command, Coal kicked off his only shoe. Biror and Jatiri removed theirs as well, and the woman smiled at them, though its warmth did not reach her eyes.

"Please follow me," she said.

The antechamber they walked through had divots dug into the walls, where lit torches guided their way into the main entry hall. The torches themselves were being held by clay tentacles similar to those that adorned the outer dome.

The robed boar led them through the short hall where they were then funneled out into a cavernous room, spanning the entire size of the massive dome. There was not a speck of furnishing anywhere; the chamber held nothing but a stairwell to their far left leading underground and the massive pit of which Biror had spoken.

In spite of the room being totally barren, Biror looked around it with awe, his mouth hanging open dumbly. Coal was left unimpressed, but this had to be a pretty surreal experience for the boar. He murmured something in his native tongue as he spun around, soaking up the chamber.

It was far colder inside the dome than out. Coal stood there shivering and was jealous of the woman's robe. He wanted that thick fabric to wrap him in its warmth.

Coal peered curiously at the pit in the middle of the room. Standing before it was two attendants wearing matching red robes, stock still. Whatever the statue was down there, it was sunken deep into the ground; all he could see from here was shadow. Total darkness.

When he had gotten his fill of the room, Biror addressed the boar who had welcomed them inside. "Thank you for granting us this visit."

The woman nodded and motioned toward the pit. "Please cast your offering." She stood aside and they stepped forward, approaching the pit with reverence.

Biror was the first to toss his token into the void, taking care to clamp his eyes shut as he did so. He then moved aside and Jatiri walked to the edge of the pit, closing her eyes and dropping her token.

Next was Coal's turn. He took a few steps forward before closing his eyes; there was no railing, and he thought it was an

easy assumption that if simply looking into the hole was dis-
respectful, throwing your entire body into it was probably a
step or two above that on the offensiveness scale.

He gripped the wooden token between his index finger and
thumb, held it over the edge, and let go. He listened for its
impact at the bottom, but he was met with silence.

When he perked his ears up and listened closer, though, he
realized it was not silent after all. There was a faint rustling
emanating from the bottom of the pit. The noise unsettled him.
He started to feel somewhat nauseous listening to it. After a
couple hasty steps backward, he opened his eyes.

"Kaya's blessing envelops you all," said the two attendants
in unison.

So Kaya was a name, apparently. Was Kaya the first
Mother Pig? Or was Kaya the tentacled thing the boars evidently worshipped? And was it worship, or fear? Coal wished
he spoke Ronog so that he knew what "vetch" meant.

The three turned to face their guide, who said, "You wish
to speak to Mother Pig." It was a statement, not a question.

Biror nodded. "Our business concerns the jade hoof."

"Yes," said the woman. "The hoof. Mother has said that at
some point, travelers would come seeking the Lodda. She did
not know when it would happen, if it was even in her lifetime.
Nor did she know what form they would take, so it pleases us
to see a fellow boar among your ranks." She glanced at Coal
and Jatiri before saying, "She was told there would be six,
however."

"There are six, but these others are away," Biror said.
"Mother was not misinformed."

Lodda must be their name for the hoof, Coal figured. It was
interesting that the boars knew there was some significance to

this artifact, unlike pretty much all the people who had come to possess the various other ones.

The woman narrowed her eyes, sizing them all up again, before saying, "Mother Pig will see you now."

She led them down the lonely stairwell, deeper into the earth beneath the dome. Given the disconcerting rustling he'd heard in the pit, Coal was not eager to travel downward, closer to it, but he dutifully followed the woman and Biror. Jatiri was behind him, keeping quiet.

The stairs led to another wide and dimly-lit chamber, with the same torch-bearing tentacles jutting out from the walls like disturbing sconces. This room was a semicircle with three closed doors on the opposite wall from where they stood.

They followed the woman across the empty room and through the central door.

Beyond it stood a woman wrapped in an elegant robe the same shade of red as the others, but with much finer detail woven into its fabric. The sleeves were decorated with pink symbols and flourishes, while the bottom of the robe bore even darker red that looked like tentacles reaching up the woman's body. She was tall as well, though not quite so tall as Biror, with long, curly tusks that had never been shaved down. Hanging from her neck was a silver diamond-shaped pendant, and a matching silver ring pierced her snout. Her eyes were a bright, blinding yellow, and she greeted them with a cold smile.

"Hello," said Mother Pig.

Biror bowed immediately. Coal and Jatiri scrambled to mimic his actions.

"*Jezwa nah shilahks,* Mother Pig," said Biror in a low voice. Neither Coal nor Jatiri repeated the greeting, assuming the man's "do not speak unless spoken to" rule was still in effect. Biror then stood up straight, as did they.

The woman who had brought them to the room showed herself out while Mother Pig walked toward them with her thick, brown fingers clasped together.

She said, "You come for the Lodda. I was expecting six of you. That was what my Lastmother told me, and her Lastmother before her." The woman's voice was smooth and syrupy, trickling languidly from her mouth. It had none of the same stiltedness as Biror's speech, which Coal had anticipated given the woman's reclusiveness.

"There are six of us, but these others are in the east," said Biror. "We will join them shortly after going from here."

Mother Pig nodded. She then looked to Coal and Jatiri and said, "You two are mute?"

Biror shot them both a glare, as if he had not been the one to forbid them from speaking.

"No, my apologies," said Coal, unsure how to address the woman. Being an outsider and calling her "Mother" felt wrong. "Thank you for welcoming us into your home."

"Of course. I have been waiting for you to arrive for many years. The Lodda has been passed down from Mother to Mother for a long time, until finally my Lastmother presented it to me. She said that six may arrive requesting it, and that I should give it to them without question. She said that those who knew of its true form and significance would be trustworthy. Its true form has never been spoken of outside the walls of Vetch Kaya."

She approached the wall to their right and pressed her palm against it. Until she did so, Coal had not noticed the thin seam in the wall; before, it had blended in with the other cracks and unevenness in its surface. The piece of clay slid backward, exposing a hole in the side of the small tunnel. Mother Pig reached her hand inside and extracted a brilliantly gleaming jade hoof. The Lodda.

Once the wall returned to its former status, Mother Pig walked back over to them with the hoof in hand, turning it over, admiring it from all sides.

"My Lastmother also instructed me to ask a question of you all," she said. "I do not understand the nature of the question, but I will ask it because my Lastmother requested I do so, and she was the wisest woman I ever knew. Like the Lodda, this question has been passed from Mother to Mother until it came time for it to be asked. Though I will say that I am displeased to find only half of you here. I hope the question still bears fruit."

"Anything, Mother," said Biror.

Mother Pig took in a deep breath and exhaled through her snout, looking at them one by one. She turned to Biror as she spoke.

"I am to ask you what your blight is. As I said before, I do not understand the nature of this question, but I do know what answer I am searching for."

Coal's eyes widened, as did Jatiri's. Only Biror appeared unfazed.

The line of boar Mothers knew about magic, but had not disclosed this information with their people.

Biror frowned, knowing he was about to disappoint the woman. "Mother, I regret to say I do not know mine."

Mother Pig nodded, mirroring his frown. "An unfortunate start," she said. Then she turned to Jatiri and awaited the saola's answer.

"I can turn invisible," she said. She held up her left hand to demonstrate, and a second later it vanished before reappearing after a couple moments.

"Incredible," said Mother Pig in a hushed tone. "That is remarkable, truly. But it is not the answer I am searching for." Then to Coal, she said, "And you?"

Coal bit his lip before replying. He took some solace in the fact that being a Flesh Eater was not as taboo here in the Mudlands as it was in the rest of the kingdom. But still, it was an uncomfortable thing to admit.

"I can speak to the dead when I eat their flesh," he said. There was no way to phrase it so that it did not sound completely ridiculous.

Mother Pig stared at him, disbelieving. She scratched her upper lip and peered suspiciously at him. "You say true?"

He nodded.

The woman chewed this over for a second, then said, "The right answer. Lucky fox."

Coal blinked. He looked over at Biror, who was glaring at the floor, fuming. They were in the boars' hallowed ground, and yet it was the fox that Mother Pig had been waiting for all these years. Coal would have been amused by Biror's anger if not for how terrified he was of the fact that Mother Pig had been looking for him.

"I must speak with you alone," said Mother Pig. To the others, she said, "Please wait here." She brushed past them and exited the room, handing Biror the jade hoof as she walked by.

Coal looked back and forth between Jatiri and Biror. "What the fuck's going on?" he whispered, panic setting in. The satisfaction of obtaining their artifact was subsumed by confusion and worry.

"Do not leave Mother waiting!" Biror barked, shoving him toward the door.

Jatiri offered a companionable shrug, but nothing more. It did not soothe his nerves in the slightest.

He stepped out into the semicircular chamber, where Mother Pig was exchanging some quiet words with the other woman who was waiting for them to conclude their business. Mother Pig turned to Coal and said, "This way."

She brought him to the door on his left. From the depths of her robe she extracted a hefty clay key, which she inserted into the unmarked door. With a grunt, she pushed it open and entered, motioning for him to follow.

Coal closed the door behind him just as Mother Pig lit a candle on a table in the center of the room. It was empty but for the table, and he was more bewildered than ever.

On the walls were paintings of countless boar women, all wearing robes similar though minutely different than the one Mother Pig donned. Coal's eyes ran along the messy portraits and found one that depicted the woman standing before him.

"All of my Lastmothers," explained Mother Pig, watching him examine the walls. "This room is where we keep Vetch Kaya's most valued treasures, and all Lastmothers watch over them. I am the only person who can enter. The Lodda was stored here shortly before your arrival."

She approached the wall and again gingerly pushed against it, sending the clay sliding back into it. This time the block was much longer, a rectangle stretching out the full length of the wall, revealing a row of darkened holes that were presumably holding numerous items.

"I must confess, I...have no idea what is going on," Coal said.

"That is okay. Though I am Mother to all boars, there is much I do not know either, and that is okay." She reached into one of the holes and pulled out—

"Oh, fuck," Coal blurted out. Only after the words had left his mouth did he stop to consider whether coarse language would be offensive in this sacred place.

Mother Pig chuckled at his outburst and set the arm she was now holding on the table beside the candle.

The limb was off-colored, but it was definitely the arm of a boar. It had the same muscular thickness of every boar Coal had met here in Vuntagonyeo. But it was lacking the same vitality, the skin closer to gray than brown, and it was wrinkled, with all the wiry hair shaved away.

"This is the arm of a Lastmother from long ago. She amputated it herself and gave careful instructions for its preservation and care to ensure that it lasted for many, many years. It was she who originally told her successor about the six, the artifact, and the question to ask, seeking one who eats flesh. Those instructions have been passed from Mother to Mother in vain until finally I held the honor of carrying them out on this day. The only other instruction I received was to leave you alone in this room until you were ready to exit."

Without giving him the opportunity to react or ask any further questions, she hastily departed from the room, red robe billowing in her wake.

Coal looked down at the arm.

The fingers were gnarled and curled up, some of the nails gently piercing the palm. Its dead skin flickered in the candlelight, sending a chill down his spine. Amazingly there was no smell, so whatever method the boars were using to preserve it, they were doing a fine job.

Am I supposed to eat this fucking thing? he wondered, positively horrified. It was a good thing he ate such a light breakfast.

There was no telling just by looking at it how old the flesh was, but it appeared to be ancient. If Mother Pigs did not name successors until the end of their lives, and this reached back past several Mothers, then...

He did not want to think about it anymore. The arm was disgustingly old, and he was expected to eat it.

Is this something Biror would be jealous of? he suddenly thought. *Would he be mad that I got to eat a Mother and he didn't?*

He pushed the bizarre, morbid thought from his mind.

For some reason this ancient boar countless years ago had hacked off her own arm in order for some poor sap to eat it way down the line and talk to her.

If that old Mother Pig was willing to do something so clearly insane, it was the least he could do to find out why. Somehow she was aware of this magical ability; was she able to do it too?

"I guess I can ask her," he muttered dejectedly.

Coal slowly reached down and picked up the arm, sending a creeped out convulsion running through his body.

He took a deep breath, brought the wrist to his lips, and bit down.

35

W ATCH YOUR STEP," YURZU called back to the others. They had crossed the bridge leading from Moonoshk to the mountaintops, where the ground was rocky and uneven. Pathways were smoothed away, but had clearly not been maintained over the years.

At the path's first branch, the signpost stated that to their right was something called Jairdin's, and to their left was the cemetery. The Buatang word for "cemetery" was "vild." Yurzu headed in that direction.

When they left city hall, they decided that today would indeed be the ideal time to check out the cemetery. Yurzu had been hearing rumblings that there would be a mass funeral sometime in the next few days, for all those lost in the blightbeast attack. It hadn't taken place yet because they were still working on cremating the bodies.

What that meant was the cemetery would soon be full with fresh ash and all the items those poor people were being cast out with. The beak might end up buried and much harder to track down. Their best bet was to search for it today.

The path was a shallow incline, bringing them higher into the Yuluj Mountains. There were scattered trees with narrow trunks on either side of them, but the greenery started thinning out as they ascended.

Yurzu had previously only visited the mountain range on two occasions. One was for his parents' funeral, but before that he had traveled with them to visit his aunt and uncle who lived up on an isolated peak. They had gotten fed up with life in the Yagos caves and decided to live on their own out in the mountains. Even at a young age Yurzu could see the appeal, but he liked being around people, even if they made him feel anxious sometimes.

There were a few more branching paths, but Yurzu continued following *Vild* and went higher and higher. The air was crisp and it was getting slightly harder to breathe, but it felt refreshing at the same time. One signpost he encountered was weathered and worn down, obscuring the Buatang scrawled on it, but Yurzu guessed that if they continued taking the path leading up, they'd be on the right track.

Lop was wheezing at the rear of the group. The thinner air combined with the strenuous hike was exhausting him. "Have we almost reached it?" he grunted. "Or should we take a break?"

"You'll be fine," Noswen assured him. "Just keep putting one foot in front of the other and you'll get there."

"How do people endure this whenever they must attend a funeral?" Lop sputtered. Every step was a struggle. "Talk about adding insult to injury."

Yurzu was feeling fine, though. He said, "Not only do they walk all the way up here, but some of them also have to carry the funerary urn. The urns we use are a lot bigger than a normal one, usually…not quite big enough to fit a person, but maybe half that size. We need space to fit whatever possessions they valued in there along with the ashes. Some people's urns are small, if their items are small too, but of course you need bigger ones to accommodate bigger things."

His mother's urn was small. He was the one to carry it up the mountain. It was painted dark blue, with a green band of clay embossed around it. Every urn had such a band, which symbolized the person's link to the valley. The act of it shattering was how the person became unchained from the earth and could fly on Vyru's Winds for all eternity.

Inside her urn was a watch gifted by her father in her youth and a packet of cucumber seeds. The latter was somewhat corny, but it had been Yurzu's idea. He'd put a seed packet in each of his parents' urns.

In addition to the seeds, his father's larger urn contained one of his favorite records. It also held his famyat, a gold piece of jewelry given by one person to another in an engagement; in a man-woman relationship, traditionally the woman gave it to the man. A famyat consisted of two thick, looped circles resting upon four columns that symbolized the pillars of a relationship: Love, Honesty, Equality, and Support.

"I'm glad my people just toss our dead in the ground," said Lop. "No hiking for us. Though I mean no disrespect," he added. He took a few moments to catch his breath. "There is a beautiful cemetery on the Palace grounds for those who worked and lived there. Large open space, full of trees and flowers. My parents are buried there."

"It's hard for me to imagine you as a child with parents," Noswen said. "I think of you as someone who has always been a fifty-year-old wet blanket."

"Well, I had parents," Lop grumbled. "I was born and grew up like everyone else. And I'm not fifty. I am forty-seven."

"My mistake."

They followed one more sign, continuing their ascent, and finally they reached the funerary peak. It was a huge, flat area surrounded on all sides by craggy mountains. But there was a gap in one section, where Yurzu knew the urns were thrown. In the gap they could see the mountain range stretching out infinitely, set against the purpling sky. Yurzu wondered if those mountains ever ended, and if so, what lay on the other side. Maybe a sea—was that the word?—like Fennigha spoke of in the Nitulo hot springs.

The peak was devoid of anything. Lop asked, "Is this it? Where's the cemetery?" He took a few steps forward but then stopped to take a seat on the ground. His breathing was ragged. "Did we go the wrong way?"

"No, this is it," Yurzu said. This was definitely the *Vild*. He pointed at the gap. "It's through there."

Noswen approached and peered down. "It's a sheer drop," she said. "I can't even see the bottom. It's just mountainside."

Yurzu nodded. He had hoped it wouldn't be quite so far down, but he knew that he would have to be the one to enter the cemetery for them. The only way to reach it would be to fly.

"I'll have to fly down there and find the beak then fly back up," he said. "I don't think you'd be able to get down there."

"Oh, I can get down there," said the raccoon. "I would probably just splat in the process and I don't think I'd be coming back up."

"My arms have their limits as well," Lop said with a haggard cough. He was in no shape to go anywhere. At least their return to Moonoshk would be downhill. "Why's it all the way down there and we're up here?"

Yurzu explained. "We carry the urns to the edge of the mountain's peak and throw it over. The urns have a stripe painted around them, and when the urn hits the mountainside or the ground below, it breaks and frees the person to fly on Vyru's Winds. The ashes are scattered, and the possessions collect below along with ash. That's what the actual cemetery is."

Lop nodded but had no comment. Noswen asked, "Are you sure you'll be okay down there on your own? Will you even be able to fly down and back up that distance?"

He'd gotten some good practice flying the other day during the blightbeast attack, so he was feeling confident. He nodded.

Noswen still looked unsure, but she accepted his answer. "Okay. We'll wait here. Try to be quick, in case someone comes."

"Right."

Yurzu stepped to the edge of the mountain and peered over. Nothing but rock below. He unfurled his wings and jumped.

It was a pleasant descent. Slow and methodical, weaving out of the way of sharp rock. The cemetery was far below, easily surpassing five or six hundred feet before he even spotted it. The flight back up to where he left Noswen and Lop would be difficult, but he would manage.

He came to a soft landing in a pile of ash.

The whole area was covered in piles of gray and white cremation ashes that shifted beneath his feet. It looked like dust to him, the mountain left uncleaned for years. Various objects and pieces of shattered clay peeked out from the ash. He saw everything from rings to the tips of candelabras to suits to anything else one could dream of. So many different items that could mean nothing to one person but the world to another. It was humbling.

Each of the artifacts they sought had a modicum of the Houndstooth's essence inside which Yurzu was able to sense, and he was picking up on it now that he was close. It was terribly faint, but if he followed it, he should be able to find the beak.

Yurzu leaned down where he saw the corner of a black rectangle sticking out from the ash. He picked it up and saw it was a framed photograph of an owl and a rabbit, their arms wrapped around each other's shoulders. He placed it back on the ground and continued searching.

The cemetery stretched on for at least half a mile. Yurzu gazed in wonder at the hills of ash as he strode past.

He saw old pieces of jewelry that were chipped or weatherworn or outright broken. It made him wonder about the condition of his father's famyat. Whether it had survived the fall off the mountain or instantly broken into multiple pieces to lay in ash for the rest of time.

Wind blew and uncovered vibrant shards of urn. Some pieces were plain solid colors, others had intricate patterns, and a few were swirls of different colors all mixed together.

Yurzu found the swirls to be the prettiest. The colors intermingling in interesting, unexpected ways that not even the artist could fully control.

Yurzu felt the beak somewhere close by. If Ranatt Waraspoke had been cast to the Winds a few months prior, there was possibly a good amount of ash covering up the beak by now. Perhaps the cold mountain breeze would displace some more ash and help him find it.

Some parts of the cemetery were piled with considerably more ash than others. Some steps he took had him sinking knee-deep into the gray.

He spent the next fifteen minutes sifting through ash, his skin tingling as he did so. It didn't feel right. Literally brushing aside the remains of people who had once lived, who had thoughts and dreams and loves and losses. The thought of someone doing this to his own parents' ashes made him deeply uncomfortable. He didn't know what else to do, though. It was necessary to save Ruska. Maybe there was a holy man he could talk to about ways he could make it up to the people he'd disrespected.

In the meantime, he continually muttered "I'm sorry" as he searched through the ashes, chasing the feeling of the obsidian beak. Reaching out for the Houndstooth's infection.

After another couple minutes of wandering, the pain in his head sharpened drastically. The beak had to be somewhere around there. He must be right on top of it.

Yurzu fell to his knees, kicking up ash with another apology, and began to dig. His knees sank into the ash and his hands were covered in gray.

It was here. He knew it.

He reached his hand underneath the pile of ash and the pain in his head intensified. The beak was calling out to him.

His fingers brushed against hard stone. He wrapped them around the unseen object and yanked it into the open.

It was solid, glassy black. Thick and curved, with a sharp point at its tip that he was glad to have avoided.

The obsidian beak.

Yurzu's mind screamed at him and he closed his eyes for a moment, concentrating on dulling the pain. Ignoring it. Pushing it to the background.

He opened his eyes and looked down at the beak he held in his palms. It was a beautiful piece of work. The precise size of a real macaw's beak and perfectly carved, all smooth curves. Not even careening down the side of a mountain had introduced any imperfections to its shape.

While he felt gross about ambling through a cemetery, at least the task had been easy enough. And in the end it had only taken about an hour, with the walk up the mountain included.

They had obtained the artifact. Ruska would be okay.

And they couldn't have done it without him.

Yurzu smiled at the thought. Proud that he had finally contributed to the group in a meaningful way. He had made a difference.

Now he just had to return to his companions. He gripped the beak tight and flapped his wings, lifting into the air in a cloud of ash.

It was a struggle to reach the peak again, and when he landed he was as out of breath as Lop. The orangutan was still sprawled out on the ground resting, but Noswen perked up at the sight of Yurzu.

Then she saw what was in his hand and a smile stretched out across her face.

"You found it!"

He grinned.

Lop sat up and looked at the beak. "Excellent work!" he said, rising with a huff.

"Did you have any trouble?" Noswen asked him.

Yurzu shook his head and asked, "Did anyone come by?"

She said no. Lop reached for the beak and offered to carry it for him. Yurzu handed it over, thankful for the man shouldering the responsibility for it. He'd been happy to locate it, but being the one to keep it safe made him nervous. It was a good thing Zsoz was in their party. He would let Lop be the one to deliver it to the slime, though.

"Our business here is done," the orangutan beamed. "Now we can return to the Palace and put all this behind us."

"We can stand to have one more night in a free hotel, though, I think," Noswen said. "Let's have one more night of enjoyment before we're back on the road again."

That sounded like a plan to Yurzu, and Lop reluctantly agreed. The man was always eager to get a move on, but after the day's long and vigorous walk, even he could not deny that a night's sleep in a real bed would hit the spot. Assuming construction did not keep them up.

They then began their descent down the mountain. From these higher paths, they could actually spot the bridge into Moonoshk in the far distance. It would be half an hour or so before they reached the city.

Lop was now in the lead, enthusiastic about putting this trek behind them. Yurzu was at the back of the pack, lost in his own thoughts. They passed by a few of the signposts, all of which bore unfamiliar words, and Yurzu was left wondering what lay down those other paths.

Now that they had finished collecting the Dirt King's artifacts, Yurzu was starting to share Lop's keenness to get back to the Palace. The sooner they did, the sooner he would return to his life in Toothshadow. His garden was certainly in rough shape, but it would only take

A bullet pierced Yurzu's skull and his head burst in a shower of brain and blood.

36

COAL RETCHED AS HE chewed the ancient preserved flesh. It was unimaginably salty, and the skin was so tough it was like eating leather. While he chewed, he looked back down at the limb and saw the dead muscle underneath and gagged again.

He swallowed, and the armless Mother Pig appeared before him.

This Mother Pig was even taller and more intimidating than the current day one, with an impressive protruding belly and dangling jowls. She too had long, curved tusks that had seemingly never been tamed. Her left arm stopped at the elbow, ending in a scarred, puckered stump.

But she appeared differently than his father's spirit had. While he had been a translucent blue, she instead was totally black. Her skin protruded in jagged clumps like tree bark. The only part of her that wasn't black were her eyes, which were a solid, mesmerizing white with no pupils.

Coal took a step back as she took in her surroundings and landed on him with a glare. But the expression swiftly changed to confusion, and then excitement.

"Palash kvo?" the ghost woman muttered. Then, seeing she stood before a fox rather than a boar, "It finally happen. *Dahnla novwa*, I can believe not this took so long!"

Her accent was even heavier than Biror's, and she clearly did not have the best grasp of non-Ronog grammar rules. But it was easy enough to understand her.

She turned on her heel, looking around the room. The slab of clay was still receded into the wall, and she took a few steps forward to peek in the holes at the valuables the boars were saving.

"That still is in here?" she muttered to herself before turning away. She took one last look around the place before returning her attention to Coal, who had decided to keep his mouth shut while the woman adjusted to being a spirit.

She pointed at his clay foot, then at the empty air where her arm would have been.

"Match!" she laughed.

"Yeah. I guess so." Her appearance chilled him. He then offered her a meek wave and said, "Hi. My, uh...name is Coal."

"Hello, Coal. I am Mother Pig. I know our time together is short, and a lot there is I must tell. But first I am ask: what year is this?" He told her, and she let out a heavy sigh, rubbing her brow. "Near one thousand year since I die. One thousand year that this continues."

Her words were perplexing, but Coal said nothing. He was too busy trying to accept that he had eaten thousand-year-old meat.

Mother Pig said, "I would find love in knowing you a little, but we must speak of things. I know how this work; I know I might disappearing at any time. You must need to eat more of my arm to make me see. If you nibble while we speak, we will be fine." She glanced down at the grayed limb Coal held in his hands and said, "I think there enough flesh is there to get us through this."

Coal found it peculiar being instructed by a person to nibble on their arm, but these were peculiar times. He said, "Sure. What is 'this,' though? Why did you…" He lifted up the arm and gestured with it. "…leave this behind? What happened to you?" He stared at her rough, ink-black skin.

Mother Pig began pacing the room, tapping her wide chin. "Where to begin…" she asked herself.

He thought he might help her out with that. "You were a Flesh Eater?" he prompted.

The woman seemed confused by his question. "Have things change? Everyone eat flesh in my time. We all were flesh eaters. Do you mean am I possess this power that you have? I am, yes. I was one of the six Blighted, Dirt King say. And I could speak to the dead upon eating."

Coal took another foul bite of the woman's arm, causing her to wince, then said, "So you left behind a piece of yourself in case another person like you came along."

"You get ahead of us," Mother Pig said. "Let's go back. What were you told about this going on?"

"With the Houndstooth?"

A nod.

Coal took a deep breath then dove into the explanation that had been recited to him. The Houndstooth was holding back a plague; it was starting to leak out and infect people and creatures; it was creating malformed monsters; there were six Blighted who had to retrieve powerful artifacts and channel their energy into them to keep the plague at bay.

"The Dirt King spoke you this?"

He nodded, then clarified, "Well, the Dirt King told some other people in the group and then they told me."

Mother Pig laughed bitterly. "It is all lie."

Coal gulped down a bit of the woman's arm. "What?" he mumbled.

"The Dirt King, he is full of shit," said Mother Pig. "I always have a bad feeling about this man."

"I did too!" Coal proclaimed. "I couldn't put my finger on it, but something about this whole story seemed off to me."

Not that hearing the Dirt King was lying put him at ease or made him feel vindicated. Quite the opposite.

"This is why I leave a piece of myself," said Mother Pig. "In case something happen to me and I must tell the next person with my power. I did not think it would be one thousand year before this happen."

Coal raised an eyebrow and asked, "What happened to you?"

"You get ahead of us again," Mother Pig said, tut-tutting him. "First thing first: the Houndstooth is sick, but Dirt King is making it this way. He...hmm, it is hard to speak this. Okay, you speak how bad the kingdom is right now. This is because Houndstooth is bottled up, not because it leaks. The Houndstooth is not a tree, truly. The Houndstooth is construct that hold energy. The energy that breathe life into Ruska, that give the kingdom its vitality and its magic. I know not how, I have not figured this part. But the Dirt King, he discovers a way

thousands of year ago—long before my time, even—he discovers a way to capture the energy at its source, trap this,
and...what is this word? Funnel? Funnel into himself. This is
why he lives for so long, because he suck the life from Ruska.
And this is why he is able to do these so many wondrous thing,
yes? All of the magical abilities you and your friends have,
what myself and my friends had—what Dirt King spoke are
blights—are abilities that were normal in Ruska. Long, long
time ago. But Dirt King captured this energy and put it into
himself instead. He has now all those abilities and more. He
can do anything."

Coal's head was spinning, and Mother Pig had to remind
him to take another bite of the preserved limb. He did so in
silence, chewing and swallowing and mulling over the mind-
shattering revelation that the woman had thrust upon him.

"Any question so far?"

"Hundreds," Coal sputtered. "But maybe it's best that I
save them all for the end."

"You are smart one. This is good. You must need to be
smart to beat him."

"Beat the Dirt King?" he choked. "Beat the immortal being
that you just said has every magical ability ever conceived of
at his disposal?"

Mother Pig nodded. "You and other Blighted are the ones
who must have to do it. I speak sorry that you are the one who
end up being able to talking to me, but this is the way this is.
Too many people are suffering for too long already. Ruska
could be flourishing if not for this man. It is time for someone
be putting a stop to what he is doing."

Coal thought over what she'd already said and asked, "If
the Houndstooth is supposed to be the vitality of Ruska or

whatever, why is it spitting out monsters? I've had to fight a lot of truly heinous shit over the past couple months. Those things look more like death than life to me."

"Let me speak you this first: are the animals dying out there?"

"Yeah," Coal said with a slow nod. "Geigexes are somewhat plentiful, but animals like retnos are almost entirely gone. There's a law against hunting them, and no one can eat meat anymore."

"See you? This same thing happens in my time. I am sure we had animals you never have heard of. As the year go on, the problem gets worse and worse. I will give him some credit for make this baby effort to save the last wildlife with his laws, but it would not be necessary if he does not do what he is doing. The energy trapped within the Houndstooth is what grants life to Ruska. Those monsters you are speaking are its attempts to keep doing so, but it so damaged is by the toxic of the Dirt King's actions, the blockage of its natural flow, it is not working. So what you get instead are monsters that only small resemble the real animals. If the magic is flowing freely, those would exist not. Or, rather, they would be as normal animals."

Her explanation made some amount of sense to Coal. Pretty much every blightbeast he'd encountered—the not-ventem in the Houndsvein, the not-retnos in the race—all looked *somewhat* like their counterparts, but unfinished versions of them. Versions that were falling apart, broken, sick.

"If this is bad enough that he makes outlaw eating of the animals, then this kingdom must be on its last breath," said Mother Pig. "I know not if it could even last until the next cycle."

Coal realized he'd been staring down at the arm. He looked up at the blackened spirit's white eyes and said, "Cycle?"

"This happens every few hundred year, it seems. Enough time pass in between each cycle for people to forget what happens the last time around. The Dirt King keeps the whole thing quiet as he can, and then the few people left behind who know anything about this are dead and forgotten by the time this comes around another."

That would explain why seemingly no one knew what was special about the artifacts they'd been collecting. No one except for the boar Mothers, all due to this woman's forethought.

"You're talking about the artifacts and the Blighted," said Coal.

"Of course. Well, the Blighted in particulars. None of you are sick. Having magic in you, this is natural. It is the people having no magic who are sick, really. You are proof that the energy inside the Houndstooth not is totally gone."

Coal was willing to bet that his prior assumption was correct, that there was no way only six of them in the entire valley had magic. It was too big of a coincidence. They just happened to be the six who found each other.

But something was still bothering him. That same nagging doubt that had made him suspicious of the Dirt King in the first place.

"How could you possibly know all this?" he asked. "If you fulfilled your duty with the artifacts and went on your merry way and are dead now, how did you discover the 'truth'?"

Mother Pig smiled, but there was no joy in it.

"I know *because* I fulfill my duty," she said. "When you have talk to spirits before, did they speak that they knew they were in the afterlife? That they could feel around them the others?"

Coal nodded. The only ghost he had previously spoken to was his father, but Von did mention that very thing.

"Yes. I hear this as well. But I am not there," said Mother Pig. "I am trapped in the Houndstooth, as are the five others I travel with. As are all the Blighted who come before, and those who come after. We us all are stuck here, unable to escape."

Coal blinked. Words were lost to him.

Mother Pig went on. "It should no longer be as a surprise to you that the Dirt King lied about this part, too. All of us, the souls of what he calls the Blighted, are the Houndstooth's indestructible bark. Take a bite of my arm."

He was glad she was keeping track. He'd forgotten again. He chewed a piece of muscle as she continued.

"The Dirt King discovers a way to use us as the very thing bottling up the energy he funnel into himself. I suppose whatever method he was using before was starting to wear off or deteriorate, I cannot be sure; there is much I know not, but I do know this much: we are all trapped here together in this place. No longer living, but unable to move on to the true afterlife. We can feel in us this energy trying to help the kingdom. Trying to make the animals, trying to bring this magic and life back. In every moment, we can feel the kingdom's pain. The energy, it is beating against us, desperate, begging, trying to break free. But we cannot be able to let it flow. We are the Houndstooth."

Coal took a step back and had to sit himself down on the floor. He leaned his back against the cool clay wall, trying to process what Mother Pig was saying.

She was a ghost. Long dead. There was nothing for her to gain from lying to him.

He believed every word that she was saying.

The Dirt King was killing Ruska. All so that he could keep himself alive and powerful.

And he was going to kill the six of them in the process.

"Those artifacts you collect," Mother Pig continued after giving him a minute to regain his composure. "They are...how I speak? These artifacts are the essence of the six Blighted who come before."

"...what?" Coal barely had it within him to say that much.

"If you are in Vetch Kaya, then one of the artifacts has something to doing with a boar, yes?"

He nodded. "It's a jade hoof."

"So one of them was a boar. What were these other objects?"

"A lizard scale, a macaw beak, a deer antler, a tiger fang, and an anteater claw. So those were the people who did this in the last cycle?"

"Yes," Mother Pig confirmed. "And none of them with the power to speak to the dead, or none who must travel to Vetch Kaya, I am supposing. I would have already speak to them and put a stop to this."

Her words stirred something inside. "That's why," he said, a realization striking him. "You said the Dirt King has pretty much every magical ability now, right?"

Mother Pig nodded. Her black form flickered, and Coal took another bite of the arm before continuing his train of thought.

"When you died, he must have gained the ability to speak to the dead. But I guess he probably already knew what you could do before then, anyway. So he knows that's a potential ability that one of the Blighted could receive. Did he know you left part of yourself behind?"

"He must," said Mother Pig. "When I see him before we bring our artifacts to the Houndstooth, I have a clay arm in place of my own."

"Maybe he guessed what you'd done, then. Left a part of yourself behind. That's why he made those laws, why he sends Flesh Eaters to prison camps. He wanted to make sure that if any of them happened to be a person born with that magic, they wouldn't be able to get to you and speak to you, on the off-chance your spirit could divulge anything."

He then recalled the letter they had sent, relaying his magical ability to the Dirt King. The man had wanted to know the ability of each person in the group specifically so he could be made aware if one of them was capable of speaking to the dead.

It wasn't Lop who had talked to the Dirt King, told him to send another Stinger after him.

They had done it themselves.

The Dirt King thought of him as a liability, so when he received the letter and learned of Coal, he dispatched more Palace Stingers to take care of him and prevent this very conversation from ever taking place.

"He's ruined countless lives just so he could keep his power and keep his secrets," Coal muttered. He slouched against the wall.

All hope drained from him. He felt used. Dried up. He looked to Mother Pig, who was respectfully giving him time to think things through, but there was a twinge of impatience in her expression. She still had more to tell him, and once all the flesh of her arm was consumed, her opportunity would be over.

"So we would've…we would be turned into artifacts too," he said. "When all this was over."

That was why it was so easy for the Dirt King to promise them anything they wanted in exchange for performing this task. No request was too outrageous, because none of them would be fulfilled anyway.

"Yes. The artifacts are being the essence of those who blindly followed the Dirt King's orders. I speak this without judgment; I too carried out this man's wishes without question, simply because I am told it is necessary, and that it was always the way things have been done. Who was I to go against this?

"When the Blighted bring the artifacts, they do channel their magical energy into them, as the Dirt King tells you. This power frees the essence from its first cage, in the artifact, but it traps it again as part of the Houndstooth. The Blighted, this energy then envelops them and destroys them, encasing them in what I must only speak as inferno. It boils you alive. This is unbearable. The worst pain I ever have felt, and I cut my own arm from me. When the white fires die, all that is left is their essence. The artifact."

"Are they alive in there?" Coal asked. "Were you alive in your artifact? Not alive, but—like *this*," he said, nodding toward her spirit form.

"Yes and no. I was not totally unaware of my surroundings, but it was not like it is here, or like how ghosts described the true afterlife to me. It was…this was like a very faint knowing that I exist, with all my senses dulled to the point of confusion. It was disorienting and uncomfortable, and it last hundreds of year."

Coal shuddered. It sounded like a fate worse than the Flesh Eater camps.

What artifact would he be turned into?

What would his essence become?

"I..." he started. "I don't know what to do." A pause, then, "I don't know how to explain all this to the others. This..."

"This is overwhelming, I know," said Mother Pig. "But you must to be told. I have been waiting so many year to tell somebody the truth of what happens in Ruska. I am sorry it had to be you, truly, but that is the way of things. Take another bite."

Coal had eaten about half of the arm by now, and so combined with the world-ending revelations he was hearing, he felt like he was going to throw up. He bit down again, tearing off a piece of the salty flesh, his fangs gnashing at the tough skin.

He swallowed the piece of meat, gagging on it, a teardrop escaping from his eye.

"So what are we supposed to do?" he asked.

Mother Pig looked down at him with a confused expression.

"I should think it is obvious now, fox," she said. "You must to kill the Dirt King."

Coal vomited into his lap.

37

A T THE SOUND OF the gunshot, Noswen and Lop both ducked down and leapt to either side of the path. Noswen turned to see where Yurzu was and saw the bat's small, limp body in the middle of the dirt path, gushing blood from a massive hole in his head.

She screamed.

She screamed so loud, her throat felt like it was tearing. She screamed until the air had left her lungs and she was crouched there, mouth open but silent. Tears raged down her cheeks.

It took Lop yelling her name multiple times for her to realize there was more gunfire. The orangutan had ducked around a corner and stretched out an arm to pull her back with him. As she disappeared around the mountain, the gunfire ceased.

A voice called, "Give us the claw and you won't have to die too."

"Go fuck yourself!" Noswen screeched. Her voice cracked, and each word was punctuated by a sob.

"Calm yourself," Lop whispered to her. It was not in a condescending tone; he was matter-of-fact. "I am angry too. I am saddened. But we need to be calm and focused if we want to get out of here."

She nodded. But then her fur started to change. A shift from the brownish gray with speckles of black into something at first yellow, then orange, then red.

Like she was heating up.

And then she was smoking.

Black smoke billowed from Noswen's mouth. All her fur was now varying shades of red and orange, but it was still changing. It was whitening.

A few seconds later, she was completely white. As if all the color had been drained from her. Even her clothes were colorless.

And then she was on fire.

Lop scrambled away from her, yelping in shock and horror.

Flames burst from her body, then adhered to the shape of it. Fire licked at the air around her as she stood heaving, catching her breath. With every exhale, smoke poured from her mouth and into the sky.

Noswen looked down at her palms. Her brow furrowed as she tried to make sense of what she was seeing. What she was feeling.

Every strand of fur on her arm was the same pale color. Like she was caked in ash. Fire engulfed her, but she could not feel it. Not even its heat. She felt completely normal. She felt in control.

She shot out from around the mountainside and was immediately fired upon. None of the shots hit, and she lobbed fireballs from her palms in the direction of the attackers.

Unlike them, she did not have to reload her weapon. Noswen continued assailing them with fireballs as she advanced. Lop turned the corner, his arms fashioned into swords. Together they marched toward the shooters.

These had to be the same people who attacked them in Lakilu Forest. They had finally tracked them down here and were trying to finish the job.

They want a claw, she suddenly thought.

It took her a second, but she realized they must be talking about the diamond anteater claw. She hadn't given the damned thing a second thought since they obtained it from the spider-back race. It was old news; they had other artifacts to hunt down.

That was when she knew who this person was.

She shot out another fireball and the man yelled out in agony.

Noswen and Lop moved past the signpost, down the path they had not traveled before. Ten feet down the path was the man she'd been expecting.

Patting out a small flame on his arm was the wolverine who had ambushed Coal, Yurzu, and herself on their way to Sadatso. Noswen wracked her brain for the man's name. She was positive Coal had said it.

Marl.

That was it. Marl. She threw another fireball at him, which he barely dodged. His rifle had clattered to the ground when she previously hit his arm, though.

With him was one of those rabbits who'd accompanied him last time. The man was even more singed, a good half of his fur blackened by Noswen's flames. She grinned at that. He had dropped his firearm too, screaming.

Marl stared in wide-eyed horror at the flaming raccoon as she descended upon him. She backed him up against the mountain wall, her flames licking hungrily at the air. Though she couldn't feel it herself, she knew heat emanated from her body. The wolverine began to pant.

Behind her, Lop walked straight over to the rabbit and stabbed him in the gut. The man fell backward onto the ground, and Lop sliced at the man's neck. His head rolled down the mountain path, wherever it led.

The wolverine looked a lot less intimidating now. Fear was in his eyes, darting back and forth between the enraged, sword-handed orangutan and the pure white raccoon wrapped in fire.

"What the fuck *are* you people?" Marl sputtered.

Noswen stuck her hand in the man's mouth and he tried to push out a scream. She shot fire down his throat.

Marl's eyes widened as the stream of flame filled his mouth, racing down his throat, burning him alive from the inside out. His screams were muffled against her hand. He bit down hard, though it burned his lips and face. Blood trickled down Noswen's wrist, dripping onto the dry mountain path.

She ignored the pain in her hand. It was the only physical pain she felt despite the flames engulfing her. Even when it appeared the man's eyes were beginning to boil, she did not stop.

Eventually, he collapsed in a heap on the ground. Her hand slid from his mouth, damp with saliva for just a moment before the moisture was evaporated by her own heat.

She stepped back and the flames died down. Her fur and clothes returned to their normal pigment. Nothing had burned away. In fact, it looked as if the fire had not touched her at all.

There was nothing left to do here. She did not want to see this man anymore.

She raced back up the path and returned to Yurzu's body. Lop was not far behind her.

They kneeled beside the small bat, their bodies shielding him from anyone who might meander down the path.

Her chest heaved with sobs again at the sight of him. Magic brimmed in her fingertips, but she knew he was beyond healing. Maybe there was in fact some way for her healing to fix him, but she did not know what it would be. It was probably impossible.

I'm sorry, she thought, too choked up to actually vocalize the words. *I tried to protect you. I did.*

Beside her, there was a tear in Lop's eye too. He placed a hand on her back, trying to console her. It wasn't working. She appreciated the gesture, but she had to let it all out.

She leaned over, her hands pressing into the hard ground. Teardrops fell onto Yurzu's small, motionless hands. She interlaced her fingers with his.

I'm sorry. Those two words would not stop repeating in her mind.

She couldn't bring herself to look at his head. It was too much to bear. Even catching the slightest glimpse of it made her want to scream in rage and sorrow. If she could, she would've killed Marl a second time. The wolverine and his companion had gotten off easy.

It was then she heard frantic footsteps approaching. A meek voice, mutterings of distress.

The thought shook her, but she thought it all the same: if anyone else tried to impose on them, she would not hesitate in killing the person.

482 • *Travis M. Riddle*

"No, no, no, no, please, no," the stranger warbled. "Am I too late? Please, no. Please tell me he is okay. I tried to get here in time, I went as fast as I could…"

Noswen looked up and Lop turned around to face this unknown person.

It was a woodpecker with striking orange eyes and thin, red-rimmed glasses. His clothes were dirty and tattered. Clearly he had a rough go of things in recent times. The red feathers atop his head were ruffled and he clutched his hands to his stomach as if he was about to be sick.

The man's eyes trailed down and rested on Yurzu, who was finally in view. His brows raised in shock.

"That is not Coal," he whispered.

"No, it's not," said Noswen. "And who the fuck are you?"

THE STORY CONCLUDES IN...

DIRT KING

ACKNOWLEDGMENTS

Last time I mentioned that I never thought I'd write a series. Somehow, since then, I ended up writing that entire series in less than a year. As you're reading this, I've already written the end of Coal and the other Blighted's journey. I know where everyone ends up, and you don't. Ha ha!

For that reason, I once more need to start by thanking all my beta readers: Emily Atwood, John Bierce, Tyler Gruenzner, Jenna Jaco, and Tim Simmons. As always, they helped me see where there were weaknesses in the manuscript as well as let me know that maybe this story isn't as stupid as I feared it might be. Their unwavering support has been a great help while trying to navigate the complexities of writing a series. And I appreciate more than I can even express that they took the time to read two gigantic books from me within the span of only a few months. Pretty much a few weeks after they sent Flesh Eater back to me, I was sending them Mother Pig. And a few weeks after that, I sent them Dirt King. Thank you so much for taking the time to read these books and not berating me for sending you so many words in such a short amount of time.

Thank you to the bloggers who have supported my work, especially with the launch of the Houndstooth series. Calvin Park from Fantasy Book Review, Ella from The Story Collector, Jordan from Forever Lost in Literature, Phil Parker from The Speculative Faction, Peter from The Swordsmith, Nat from Booknest.eu, and Ollie from OllieSpot. It's always an honor every time anybody decides to take the plunge on one of my books, let alone when they then dedicate the time and effort to write about it and spread the word. All of these folks, as well as any reader who's taken the time to write and post a review, have my unending gratitude.

And thanks again to the crew of authors I've befriended over the past few years. Jon Auerbach, John Bierce, Angela Boord, Josh Erikson, Barbara Kloss, Devin Madson, Steven McKinnon, Richard Nell, Kayleigh Nicol, Carol A. Park, Clayton Snyder, Aidan Walsh, Phil Williams, and Dave Woolliscroft. Your insights into the publishing world (especially with audiobooks and Kickstarter) and your support are always appreciated.

Last but not least, thank you for buying this book. For taking a chance on an indie author and seeing where Coal's journey takes him. Without your support, I'd be nowhere. If you can, please leave a rating or review on Goodreads and Amazon, and if you think your friends and family would like these weird stories of mine, perhaps gift them a copy. I'd truly appreciate it.

See you at the finale.

RECOMMENDED READING

PIRANESI by Susanna Clarke. It seems like everyone has read Clarke's debut novel and loved it, but her second outing was the first time I read anything by her. I was positively blown away by this book, which is relatively short but packs a powerful punch. It follows a man named Piranesi in a strange, otherworldly house as he spends his days exploring and tending to his things. That description may sound quaint and boring, but this book is anything but boring. The character of Piranesi is beautifully written, and it's a joy being in his head, seeing the world through his eyes. Plus, there's some great mystery and a truly moving ending.

SYMPHONY OF THE WIND by Steven McKinnon (The Raincatcher's Ballad). This is a rollicking steampunk adventure filled with magic, gunplay, airships, and even zombies (kind of). It was a finalist in 2018's Self-Published Fantasy Blog Off, and it definitely earns that finalist status. McKinnon weaves a tight, complex narrative with a cast of fascinating characters and filled with explosive action sequences rivaling any Hollywood blockbuster.

BANEBRINGER by Carol A. Park (The Heretic Gods). The Heretic Gods series boasts one of the most interesting magic systems I've read in fantasy, and it examines it in a way I have never encountered before: scientifically! Well, fantasy-scientifically, anyway. But still. The world of Banebringer is dark and brutal, but there's nothing bleak or oppressive about this series with its hopeful tone and likeable characters. It also contains one of the most realistic romances I've read in fantasy, which actually had me invested in seeing how it develops even though it's only a small part of the overall story.

BLACK LEOPARD, RED WOLF by Marlon James (The Dark Star Trilogy). The main character, Tracker, has one of the most distinct voices I've ever read in a book of any genre. James has crafted a fascinating and unique character in Tracker, as well as a hugely compelling story about trying to find a missing child. The entire cast of this story could easily get an entire book dedicated to them, my favorite being Sadogo. What sets this book apart from most fantasy is James's insertion of African myths and versions of classic fantasy creatures—I'm not going to describe his version of vampires, but man, they are horrifying. The structure of the trilogy also differentiates itself from others in that this book tells the entire story, and books two and three are going to tell the same story but from the perspective of other characters in the group. I can't wait to see what secrets are revealed in the following volumes.

SENLIN ASCENDS by Josiah Bancroft (The Books of Babel). I've sung praises for this series for a few years now; I think it's absolutely brilliant. Book one gets off to a slow start, ingratiating you into its bizarre, complex world, but it has a propulsive second half and books two and three are breathtaking, cementing it as one of my all-time favorite series. It follows the exploits of a schoolteacher who travels to a gigantic tower filled with tons of different societies on each level for his honeymoon, only to lose his wife before they even enter the place. His adventure trying to find her goes in a multitude of unexpected directions and involves a huge, wonderful cast of characters. If anything bad happens to Byron in the final book, I am going to lose my mind.

RING SHOUT by P. Djèlí Clark. Hands down my favorite novella by Clark, who's now an author on my insta-buy list. This takes place in Prohibition-era Georgia, following Maryse Boudreaux and her associates as they track down and slay members of the KKK, who in this reality are literally hideous, hulking monsters. There's a ton of great social commentary as well as exciting action sequences and gross eldritch creatures, so this is one you are not gonna want to miss.

ABOUT THE AUTHOR

TRAVIS M. RIDDLE lives with his girlfriend and his pooch in Austin, TX, where he earned his bachelor's degree in English Writing & Rhetoric at St. Edward's University. His work has been published in award-winning literary journal the Sorin Oak Review. He is the author of such works as *Balam, Spring* and *The Narrows*, which Publishers Weekly praised for its "intricate worldbuilding and familiar but strong narrative arc."

Find him on Twitter and Instagram @traviswanteat
or at www.travismriddle.com

Made in the USA
Monee, IL
29 May 2021

69761432R00291